# COLONIZATION

## HUMANITY ISN'T ALL THEY LEFT BEHIND.

# SEAN PLATT
# JOHNNY B. TRUANT

# COLONIZATION
**Sean Platt & Johnny B. Truant**

**REALM & SANDS**

*To our Platinum Readers. You make our lives awesome.*

# COLONIZATION

SEAN
PLATT

JOHNNY B.
TRUANT

TWO YEARS LATER

# CHAPTER 1

The gray fighter jets made another loop. Piper watched them screech through the clear blue sky, near the fence surrounding Heaven's Veil, a nervous flutter in her chest.

She couldn't place the source of her nerves. Part of it was probably fear for the pilots. The resistance kept playing with fire, but at least she could usually understand what they were trying to do before they failed. *These* fools, on the other hand, were begging to be slapped by the patrolling Astral shuttles, then sent down in scraps. From the occupation's first day, humanity had been testing the alien ships' defenses. They'd never come close to making a dent. Even Black Monday hadn't made a ding. So why, after all this time, did dissenters continue to spit in Fate's eye?

*Maybe that's just how humanity is,* Piper thought as she watched the circling planes.

Humans never gave up, no matter how stupid or futile their attempts might be. A strength and a weakness — an obsessive-compulsive breed of obstinacy. Those who couldn't accept the obvious would slam their heads against the inevitable until they exhausted their numbers and dwindled to nothing.

That's what Meyer always said anyway. As much as violence still bothered Piper, none of it seemed surprising to the alien envoys. Resistance had been assumed from the start. It had been factored into the Astrals' grand equation as predictable. Inevitable. Maybe even essential.

Piper stood on the mansion's porch, watching dead men circle in their obsolete tin cans, feeling something like pity. Meanwhile, the shuttles protecting the city beneath the mothership remained at their posts, not bothering to intercept, apparently unimpressed.

Once the formation again vanished behind the enormous, shimmering blue-glass hulk of the Apex at the city's center, Piper turned to go inside. The day was warm, so the large doors had been propped open. The home's doorway was downright titanic without at least one door closed, and Piper felt uncomfortable walking between them in her simple blue dress, as if she were entering a cathedral without proper attire.

But of the three Astral classes, only the Titans might have passed judgment on her wardrobe. And of course they never would.

Two of the stoic figures were standing just inside the foyer, turning a small, transparent cube in their hands, passing it from one to the other as if trying to solve a puzzle. The Titans looked up without comment at the clacking of Piper's low heels. Maybe they thought her clothing was fine for the lady of the house. Maybe they didn't, but were too polite to say anything. She almost wished the cloaked figures spoke so she could ask, but in two years of living among them she'd never heard a word. Meyer had heard them all in his own way, of course. But Meyer was different now.

Piper wound through the home, fingers brushing stone columns, her path through the maze practiced but still not quite comfortable.

In the west hallway she passed another Titan, this one

female. The creature's pale bald head inclined toward Piper atop her massively sculpted shoulders. As she looked back up, her pale face affected the vaguely polite smile they all wore, seemingly all the time. She wanted to take the smile as genuine, and maybe it was. Unlike the Reptar Astrals, Titans were so human-looking. Two legs, two arms, ten fingers and ten toes, two eyes, a nose, a mouth. Massive, muscular, powder white and hairless, yes — but humanlike nonetheless. Proof of Benjamin Bannister's seeded-human-origin theory perhaps.

But the Titans *weren't* human, no matter how much respect they seemed to show the Dempseys. Piper always tried to keep in mind that they hadn't been as respectful to the rest of the planet. Plenty of people saw Piper Dempsey as a traitor to her species for all her privilege, and maybe she was. Getting friendly with the house ambassadors only made her feel worse.

Piper flashed an unnatural smile.

She found Meyer in his elegant but humble office, unattended, without even Mo Weir to answer his questions or take his orders. Stalking the room alone, Meyer looked like the giant he'd been back in the old world. Seeing him this way, in this human room so like his New York office, settled her slightly. She allowed an exhale, but still felt the bunching in her chest.

Meyer looked up as she entered and smiled. After watching the Titans, Meyer's genuinely human expression felt like a breath of fresh air.

"Hello, Piper."

"Those jets are still out there."

"Yeah?" Feigning interest. Meyer held what looked like a glass tablet and was barely offering lip service while he worked on something else. But the tablet *wasn't* glass, same as the Apex. Piper also knew she couldn't operate the thing if she tried, whereas Meyer used it for most of his work when he wasn't using the office terminal or his human cell phone. It didn't matter because she hated to touch it. Living here, surrounded by the enemy, was bad enough.

"It's making me nervous," she told him.

"I could have them shot down, if you'd like."

Piper watched Meyer, but he kept his eyes on the tablet. His casual comment chilled her.

"No, please."

"Okay then." He looked up, the slow smile returning. Almost the old Meyer. *Almost.* "How's your day?"

"Meyer," she said, "what do you think those jets are doing out there?"

"Does it matter?"

"Aren't you concerned about them at all?"

Meyer set the tablet aside, looked at Piper, and shrugged. "Should I be?"

"It doesn't make sense. When's the last time there's been such an overt attack?"

"It's not an attack, if I'm understanding you right."

"They're *fighter jets.* You think they're just circling the city for kicks?"

Another shrug. "Maybe. We can't police everything that happens, Piper."

Piper didn't know what bothered her most about that simple statement: Meyer not seeing the fighters as a threat, his lack of concern over the resistance's possession of jets in the first place, or his casual use of the word "we" in conjunction with humanity's enemy.

"It's just ... what is the resistance thinking?"

"Who knows." He laughed.

"No — *I'm actually asking you to tell me what they're thinking.* The Astrals still have their mind-reading stones lined up all over the outlands. So what are the pilots thinking? Why are they just circling, asking to be blown from the sky?"

"I keep telling you, the monoliths don't work like

4

that," Meyer said. "They don't read every thought from every person. They can't be tuned in like a radio tuning a frequency."

"Then what good are they?"

"It gives them an average. A temperature of an area as a whole."

"So what's the 'temperature' of Heaven's Veil?"

"Pacified. Compliant."

Piper sighed, her fingers rifling through a stack of important-looking papers on Meyer's desk, looking for nothing. She wondered if the Astrals had authored any of these pages. If so, had they committed to paper for human benefit? Or was this human-to-human bureaucracy — the metropolis running as any human city ever had — under human hands, ignoring the alien bosses above?

"I think they're up to something," Piper said.

"The people?"

"The jets."

"Maybe they are. It's fine. As long as the guard shuttles intercept them outside the borders, there won't be any debris falling onto people's homes. That was a mess last time."

"A *mess?*"

"Yes, a mess." Now he seemed impatient, probably exasperated by Piper's intrusion. This was classic Meyer, as he'd been even before Astral Day. Clever, intelligent, and occasionally too arrogant to see past his own absurdity. His family was safe, and the overlords had successfully made contact. Now it was time for business.

A klaxon blared. Piper's heart stuttered at the alarm. Meyer rolled his eyes.

"Goddammit," he muttered.

"What is it?" Piper yelled above the bray.

Meyer touched his finger to his temple and closed his eyes.

"Meyer!"

"Hang on."

"Is it the jets? What's going on?"

"Hang on." Finger still to temple. Eyes still closed. As if he had all the time in the world.

"Do we need to hide in the—"

*"Piper, if you don't shut the fuck up, I can't listen!"*

Piper's eyes were on the hallway, toward the alarm and stomping feet. The house was a place of business during the day, and now she could hear administrators rushing by. She didn't need to peek at the chaos to imagine the panicked humans rushing about like dumb animals, Titan guards marching into assigned positions. Outside, Reptar peacemakers would be finding their stations, looking hungry.

Piper watched Meyer turn his attention inward, listening to Divinity's voices in his head as the klaxon filled the home with fear.

His eyes opened. They were the same human eyes Piper had fallen in love with — and yet she fell a step back, nearly as afraid of Meyer as she was of the blaring alarm.

"Yes, they say it's the jets." His finger fell from his temple. "But this time, they've brought something with them."

# CHAPTER 2

Trevor heard the blaring alarms and stood from his chair fast enough to knock his water to the floor.

Despite the tumult, Trevor paused to watch the glass shatter. It was okay; he didn't want the water anyway. He'd been trying for over a year to transition to drinking only water but still didn't like the taste, forcing himself to hydrate only because his body needed fluids. Supposedly, the systems installed by the Astrals when they'd built Heaven's Veil did something to flawlessly purify the water, but to Trevor it still tasted fetid. Secretly, he'd have given anything for a Coke. He'd been meaning to flaunt his position as Heaven's Veil royalty and command a shuttle to seek caches of sweet carbonation in the outlands, but he hadn't mustered the guts to ask. Speaking to the muscular, white Titans (who supposedly understood English even though they never replied with words) always creeped him out.

Trevor ran to the window. Whatever was happening seemed to be on the home's other side, so he rushed into the hallway, realizing the irony of running toward the alarm rather than away from it.

Lila burst from her room, and Trevor collided with her,

knocking the breath from his lungs.

"What's going on?" she asked, her eyes wide.

"I don't know. Didn't you look out your window?"

"No." She sounded rushed, panicked. "Do we need to get to the basement?"

"*You* can go to the basement. *I'm* never going into a basement again."

"Have you seen Raj?"

"Why would I have seen Raj?" Annoying Lila, wasting seconds while something important unfolded. He shoved at her, trying to get into his sister's room and her precious front-facing window.

"Get out of my way! I don't care about Raj and his stupid—"

Trevor stopped when he saw his niece on the floor of Lila's room behind her, surrounded by letter blocks. "Oh, hi, Clara." Then, back to Lila, hissing: "Take her downstairs, stay here, find Raj, whatever. Do you know where Mom is?"

"Probably in her house. Or maybe pacing the grounds between like she does."

"Hi, Trevor," Clara said from behind Lila, barely audible.

Trevor smiled at the two-year-old. Her voice was small and, when klaxons weren't blaring, adorable. Even Trevor, as a teen boy, wasn't immune. Some people were a little afraid of Clara, but Trevor didn't understand why. So she'd walked early. So she'd talked early. Who cared?

The alarm died. With the air silenced, Trevor could hear a commotion coming from outside Lila's window. He desperately wanted to see it — partly because it was surely exciting and partly because he was number two around here, the second Dempsey below his father in the media's eyes. He should be up front, where he could make decisions. Where the cameras could see him.

"Mom's not at her house. I saw her in the mansion earlier. Downstairs. Talking to Dad."

"I didn't see her," Lila said.

"Hi, Trevor," Clara repeated.

"Hi, Clara." Then to Lila: "Go and find Raj, but see if you can track down Mom too. Don't go outside. You hear me?"

Lila looked like she might protest. She didn't like taking orders from Trevor, but she'd been exhausted almost nonstop since becoming a mother.

"Fine. What are you going to do?"

"I'm going to look out your window. Then I'll go outside."

Again, Clara said, "Hi, Trevor."

Trevor nodded to Lila then crossed the extravagant bedroom to greet his niece while approaching the window. He patted her on the head as he passed. Trevor was beyond her, halfway to the window and able to see the first fireworks outside, when Clara said, "Don't be afraid."

Trevor turned back. Lila's arms were out, reaching for Clara to smuggle her downstairs. But Lila had stopped, staring at the blocks around the little girl, her mouth open.

"What did you say?" Trevor asked.

Lila broke her paralysis and lifted Clara into the air, Trevor looked where the girl had been sitting. Where Lila had been staring.

Her blocks were arranged to spell *DECEPTION*.

# CHAPTER 4

Heather saw Meyer striding through the home's foyer as the alarms fell quiet. Piper chased him like a yappy dog, in heels and a little blue dress. *Surely*, Heather thought, *because that's how Meyer likes her.*

"Stay inside, Piper."

"Tell me what you mean!" Piper grabbed his arm. "What 'new' do they have? Is it a problem?"

"Stay inside! I'll handle this!"

But of course, Piper didn't stay inside. When Meyer went out, she followed. Heather followed too. It was ironic: Heather following Piper for her turn with Meyer, just like in the old days. But then of course, Heather had been there first. And Heather, unlike Piper, wasn't arm candy, and didn't dress like she was.

"Meyer," Heather said, more projecting her voice than shouting.

Two of the bland-faced Titans (Heather sometimes called them "albino Hulks," always followed by smashing sounds) turned at the sound of her voice. They didn't twitch toward her any more than they'd twitched toward whatever was happening outside. Heather was permitted to be in the viceroy's mansion — and just as she must have made sense to them, their lack of action made sense to her. Heather couldn't tap into their ESP any more than anyone else (although Meyer seemed able), but you didn't need to know what they were saying inside their minds to see the patterns. Some of the Titans had gone outside without hesitation. These two had stayed inside. Apparently, they weren't needed. The proper force had been deployed. Nothing with the Astrals, it seemed, was ever wasted. These two seemed to be at work despite explosions on the lawn, puzzling over the meaning of a small glass cube.

"That's right, you heard me," Heather said to their unheeding forms as she rushed past and through the open door. "Hulk smash!"

The Titans didn't respond.

Outside on the lawn, Heather gaped at the sky. The usual immaculate blue was a mess of winding contrails, as if a scattered air traffic controller had been put in charge of the flight paths. Every few seconds, something exploded. She seemed to be seeing planes, rockets, and something else — swirling, twisting things that appeared to have lives of their own.

She stuttered up to Meyer. Piper clung to his arm below the explosive ballet. For a second, Heather hated Piper. Then the flash of hatred vanished, like always.

Meyer seemed to notice Heather's presence with Piper's.

"Get inside," he said to them both.

"Not until you tell me what's going on." Heather tipped an invisible hat to Piper. "Hey, Piper. Lovely weather, isn't it?"

"Get back, Heather. You'll get hurt."

"*You'll* get hurt too."

Heather looked at the sky. What had to be rebel rockets weren't simply exploding on their own; they were being shot down by the round shuttles tasked with protecting Heaven's

Veil. The spheres were zipping about faster than her eye could follow, homing in on the contrails, seeming to reach out for the altered rockets and breaking them like sticks. The sky dance seemed effortless, but still shrapnel rained onto the city beyond the lawn. She could hear it striking roofs, landing on concrete — or whatever the aliens called the modified stone they'd laid for streets.

"I won't get hurt," he said.

"Because you're Superman?"

Meyer turned and glared at Heather. His eyes, usually green, seemed almost gray. She'd seen that happen in the past, well before the Astral telescopes had spotted the approaching fleet of spheres. You didn't mess with Meyer Dempsey when he gave you that look. Business rivals trembled beneath it. *Even hungry wolves*, Heather thought, *might do the same if they found him in the wilderness.*

"Get inside. *Now*. You too, Piper."

Heather paused long enough to let Meyer know she wouldn't go easily then began walking backward, keeping an eye on the skies. Piper did the same, and Heather took her hand. What she'd taken for Piper's subservient fear, she now realized, was conflict. Piper wasn't terrified. She was something else.

"You okay?" Heather asked.

"No."

"Meyer?" Heather's one-word question carried thousands of smaller queries inside it.

"He's right, you know," Piper said, now looking at her husband's back. He was at the front of the sprawling lawn, a dozen feet from the palatial home's front gate, in the middle of nothing, wholly exposed. His body language held all the mortal terror of a man waiting for a bus.

"About what?" Heather asked.

"He *won't* get hurt."

"How do you know that? I have half a mind to go out

there and haul his ass back in here. If a stray explosion doesn't hit him, an on-purpose one will. If I were out there with the rebellion, my first target after the aliens would be their chief toady."

"*I* don't know he won't get hurt," Piper said, "but *he* does."

Heather wanted to reply that Meyer didn't know dick, but she'd felt his changes. He couldn't see the future, but sometimes it seemed like he could *calculate* it just the same. The shuttles were intercepting rockets from the jets and from bunkered installations past the city's edge — but keeping up with the rockets wasn't challenging at all. If the Astrals knew which weapon would strike where next, then Meyer knew, too.

"He's full of shit," Heather said anyway, glaring at Meyer's stoic back. "Where's his adoring public to witness this? Out carving effigies?" She turned to Piper, scooting them back as a ball of fire bloomed overhead. Then, less bitingly, she asked, "What did he say this is?"

"I saw the jets and told him. He wasn't bothered at all. Then the alarm started, and he told me they had something new this time."

"By 'they," you mean the rebellion."

Piper nodded.

"Who are we rooting for here, Piper? Us or them?" Heather pointed at the jets. At the human pilots trying to save humanity while Heather and Piper watched its eclipse.

"*Them* or them," Piper corrected.

Heather looked up. There was another explosion — one more rocket intercepted on its hurtling path toward the mothership. The next few rockets struck the giant sphere, but did less damage than the Black Monday nukes.

The jets were still streaking by in a taunt, staying beyond city airspace. Heather looked toward the trees and hills at the horizon. She followed a few of the stray contrails toward their hidden, secondary sources: rockets fired from pits, trucks, or mobile launchers. A coordinated attack on the ships above Heaven's Veil in Colorado using intelligent weapons that were, of course, useless as anything else.

"Why aren't they — ?"

Piper didn't finish her thought. Shuttles finally broke ranks and headed away from their stations. Apparently tiring of chasing projectiles, they were heading out to decimate their bunkered sources instead.

Shuttles blurred toward the city's edge, bringing the jets within range. Heather didn't think they could fire very far. Why would they *need* to, given the shuttles' speed? If they could close on a target in under a second, why use long-range weapons?

The first strike happened in a one-two clap that made both women flinch — though Meyer, still exposed on the lawn — didn't twitch. A burnished metal sphere blurred into position mere feet from one of the fighters, at its nose, causing the pilot to compensate by attempting to bank away. He wasn't close. The gray bird struck the sphere like a car crashing into a bridge stanchion and broke apart like a toy. Metal spun away with a tremendous crunch. Beams lanced from the craft like quills from a porcupine, spitting in a dozen directions, annihilating the remaining shards of plane.

Two more shuttles. Two more planes turned to balls of fire, moving close enough to fire their weapons point-blank with no effort at all.

With the fighters destroyed, the guard shuttles vanished from their positions overhead, zipping into the distance. Fire plumed beyond the trees, the explosion's source unseen.

The shuttles moved like the aliens themselves: coordinated without speaking, decisions made as if by one brain, artillery moving out to follow that single common command. The mothership, unmoving, seemed to watch it all.

"Jesus," Heather said.

Meyer was still on the lawn. Rooted. Staring into the distance where clouds of black smoke bloomed like rancid weeds.

A noise filled the air. A horrid, screaming, rending sound. To Heather, it was the grate of an engine desperate for oil and grinding its parts — an ancient machine approaching with reeking death on its breath.

"What the fuck is *that*?"

Trevor ran up from behind, shouting, his footfalls like hollow gunshots.

"Get inside! Get into the basement!"

Trevor started grabbing, but Heather and Piper were looking up, transfixed, seeing the rebels' approaching surprise.

"Get inside, Mom! Piper! *Get inside! DAD!*"

Trevor pushed past them to run for Meyer, but Heather, snapping out of her hypnosis, grabbed his arm hard. Fear dawned as her eyes again found the sky and its grotesque bird: an enormous, ancient plane, cobbled together from history's parts and quietly launched, engines unable to hold their stealth as it banked above. The goliath's flight path doubled back in a wrenching, shuddering turn, having come from behind while the shuttles were occupied up front.

Headed directly for them, surely brimming with death.

The plane's nose wrenched slowly around, peeling the air, lining up with Meyer and the house behind him.

The rebellion couldn't fight the Astrals, so they'd fight the aliens' allies and what they'd built instead.

"*Meyer!*" Heather shouted.

He didn't move.

Seconds passed, too fast — and yet timeless.

Above, the mothership didn't flinch. Why wasn't it coming? Could it only decimate, lacking the shuttles' precision? Or was it simply content to allow this — to let a flying pipe bomb strike the city's center without a care?

Meyer, his back to Piper and Heather, watched it come.

Trevor continued to tug and shout as Heather tried — now with Piper's help — to yank him away.

The plane was almost falling from the sky as it turned, not trying to launch an attack so much as *be* an attack. Surely, it was loaded with explosives and flammables, the pilot a kamikaze. They didn't have time to get deep below the house, but they had to try.

Meyer raised his arms. Unable to turn away, Heather watched the plane bank and roll, its massive wings now striking trees in its final deadly approach. She could see the pilot and his hateful human face.

"DAAAAAD!" Trevor wailed.

All of a sudden, the plane struck nothing.

Less than a hundred feet from the mansion gate, the enormous craft detonated as if it had collided with a mountaintop. Fire consumed it — so much that for a few seconds, Heather couldn't see the plane's shining skin at all. She waited for the shrapnel and fallout, crouching as Meyer failed to cower, wrapping her arms around Trevor as Meyer raised his own arms high.

A vast sphere of yellow and orange bloomed as if the plane had exploded inside a transparent shell.

Shrapnel didn't fly.

Fire didn't spread.

The huge bomber died its spectacular death inside the invisible shell, its damage contained. The sphere, with the old bomber's ruins inside, hovered in place, its contents burning. Eventually, Heather, Piper, and Trevor stood to watch, knowing the floating inferno — whatever force field had surrounded it, wherever it had come from — could no longer harm them.

Meyer lowered his arms and turned then approached the trio. Explosions boiled and rumbled in their transparent prison behind him.

"Trevor," he said.

Trevor couldn't speak but managed to nod.

"Call Police Capt. Jons for me. Tell him I'll be doubling peacekeeper presence in the city effective immediately following this attack, and that he's to align his officers to comply."

Heather shuddered: Peacekeepers. Reptars. *Doubled.*

Trevor nodded. Meyer stalked past, leaving the floating sphere beyond the gate to burn.

Trevor called after him. "What's going on, Dad?"

Meyer paused then turned to look at his son, wife, and former wife in the eyes.

"I think the rebellion knows something they shouldn't, and are getting desperate." Again, he turned to walk away but paused at Trevor's fresh question.

"*What* do they know?"

Meyer looked for a moment like he might not say, then his body language changed in a way Heather recognized. His way of saying, *I guess the cat's out of the bag, so what the hell.*

"I think they know the Astrals have lost something they need," he said, "and now they're digging."

# CHAPTER 4

"Anything?"

"No. Nothing. Wait. Hang on."

Cameron watched his father and Danika bustle between stations in the Moab research facility's "communications room" — a place Cameron still thought of as the coffee room. When they'd hooked up with Ivan (and his serious attitude, strong enough to be a second person), he'd dragged his quasimilitary equipment in to join what Benjamin already had and insisted on a "nerve center" from which all communications could be monitored and coordinated. Cameron was a by-the-way kind of guy; he thought communications could be "done" rather than "monitored and coordinated." But Ivan had won, and now this was the comm room. But there was still a shitty coffee vending machine against the wall, and although it had run out of supplies long ago, it was plugged in, and its front was lit like always.

"Anything?" Benjamin repeated.

"I said hang on."

"I'll hang on. But did you hear anything or not?"

"If you'll just *hang on*," Danika repeated, "I'll answer that question."

Ivan reached out, his fingers beckoning for Danika to hand him the headset that had started life as Charlie's personal headphones. The headset on the ancient radio that had accompanied Ivan to the lab had glitched out a while back. Ivan had commandeered Charlie's headphones as a replacement. Charlie, still holding a grudge, stood in the corner, his gray-brown beard particularly unkempt, bug eyes disturbing behind his glasses, not so much as leaning against the wall. He stood like a statue, his social retardation on full display. Cameron, for his part, wondered what Charlie used to listen to on those headphones. He listened to nothing now, and that told Cameron he'd been listening to something secret or embarrassing — something that wouldn't translate to out-loud play. Probably, it had been both secret *and* embarrassing, like square dance fiddle rap.

"Give it to me," Ivan said.

"Because you can *hear* better than me," Danika said.

"Just give me the goddamned headset." Ivan snapped his fingers.

Ivan was tall and rail thin — the kind of man you could knock over by accident and barely feel it. It was hard to believe he was military at all, let alone had once ranked highly before the nation had been decimated and turned him into what was essentially the head of military resistance for a four- or five-state area. Ivan's intense blue eyes were the only thing keeping Cameron from disbelieving any of it. The man had only to hold someone in his gaze for a few uncomfortable, uncompromising seconds, and they'd follow his every command.

It might have meant something if the resistance mattered, but Cameron had never shaken the impression that they were playing house. The Astrals knew where the lab was; a mothership had hovered above for months. It was possible they didn't know what the lab did or that Benjamin had spent his life researching Earth's visitors and their past work, but they couldn't be total idiots. Shuttles flew overhead all the time, but the ranch earned no special attention.

Benjamin said the aliens hadn't pursued them because they were doing a good job of hiding their intentions. But Cameron was positive the Astrals had left them alone because to them, the ranch was no different from the rest of the outlands.

They'd been left alone, in short, because the resistance was a joke.

Danika looked for a minute like she might hold onto the headset for spite (she could listen to static for Franklin's voice, same as anyone), but then Ivan's stare did its work, and she handed it over with an annoyed grunt. Cameron felt relieved. Even at an oblique angle to Ivan's eyes, he'd felt uncomfortable.

Ivan slipped off his usual stocking cap in favor of the headset. Then, despite any signal being listen only, he adjusted the small mic he'd jury rigged in front of his reddish stubble.

"Anything?" Benjamin asked.

"Hang on."

"He's *sooo* much better at this," Danika said, rolling her eyes.

Danika was no match for Ivan: small and feisty, with a pixie face and a tiny upturned nose. Cameron was reasonably sure his father had a crush on her despite her being closer to Cameron's age, and despite her position under Charlie in the lab's hierarchy.

"Hang on. I'm getting something."

"Did it hit the pyramid or not?" Charlie, as usual, sounded annoyed. Though he could've just been being Charlie.

"Or did it miss?" Cameron asked.

Benjamin looked over, his intensity momentarily broken.

He knew exactly what Cameron was asking and what he feared but spared Cameron the indignity (in Ivan's hardline presence) of stating it. Internet inside Heaven's Veil (though heavily censored and filtered) was nearly as good as it had been before the aliens' arrival. Terrence and Ivan, working in tandem, had managed to hijack an air signal that gave them limited access to that network. In all likelihood, the aliens knew they'd managed a connection and had simply allowed it, but when the jets and mobile launchers around Heaven's Veil had finally forced the shuttles guarding the cities to break formation and give chase, their hijacked camera feeds had flipped off like a switch. *No sense in giving eyes to the resistance,* the Astrals seemed to have decided, *if they're going to force us to kill them after all.*

The guard shuttles had broken away from the city's airspace, and Ivan had cheered despite knowing those good men and women were going to die — "for the cause," he'd said. But Cameron couldn't help noticing that they were still alive here in Moab. Just not worth the effort to exterminate, given the "merely irritating" nature of their best efforts.

In the seconds before they'd lost the feeds, it had looked like the suicide plane wouldn't be able to bank hard enough to strike the Apex and would instead slam into the mansion.

Where Meyer Dempsey lived. With Piper.

"Hang on. I can hear him."

"Franklin?" said Benjamin.

"No. The deejay on Q106.4." Danika was sitting sideways in one of the coffee room's wooden chairs around its chipped wooden table, wearing an unflattering gray hoodie with her brown ponytail wagging behind her. She was in her thirties but had a college girl's posture and temperament. She'd worked for Benjamin as a researcher for over a decade. After Piper left in the mothership, Cameron had developed a brief crush on her, too.

"Shh."

"Holy shit, Ivan. The suspense is killing us."

"Shut up, Danika."

"Wait." Something had caught Cameron's eye. A blinking light.

"Almost got it." Ivan used one hand to press the headset to his ear, the other to turn a dial.

"Something's going on over here." Cameron approached the network interface area in the corner (the place where sugar, coffee creamers, and stir sticks were kept) and knelt below the desk. Nearby, Ivan hit keys on the open laptop's keyboard and scribbled his finger across the touch screen.

"If you people don't shut up ..."

"Ivan. Do I need to reset the router or anything? Is it like normal Internet?"

"Power cycle," Ivan said impatiently, pressing both hands to his headphones to muffle the noise.

"He means to turn it off and on," Benjamin translated.

Cameron unplugged the device, plugged it back in, then waited. Green lights climbed its front. A page reloaded onscreen, and Cameron found himself looking at an image of an immature but populous city made of mostly perfect lines: simple houses and a few larger, impressive structures. The camera was high up. Near the middle there was ...

"Guys. Look at this."

"Quiet, Cameron!" Ivan hissed.

"Okay, Ivan," Danika said. "You keep listening. We'll look at the video showing us exactly what we want to know."

Ivan turned. Charlie, Benjamin, Danika, and eventually Ivan clustered behind Cameron, now operating the small computer from his knees on the floor.

"The Internet's back?"

"No," Danika said. "I made this image in Photoshop."

"Standard communications blackout," Ivan said. "They cut us off during the attack, but—"

"Oh, shut up, Ivan."

Benjamin pointed at a round thing near the unharmed mansion (near the predictably unharmed blue pyramid) that seemed almost superimposed on the monitor. It looked like something burning inside a transparent glass sphere, hovering maybe fifty or a hundred feet in the air.

"What's that?" Benjamin asked.

Ivan zoomed in on what looked like twisted, blackened metal sitting on the enormous sphere's bottom.

"Shit."

"What?"

"It has to be the bomber."

"What did it hit?"

"I don't think it *hit* anything. They must've surrounded it with a force field or something."

"But the shuttles ..." Benjamin began.

"We're clearly not entirely capable of understanding the complete defensive abilities of a race that is able to travel through space and occupy a planet," Charlie said as if reading from an instruction manual.

"It was worth a shot," Ivan said, as if that shot hadn't just resulted in maybe fifteen or twenty deaths. The bomber's pilot hadn't taken that shot. It was also the fighter pilots and the people who'd fired Ivan's modified rockets from mobile launchers nestled in the nearby hills. All the people Charlie had argued would pointlessly die, seeing as it would take more than a simple, guard-drawing distraction to launch a suicide attack on one of the occupation's nine global capitals. But Ivan was a strategist first and a human second. The decision had been reduced to a simple equation: the probability that an attack on the city (instead of the mothership) would be successful versus a handful of soldiers' lives. A cold thought, but if it worked, Ivan would have been saying *I told you so*, then toasting to the first chink in the Astrals' armor.

"No, it wasn't," Charlie said.

23

"It's made of *glass*, Charlie." Ivan jabbed a finger at the gigantic blue pyramid dominating the city shot on the laptop's screen. "It wasn't unreasonable to think we could break something *made of glass.*"

"First of all," said Charlie, raising a finger as if preparing to tick off points of a forthcoming argument, "you're *assuming* it's made of glass. But what you don't understand because you haven't spent your life studying extraterrestrial visitation — or cultural and genetic interference — is that there's no evidence of anything as fragile as *glass* being used in monolithic constructions in the past, and—"

"This isn't the past," Ivan snapped.

*"And,"* Charlie said, raising his voice in a rare display of emotion, knowing Ivan didn't have a leg to stand on and eager to prove it, "given that their first monoliths this time were stone, simple logic assures us that if they're not using stone now, it's in favor of something stronger and *more* permanent, not less, and that despite what you may think, the pretty blue look of the Apex structure doesn't mean it's actually just an Apple Store, but is something important and *not* fragile."

"You can't assume—"

*"Thirdly,"* Charlie interrupted, ticking off a third point on his raised fingers, "you insist on giving them less credit than you'd give any human enemy. If the Apex is the site we think it is, and if it's as important as we believe it to be, why would they leave it unguarded?"

"Because they'd be chasing shuttles!"

"Oh, come on, Ivan," Danika said. "If you were defending your own flag, would you let the other team wave their arms to distract you, then send everyone after them and leave your base unguarded?"

"It's easy to second-guess now." Ivan crossed his arms. "But I'm the only one willing to—"

"Okay, okay," said Benjamin, straightening and raising

his arms for order. "Mistakes have been made by all of us. As a *team*, because no matter whose idea this was—" He looked at Ivan. "—we *all* agreed to it." He glared at Danika and Charlie in turn. "Like Ivan said, it was worth a shot."

Benjamin sighed, possibly feeling the weight of those many deaths partially upon his shoulders. If this had worked, those deaths would have had meaning despite their sadness. But it hadn't, and now the loss was so terribly worthless.

After a moment, Cameron said, "Do you still think the Apex is important?"

Benjamin seemed like he might waffle, so Charlie said, "Yes."

Cameron looked over at the shaggy-bearded man.

"From the moment we saw they were interested in Vail," Charlie said, again finding a coatrack's emotion, "there was something that bugged us." He looked at Benjamin meaningfully. His eyes ticked briefly toward Danika. Then he added, "*All* of us."

"'What makes Vail so special?'" Cameron recited what might as well have been the lab's slogan for the last two and a half years.

"The other nine capitals all have something obviously alien about them," Benjamin said. "All but Vail. There are pyramids, old cities, temples made of massive stones ... but Vail has nothing at all that we know of. And the more research I do — the more we compare notes with our colleagues around the world — the more I worry that Vail might be special because it's the resting place of something powerful, left behind from all their past visits. Something they don't take when they leave, but that they need to access each time they return in order to force a—" He made an uncertain gesture. "—a *reset*, I guess."

"What kind of thing?" Cameron asked.

"There are a few ways it's been described, both directly and indirectly," Benjamin said. "I call it Thor's Hammer."

# CHAPTER 5

Sometime after the commotion died down and her father assured everyone that the threat of danger was an exaggeration, Lila caught a glimpse of motion outside her window. She stood and walked over in time to see two of the round silver shuttles flank the now-mostly extinguished sphere of fire and tether it with energy beams. Moving much more slowly than shuttles normally moved, as if afraid to drop the thing, the ships towed the big plane's remains inside its capsule. Where they'd dispose of the behemoth, Lila didn't know or care. Probably in the outlands, beyond the city perimeter.

After the ships were gone, Lila watched the sky. Once upon a time, the air had been filled with vapor trails from commercial airliners. Then for a while, there had been motherships and shuttles. Now there were both. Aliens had colonized the globe, but that didn't mean people had stopped needing to travel. It was almost possible to believe this was all the new normal.

Lila's eyes flitted to trees and mountains. Rifts of smoke in the distance had gone, but she still didn't like to be here, in her room on the second floor of this large civilian target.

She'd also never really grown comfortable *here* in general: below her father, at the head of the occupation's human wing. Dad said the Astrals had good intentions despite all that had happened, and that mankind's insistence on violence had made bloodshed necessary. Everyone would understand in time, he insisted, and see that this had all been for the best.

But Lila had her doubts. Even though she merely lived in the giant house near the heart of a North American capital, she still felt like her life was lived on the wrong side. Cameron was out there somewhere, and Piper would have been with him if the mothership hadn't brought her home. Cameron was against all of this, and Piper would have been, too. Maybe she was anyway. Lila had heard Piper and her father fighting plenty, always making up inevitably. And like Lila, Piper's love of the viceroy seemed to go hand-in-hand with fear of his changes.

Lila sighed, turning away. She tried to settle her wandering thoughts. The strike had unnerved her. Rebels had attacked many times in the past but hadn't bothered for years. Black Monday's assault had silenced mostly everyone. But earlier rebel attacks had focused on the ships, and this was the first to feel personal. Now it seemed like they were after Lila's family — traitors that they were.

The door opened. A familiar face peeked through the gap.

"Can I come in?" Christopher asked.

Lila heard his actual question: *Is Raj in there?*

It wasn't the kind of thing he could ask outright because if Raj *was* there, he'd easily read Christopher's subtext. And while Lila was pretty sure Raj assumed Lila was habitually unfaithful (he wasn't stupid, after all), he didn't know for sure, and didn't know the culprit was Christopher. She'd deflected that idea before they'd moved here, when she'd allied with Raj and complained about their old bunker mate. But so much had changed since then. Mostly *Raj*.

"Yeah, come on in."

Christopher pushed the door open but hesitated at the threshold. Lila's room was enormous, like all the mansion's many bedrooms. She had rooms within rooms — an enormous suite easily as large as the starter house she'd one day dreamed of having with Raj, back when he'd been the sweet, shy boy she'd fallen in love with.

"Come in," Lila repeated, now beckoning.

"What about Clara?"

"She's asleep."

"Asleep? I thought she was done taking naps." Christopher came inside, careful to leave the door ajar. The only thing worse than Raj walking in to find Christopher in Lila's room would be Raj walking in to find Christopher in Lila's room *with the door closed for privacy*. It seemed likely, in a Raj/Christopher conflict, that Meyer would take Lila's wishes into consideration, but it wasn't worth the risk if they could avoid it. Ironically, their new life was like their old one in that Meyer's public image was everything. If there were magazines, Meyer Dempsey would still grace their covers. And to Meyer and his public image, his granddaughter's father probably belonged in the picture more than the captain of the unnecessary human guards. If it came down to choosing, Lila was sure Christopher would find himself out of a job at best. She didn't want to consider the less appealing possibilities.

"She got really tired after the recent ... excitement," Lila said.

"She saw it happen? You didn't take her into the basement?"

"She doesn't need to see things to get excited about them, Chris."

Christopher bobbed his head as if to indicate a fair point. But he didn't like to discuss Clara's differences from a normal child any more than Lila, and they seemed to have mutually decided to ignore the topic and hope it would go away. Only Meyer treated Clara as truly special, but it was because of her pedigree as new royalty, not anything more troubling.

Christopher sat in Lila's chair. She sat on the bed, squeaking the springs.

Christopher glanced through the open door, into the hallway.

"Where is Raj anyway?"

"I think he's up on the fourth floor, in the network center. He wanted to go off with Trevor to talk to the cops, but Dad said that's more your job, and that Trevor could handle it fine on his own. That went over well, seeing as Raj technically outranks you in the guard."

"He's gotta see it wasn't really necessary to send him on an errand like that."

"Is *anything* my dad gives Raj to do necessary?"

"Fourth floor, huh?" Christopher looked up, knowing that only a staircase separated Raj from his cheating wife. "How long will he be gone, and how well do you think they can hear up there?" Christopher looked down at the bed.

Lila smiled, despite knowing Christopher wasn't joking, even though he should have been with Raj so close. "Not today. I'm beat up."

"Maybe I can help you relax."

"Not today." She reached out to soften the rebuke and briefly held Christopher's hand.

"So. Trevor," said Christopher. "Stepping up as the big man."

"Like father, like son. He'll be declaring himself lieutenant viceroy if I don't keep him in line."

"Is there such a thing?"

Lila rolled her eyes, giving Christopher an *I could give a shit* look.

"They told us to tighten security around the house, too," said Christopher. "But not *how* to tighten things up — probably because we're not the security force that actually makes any difference. But ... the police? What, they're going to add beat cops to keep F-14s from attacking again?"

Lila had no idea whether those had been F-14s or if Christopher was talking out of his ass. She decided not to ask herself how the rebellion had secured F-14s or anything like them, or what other aces they might still have in their deck.

"I think they're increasing the number of peacekeepers. Not just cops."

"You mean Reptars?"

"What else would I mean?"

Christopher looked like he wanted to slide beside Lila. Instead, he glanced at the door and stayed where he was.

"I just don't buy that name. Peacekeepers. They're more like animals. *Dangerous* animals."

"I think that's the point," Lila said.

"That the city is patrolled by animals?"

"That they're dangerous."

Christopher sighed then picked at his black uniform pants leg, looking out the window. Lila could see the Apex's transparent blue form beyond him, the pyramid's partially finished side eclipsing the window's left quarter.

"Oh, just ask what you're here to ask, Chris."

"I'm here to see you."

"And we're going to sit like diplomats. Sounds like a fun date."

"Wanna go to the coffee shop?"

Lila almost laughed. It was such a normal, average, ordinary thing to say. Problem was, these had stopped being normal, average, ordinary days a long time ago. To Meyer, the reestablishment of human trade, commerce, and global communication made perfect sense because he kept saying the Astrals were here to understand and observe humanity — to help it improve as a species. But Lila, to whom that sounded like the thickest of bullshit, thought the idea of grabbing a coffee in a city watched over by an alien mothership and patrolled by alien animals was like singing in sinking lifeboats. Her odd sense of prescience had departed with Clara's birth, but she couldn't shake a strong mental image of cows fattened for slaughter, or masses kept dumb by social opiates. Getting coffee under the eye of Reptar peacekeepers didn't feel any different to Lila than joining one of the new religious orders and lending help to build their absurd effigies in the wasteland.

"I want you to tell me what's on your mind," she said.

"What makes you think I have some evil intention in being here?"

"Because you *always* have evil intentions."

"Like how I shot my way into your house just to get into your pants?"

Lila snorted laughter and covered her mouth, big eyes darting to the hall.

"Okay, fine," he said, shifting in the chair. "The guys are bugging me for information."

"And by guys, you mean Terrence."

"Mainly Terrence."

"And he wants to know ... what, exactly?"

"Trevor said your dad said something about digging."

"Digging? I don't know anything about digging."

"*Nothing?*"

"Why does Terrence want to know?"

"You know how Terrence is," Christopher said. "He's curious."

Lila raised an eyebrow. "Why is he always so curious?"

"He just is."

Lila turned her hands over, palms up. "Well, I don't know anything about digging. Tell Terrence to ask Trevor."

"He did. That's all Trevor knew."

"Then he can ask my dad."

Christopher looked at Lila as if to say, *Touché*. Maybe what Terrence wanted to know was for public consumption and maybe he was being nosy, but Christopher's look now told Lila that he didn't particularly want the viceroy to know he was curious.

There was a knock at the open door. Lila flinched.

"Hey, Trevor," Christopher said, turning after a flinch of his own.

Trevor looked embarrassed. He'd known about Christopher and Lila from the beginning. He'd always liked Christopher more than he liked Raj, and that gulf had doubled after his new brother-in-law adopted his current position under Meyer. But he still didn't like lying — or thinking about his sister and one of his best friends having sex.

"Hey, Christopher." Then: "Have either of you seen Piper?"

Lila shrugged. She didn't track her stepmother at all hours. "No."

Christopher shook his head.

"Why are you looking for her?" Lila asked.

"Because nobody's seen her since the attack," Trevor said. "She's gone, and nobody has any idea where she is."

A terrible noise swelled from outside and killed her response.

Lila thought she knew what it was but had no desire to find out for sure.

# CHAPTER 6

"Penny for your thoughts, kiddo?"

Cameron was outside, sitting atop a picnic table between the half-cliff lab and the old ranch house he'd once shared with Piper — as cohabiting civilians at first, then as lovers once they'd finally stopped kidding themselves. They'd lived in that house for three months before the mothership had taken her. That riddle, at least, had been solved in short order. The motherships connected to their stone network and began to colonize. Communications resumed, making it immediately obvious who'd become Queen of Vail — of Heaven's Veil, today.

Cameron turned to the voice behind him. It was Benjamin. He wanted to sigh at his father's choice of words, but that wouldn't be fair. Benjamin was just doing his best. The way he always had, even back when Cameron had abandoned him to his ancient rocks and dreams of little gray men. He'd been right about the rocks. The little gray men? So far, not so much.

"Dan used to call me that, you know," Cameron said.

"Penny?"

"Kiddo. The penny for thoughts thing — that was Mom's

expression. It's like you have nothing of your own."

"I used to tell you bedtime stories about carbon-dating limestone."

"Just sit down, Dad."

Benjamin looked touched as he took a seat. Cameron sometimes still referred to his father as "Benjamin" or "Ben" when he talked about him to others but usually didn't refer to him as anything when they spoke directly. Calling him Benjamin to his face felt cold, but "Dad" always felt too familiar. It wasn't lost on Cameron's father that a few years of reacquaintance was all it took to begin healing the gulf between them. Given a decade, they might share a hug.

"You know someone has to try getting into Heaven's Veil, Cam."

"I figured. I assume it's going to be me?"

"Charlie wouldn't last a day. I need Danika to help run the lab. The other assistants might consider it an imposition on their jobs. It's not worth the money I don't pay them anymore. It's down to you or Ivan, and I doubt you think Ivan leading this is any better an idea than I do."

Benjamin had situated himself on the bench seat. Cameron was on the top, feet where his ass should be. He wondered if it was an improvement or a worsening of their relationship that Benjamin assumed Cameron should be the one to cross the 250 miles to Heaven's Veil. On one hand, it was a dangerous trip that Cameron had already taken twice, there and back, on his old man's request, and the kind of thing most fathers would try to protect their sons from. On the other, something lit a little inside Cameron whenever he was included in the unfolding plans. It's how he and his dad had been in his teen years. It meant he'd been forgiven for walking off, for leaving one father behind to find another in his agent, Dan.

"Ivan would go in with guns blazing," Cameron said.

"He wants to stay anyway, to coordinate the resistance. But

you ask me, they need controlling more than coordinating. Anyone who prefers living here in the outlands and declares him- or herself a revolutionary is questionable." He waved the idea away. "Bah, that's not fair. I'm sorry. They're good and noble people."

He didn't say more, but Cameron could read a bloom of guilt on his father's face. The people who'd died in the failed raid — the one Benjamin had agreed to, even though Ivan had dreamed it up — wore heavy on his conscience. The lab and the group of rabble rousers had always worked toward the same basic goals but remained fiercely independent. Benjamin's small crew needed the lab and found the Moab ranch land worthy of their intense study, but the revolutionaries feared it. This property was an alien place and always had been, from its haunted grounds to the plugged-up money pit under the stone arch.

Cameron looked across the flat landscape, then the miles-wide sky. He'd come to this place through the canyon, and at that time, the vast openness had sneaked up on him. It had taken months to get used to the wide-open skies. Everything felt so unprotected. But the point had been moot on arrival; there'd been a mothership over this place. Today, the ships didn't seem to care about it at all. As if to put a fine point on his thoughts, Cameron saw the tiny silver flash of a shuttle passing in the far distance, out on patrol. The shuttles had come here, too. He felt almost insulted by the spheres' blasé attitude toward the ranch.

"You know," Cameron said, "most fathers and sons aren't like this."

"Aren't like this how?"

"One always leaving. One always sending the other away."

"Oh, I don't know that it's so bad." Benjamin shifted on the bench, watching a second far-off shuttle as if they were at this table to have a picnic in better times. "We live together. We work together. We're seeking common goals. We collaborate."

Cameron wondered if his subconscious mind was trying to pick a fight — if he wanted to find a way to be angry so he could justify leaving ... which, he'd realized over the past half hour, he very much wanted to do. Benjamin was right; they *were* close right now. Cameron *shouldn't* want to leave. Even though Cameron had already figured out that he'd be going to Heaven's Veil, he wanted that announcement — that command and order — to come from his father. If it was Benjamin's decision, Cameron would *have* to go. He wouldn't be going because he desired it. The old guilt of leaving the first time was still too pungent a memory.

But he *did* desire it. He *did* want to leave. And his reason had nothing to do with the mission.

"It's fine. I can go," Cameron said.

"Ivan's already talked to Saul. Three of his people will go with you."

"No," Cameron said. "I'll go alone."

"Cam ..."

"I'm faster alone. You taught me to hide and keep a low profile, and I got damn good at it."

"Last time, you had—"

"Vincent, Dan, and Terrence," Cameron finished. "How did that work out?"

"You can't possibly be blaming yourself for Vincent and Dan. You weren't even there when—"

"Oh, I agree it doesn't make sense. Or change my feelings. You sent Vincent and Terrence to meet up with us. And Dan ..." Cameron sighed. "Well, Dan stuck with me for long after he should have. You sent *me* to Meyer's ranch, and they were only there to help. Whether it's my fault or not, they were there because of me. This time, I go alone or not at all."

"Then don't go."

Cameron gave his father a look. He'd never been good at bluffing. *Of course* Cameron would go. It wouldn't be an assault, so an army wasn't required. Just intelligent reconnaissance and a good pair of hands. They'd tried repeated assaults. The Astrals didn't so much as bother seeking the source to stop further incursions. Their best brute force efforts were *that* insignificant. This last attack — on the blue pyramid rather than on the impervious ships — was supposed to change things, but again they'd been swatted like flies.

"Fine," Benjamin said, looking down at his hands. "Go alone."

"When?"

"Tomorrow, if you're ready. I always assumed someone would need to go in. I didn't think Ivan's stunt — *our* stunt, I suppose — would be some sort of death blow, but I did believe that it might buy some time. Seeing as it didn't even start so much as a street side trash fire, I feel the clock ticking. I have since they started building the Apex, and look how quickly it's progressing. If they're working this quickly on the visible structure, I worry they'll be working as fast underground."

"But why would they build a big thing like that to dig under it? How do you even know that's what they're doing?"

"It's complicated."

"Why did they wait? If they wanted to dig up this old thing, why didn't they start when they got here? Or the minute they docked at the capitals?"

"Charlie thinks they needed to establish their colonies to control the capitals first. And if the Hammer is down there, it might be inside a larger structure. Something they need to excavate the door of, and feel no hurry to do in the way we might.

"But *why*, Dad? Why about *all* of it? You told me — me and Piper, actually — that there are records in the past of mass die-offs, but—"

"Mass *exterminations*," Benjamin corrected.

"But if they've just come here to ... I don't know ... just *wipe us out*, then why the stone network? Why the abductions? Why go to all the trouble to narrow it down to the Nine? Why set up the capitals, the outposts, the patrols, all of it? I mean, shit, there are planes in the air again. The Internet is back. Why colonize if they only want to find the master kill switch and erase us all?"

Benjamin sighed. "I don't know."

"You're the expert! You spent your life researching this stuff, all over world, in every—"

"*I don't know, Cameron.*"

Cameron looked again at Benjamin — his father's kind yet serious hazel eyes. His mop of still-mostly brown hair. His full beard, surprisingly devoid of gray. Benjamin had never had an ill intention. He'd accidentally destroyed the lives around him through what had once seemed a selfish pursuit but had since proved itself to be the most important hobby in history. Researching the past and extraterrestrial visitations was the one thing his dad had always excelled at, far outstripping his aptitude as a husband and father. The idea that he'd come up blank now yet feel a pressing need to surge blindly forward wasn't just maddening. It was a living, breathing terror.

Cameron watched him for another few seconds then shook his head, resigned. He'd made the trip before and could make it again. Off he'd go, no matter what was known. Because even beyond the mission, there was a prize at the end of this particular rainbow.

"I can leave at sunrise." Cameron sighed. "I'll go back the way I came last time. Just tell me what you need once I'm there."

Benjamin nodded. "It's simple. I have something you'll need to take with you, then either install it yourself, or get it into Terrence's hands. But there's still something we need to discuss about the trip itself. About which roads you should take to get there in one piece."

"I won't take roads," Cameron said. In this day and age, roads were for dead men.

"That's what we need to talk about," Benjamin said. "About you — and the Andreus Republic."

# CHAPTER 7

Piper went to the fourth little white house beyond the viceroy's mansion, staying low and feeling stupid. She ducked behind the long row of hedges out front and felt even stupider. The grounds were surveilled. The alien network supposedly couldn't read individual human minds, but she'd heard Cameron's thoughts plainly once upon a time.

It was hard to believe she was successfully hiding from anyone, but standing upright and being seen by naked eyes was an idiot's game.

Piper's body tingled with nerves, watching the front porch past the hedges, wondering if she should walk up and knock. Houses to the left and right — Christopher's and Heather's, though Heather's was necessarily larger — were quiet. So was the one Piper was steeling herself to approach.

Homes inside the sprawling grounds were made of wood, built entirely by human hands and human equipment, unaided by alien ships. None of the Titans had so much as glanced toward the construction, so far as Piper could recall. It was as if they'd been saying, *Sure, build whatever, we don't care.*

But they'd needed the structures, due to pride if nothing else. Heather was first to insist, saying that if she wasn't wanted in the main house, she'd need her own — not out with the commoners, but close to her children. A classic Heather Hawthorne power play, passive-aggressive in perfect measure (Heather wasn't unwanted in the mansion at all, and even had her own suite), but Piper hadn't argued. They'd all felt raw, and she'd felt desperate for peace. It had taken months following her abduction before Piper could finally settle into her new normal and feel something close to surrender.

As the sea of hippies around Meyer's old house had grown to include well wishers, refugees fleeing the dangerous outlands, and sycophants of all stripes, willing human labor had become simple to find. That was the thing about Heaven's Veil citizens: to a greater or lesser extent, everyone was here because they agreed to lie down as pets. Getting those hands to build not just Heather's house but also several more (for other should-be-close-but-not-in-the-mansion staff) had been simple.

Piper glanced around, searching for cameras out of habit. There would be some, yes. But getting caught would require something less pedestrian than glass lenses. And it would mean she'd have to admit to wrongdoing, which she may or may not have been up to.

The thought made Piper touch her jeans pocket, brushing the hard lump of plastic and metal inside — the tiny slip drive she'd taken from Meyer's office after the attack.

*This is ridiculous,* she told herself.

Still, Piper fished the drive from her pocket and held it in the hand nearest the shrubs while mounting the small white home's porch. At least this way she could toss it casually into the bushes at the sound of a shout.

Piper knocked. After a few seconds, a huge head of

poufy black hair greeted her, stylish sunglasses poking into its massive halo as if saved for later.

"Hey, Piper."

"Terrence. Hey. Can I come in?"

"Uh ... sure."

Terrence stepped aside to let Piper enter then left the door open with the screen closed to summertime insects. He looked perplexed, but of course he would. She'd always been cordial with Terrence but had missed the intense bonding period he'd spent with everyone else. Thinking this now, Piper felt more alone than she had in while. People living on the grounds could easily be partitioned into two groups: Piper and Meyer in one, those who'd remained in Vail when she'd left in the other. Even the children weren't really in Piper's camp. Not anymore. Meyer was her only confidant, and her feelings for him were ... *complex.*

Terrence turned from the door after Piper was sitting in one of the wooden chairs around his kitchen table.

"Can you close the door?"

Terrence looked at her strangely then pushed the solid door closed. After the lawn's brightness, the LED-lit house seemed dark to her unadjusted eyes.

Terrence walked over and sat opposite Piper.

"What's up?"

Piper didn't know where to start. The minute she pried at one edge and found it loose, this whole thing would pop wide open. Her question wouldn't be easy to ask — and without the answer Piper wanted, she might be hanging herself.

"You saw what happened with the plane?"

Terrence nodded slowly. Despite all the changes, he hadn't lost his ability to be cool.

"Of course."

"Is everything ... okay?"

"Okay how?"

"With security."

Terrence nodded. He responded slowly, his deep voice falsely casual. "It's fine. Not a scrap of debris. We didn't have to do anything. A couple of shuttles just carried it off."

"Did you see the plane come in?"

Terrence nodded. "We came out at the general alarm."

"Did you know that was going to happen? With the ... the force field or whatever?"

"No, I was pretty surprised."

"You seem blasé about it all."

"It's over now." Terrence shrugged.

"But we almost got suicide bombed."

"Apparently, it was never a threat." He tipped his head. "You know, if you're worried about security, you should maybe be talking to Christopher."

Piper didn't want to talk to Christopher. He was too much of a wild card for this, and Piper had no idea where his loyalties lay — if they were where they were officially supposed to be, or elsewhere. And Christopher, unlike Terrence, had never hot wired a radio connection across a hundred miles for her.

"You know what I was thinking about the other day?"

Terrence shook his head.

"Raj's watch."

"Why were you thinking about Raj's watch?" Then Terrence's cool dark eyes grew uneasy. "Was he asking about it? Was Raj asking about his watch or something?"

"No, no ..."

"Because I gave it back to him. *Years* ago, I mean. Before that all happened with the ship. He might have lost it when—"

"Not literally about the watch, Terrence," Piper said, strangely calmed by his unease. An angle occurred to her — a way to ask what she wanted — and she grew calmer still. "I was remembering the way you used that watch to get through blocked communications when Cameron and I were on the road."

Terrence hummed acknowledgement but didn't say more, clearly uneasy. Back then, he'd been subverting the Astrals (before they'd even been called Astrals) and working with Cameron. Now, he was more or less employed by the aliens and was supposed to consider Cameron an enemy. Everyone seemed to hide those facts in front of Meyer, more comfortable saying they were allegiant to *the capital* and its *viceroy* than to the ships pulling the strings. But in the end you took one side or the other, not both. Sometimes, it seemed to Piper that everyone in Heaven's Veil had chosen security over their species. Ironically, few seemed at peace with that choice, but the contents of a person's heart didn't determine morality or bravery. Actions spoke louder, and they'd chosen to act for the colony — and therefore against people like Cameron. Herself included.

"Well," Piper went on, "don't you think that the ... the insurgents—" Careful to use an official word, rather than something biased. "—might be using some of those same old ways to communicate?"

"The airwaves are open. Phone, Internet, radio, you name it."

Piper decided not to call Terrence on his bullshit. Terrence, of all people, couldn't possibly believe all the old channels were truly open — or that they weren't being scrutinized with incredible efficiency thanks to the assistance of the neural net threading the globe in double lines of monolithic stones.

"But the rebels would want to hide, right? If they're communicating, they wouldn't want to use open frequencies. They'd need secret ones they could keep on the down-low."

"Maybe." He looked like he thought Piper might be ready to hurl an accusation.

"If you wanted, could you tap into what you were doing

back then?"

Terrence's cool had fragmented, now it looked ready to break. There was no obviously correct way to answer. He clearly didn't know where Piper stood. She was Meyer's wife, queen of the city's stone mansion. Her family was the new royalty. Everyone knew Piper Dempsey just like everyone knew the beloved and godlike Meyer. If she was asking about old subterfuge, Terrence probably thought, it might be because she suspected something about Terrence — and was here to call for his head.

"I *could*, maybe," he said, "but I *wouldn't* ever—"

"Those channels you were 'tunneling' for me and Cameron, through devices like Raj's watch, using the old cell networks ... have they been blocked?"

"I don't know." Defensive now.

"But did you tell someone, Terrence? Did you tell anyone about the vulnerabilities, so someone else — not you, necessarily — could see about plugging the holes in security?"

"Well ... no ... but—"

"So they could still be accessible? The rebels could still be using them to talk?"

Terrence looked at his feet, touched one hand to another, spoke quickly without quite meeting Piper's eye. "Well even if they could, it's nothing that would affect us here, in the city anyway; they'd just be using it out in the outlands, among themselves I mean, and there's no evidence that they're coordinating among pockets of people in different places, so it's not like—"

There was the sound of a door closing outside. It was the house next door — Christopher's maybe — but still it broke Terrence's hypnosis. He stopped speaking, after inadvertently spilling his guts. Piper felt sure Terrence was hiding something. And maybe that was good.

"Terrence," Piper said slowly. "Have you talked to them?"

"Who?"

Piper watched him carefully. Whatever power existed in this discussion, it had started with Terrence and now resided wholly in her hands.

"Cameron and Benjamin."

"No."

"Or Charlie? Any of them in Moab?"

"Of course not. If you're implying that I somehow had something to do with—"

"It's okay, Terrence. I'm not accusing you of anything."

Piper knew one thing for sure. Those lines of communication had never been divulged. They'd still be open. And Terrence, if she could read behavior at all, was either still using them or trying to. And that was okay. Ideal, in fact.

Terrence relaxed but still seemed to be reserving judgment. As if he didn't truly believe her. Outside, the door slammed again, and Piper heard someone shout.

"And no," she added. "I haven't talked to Raj."

He relaxed a little more.

Piper shifted on the chair and slipped fingers into her pocket. Her fingers touched the stolen drive, but her jeans were tight, and she'd have to stand to retrieve it.

"*If* you thought talking to Moab was possible—" Piper paused to give Terrence an out, knowing it might help him speak with a thinner guard. " — Or if you found a way to monitor any of *their* communications, as part of your job in security, I'd be interested in knowing."

"So we can know what future attacks the rebels might launch on the city." His eyes ticked toward the window, and the blue hue from the enormous under-construction glass pyramid. "Or on the *Apex*, or your house."

The way he'd stressed the word Apex told Piper something more. Something Terrence might know about the pyramid or Moab, or Moab's thoughts on the pyramid.

46

Something, Piper decided on a leap of faith, that meant she could trust him — or try to anyway.

She stood then had the slip drive mostly out of her pocket when another shout seemed to echo much closer. Almost outside. Her fingers stopped between denim and denim, the drive still hidden.

"Could you get something to them?" Piper asked, her voice now rushed. "Could you get something to Benjamin for me, if you had to?"

An ugly noise chattered from beyond the front porch. A vast, deep sucking sound, slightly guttural, chattering, like a demon inhaling. It turned Piper's blood and widened her companion's eyes like saucers, instantly stealing his cool. It was a sound they'd both heard many times, when the ships had first established order on the ground. But she'd never heard a purr so close, or felt so sure she was the target.

"*Yes,*" Terrence answered, nodding.

The front door swung inward. Locks didn't slow them, and privacy didn't matter. A blue glow illuminated the door's bottom and bled into the gap along the floor. The tip of an appendage teased its horror, black skin crawling as if covered in a billion writhing insects. The deep, inhaling sound grew louder as the glowing gap at the small home's entrance yawned from an inch to two, then six.

"Go!" Terrence hissed, shoving a small card into her hand. Then, his brown eyes steeled but terrified, he added in a harsh whisper, "I can make it believe me."

Piper knew that wasn't true, but she sprinted for the back door anyway, ignoring the rattle of death growing louder behind her.

# CHAPTER 8

Nathan Andreus stood on the widow's walk atop his second commandeered house, sipping black tea, watching the gap amid the hills as the enormous mothership drifted between the peaks.

Feeling meditative, he wondered which ship he was seeing.

It wouldn't be the Vail mothership. Nathan had never seen a capital mothership leave her post. According to his network — not the public Internet but the special one beneath that only trusted people like Nathan could access — those nine keystone motherships hadn't moved since they'd made their first connections, dropped off their first contact teams, and reestablished themselves in the skies.

Nathan sipped his tea, watching the thing, knowing its identity didn't matter at all. But a curious man wondered for spectacle's sake. He'd been inquisitive when average — and was still curious as a baron today.

It might be one of the outpost motherships. They were nomadic, circulating among a handful of cities rather than remaining tethered to one. Nathan hadn't worked out their patterns — even the privileged network was clearly censored

— but he had his guesses. Aliens behaved like territorial animals — wolves, say, which staked out an area and patrolled it in a circuit. But that territorial thinking was meshed with something higher, which coordinated the ships' efforts on a global scale. The motherships assigned to the larger, non-capital cities (New York, Chicago, LA, Dallas) seemed to stay put like those above the capitals. As a whole, the system of motherships and shuttles behaved more like a colony of ants than wolves. They surely communicated ship to ship, but there was more at work than sci-fi phone calls. Ants worked like parts of a single organism, aware of a group goal that transcended the individual. Those goals served a purpose that no single ant could know or understand. The Astrals, who sometimes seemed to share a common mind, were like that.

"Mr. Andreus?"

He turned. Coffey was behind him. She hadn't always been Nathan's lieutenant and number two, but Coffey was loyal, greedy, and more afraid of her boss than the alien occupiers. As it should be. The outlands were lawless, and if shuttles flew by and saw you out there, you were likely to be vaporized without ceremony or cause. And because of that, there were only two truly safe places. The first was within an alien colony, sucking alien cock and swallowing your pride as a human. The second was in organizations like Nathan's — those groups tapped by the overlords as being worthy of leaving alone. The Andreus Republic and similar groups didn't have to suck alien dick. Coffey was second in command at the best place to be during an alien apocalypse — comfortable, safe, and clinging to dignity, so long as you stayed in line. Coffey *should* be respectful, and fear was adjacent to respect.

"I keep telling you, call me Nathan."

"Yes, sir, Mr. Andreus." She stammered. "*Nathan.* I'm sorry to disturb you."

"Well, that's not a problem," Nathan said, turning but not coming closer. "Really, the only thing worse than disturbing me would be disturbing me *for no reason* and then *not getting to the fucking point.*"

"Oh. Yes. Of course. I'm sorry. There's—"

"Jeanine?" Nathan said.

"Yes?"

"I'd like you to breathe."

"Of course."

"You like it here, don't you?"

"Yes. Of course. *Hail Andreus!*"

Nathan rolled his eyes. "Jeanine?"

"Yes?"

"I know you're trying to be loyal. But don't ever do that shit again. Don't ever tell me 'Hail Andreus.' I don't like it. They can salute out there, fine; that crap helps them belong and gives them a sense of unity. But I don't want to be a god. I'm not Meyer Dempsey or Zhuo Feng Huang."

"Oh. Okay."

"But you like it, I mean. Being here. Hail or no hail."

"Yes, sir."

"And you like being near the top. Being my second in command."

"Yes."

"My most trusted compadre."

"Yes, of course."

"Number two. My right hand. The second most important person around here."

"Yes, sir."

"Then I need you to get two things through your head."

"Okay."

"I don't want a toady in your position. I moved you up because you were an insubordinate bitch who always did what she thought was smartest even if it wasn't what her commander wanted. I have plenty of toadies. It's been a

50

week, and you keep calling me sir. You're practically bowing. I want you to respect me and listen, but if you don't stand up and be the person I promoted, you're out. We'll use you for mission fodder, and I'll bring in someone with some balls, no offense to your literal lack thereof. Do you understand me?"

Coffey stood taller. Her eyes found some of the disobedient sheen he'd first seen in her. You didn't kill your way to the top in the Andreus Republic, but Coffey had killed enough people either outside the Republic or below her in rank to have earned some self-respect.

"And I hate pleasantries," Nathan added. "You used to understand that."

"I still do, s — Nathan."

"Then let's start over." He pointed both index fingers at her, smiling something that probably looked more sinister than friendly. He'd once smiled for a living, back when he'd run a business instead of an army — but the world had changed despite so many principles staying the same.

"Go."

"There's someone to see you." She hung on that for a half second then pushed on. "His name is Cameron Bannister."

"I don't know any Cameron Bannister."

"He asked for you specifically. And he came here — to the house, not to HQ."

"What, right here?"

"To the front gate."

"Nobody knows this is where I live." Nathan felt his eyes inadvertently narrow. "Nobody outside the High Guard anyway."

Coffey should have flinched. It was a direct accusation of the elite few who guarded the home. Those people were supposed to be undyingly loyal. There was no reason for them to betray Nathan Andreus. Doing so threatened the power structure they were trying to reach the top of. Nathan, who'd earned one of his college degrees in psychology, knew mutinies in an organization like his were almost impossible. Mutineers were killed outright by those wanting to please the boss, eager for a safer way to grab the brass ring. You didn't mutiny to get ahead. You curried favor like a kid seeking a stern parent's approval.

But Coffey didn't flinch. Now that Nathan had reminded her why she was in her current position, she seemed to have reverted to the person he'd known her to be. If she'd done nothing wrong, she wouldn't back down. She'd probably stand tall and bluff even if she had.

"He knew on his own."

Nathan looked toward the hills, toward the place where the mothership had been a moment ago. He could see the perimeter gate, guards circling the house. Once, he'd had none of this.

"What does he want?"

"He claims to have important information about the Astrals' plans."

"Everyone claims that."

"He told me to give you this. Said you'd understand."

Coffey held out her hand. Nathan extended his. She dropped something cool into his palm. He unfolded his hand to a thin silver chain, a sort of charm hanging from its front. Two delicate silver lines dangled from beside the charm, which looked like a coin engraved with a crescent moon. On the back, barely readable, was an inscription. One he knew well.

Nathan pushed down a surge of emotion. In the moment, with Coffey still watching, he couldn't place that emotion. He might have been angry. He might have been wistful. He might have been (if he didn't cling to rationality and sense) about to shove Coffey from the widow's walk to her death.

He slid the sliver necklace into his pocket, ran a hand over his shaved head, and looked at the hilly horizon for another few seconds.

"Have him wait for me in the front study," he said.

Coffey nodded and turned. When she was gone, Nathan took another few deep breaths, trying to center himself as if he'd never been interrupted. The flash of anger slunk back, awaiting judgment. His fingers trailed idly across the fabric of his pocket. This could mean anything. It could be nothing — although God help this Cameron Bannister if it didn't.

He took the steps slowly, making his way down to the third floor then to the second. He detoured to the washroom off the hallway and splashed his face with cold water.

Nathan toweled off and stared at the reflection feared by thousands of people inside the Republic's ranks. Tens of thousands more feared it on the streets and in the outlands sprawled across three states. But it hadn't always been that way.

He re-hung the towel and rounded the central hallway to the staircase on his way to the ground floor. Several underlings milled in the corridors, but for the most part this was a house, and soldiers didn't patrol homes. HQ was for HQ business. This was Nathan's place first, and a quiet spot for high command meetings second. Whenever he had to do business where he slept, Nathan hated it. Having to meet someone bringing this particular nugget of possible news to the house where he'd always planned to make a proper home? Where he'd carefully chosen to raid a place with such a fine master bedroom and separate vanities in the bath? That was repugnant.

Coffey and a Republic soldier stood outside the front study. The place was arranged in an odd position, Nathan always thought. It was at the home's front, beside the door, walled mostly in glass. It had always seemed mostly soundproof, and Nathan had never minded everyone seeing what he was up to. It was instructional for the others. A way of showing how powers lay in the Republic — with no additional words.

Inside the room, sitting with his back to the door, was a kid with a mop of messy brown hair. Thick as a twig, with a lean, conniving look — the kind of build that made Nathan think of an agile animal, faster and smarter than it looked.

Coffey nodded to the soldier. He opened the door.

Nathan stepped inside then stood above the kid, who was seated in one of the soft red, distressed leather chairs. Meeting his visitor's patient gaze, Nathan realized the man was older than he'd seemed from the back and side: midtwenties at least, maybe upper twenties or thirty. But he'd be able to pass for his late teens, Nathan thought, if he put on a baseball cap and let some of the experience leave his eyes.

The kid's look was placid, not nearly as afraid as most of Nathan's visitors. As he'd felt earlier with Coffey, Nathan wasn't sure if he admired the kid's unwillingness to cower and snivel before the great Nathan Andreus, or angered.

A lot depended on his answer to Nathan's first question.

"Where are they?" His own bluntness surprised him.

Cameron Bannister stood and — unbelievably — offered his hand to shake.

"I'll tell you," he said, "but seeing as that bit of trivia might be the only thing keeping me alive, there's something I'd like to discuss first."

# CHAPTER 9

Cameron shook Nathan Andreus's hand, noting the hard calluses on his palm. Andreus wasn't a soft despot. Two and a half years of living at the top of a seized kingship was long enough for a man's hands to smooth with disuse, but this tyrant clearly still worked for what he had. He still built. Still walked the trenches. Still did, Cameron was sure, many other unthinkable things face-to-face without flinching.

He let Cameron reclaim his seat before sitting in the largest chair, his posture subtly solid and unmoving. Andreus's bald head gleamed above his neatly trimmed goatee. Forty odd years had added a scatter of salt to the brown. If what Benjamin had dug up on Andreus were true, he'd run a successful software business before Astral Day, helping to pioneer many of the technologies people like Charlie and Terrence had twisted to form their subversive network after the fall. It meant that Andreus held a thug's facade in front of his brilliance. It told Cameron that Andreus had once been rather ordinary, perhaps unremarkable.

And as Benjamin had warned, it also told him that the Andreus Republic could listen in to an all-they-could-eat buffet of below-the-wire communications — and had been able to from the beginning. The expression said that knowledge was power, and that seemed to have been literally true for Nathan Andreus. While the world had been scrambling to find its bearings, Andreus had used his software to rig a rudimentary protocol that he'd later released onto the web like a virus. The Andreus Republic had been first to manage communication — and once others found ways to plug in, Andreus had sat behind the switchboard, watching and hearing it all.

But to Cameron, he didn't look like a criminal. Beyond those narrow, experience-hardened eyes, Andreus was a man.

"Are you from the Moab research facility? The group allied with those assholes who led the attack on Heaven's Veil the other day?"

Cameron felt his eyebrows rise. "You know our lab?"

"Of course I know it. At the top of Snake Canyon. There's a house and a building stuffed into a cave. It's where the mothership above Vail sat before sliding over to the capital."

Cameron felt blindsided. He'd come in with what he'd thought was an informational ace, and yet Andreus had taken fifteen seconds to flip the conversation. He was sitting in the big chair, with one leg crossed over the other, his face serious but not intimidating or angry. Everything in the leader's body spoke of strength and certainty. It was easy to see how he'd risen to power. This was the kind of man people assumed was in charge simply because he seemed to be, and few had guts enough to ask.

Knowing he was only feeding the fire, Cameron said, "How do you know all of this?"

Andreus gave a humorless smirk. If Cameron wasn't withholding something sensitive that the bastard across from him was desperate to know (and resented Cameron for holding it back), he felt sure the smirk would have held genuine humor, maybe respectful companionship. But right now the smirk was laced with ire — a power play more than a mention.

"There's a backdoor to the protocol you've been using to reach your worldwide network, for one. Failing that, I can see you on the satellites."

"You have access to the satellites?"

"I have access to those who control the access."

There was a quiet, assessing moment wherein Andreus seemed to be asking whether they understood each other. Cameron did, and didn't like it at all. He'd come here because the Andreus Republic controlled the outlands between Moab and Heaven's Veil, and those who controlled the outlands owned the roads. If he tried to sneak through the underbrush, making the trip might take a week or two, but using the roads he could make it in a day.

But this changed things.

The idea of getting the man's attention with the necklace (proof that Cameron knew at least one thing Andreus didn't) had sounded logical back at the ranch. Now he felt himself wanting to sweat. New information had just been added to the mix — information about *communication*, of all things. But this wasn't someone Cameron wanted to bring deeper into his father's plans than that of gatekeeper — especially considering Andreus's soldiers had almost killed him and Piper once upon a time.

Andreus sat back in his chair, chin slightly lowered, his gaze intense, blazing from the top half of his eyes rather than their dead center. It was a *sure* look: one that made Cameron feel that handing over the necklace hadn't bought him a free ride so much as quicksand.

*I have access to those who control the access.*

Did they understand each other? Cameron was afraid they did. The aliens and their beast peacemakers patrolled the cities and outposts, but they had an entire planet to occupy. The best way to watch the vast outlands wasn't to survey everything themselves. It was to enlist help. *Human* help, provided by people with something to gain.

"I used to own a small company," Andreus said, now dominating the discussion and leaving Cameron feeling stupid and meek. "Everyone around me had contracts with all their partners, but I always did my business with a handshake. I just shook *your* hand. I'm sure that means we're on the same page, and that I can trust whatever you came here to tell me. Am I right?"

Cameron nodded slowly, unsure where Andreus was going.

"Because the way I see it, there are two reasons you might have brought me my wife's necklace. The first is as a peace offering. Maybe you know where she and my daughter are and have come to tell me we can all be reunited as a big, happy family. The second possibility says you meant it as a threat. Or an implied threat, like a bargaining chip. Like you wanted to hold this over me—" He patted his pants pocket, indicating the necklace. "—as some sort of leverage. But I hope it's not that second choice ... *Cameron*. Because it would insult me if you thought you couldn't just come here for a chat. That's the kind of thing that might make me more allegiant to my silent partners. The kind of devotion that would make me eager to report a band of malcontents rather than letting them continue with what I'd previously believed to be sensible work — in the interest of universal checks and balances, I mean."

Cameron felt all his carefully arranged cool coming unraveled. He'd steeled himself while the woman went to get Andreus, and he'd thought he was in control — of himself first, and of the ensuing negotiation second. This was supposed to be simple: *You get me to Heaven's Veil, and I'll tell you where your family is hiding from you.* A betrayal, sure, but once Ivan realized who was among those at the rebel camp, he'd had no compunctions about using that knowledge for the greater good.

As Cameron prepared his response, Andreus derailed his question with a new one.

"What do you want?"

Cameron had been thinking of the Moab ranch and of how he'd barely escaped warriors from the fledgling Andreus Republic two years ago. He'd wondered what had happened after they'd fled. Had Andreus been in contact with the Astral ships back then, too? Had they watched Piper and Cameron arrive at Moab, and decided not to pursue them? The man had nerves of steel. Anything was possible. Cameron couldn't tell which side the man was on, other than his own.

"I need transportation to Heaven's Veil," Cameron blurted.

"Why would you want to go to Heaven's Veil?"

"Why do you care?"

"Because it affects my territory."

"Heaven's Veil isn't your territory," Cameron said.

Andreus smiled then rose from his chair. He went to the window, looked back, and said, "Have you ever heard of a biodome?"

Cameron wanted to blink and ask the man to repeat himself.

"They kept trying them, before all this started," Andreus continued. "In the years before the first Mars missions, they ramped up. There was one in Canada, another in Europe. Truly isolated environments. But do you know why they're so difficult to pull off in the long term?"

The question was several paces ahead of Cameron. He knew nothing about biodomes beyond the concept: to wall off a piece of nature and see if it could sustain itself with no exchange beyond the bubble.

Cameron shook his head.

"It's because nobody really understands the complex interactions of an ecosystem," Nathan said, still glancing toward the window. "There's the question of what eats what and what breathes what — biologist, ecologist stuff. But I think there's a lot they're forgetting, because it's on a higher level. A *thinking* level perhaps. Like how a zoo animal will never truly behave like a wild one simply because it's not free to wander."

"Okay."

"What the Astrals are trying to do by colonizing the planet, if I had to guess," said Andreus, folding his hands behind his back, "is to control us. Not exploit or destroy us — not yet anyway — but simply to keep us under control. But like with a biodome, there's a lot of 'thinking stuff' that's maybe too chaotic to account for, if their little colonization experiment is to work. Stuff in the way we communicate person to person. The way we interact, cooperate, and think in pieces along with collaborators who pick up other pieces. And things like healthy rebellion."

Andreus turned to Cameron.

"This Republic isn't the only game in town when you consider the whole globe, but it's definitely the only game in *this* town. That puts me in a curiously responsible position. I'm supposed to control the outlands to keep the Astrals happy, which in turn makes them want to leave *me* alone and keep *me* happy. But even that control has limits, because too much upsets necessary elements within the ecosystem. Does that make sense?"

It didn't, but Cameron kept his mouth shut.

"Someone was always going to fill the void that was once filled with police, government, and other authorities. I didn't want this position, if you can believe that. But if it wasn't me, it would have been someone else — someone who maybe wouldn't have understood that cooperation has its place in a balanced society — as does dissent."

Cameron wasn't sure he could keep playing along. His mission had been completely upended. "What are you talking about?"

"In your shoes, I'd be trying to work out which side Nathan Andreus is on. Is he helping the Astrals by acting as sheriff or helping the rebels by deliberately allowing their activities to proceed — even when they do stupid shit like trying to launch a 9/11 suicide attack on the viceroy's mansion?"

Cameron couldn't help himself. Andreus's manner was hypnotic. "We were aiming for the pyramid."

Andreus turned. He seemed not to have expected that. "Why?"

"That's what I came here to tell you about. The Astrals seem to be ..."

*Oh, just tell him.*

"They're looking for something. Deep underground. Something to help finish off whatever they're doing here on Earth. Something not good for us. For *any* of us." He gave Andreus a look that said, *Not good for the Andreus Republic, and certainly apt to shatter whatever biodome it's trying to keep whole.*

"Is that why you want to go to Heaven's Veil? To destroy the Apex?"

"To find out what it's for," Cameron said, admitting a half truth. It would be folly to tell Andreus about the digging if curiosity about the pyramid itself was reason enough. And it would be the height of folly to convey his *real* mission — as unsure as he was about which side of the information war Andreus truly meant to play.

"What about the other eight capitals?" Andreus asked. "They're building structures like the Apex at all of them."

"The leader of our group thinks there's something special about Heaven's Veil. A reason this structure might be different." Cameron could continue, but he'd said too much already.

Fortunately, Andreus didn't ask. Instead, he looked out the window again, quiet for a while. Finally, he returned to his chair without sitting and again veered the conversation in a fresh direction, disorienting Cameron just as he was feeling settled.

"Are they alive?"

Cameron looked up, his face pinched.

"My wife and daughter. Are they alive?"

Cameron nodded slowly.

"Where?"

This was Cameron's ace. But for some reason deep down, he knew it was also the tipping point, and the place to surrender his ace. They were still at a standoff, new information notwithstanding. One of them would have to budge, and trust the other to follow. It might as well be Cameron. If he refused to answer, Andreus would probably have him killed — a long-overdue punishment for trespassing that Cameron had already narrowly escaped once.

"There's a camp not far from our lab. Just to the east. It's—"

"I know it."

"They're both in that camp. Healthy and fine, according to our people."

Andreus took a moment to digest then sighed. It was a curiously vulnerable thing to hear from the man Cameron had always imagined as a mindless warlord, but the past twenty minutes had changed his impression of who Nathan Andreus was and who he'd once been. *Violent?* Yes. *Ruthless?* Yes. *Cruel?* Perhaps. But *mindless?* Not in the least.

"I won't help you, but I won't get in your way, either. Due east along Route 70, there was a biker gang stupid enough to try and gate crash one of our barricades. It was unmanned at the time, but as soon as they passed it, the shuttles picked them up and put an end to their joyride.

I imagine one of those bikes will get you most of the way to the capital, if it's fueled or charged. You'll want to steer it manually. Self-driving bikes rely on GPS, and that's a protocol I won't show you how to open. I'll tell them to let you pass along the way. But once you reach the gates of the capital, you'll be on your own. Understood?"

Cameron nodded. He wouldn't trust a bike to drive itself anyway, and he'd always assumed he'd need to find a way to talk himself into the city. He felt upended and out of sorts. He'd come in here thinking he had the situation under control, had ridden through its middle terrified that he'd misstepped, and was now leaving with the despot's blessing. How it had happened and what had persuaded Nathan Andreus to — well, not *help* him, but not *hinder* him either — was a mystery.

"So ..." Cameron eyed the door and the soldiers beyond it.

"Out the way you came. I'll send word to let you go."

Andreus wasn't going to escort him out. Cameron was on his own. He'd surrendered his information, and now had to trust the man at his word. Soldiers outside the study might knife him in the belly the second he stepped into the foyer, but somehow Cameron doubted it. The Andreus Republic was the main reason few people tried to cross the outlands in this area, and there were still severed heads on pikes near the headquarters. But that was the work of zealous worker bees, not the man himself. And as frightening as the cabal was, everything Cameron had heard said it valued honor above all.

Not because Nathan himself was sentimental, Cameron thought, but because honor was an excellent way to maintain loyalty and control.

Something struck Cameron at the door. He turned to Andreus.

"Don't blame the rebels," he said.

"Blame them for what?"

"For hiding your wife and daughter. When you go in ... keep in mind that they were only trying to keep people safe—"

"I'm not going in," Andreus interrupted.

"Why not?"

"They don't want to see me. They ran away. I won't break into that camp and drag them back here. They're always welcome if they choose to come to me on their own, but I won't force myself on them. For now, it's enough to know they're safe."

He watched the man's stern face for a long moment, but apparently their conversation was over.

Cameron left the room, realizing he'd somehow managed to get what he came for without giving Nathan Andreus anything other than peace of mind.

Maybe there was hope in the world after all.

# CHAPTER 10

Trevor was out the door before he realized that Christopher seemed to have forgotten all about him, and that Trevor's summons from Lila's room had them running in the first place.

"Christopher!" he shouted.

Christopher paused long enough to let Trevor catch him, and they both ran toward the estate's front gates. Trevor wasn't in uniform, but that was okay; his was more ceremonial than anything, seeing as he was family more than Guard. More like a protégé to his father than Christopher's boss — though if push came to shove, Trevor was probably both, technically speaking.

They ran through the gates and into the strangely perfect city streets. Everything was pristine and square without being precisely nice, in contrast to the Apex pyramid's useless extravagance. The city's buildings had the look of better-than-average barracks — but barracks nonetheless.

Trevor had a hard time imagining the place as it had been beneath the footprint of Heaven's Veil after the ground leveling and slight terraforming, but he thought they might be running near the old location of his father's Axis Mundi

— the home they'd all once thought was just a home. If so, the barrack-like homes and small, almost-businesses were an upgrade: hippie tents replaced by socialist bunks. Nobody had to pay their way inside Heaven's Veil, but many tried to make a living anyway. *The American spirit hard at work,* Trevor's father sometimes said with what always sounded like a politician's falsely positive voice. His mother had a different interpretation. *Assholes will be assholes,* she said.

Trevor and Christopher ran side by side, making their way through the streets toward the precinct. Christopher was part of the Apex Guard, and Trevor was son of the viceroy, but the city's human nexus of authority was still the precinct five blocks up. They could simply call in, but neither wanted to receive assignments and shatter the illusion that they were masters of their own fate.

So they ran. And as they did, Trevor felt like he was using his legs to burn worry.

Things had happened one-two back at the house: Trevor's curiosity about Piper followed by the sounds of outside activity, as if someone were searching. The pair of events, side by side, made Trevor uneasy.

Purring Reptar patrols filled the air, making Trevor's skin crawl. He forced himself forward, seeing black flashes as the beasts passed intersections, making their horrible sounds. The things acted like animals (huge, shambling timberwolves or cats perhaps, moving like insects), but Trevor tried to remind himself that they were supposedly every bit as intelligent as the Titans or even the rumored Divinity class.

But that, Trevor supposed, was why they were used as peacekeepers in the city. Nothing kept the peace quite like terror.

They arrived at a precinct in chaos. A dozen human city police jockeyed with an equal number of Reptars for the same positions. The precinct only had the one main set of double doors — if the action was inside, they'd bottleneck in confusion. Reptars were supposed to stay out of the precinct. Human and Astral patrols were supposed to do their jobs to the same technical ends, but cops didn't like the alien creatures any more than the Reptars seemed to care for them.

As Christopher and Trevor neared the precinct, they saw the bottleneck's heart. Cops and Reptars weren't shoving to get inside after all. *Nobody* was getting inside because there was a black man with arms as large as a Titan's at the double doors, his hands raised and a no-bullshit tenor in his voice: Malcolm Jons, captain of the Heaven's Veil police force.

"Get out of here, goddammit!" He shooed the enormous, crawling peacekeepers like obnoxious houseflies. "Go back to your fucking posts, and let us handle this!"

One of the creatures lunged toward Jons — the equivalent of an attempted tackle, if the Reptar had been a person. Jons punched the thing in the side of its yawning jaw. He seemed to realize his error immediately and stepped back as the Reptar bellowed its hollow, purring breath and took another pace forward. Then it fell back, apparently chastised.

"You hear me?" Jons yelled, emboldened. "This is a human precinct! You want to take it, then fucking take it, and be done with it all! Go ahead! You want to vaporize my ass and stop pretending we have anything to do with this city's protection? Do it!"

Several of the massive black Reptars — each the size of a midsize car — prickled at the offer. For a few seconds, Trevor thought the encounter would end in death, but one of the Reptars backed up instead, swishing its head with irritation. It must have sent a psychic command to the others. Soon, they all turned and pawed their way out in an expanding circle, moving away from the building. The human police swiveled away to let the things pass.

Trevor and Christopher did the same as one of the Reptars came directly at them. It paused to assess Trevor. He felt his heart leap into his throat. Its eyes were like a giant serpent's. It blinked as it took him in, dual sets of eyelids fluttering as the irises underneath shifted from yellow to red to blue to a dazzling emerald green.

"Hey," said Trevor, watching it, trying to see it as the intelligent being they supposedly were. But he couldn't get through the single syllable without swallowing, his hand subconsciously raised in surrender.

Unbidden, he felt a thought forced into his mind. This was the way the Reptars "spoke," such as they ever did. To Trevor, who'd felt it a few times before, the sensation was intrusive, like having a blade's tip pressed not just to his neck, but through its meat.

The thought came as a series of three bursting images, each lasting a fraction of a second but visible in full detail: a dark place with half walls wet with moisture, a man with black pits for eyes and a ring around his head like a halo, a woman (not Piper) draped in shadow who'd been bisected down the middle and yet remained alive. Trevor got a heavy sense of *settling* to accompany the blast of images, as if something enormous had sighed its weight upon him.

Then the thing flicked its head away, trailing that guttural, rattling growl they all made while stalking their rounds. The creature was through with him, its cryptic message conveyed.

The precinct's courtyard drained, becoming just another building surrounded by milling humans. Christopher turned to Trevor.

"What did it say?"

Trevor shook his head, trying to clear it. He closed his eyes, inhaled, then let the breath escape.

"No clue. I *hate* when they do that. I think I'd rather it bit me."

"Watch what you wish for, bro," Christopher said.

"You all," bellowed Malcolm Jons in front of the doors, waving at the baffled-looking officers. "Get in here. You stay outside wobbling around like you just got your dicks kicked, you make us look like assholes. Except you, Garcia and Niles. You don't look like you got your dicks kicked, but only because you don't have 'em." His eyes lit on Trevor and Christopher, still near the small group's back. He nodded to another officer to keep shooing the others inside and walked over.

"What are you two doing here?" Jons asked Christopher with his fathoms-deep voice. "There wasn't a general alarm."

"We heard it start to happen," said Trevor. "Ran down to see what we could see."

"No offense, son," Jons said, "but I don't need any help. We're still cops."

"There was one of those things on viceroy's property." Christopher nodded toward the departed Reptars.

Jons's large jaw worked, considering. "You're Apex Guard. I suppose you should have been alerted anyway. *They* were, after all." He nodded toward the absent peacekeepers.

"Alerted to what?"

"There was some sort of security breach. Looks like it was in the house itself."

"What kind of security breach?"

"No idea. But we're already on alert, and now there's this blast of instructions to fan out and await further orders."

"Await further orders on what?"

"Fuck if I know, Christopher! I'm just some gumshoe motherfucker who *pretends* to be in charge of keeping order around here. I'm sure *they* know exactly what they're after, but we're on a need-to-know basis." The big cop affected a servile voice. "Yes, sir, tell us what to do, Mr. Alien Overlord!"

"So what was all this? Why did they come to the precinct?"

69

Christopher gestured at the courtyard. The situation had been quickly devolving before Jons flushed the Reptars — or until they'd been called back.

"It's a computer thing. The city backups are here."

"*Here?*" Trevor looked at Christopher. "I thought Raj kept that stuff up on the—"

"*Our* backups," Jons clarified. "One of the downsides of the Astrals letting us get about our business is that we have our own brains and don't always play it exactly as they would. But until they want to drop the act and wipe us out, then yes, we still have our own records. Surveillance plus a hard backup of the local network."

"They don't have access to our network without you letting them in?" Trevor asked.

"Oh, sure they do. That's where they're off to now, I'm sure. Or maybe they don't need to actually *go* anywhere. They just talk right on up to the ships or the shuttle or whatever the fuck with their scary ESP — or, hell, just rape it right out of our minds with their magnet rocks, I don't know. But that's my whole point. That's why it's so fucking obnoxious, the way their first reaction was to come here. 'Hey, it's just the humans. It's just their only fucking farce of privacy. The one fucking place they pretend to actually be doing anything.' But I'll be goddamned if I'm going to open the doors and let some spider panther things paw around my files. Shit, like they could even use a touch screen or a keyboard!"

Trevor wasn't sure if that was supposed to be a joke, so he kept his mouth shut.

"Anything we can do?" Trevor asked.

Jons gave Trevor a patronizing look. He wasn't trying to be disrespectful, but Trevor felt it just the same. Kid of privilege, good only by virtue of sharing half his famous father's genetic code. Maybe not even then. "I'm sure we can handle it," he said.

"But a security breach involving the house ..." Christopher trailed off.

"Well, sure Apex Guard would have to be involved." Jons deferred to Christopher's position as quickly as he'd dismissed Trevor's. But that wasn't fair — Trevor had been the one to come over earlier about all of this, to inform Jons that his father wanted to double the peacemaker presence. Although now that he thought about it, Trevor realized that was maybe why Jons didn't want to talk to him, or hear what he had to say. There would always be power struggles, and the debate between those who made public proclamations (Trevor's father) and those who had to live with and enforce the consequences (the human police force) was one of the oldest among them.

"Trevor's part of my team," Christopher said.

For a half second, Jons looked like he'd bitten into a lemon. Then he reluctantly softened, and Trevor throttled his gut reaction: It wasn't Trevor who was on Christopher's team; Christopher was on Trevor's. He let it go. They were all ultimately on the same team — Team Humanity, which was supposed to oppose any ill intentions by Team Astrals — but played along because it was easier.

"All right. Look. Like I said, I don't really know anything other than there's some sort of problem they care about, which means it's not a bar brawl. They let us handle human on human, even if it's a riot. If the cats are all worked up, I'd guess it's something on the order of an info leak. Gun to head, if I *really* had to guess, my gut says they've got ideas about an insider helping with the recent attack. Whatever it was centers around or in the viceroy's mansion, so I'm sure we'll need your eyes. But right now, I don't know what to tell you, other than hang tight."

Christopher nodded.

They were turning around to head back when something prickled at the back of Trevor's head. "Captain Jons."

71

The big man turned.

"My father wanted me to check in with you anyway."

Jons looked ready to roll his tired eyes. "What about?"

"One of the officers was mentioning problems with surveillance feeds," Trevor lied. Christopher looked over, confused.

Jons's eyes scrunched down. He looked perplexed then seemed to maybe recall something barely worth mentioning — a minor distraction that had taken a back seat to the current chaos. Which was expected because Trevor hadn't heard anything about surveillance from his father at all, and had been anticipating a no.

Instead, Jons said, "Yeah. We did have a glitch. But it was just this morning. Like, a minute before those fucking things swarmed the station. How did you even hear about it?"

"Doesn't matter." Trevor puffed his chest. "Just get it fixed, okay?"

"Sure," said Jons, mystified. And ordinarily, Trevor would have been mystified too, except that one of the images forced into his mind by the passing Reptar had looked an awful lot like an alien mind might see Terrence: dark sunglasses looking like deep eye pits, his head surrounded by a wide halo of giant black hair.

The Reptars had been to see Terrence today — and if Trevor could trust the feeling behind the impression, they didn't quite believe whatever he'd told them.

Disturbing camera feeds to bury the truth sounded *exactly* like the kind of thing Terrence might do after being questioned by Astrals — Terrence, whom Trevor had been suspecting for months, was up to something.

"Which feed has been glitchy?" Trevor tried turning the question into an afterthought.

"Northeast, at the border." The captain pointed, and Trevor knew what was coming — what Terrence had been trying to hide from prying eyes.

"Near the church," he added.

# CHAPTER 11

"Here."

Benjamin looked up. Charlie was above him, having made his delivery of important information with all of Charlie's trademark tact. The bug-eyed scientist was standing beside him, his hand still planted on the colorful printouts he'd slapped onto Benjamin's desk, his brown-gray beard a tidy mess. His bespectacled eyes were meeting Benjamin's as if in accusation.

"You run these by Ivan?" Benjamin asked.

Charlie shook his head. "Ivan would try to find nukes if he were smart enough to understand what you said — and didn't say — about Thor's Hammer. There are plenty of nukes left out there even after Black Monday, and if anyone knows how to launch them, it's a guy like Ivan."

"You don't like him, do you, Charlie?"

"This used to be a place of research and knowledge, not war."

Benjamin shrugged. Through the office window, on the main laboratory floor, Danika was watching them. Benjamin gave her a slight nod, telling her it was okay to come over and see what they were discussing — but as Charlie had indicated, not to inform Ivan. Between the three of them, "don't tell Ivan" was the default.

"It's still a place of research," Benjamin said.

Charlie sat like a mannequin, or possibly someone whose bones had been replaced by rods. "I don't want Ivan seeing those maps."

Danika arrived. She closed the office door behind her, intuiting the room's mood.

"What maps?"

"Charlie got these off of GeoSurvey." Benjamin tapped the stack of documents. "Topological, but also seismics and a handful of others."

Danika picked up the stack and leafed through the maps. All were of Heaven's Veil and the surrounding mountains where Meyer Dempsey's Axis Mundi had once stood.

"Who don't you want to see them? Ivan?"

Benjamin nodded.

"Are they what I think they are?"

"You see what they are."

Danika looked at Charlie, annoyed. "I meant, are they *for* what I think they're for?"

"Maybe you could propose what you think they're for instead of playing guessing games?"

"Shut up, Charlie."

"Some scientist you are."

"Shut *up*, Charlie!"

"*Yes*, Danika," Benjamin said, eyes on Charlie. "I wanted them so we could get an idea what's underground at Heaven's Veil. And as you indicated, we don't have Ivan here because—"

"Because he'll nuke the mountain."

"Right."

Benjamin had already sifted through a similar set of maps and was reasonably sure of what he'd see. But he'd wanted to be thorough. And per the typical scientific investigation, thorough meant boring. Movies made it look like science was filled with the flash and dazzle of discovery, but Benjamin had been doing this for his entire life, usually with Charlie by his side. Most of the time was spent eliminating dead ends and verifying things they already knew rather than finding new information. It was like searching for your car keys by checking everywhere in the world you were sure you *couldn't* have left them, just to be sure.

Not surprisingly, the new maps were as unhelpful as the previous ones.

"There's nothing here," Danika said.

Benjamin nodded. Across from him in the chair, seeming snug in his discomfort, Charlie did and said nothing.

"Right," Benjamin answered. "Because why would anyone do more than the most rudimentary survey on an area with nothing special about it? You can find all sorts of sonic soundings and blast analysis on the world's buried cities, but who scopes a random mountain? A mountain in the middle of a bunch of hoity-toity real estate?" Benjamin set the maps on the desk. "So we're still at zero."

"But you're sure it's there. A buried temple or something," said Danika.

"Of course I'm not *sure*. Charlie, are *you* sure that Thor's Hammer is hidden at Vail?"

"I have neither confirmed nor rejected a single null hypothesis."

Benjamin gestured at Charlie as if his eloquent answer said it all. "But they're digging. You know they're digging."

"The footage Terrence's people sent us shows excavated soil and rocks leaving the Apex."

"But does that mean they're looking for Thor's Hammer?"

"What else would they be looking for?"

"Point of consideration though," said Charlie. "This is the race that built the pyramids. Not the new ones. The old ones. Are we really to believe they need to get in there with shovels and hunt around like nineteenth century coal miners?"

"Maybe it's delicate," Danika suggested.

"Maybe there's interference or something," Benjamin said. "Maybe they're working blind."

Charlie slapped a hand on the table. "Oh, come on. *Humans* can set up explosives and observe the echoes to see what's down there. These beings travel through space in ships that defy conventional physics. We can't even imagine how what they do is possible — or why, when they can fly so fast, they took so much time to arrive in the first place. I have a hard time believing that if they want to find something under Vail, they can't just look through that mountain as if it were glass."

"Maybe they know where it is but need time or precision to reach it."

Benjamin ignored Danika and spoke to Charlie. "Come on, Charlie. You of all people know you can't make an assumption like that. We've seen extensive evidence of a doomsday weapon throughout the historical records, and those are just the records that survived. The Library of Alexandria, when it burned, surely contained a lot of documents detailing what humanity knew then but will never know now. Even without more evidence of a Thor's Hammer, what we have is clear enough. The pattern's been the same forever: They come, they build, maybe they teach. There's a brief period of maturity, sufficient that later cultures don't understand how the growth could even be possible. Then, all at once, there's a reset. Those advanced cultures — Egyptians, Mayans, and on and on — vanish, leaving a handful of dumb ancestors who grow up able to do none of what the old cultures could." He raised a hand and ticked off points. "Not just the megaliths, but monuments like the Nazca lines, Sanskrit texts describing Vimanas and other obviously flying craft, the writings in the Zohar of the manna machine, the list goes on. Maybe past visitors have just wiped memories and destroyed records to erase all this knowledge instead of invoking a mass extinction, but then why do we sometimes hear the Ark of the Covenant described as if it were a radiation weapon?"

"Your point?" Charlie said.

Benjamin tapped around on his computer, displaying images of blue faux-glass monoliths in the nine worldwide capitals.

"They *come*. They *build*." He tapped the under-construction megastructures, all similar to the Heaven's Veil Apex. "And based on some of the new tech blips coming from the cities, sufficient that we can get them, I'd say they're *teaching*. But what's next? Maybe there's nothing under Vail, fine. But we can't just dismiss the possibility because it seems unlikely based on, 'Well, they'd just use The Force to get at it if something was there.' Every one of these eight other spots, investigators have already known there's been alien contact. *Every one* of the modern capitals other than Vail is a place we know they've visited before. So doesn't it make sense — not as proof, but as a reason to not give up and say it probably isn't so — that there might be something at Vail, too?"

"Giant spaceships," Charlie emphasized. "*Psychic* giant spaceships. And this is how they conduct business. They build a pyramid then dig for gold like humans."

"Excuse me," Danika said, raising a hand.

"Yes. Danika has the floor." Benjamin gestured for Charlie's benefit.

"I said, what if they *do* know exactly where it is, right there under Vail, but can't just 'use The Force' because it needs to be carefully excavated?"

"Like nineteenth century coal miners," Charlie said.

"Like intelligent beings who know to be careful when

unearthing an ancient weapon," Danika retorted.

"That's another thing," Charlie said. "They can incinerate us no problem, but for some reason they need a doomsday device to finish us off. And they don't just *require the device*; they *leave the device behind for thousands of years* instead of taking it with them."

"You *know* there's evidence of a shift in the Earth's axis after each incursion. Maybe it's something that's necessarily planet based."

"Now who's grasping instead of using the scientific method?"

Danika sat on the edge of Benjamin's desk, her always-thin patience snapping. "Okay, Charlie. So you don't want to keep scoping GeoSurvey for maps to help us find what's *obviously* not there. You don't think we should have sent Cameron. You—"

"I didn't say we shouldn't have sent Cameron. I also didn't say we shouldn't keep looking. I'm just saying it seems unlikely."

"Well, then, duly noted. Charlie doesn't have an alternative plan. He just wants to bitch about the plan we *do* have while the rest of us go about our business."

Benjamin waved his hands, asking for peace.

Danika and Charlie stopped bickering, both turning to find his eyes.

"Look, none of this changes our plans. Maybe there's nothing to the Thor's Hammer theory, but it definitely seems possible, and we can't just reject it on circumstance. It's *also* still possible they're really here to understand us and have no ill intentions. But I have trouble believing the benevolent-visitors angle these days."

"Considering they keep killing humans and herding them into what are essentially internment camps," Charlie said.

"Maybe they just have really bad people skills," Danika

offered. "Get it?"

"Regardless, it's all just guesswork because we don't have enough information. The best we can do is to—"

Danika cut him off.

"Information is the problem. It really *is* just guesswork. The Internet's back up, but so what? It's clearly being controlled. I can't raise half the sites I need, and we're definitely being filtered from the Middle East and Asia, maybe Europe. I get the distinct impression that even what we're getting from Central America is being ... I don't know ... altered somehow? There's just no way to parse fact from fiction."

"We know they're interfering," Charlie said as if rehashing an exhausted topic. "Censoring, blocking IPs, actively changing what's out there. It's almost random. That's what makes it so hard to work around. You don't know what you don't know."

"Well," said Benjamin, "then maybe I should tell you about something else I discussed with Cameron." He tapped his fingers on the desk. This part had always been controversial, which is why he'd waited to mention it — until *after* the ship had already sailed.

Danika said, "What," but it wasn't a question.

"Something I sent with him. Something we need handled, no matter what."

Danika's dark-blue eyes regarded his. "What are you saying, Benjamin?"

He looked at Charlie then Danika. "I gave him Canned Heat."

"Oh, hell." Danika sighed then turned away.

"Well," said Charlie, "I guess we can expect that worldwide network failure any day now."

"*Dammit*, Benjamin. Terrence wasn't even finished with it. That thing's based on years' old technology. Even *then* it was a risk."

Calmly, Benjamin said, "Terrence says there seems to be a communication hub in Heaven's Veil."

"Obviously," Charlie said.

"But he thinks it's run through the network center right there at the viceroy's mansion."

Charlie was about to say more, but something stopped him cold.

"The hub and Heaven's Veil database are sending the native connection off the ground unfiltered and out into some sort of unfamiliar wireless network. We don't have to understand the way the ships communicate; we just have to cut them out of the loop. The Canned Heat virus can do that. And don't worry about it being old technology, Danika; I don't think the Internet's evolved a lot during the occupation. Hell, the Astrals don't even seem to *understand* the Internet. Why do we do our thinking out in cyberspace instead of in our heads like they do? It's collective consciousness without being conscious. Terrence can modify the virus, once he has the code and hardware from Cameron. If he can plug it in and find what he expects to, the virus's release should give us a window without the Astrals knowing. We'll grab zettabytes of data before they can fix it, and create secure tunnels under the surface for after. Terrence has plans for those tunnels already. He just needs the Heat."

Charlie huffed. "If it works."

"It'll work. I trust Terrence. I trust his work."

"You'd better," said Charlie, "or we can say goodbye to whatever connections we've managed to cobble together so far — and to Terrence and Cameron when they get caught trying."

The office fell silent. Benjamin didn't respond because there was plenty of truth in Charlie's words. But that didn't make the risk less worth taking; it was pretty much all they had. If they wanted to know the Astrals' true colonization plans — especially the daunting revelation of what might be happening under the Apex in Heaven's Veil — this was the only way.

"You could have just emailed the virus to Terrence and saved Cameron the legwork," Danika said. "Forget the hardware. Just compress Heat into an image file and tell Terrence it's a lost nude picture of Pam Grier from the 1970s."

"Funny," said Charlie, not at all amused.

# CHAPTER 12

Piper clutched the small card, bobbing between buildings, staying low and still feeling stupid. She'd crouched her way out to Terrence's house, ducked behind his hedge before knocking, then stooped her way through his door before closing it like a conspirator.

And look how that had turned out.

She hadn't heard the low, rattling sucking of the Reptar since she'd made her way out the back of Terrence's house, around to the public gate, then sauntered into the city with a nod to the guard as if everything were perfectly ordinary. She had no idea what she was doing. It had been two years since she'd done anything other than stand beside Meyer and pretend he was unchanged and fabulous. But even during the exodus from New York and all their adventures thereafter, she'd never truly been on her own.

This was all so odd, only having herself to rely on. She'd always had *someone*. First, she'd had Meyer, followed by the kids, Raj, Heather, and eventually Cameron and his crew. Then she'd had Cameron — including the months when he'd had *her*.

She still felt guilty about that, even though Meyer had

been gone. She still loved her husband, but it was hard to feel she'd been out of line with Cameron. There were things Meyer hadn't told her, and places he'd gone alone. There was little difference between them.

Although really ... was Meyer as ignorant about what had happened between her and Cameron as she hoped?

Piper stopped behind a building that was as anonymous as all the others. Without circling to the front, there was no way to tell if the place was a residence, a restaurant, or a quasi-black market hardware store. Heaven's Veil had sprawled a lot since its days as Vail (or, more specifically, Meyer's small corner), and with increased growth had come the usual human downfalls: crime, menace, even a proliferation of have-nots in a supposedly idealized socialist city.

But appearances could be deceiving. She'd learned that during her time as the viceroy's wife, queen in all but name.

There was poverty even without circulating currency, just as there was wealth.

There was crime despite the peacekeepers.

There was corruption, even though the authorities were supposedly beyond profiteering.

For a second — seeing graffiti on new walls, and the slinking forms of undesirables in what was supposed to be one of nine global utopias — Piper saw her species through the Astrals' eyes. The ships had changed their world, but what she was seeing now would have existed anyway, somewhere, in some form. Evil bloomed where humans gathered, like rust in oxygen. It only required time.

She shrugged the thought away and peered again at the card Terrence had given her. Flimsier than a business card but too small for a flier. A sticker without adhesive.

It read:

NEW REDEMPTION CHURCH
401 Dempsey Avenue

Come and Be Elevated

A curious thing, Piper thought, for Terrence to have
in his house. An even more curious thing for Terrence to
hand Piper on her way out, when time and nerves were in
short supply. Terrence had never struck her as particularly
religious — or religious at all, to tell the truth. He was a man
of logic, not faith. He'd even openly laughed at the new
religions that had sprung up after the colony's formation.
*People always need something to believe in, even if they know up
front it's bullshit*, he'd said.

But Terrence had handed her this card. A tiny
advertisement to have her spirit lifted in times of crisis. It
was as if she'd been abused and he'd suggested heading to
a shelter.

Piper clutched the card like a talisman, trying not to feel
the depth of her loneliness. She'd always had someone to
lean on. Or take care of. She was great as half of a whole,
terrific with a partner. Piper had learned she was a capable
leader — but even a leader needed someone to follow.

Here, in the increasingly bad part of Heaven's Veil,
Piper had no one.

Nobody except the little card given by a friend.

She thought back to Terrence — and thinking of him
took her mind to Meyer, from whom she'd so recently stolen.
The man she loved, desired, and feared in equal measure.
Here and now, Piper wondered if she was in trouble with
her husband. She'd walked by the gate guard. *Was* she in
trouble — had she been discovered?

Maybe they'd never let her return. Maybe this was her
new life.

Oh, how the mighty have fallen.

Piper thought of the Reptar at Terrence's door and its
death rattle breath. The black paw; its twining, shifting skin.
The way the creatures moved. Those movements were so

(go ahead, say it) *alien*. The way she'd seen Reptars swarm: not civilized like the quiet Titans, but as a frantic mass, like feeding piranha. Titans carried discreet weapons just like the shuttles that could supposedly vaporize enemies, though Piper had never seen or heard of a Titan using one. The Reptars carried no such weapons. Maybe they had brains and logic, as those in the know swore they did. But it was hard to remember that after seeing them swarm, tearing heads from bodies, arms from torsos, shredding skin from limbs in long, red-ribbon curls.

If Piper returned, would the peacekeepers be there to meet her?

Did someone, somewhere, know what she'd done — what she'd *learned?*

And if they did, would she be tried and found guilty, ripped to bits? Or would she be propped up again, secretly watched, kept as the necessary companion to the powerful Meyer Dempsey? Meyer had done that with Raj, after all. His granddaughter needed a respectable father, so Raj had officially (and compulsorily) become family. Piper's visibility and public popularity might be her get-out-of-jail-free card. If so, maybe the worst she'd endure would be a sort of slavery at home.

Piper was consulting the card, trying to work out the unknown church's position relative to hers, when she heard the tapping of stone on stone.

She knew the rhythm: a peacekeeper behind her.

Piper's breath quickened. Her heartbeat doubled its speed. She pressed her back to the building.

Piper could hear the thing coming. Then she could see it.

The Reptar was facing the opposite way. Piper fell back slowly, without any idea of how well the creature could hear. Did it sense every step, biding its time before turning to confront her, its skin giving off its curious blue glow between ebony scales, eyes dialing in and shifting their colors, its mouth open to display row upon row of teeth like thorns? Or would she remain invisible to its senses unless it turned?

Could other senses give her away?

Peacekeepers had bodies not unlike a large dog, but they moved like bugs on four legs. Limbs skipped too quickly, at odd angles, buckling and twitching, pausing and reanimating when their interest was captured. They could bound like predators, but their movement had a curious burst-pause-burst pattern, like a scurrying spider.

If it turned now, the Reptar could be breathing down her throat within a second or two.

Or — since the creatures seemed to always breathe in rather than out — it might be *sucking* down her throat. Subtly pulling her into its too-far-unhinged jaw, toward that needle teeth forest.

Could it smell her?

Could it somehow taste Piper on the air, like a snake's bifurcated tongue?

The Titans looked like idealized men and women — strong, powerful, almost Zen. Reptars were the opposite.

Maybe they saw through compound eyes, like a honeybee.

Maybe they saw through sonar, like a bat.

Maybe they saw in infrared or ultraviolet or X-rays. Maybe it could see Piper now, as she slipped around a corner.

She'd never imagined that a Reptar could see through walls, but who knew what senses an alien species might have evolved?

Piper waited, her breath shallow and held, heartbeat like a snared rabbit's. She listened. She heard the clack of its somehow hard-ended feet on stone. She heard the short inhale as purred — smelling for her, perhaps.

Or maybe it was out on a normal patrol, minding its normal duties to the city: allowing those who didn't cause trouble to stay, while slaying the troublemakers.

Maybe she could walk right by the thing, and it would let her go. But Piper didn't want to find out. Reptars weren't dumb animals. They'd stop you. Assess you. Interview you in their invasive way ... but because humans couldn't communicate directly with Reptars in any meaningful fashion, it was hard to plead a decent case.

The clicking, inhaling, rattling sounds receded. After a breathless moment, Piper exhaled, her eyes closing of their own accord.

She had to reach the church. The place Terrence had so heartily dismissed in words — then endorsed when push came to shove.

She ran through the guts of Heaven's Veil, hearing the rattle of bones at every corner.

# CHAPTER 13

It took Piper a while to find the church. She had no familiarity with this part of Heaven's Veil and felt somewhat guilty for her ignorance. She was apparently too fancy for the city's lesser quarters — and this despite the sector being just an hour away on foot. It was a breed of guilt she'd once associated with being white and relatively privileged, but now she felt it for being one of only a handful of humans used by the Astrals as puppets.

At each turn, Piper paused and peeked around, stopping to listen like an old school bus at a railroad crossing. She saw peacekeepers a few times and human police a few others. She avoided them on a hunch, still unsure whether they were looking for her or merely on their usual rounds. There were a few close calls. Once, Piper found herself in a Reptar's direct line of sight. The thing crossed a street two blocks down, and she froze, trying to appear occupied by something on the street by her feet. It halted, slunk closer, then suddenly lost interest and turned, off to find other prey.

After the close call, Piper darted into a residential backyard (really just a stone courtyard) and snatched a black shawl from a clothesline. Feeling ridiculous, she wrapped the thing over her head like a babushka, allowing it to hang over most of her upper body. An absurd look: she was still wearing one the pretty dresses Meyer liked — something that didn't complement the half burka even a little.

Piper finished her journey sneaking, sure her efforts to hide were making her more (rather than less) obvious.

Eventually, she found Dempsey Avenue, felt disgusted by its existence, and found that once on the street, the church's spire was plainly visible. Piper was at the door ten minutes later.

The church was adjacent to the city's outer wall, which in this quarter was nothing more than a fence with barbed wire at the top. Fences weren't meant for security. Piper, as wife of the Heaven's Veil viceroy, had more insight into city security than the average citizen — not *all*, of course, but enough to know the shuttles kept the place safe, not the fences. The fences were there to make a point: *if you leave, it won't be so easy to come back ... so maybe you'd better stay put.*

Few people ever wanted to leave anyway, and visitors would be stupid to try and climb in without going through the official checkpoint — but new arrivals were rare these days. There had been a time of great migration, influx, and exodus, but capitals and outposts had mostly stabilized, and citizens knew to play by the rules, lest they end up as a pile of blackened ash, or a peacekeeper's dinner.

Before trying the door, Piper paused to peek through the fence at the first of the enormous effigies in the parched land beyond: one of many religious artists' stabs at a portrait of Divinity, the rumored Astral class that never left the motherships.

The door opened. Piper's hand had been resting on the wood while she looked through the fence at a twisted, angular black-marble monstrosity, so the door's sudden retreat surprised her. But it was only a Rational Monk — a man in a brown cloak, his chest bearing the symbolic lever and fulcrum.

"Oh, I'm sorry," the monk said, watching Piper jump. "I didn't realize you were standing there."

Piper's hand had gone automatically to her chest. Her head shawl had come askew, and now her hair was mostly in her face. From the neck up, she probably seemed like a crazy vagrant. From the waist down, she probably looked like she was ready to go skipping in the park with her parents on the better side of town.

The monk didn't seem to notice her odd attire or care. He appeared in his forties, with small, round glasses beneath his hood and short, graying hair. He lowered the hood then looked at Piper's quasi-babushka, seeming to encourage her to do the same. She did not. She'd spent almost two hours on high alert, jumping at every sign of possible pursuit. Relaxing would take a while to come.

"Are you seeking elevation?"

It was a ritual greeting. Piper had seen the monks around and thought they were nut jobs, but the duality of their garb always made her wonder if she was being fair. On one hand, the New Redemption Church and others had formed their cult-like religions within months of the city's formation and begun praying at the altar of Interstellar Jesus. That unseated Piper a little, whose relationship to Traditional Jesus had always been complex. But on the other hand, they wore that insignia on their robes — supposedly a nod to pragmatic realism. The lever was one of the simple machines — a group of concepts that first helped mankind master its physical world.

"I ... I'm not sure why I'm here."

The monk took Piper's hand. "Many who find us feel the same. Were you admiring the images?"

Piper wasn't sure what the monk meant, but then saw him looking through the fence at the black stone creature, buried to the waist with its hands raised as if in greeting.

He didn't wait for her answer.

"One tenant of our predecessor faiths was to refrain from creating graven images. The intention, as we interpret it, was to not worship false idols." He gestured. "But we believe these are the *true* idols."

"You think God was an alien?"

"We seek the truth. Whichever form it may end up taking." He gestured again. "This is only one guess as to how our deliverers may appear."

"Well, they don't look like *that*," said Piper, who'd lived around Titans and run from Reptars in just the past few hours alone.

"I refer to the unseen class," said the monk.

"That's a lot of work for a guess of something you've never seen." The effigy was huge — the size of a moderately sized building in the New York of her not-terribly distant past. She'd heard cranes at work on this side of the city before. She didn't think permission to work outside Heaven's Veil fell under Meyer's purview, but clearly the Astrals had no issue — allowing the church to build as it wished as a tribute or possible warning. Piper hadn't been outside the city since the fences had gone up, but she'd heard there were church-built effigies surrounding it. All were different — each a specific artist's attempt to capture the unseen face of his new god.

The monk had apparently finished discussing the statue. He took Piper by her shawl-covered upper arm and gently steered her toward the door.

"Come. It doesn't matter *why* you've come. Only that you seek elevation. We welcome all who are interested in the truth."

Piper was suddenly unsure she wanted to enter the

church after all, no matter what Terrence had shoved into her hand. It seemed dark in there, and was sure to be filled with weirdos in robes who thought God looked like a praying mantis.

She moved opposite the monk, not quite pulling away but not going with him either. The slight tugs in different directions resulted in a stalemate, but it did unseat her shawl. It spilled from Piper's head and pooled in a drape across the monk's beckoning arm.

His gaze met her big, blue, famous eyes.

"You're Piper Dempsey," he said, his mouth slightly open.

"I ..." Piper couldn't finish. The monk's grip had tightened slightly — just enough to inform her that he wouldn't be letting her escape so easily. She tried again. "I made a mistake. I need to go."

"You are, aren't you? I've seen you on television. On the city network. You're the viceroy's wife."

She tried to pull away, but the man's grip tightened further. He wasn't overly large, but she was small. Piper could flee, if she hit him.

"That's right," she said, trying to puff up. "So you'd better let me go right now."

The monk shook his head then pulled her hard, his grip certain. Piper found herself stumbling into the church after him, the big wooden door falling closed behind them.

With the door closed, the stone room's silence was palpable. An empty silence didn't permeate the cathedral; it was a thoughtful, contemplative quiet. The place was inhabited by no fewer than thirty monks, men and women, all staring directly at Piper.

She opened her mouth to protest, scream, or bluff her way out, but nothing came.

Piper was caught, quite literally.

She felt herself twisted, then looked back to see the monk holding her leaning back to slide a heavy bolt into place on the church door.

"Tell Gloria to call off the search," he told the others. "I've found her."

# CHAPTER 14

The motorcycle came with a helmet. Cameron had to yank it from its dead rider's head — simple because the head, like the rest of the body, had been transformed into shiny charred cinders like those on a campfire floor.

Cameron shook the helmet out and blew inside to clear the dust. He set the thing on his head, then heard a chirp and realized it was active, still paired with its bike. It took him a while to figure out which bike the helmet matched, but he found it soon enough. He righted the heavy vehicle, kicked it to life, then threaded it back past the barricade its rider and his companions (*Her* companions? It was hard to tell gender from ashes) had unwisely decided to cross.

Passing the barricade made Cameron nervous. Nathan Andreus had promised him clear passage to the Heaven's Veil gates, but he'd offered no escort. Cameron was trusting Andreus about two things — one he hoped was true, and one he hadn't even thought to ask. He was trusting that Andreus was a man of his word, and would prevent his men from waylaying Cameron — hopefully also keeping the roads clear of human marauders outside the Andreus camp, if there were any fool enough to cross without permission.

But Cameron had also assumed that safe passage meant clearing the road of human interference. The bikers, however, had been incinerated by a shuttle. Did Andreus have sway with the shuttles? Or was he only promising to keep *himself* out of the way, leaving Cameron to roll dice with the rest?

He looked slightly upward, afraid to properly scan the sky and topple the bike. He'd only ridden a motorcycle once before and felt uneasy atop it. He straddled it to look above. The sky was empty. But shuttles moved like hummingbirds; one might blink into position any second. He'd never know what hit him.

Cameron could only keep moving.

So he did. The roads were vacant except for a few broken-down hulks the Republic must've cleared away with tow trucks or heavy machinery.

At the first roadblock, Cameron's heartbeat had quickened and he'd reached for the pistol at the small of his back — the one Andreus's lieutenant had taken upon arrival and returned at departure. Before Cameron could get close enough to merit withdrawing the weapon, the blockade shifted. Soldiers pulled an orange-and-white highway barricade aside then flanked the gap like ushers. Cameron practically expected them to salute as he passed.

The second roadblock was the same.

The third was slightly larger, on the periphery of one of Andreus's many unofficial settlements in the outlands. Cameron could see paths that were almost roads (some floored in gravel), buildings, and cleared sections of trees. Guards wore official-looking uniforms, unlike the ruffians Cameron had previously encountered.

He rolled through their gap then stopped the bike and turned toward one of the guards. Cameron tapped one of the circular gauges on his dash panel.

"I'm low on fuel. I don't suppose you can set me up with

any?"

Cameron fully expected a "fuck off" — in which case he'd roll on, hoping to siphon from a dead gas station, cursing himself for not grabbing an electric bike and harvesting charges from the others. His chances if he had to siphon were, he thought, rather slim. He'd probably end up walking the rest of the way. The world's gas had gone bad months ago; you were lucky if you could fire an engine.

But the guard nodded and beckoned. Cameron puttered forward, only now realizing that he'd ridden a hundred miles without a hitch. The bike was a hybrid, of course, but still the gas had ignited, hadn't misfired or given him any trouble at all.

The guard stopped at what looked like an old oil barrel suspended six feet in the air on a lashed-together wooden stand. He removed a hose with a nozzle and looked at Cameron, waiting for his next move.

Cameron killed the engine, and the guard filled his tank.

"Where is this gas from?" Cameron asked.

"We have a supplier," the guard said without looking up.

"Who?"

"Who do you think?"

The guard's tone was terse, so Cameron didn't press further. The guard's question was likely rhetorical, but Cameron didn't *think* anyone at all, and had inquired because he didn't know. Did the guard mean the aliens were manufacturing fuel? If so, why? They didn't use gasoline. Its use polluted the atmosphere. But if the ships were using their technology to refine oil or allowing human refineries to regrow and do the same, Cameron hadn't a clue. And, he supposed, it didn't matter.

Before pulling away, he chanced a final query.

"How are you communicating with your headquarters?"

"None of your business."

"He's letting me pass," Cameron said, trying to sound braver than he felt. "I think he'd want you to tell me, don't you?"

The guard's eyes flicked to the side. "The Republic has its own communication system."

"Is it over the air?"

"That's classified."

"Look," Cameron said. "I just want something to listen to. I can't get the radio to work on this thing."

"There's no radio out here, you asshole," said a second guard. He didn't elaborate, but Cameron knew he wasn't referring to the bike's lack of receiver — but to the lack of public radio broadcasts this far out.

"You can listen to the pirate bands if you want," said the first guard, probably remembering what Cameron had said about Andreus and where his favors had fallen.

He tapped the console a few times, and Cameron heard a burst of static in his helmet speakers. The pairing between helmet and bike suddenly felt purposeful. Until now, he'd only been able to listen to system notices, like the low fuel warning that had caused him to stop in the first place.

"Tune it here." He tapped the console again.

Cameron tapped around but realized something delightfully unexpected: He could enter a manual frequency into the receiver. Most radios weren't like that, restricted to the public range of both the frequency- and amplitude-modulated bands. But Cameron had memorized a number before he'd left Moab (a slow frequency that would carry low-fidelity voice outside the normal ranges) but hadn't thought he'd be able to use it until reaching the city and Terrence's equipment.

Cameron thanked the guard, who seemed annoyed, then steered out and was again on open road before he dialed the frequency and spoke into the wind-dampening microphone that lowered from his helmet on a boom.

"Hey," he said. "Hey, Ivan. You suck."

It wasn't official protocol language but whatever. Nobody would be listening at a frequency this low and so far outside the normal range. Maybe the Astrals, but that only meant he'd have to watch what he said, not the official manner in which he said it.

"Cameron?" came a woman's voice.

"Who is this?"

"Danika."

"I thought I'd get Ivan."

"Predictably, Ivan found something better to do. He's all for the comm room, except when he has to sit here for hours waiting. So I'm doing it. But I was listening for Franklin or Terrence, not you."

"You got me," Cameron told her.

"I'll take you."

"Oh. Well, thanks for looking out for me."

"Don't get too excited," Danika said. "I'm only in here because I'm heating up a burrito."

"Oh."

"Are you there?" Danika, like Cameron, knew the limits of what should be said over the air and didn't specify where *there* was. Terrence had cobbled together secure protocols in the past, but this wasn't one of them. Most of the time, Terrence ushered them into an existing system, allowing them to piggyback rather than generating something brand new like this one-on-one radio show. But Cameron's options had always been limited, and both sides knew it.

"I'm on my way," Cameron told her.

"You're calling from halfway?"

"I'm on a motorcycle."

"A motorcycle, huh?" Cameron imagined Danika putting a hand on her slim hip through the pause. "I won't lie. I'm a little turned on."

"Is ... is the main man there?"

He meant Benjamin, but flinched from using his name. He'd already used his own, and Danika had used hers, but for some reason Cameron thought there was a possibility the Astrals might know a Benjamin who knew too much information, out there in the desert. Piper might have told Meyer, who might have finked. But then of course, Meyer would know and be able to tell the aliens about Cameron, too.

"You mean Benjamin?"

*Sigh.* "Yes."

"He's outside somewhere. I think he's trying to look at the ... the hole thingy again."

Danika meant the old money pit, which the ship had used to recharge while hovering above Moab. The same ship, Cameron sometimes thought, that was now over Heaven's Veil and yet never bothered to float back over for long enough to incinerate the camp of dissenters it had spent so much time floating above. They must have better things to do, or found them unworthy of notice.

"How long for you?" Danika asked. Meaning: *How long until you reach Heaven's Veil?*

"Hard to guess. Unless I run into something, maybe two or three hours."

"That close?"

"Yeah."

"Hey, when you get there, can you also — ?"

A flash of something caught his eye. Cameron cut her off. "I've gotta go."

"Why?"

Cameron swallowed, looking at the shimmering cluster ahead.

"Because I've run into something."

# CHAPTER 15

The monk, who'd introduced himself by the name Thelonius (said with a smirk, as if it were a joke), led Piper past the group of milling robed figures, toward the large doors of a back room. Chanting hummed from somewhere — a sound Piper now realized had been forming a subtle buzz in the background for the final few blocks of her journey. She had no idea what times of day the Rational Monk choir did their rational chanting, but if done at night, the area's people must sleep well.

Heads continued to turn toward the dignitary among them as Thelonius dragged Piper through the gathering. They were nearing the choir room, and Piper had a bizarre hope that she wouldn't be asked to sing. The chanting was in Latin, for one. For another, it would have to be about aliens or rational science. She knew some about the former, less about the latter, and none of it in any dead or foreign tongues.

"Unbar the front doors once we're through here," he said to a brown-haired woman, before seeming to reconsider. "Actually, prop them open. I don't think anyone saw us out there, but I feel a sudden urge to appear open and holy."

The woman nodded and crossed the shadowed space to stand by the door. Thelonius stopped in front of the large inner doors as Piper remembered her reticence and pulled against him.

"Who are you?" she asked.

"We're friends. Friends of your friend. Of Terrence."

"How do you know Terrence?"

"It's not important." He tugged again, but Piper resisted. Behind the closed back room door, the rich, deep sounds of the choir continued to roll like soothing tides.

"I have no idea who you are, why you're looking for me, or what you think I—"

"He sent us a message, Mrs. Dempsey. Terrence. He told us that he sent you our way but was concerned that you either wouldn't make it or would fail to understand. You've seen our pilgrims walking the streets?"

Piper nodded.

"Today they walk and search for you."

"Why?"

"On that, I'm trusting Terrence."

Piper looked at the door. This was all too strange. She felt snared in a trap, and took a step back. "Prove it."

"I don't have details."

"Who is Terrence to you?"

Thelonius, who'd seemed so serene outside, now looked urgent, maybe annoyed. He grabbed her again with a glance at the barred front doors.

"*Terrence,*" he said, "is the man we trust enough to believe when he asks us to show the wife of this city's viceroy *this.*"

With Piper's now-bare arm firmly in his grip, the monk leaned back toward the choir room door and rapped a complicated knock on its surface. A loud metallic clang preceded a swinging door and a sight that was nothing like Piper expected.

She'd heard a choir that sounded fifty monks strong, but

there were only three people in the large room. None were singing. They were all working at the strangest computers Piper had ever seen. Each had a touch screen embedded in a large slab of wood, like an ancient console television. The monks were in the same brown robes as the others, but their expressions as they turned, Piper thought, were anything but Zen. There was no serenity or peaceful contemplation. Instead, there was hard light and skeptical intelligence. One was at rolltop desk, holding a plastic device that looked like an enormous syringe with a plunger under his thumb. On the desk, its top open, were dishes, trays, and some sort of electronic fluid-containing device that Piper didn't recognize.

She watched the choir room doors sigh closed behind them, the reticence shocked from her body. Large metal bolts extruded at the edges — bolts that would extend and seat once the doors were closed, but would be mostly invisible when fully recessed. The door itself was much thicker than it appeared, and the monk closing it now was sliding a compartment closed on the right door's surface, hiding a high-tech-looking control panel.

Piper stopped resisting, and Thelonius released her. She looked around the room, noticing something else amiss — just one among many.

"Where are the windows?"

"They're stained glass lightboxes on the outside." His temper seemed to settle with Piper's mood.

"The chanting. Where is the chanting coming from?"

"It's a recording. There are about a dozen speakers in various places, leaking the approximate amount of sound your ear would naturally expect from any given place around the perimeter. Fortunately, that many sources facing out means it doesn't have to be deafening in here to sound loud enough out there."

Piper felt her head shaking. She stepped into the room's

center, baffled. The monk scientists returned to their work, apparently less interested in Piper than those outside.

"What is this place?"

"A place of science," said a voice behind her.

Piper turned. She hadn't seen the large Hispanic woman when she'd entered, but now she saw an alcove to the right filled with a paperwork nest. There didn't appear to be a computer. Just paper.

The woman was dressed in a robe similar to the others, but her hood, also down, appeared much fuller, its color a deep maroon. Her insignia was slightly more ornate, edged in golden thread. That struck Piper as strange, too, considering that traditional monks were supposed to eschew flair to celebrate modesty and homogeneity. But then again, these weren't traditional monks.

The woman held out a hand. "I'm Gloria Reyes, this order's abbess."

"Abbess?"

"Spiritual leader of a monastery," Gloria explained.

Piper looked around, feeling more out of place than at any time in her life. She was wearing a girlish summery dress and half of a draped shawl on her shoulders. Her hair was askew but carefully brushed. She must look immodest amid the monks, city royalty among the poor. Famous among the anonymous. Infamous while the monks, apparently, championed the resistance.

"But you're not a religion," said Piper. "It's a cover for ... for whatever I'm seeing."

"We're very much a religion," Gloria said. "Honest religions seek the truth."

"Then what is all this?"

"The search for truth."

Piper paced the room, drawing glances from the working monks. Thelonius waited, silent behind her.

"We're able to convert this room if needed." Gloria

gestured at one of the huge, wood-framed touch screens, which Piper now saw was backed by some sort of even larger wooden base. "These fold down into pews, hiding the screens at their bottoms," she said, nodding toward a long hinge at the consoles' bases. "Where Michael is working, the rolltop folds down and there's a compartment toward the back, hollowed into the wall behind, to stow his equipment. The door keeps curious eyes out. And if we have time, there are freestanding pews in the narthex we can move into this area here."

Piper looked around. It wasn't like a spy movie. Maybe the space could be made to look like the choir chamber it sounded like, but it wouldn't happen at the pull of a lever.

"What if you don't have enough warning? How did you build this place? Where did you get the big doors with their huge bolts?"

"It's not relevant," Gloria said. "What's relevant is that Terrence sent you to us. The message was limited, but it did suggest that you have something we should see."

The woman held out her hand, softly smiling.

Piper met the abbess's brown eyes. Terrence had sent her here, yes. But there was still far too much unknown to surrender herself so easily. She was tired of the dark. She'd lived in it under Meyer during their flight from New York, then under Cameron. Now she was in the dark yet again under a new Meyer, who kept personal secrets as well as the more tangible sort she'd seen then copied from his office terminal. Piper was tired of not knowing. Tired of not deciding. Tired of being another person's pretty thing to command.

"Did Terrence have this church built?" Piper pretended she didn't see Gloria's open hand.

"No, of course not. A faction here had it built. But in a city this size, under duress, it's never long before curious minds find similar thoughts. Since then, along with us, he's been communicating with others from here."

"Who?"

"We should get started, Mrs. Dempsey." Gloria extended her hand farther.

Piper clasped the drive in her pocket, aware too late that she was drawing an X on her treasure.

"Not yet. First, you tell me who Terrence has been talking to." Piper figured she knew the answer but wasn't about to volunteer information these strangers might not yet have.

"Very well. It's a group in the Utah desert. The principal's name is Benjamin Bannister."

"You know Benjamin?"

"Somewhat. But Terrence knows them best."

Piper's eyes darted around. She urged herself to relax. What were the odds that these people would bring her in here, show her their treason, speak of both Terrence's dual allegiance and Benjamin by first and last name ... and still be playing Piper into a trap? The Astrals wouldn't go to these lengths; they'd have killed or detained her outside. Meyer wouldn't go to such lengths either. His approach to disagreement was simpler and surprisingly effective. He bullied the other party into seeing his way of thinking.

Piper found herself willing to deliver the drive (she'd wanted to reach Benjamin and was now at the source), but Gloria lowered her hand from its beckoning then gestured to a second alcove and a pair of comfortable-looking chairs.

"Please have a seat," she said. "You seem uneasy."

"I'm okay."

"Nonetheless." She gestured more firmly.

"Really, I'm okay."

"You have questions."

"It's fine," said Piper, now fearing a conversion sermon. They were scientists, sure, but the abbess had made it clear this was also religion. Piper had grown up religious, giving her mixed feelings today. In Piper's experience, the pushiest among the faithful saw the unenlightened as filled with questions. Conveniently, the church always had answers.

"Please, have a seat. Time is always short, but it's important that you're comfortable."

"I'm okay," Piper said for the third time.

The abbess approached, using her superior bulk to herd Piper toward the chairs.

Piper sat. Gloria followed. Scientists continued to work in the background.

"Are you going to tell me why your people carve those stone effigies around the city walls?" Piper asked, unsure what to say.

"The artists among us believe in something they cannot see, and hope to reach it through the journey of spirit."

"Oh," Piper said.

"That's the perfect place to begin," the abbess said. "We believe this is happening because your husband did the same thing."

# CHAPTER 16

"Mommy," said Clara, "what did Grandpa lose?"

Lila looked at her daughter. Once upon a time, she would have been shocked by the child's ability to manage a sentence like that at two years old. But given the other developmental leaps Clara had taken ahead of time (early crawling, early walking, an eerie inability to be fooled while playing peekaboo), Lila usually thought of Clara as *normal in advance*. It wasn't like she had a talking infant — just a precocious toddler. She could almost close her eyes, pretend she'd given birth five years ago instead of two, and forget for long periods of time that other mothers had it different.

Instead of noticing the girl's words, Lila found herself wondering how to respond to the question's oddity.

"I don't know, sweetie. His wallet?"

"What's a wallet?"

Right. That didn't make sense. Her father had lost his wallet in the past because he didn't carry it in his back pocket like most people, but now he didn't even have one. Same for car keys. Maybe the world was on its way to perfection: a place with literally nothing to lose.

Lila squatted next to Clara. "I don't know, sweetie. Why

don't you tell me?"

"I don't know what it is."

"Then how do you know he lost anything?"

"*No*, Mommy," Clara said, giving her a look well beyond even her seeming years — a look straight from the derisive face of Grandma Heather. "I mean I don't know what the thing he lost *is*."

Lila stood. She didn't like questions like this and usually responded the way many parents answered their children's questions about sex: by pretending they hadn't heard then changing the subject.

Clara's question filled Lila's awareness with a dark cloud. Clara knew Meyer had lost something and could picture it just fine. But unlike a remote control or a tablet, Clara didn't recognize the thing. She wasn't asking *if* something was lost; she *knew* what was lost but couldn't identify it. Maybe it was a wallet after all.

"Oh, I don't know, honey." Lila looked toward the window. "It's such a nice day outside. Would you like to play in the yard?"

Clara brightened, her thoughts easily distracted. "Sure! Can Daddy come too?"

"Which Daddy?" Lila, hearing herself, flinched. It was a habit she was supposed to discourage, not off-the-cuff perpetuate. If Raj ever heard Clara (let alone Lila) refer to Christopher as "Daddy Chris," he'd lose his head. He might even request that Christopher lose his.

Clara beat her to the punch. She sprang up and gave Lila another of those condescending Heather looks.

"*Daddy* daddy, Mommy."

"I'm sorry, honey, Daddy can't play right now."

"Why not?"

"He's working," Lila said. Though *that* was a laugh.

"Oh, Daddy is *always* working!" Clara pouted.

"Well, we'll just have to play without him. Want to go to

Grandma's house and—"

A voice behind Lila cut her off. "Play without whom?"

Lila turned. Raj was behind her, wearing his ridiculous robe and even more ridiculous canvas shirt beneath. He claimed the outfit was culturally Indian — and that now more than ever it made sense to honor their old cultures as the world melted together. But in Lila's opinion, the world wasn't *melting together* so much as *melting*. It was true that cultural borders were decaying into multicultural cityscapes worldwide, almost as if humans were being deliberately shuffled. But that didn't make his get-up any less ridiculous, or make her want to wear lederhosen and a cap with a green feather to celebrate her German-Irish roots. And besides, since when was canvas beneath a robe Indian? He did that because the shirt was warm and Raj was always cold — and never mind the incongruity.

"Daddy!" Clara ran to Raj.

He scooped her up. "You weren't going to play without me, were you?"

"I thought you were working," Lila said.

"It's under control. Interestingly, it looks like your stepmother was the problem."

"Piper?"

Raj nodded.

"That's ridiculous. The peacekeepers are just riled up after that plane attack. There are too many out there on the streets. They're going to cause more problems than good." Lila couldn't help adding, "As always."

"I see," said Raj. "So your solution is to just let Piper go."

"Let her go for what? Are you saying she did something wrong?"

"Perhaps."

"How the hell could Piper do anything to merit all the ..." Lila stopped herself from saying "shit" then took Clara from Raj's arms and set the girl aside with her toys. Raj looked angry, but Lila didn't feel like caring.

She whispered, "How Piper could merit all the bullshit out there is beyond me, Raj."

"Fortunately, you don't have to agree since it isn't your call."

"It's not yours either."

Raj's brown eyes hardened. Lila wasn't surprised to feel a flash of fear. Still, her irritation was stronger. As she'd reminded him before, Raj should never have made it to Colorado and had only been saved by the grace of her father. What's more, Old Dad would have punched a hole in Raj's face after learning that he'd knocked up his daughter. The fact that things had turned out different were just Raj's good luck.

"I'm Commander of the Guard."

"Christopher is *Captain* of the Guard," Lila said. "Sounds redundant, but what do I know?"

"Are you questioning my position?"

"I've questioned your position for years, *hon.*"

His jaw worked. Lila's heart beat harder, but she kept her eyes on his. And to think: she'd gazed into this man's eyes with love, back when they'd been stupid kids together.

"You're right," said Raj. "I guess I *don't* have time to play today."

"Shocking," Lila said, tallying off a mental point won.

"What does that mean?"

"It means that I'm a single fucking parent, Raj. *That's* what."

"Really? That's my bed in there, too."

"Oh, and how happy I am about *that.*"

Again, Raj's eyes watched Lila's. She reminded herself that even though the man across from her was commander of the guard (and chief network nerd, among many other useless titles) and the viceroy's son-in-law, *she* was the viceroy's daughter. Her father might think this family needed to appear shiny and happy for the laughably named free press, but that didn't mean Lila had to lie down and take it from someone whose only relation was through the viceroy's granddaughter.

Raj's head twitched toward Clara, who Lila hoped had managed to miss every word, despite her excellent hearing and astonishing powers of comprehension. Her father's voice, when he spoke next, was saccharine sweet.

"Hey, honey," he said to Clara. "I'm afraid I won't be able to join you after all."

"What? Why?" Clara snapped.

Despite her fury at Raj, Lila had to cover her mouth to hold in a smile. Hearing her husband abused by his barely-out-of-diapers daughter was funny in itself, and it got funnier when she did it in Heather's caustic, mocking tone. Lila half expected a racial epithet to follow — possibly something having to do with spicy food or math skills.

"I have to work," Raj said, his voice still pleasant. He crossed to the girl, stooped, then gave Lila a look before kissing Clara and straightening again. Lila recognized that look, too, and tallied it as another point in her favor. It was his old look: pathetic and sad, as if she'd wounded him and should feel awful about it. Fortunately, Lila had grown immune.

Raj paused at the door then spoke quietly to Lila, his voice edged with spite.

"I know you're close with Piper."

Lila didn't reply, not wanting to play into his games.

"As it turns out, your father seems to think she copied something from his office computer. He won't go into detail, but it seems to be of some importance. Something new from above."

Raj looked up, indicating the mothership. Lila tried to keep her face impassive, but doing so was becoming hard.

She knew her father's modified mind was somehow able to talk directly to the Astrals — not to individuals, but to the hive mind they all seemed to share — but that some information still came down in traditional ways. Before now, that information usually had to do with insurgency and pending attacks, because those things most directly required human involvement and assistance. Raj's assertion that Piper may have stolen from her father — perhaps claimed by the Astrals above — filled Lila with chills. If it were true, Piper would have some serious explaining to do when she returned.

If, that was, she ever *did* return — something a few piecemeal comments by Clara had already caused Lila to doubt.

"So?" said Lila, not feeling the word's intended apathy.

"If it turns out to be a problem, I imagine the questions could extend to others who are friendly with Piper. In the interest of being thorough, you understand."

Lila chewed her lip for a second then stopped. The nervous habit betrayed her.

"Whatever you say, *Commander*."

Lila turned back to Clara, waiting for Raj to leave.

"If the Astrals themselves feel they've lost something to Piper and those who might have helped her," he told Lila's back, "I wonder how far a viceroy's protection could possibly extend?"

# CHAPTER 17

Cameron killed the connection before considering that he should have maybe kept the radio on. But before he could move his finger to reactivate the connection, he realized that the large, burnished-metal spheres above the road ahead weren't the problem. The problem was that he was still screaming down the highway at nearly forty miles per hour, and someone had covered the road with thousands upon thousands of ball bearings.

Cameron used his final moment of wobbling stability to jockey a few inches closer to the left-side berm and gently apply the brakes then surrendered to the inevitable skid.

He managed to slow some but not enough.

When the bike bit the dust, canting hard to the left as the bearings overwhelmed its traction, he struck the ribbed concrete first. He bounced farther left, and his helmet smacked the ribs like keys on a xylophone. Then he rolled into the grass, trying to form a ball to protect his guts from harm.

The bike stalled. He wedged to a stop then lay on the grass, breathing heavily.

Rolling, Cameron managed to extricate what turned out

to be a rather thrashed leg from under the bike. He paused to wonder if he was still alive. He was. By luck, not fate.

Now looking around, Cameron counted himself fortunate — first to have had the helmet, which now had a sizable crack down its middle, then for the grass itself. Back when this road had been maintained, the berm would mostly be hard-packed dirt and gravel. Today, it had sprouted a bushy coating.

Which, for the time being, was also hiding him from sight as long as he stayed mostly flat.

But thinking of the grass as cover was stupid. Someone had placed those ball bearings, and whoever had — likely Andreus's people — would be watching for someone to fall into their booby trap. The spheres ahead, too, had almost certainly seen him coming. And even if they hadn't, they'd surely heard his engine. He'd seen as few Astrals in person as possible but knew from their pirate connection — the censored Internet he was currently on a mission to free — that the two known classes of Astrals could hear just fine.

But even after Cameron sat up, nobody came for him. He could still see the shuttles ahead — not sitting on the ground because the things never seemed to, but floating a few feet above the road — and they hadn't flinched.

They gave no indication that they knew he was even there.

Cameron looked around, not trying to hide, figuring that he almost certainly *had* been noticed, and that the ships simply didn't care, just like they didn't care about Moab. Like they didn't seem to care about the rebel camp nearby.

It was almost insulting.

Cameron looked at down at his leg. He'd been wearing jeans and boots. The denim was shredded, but the damage appeared superficial. He'd managed to slow some and had heaved toward the berm. His jeans seemed to have taken it worst. His skin was still raw and bloody. He'd be picking gravel from wounds for a while and really could use some hydrogen peroxide and Neosporin, but he'd live.

Still leery about exposing himself too fully, Cameron crawled farther over the down-sloping berm and into a drainage ditch before kneeling to give the leg some weight. Tentatively, he stood. It ached, and his jeans seemed to be sticking to the wound even now, but he could walk. And if he could get past, he could still definitely ride. At least far enough to pick up some salve and an assload of Band-Aids.

Now fully upright, he looked at the shuttles above the road ahead. There were five of them, huddled together like beads on a string. Three mostly covered the breadth of the eastbound highway, with one hanging over the grass on either side for good measure.

Still, none had moved.

Cameron looked at the road's surface. There were *thousands* of ball bearings. They were everywhere: some asshole prankster's idea of an excellent time. Even now, he could see the swath he'd disturbed while fishtailing in, rocking before settling and rolling into clusters.

Cameron looked ahead at the shuttles still blocking the highway.

But really: Were they *blocking* it?

Farther down the hill, Cameron could see that the alignment he'd taken to put five ships perpendicular to the road was more of a diagonal. They weren't side by side; they were one slightly behind and to the side of the other, lined at an angle rather than perpendicular to the highway.

Cameron looked to the side. Grass was tall all the way to the trees — and there *were* plenty of trees now, farther from the desert, and into the forested area. He should ditch the bike and walk away — or better yet, right the bike, walk it a bit, and re-key the engine once around the odd alien obstruction. He had no idea why the spheres weren't reacting, but should he question it, or count his blessings and move on?

Something nagged at Cameron. Something on the same frequency he remembered from years ago, when he and Piper had crossed that double line of stones not far from here, south of the highway.

That sense of psychic connection wasn't precisely returning, but the deserted stretch of Andreus-controlled highway felt like a double exposure. There was more here than met the eye, and Cameron's mind was tuning into some of it — whatever *it* was.

He ascended the hill, now standing tall at the road's edge, fearless. Now, his sensation felt closer to curiosity.

But that curiosity wasn't his own.

And considering that there was nobody else here — no Piper to sense, as there had been during his previous psychic inklings — it wasn't those absent people's curiosity, either.

There were no sights, no sounds, no images beyond Cameron's own senses.

But there was that sense of wonder. Or rather, of wonder*ing*.

There was a large building not far from the road. There was also a highway maintenance garage on the left. There would normally be cars here, Cameron supposed, but the Andreus Republic made sure that there weren't. Several dozen thick black cables emerged from boxes on the building's roof to the left. They formed a thick almost-braid, suspended from towers and crossing the roads above ...

Well, right above the line of Astral shuttles, in fact.

With that thought, Cameron realized where he was.

And he realized what the building was.

And then, he realized whose curiosity he must — against all sense — be feeling.

*It was Astral curiosity.* He was feeling a sense of wonder and befuddlement from ... from the alien ships themselves.

There was a strange rattling behind him. He almost

jumped, wondering if a rattlesnake had crept up from behind. Or dozens of rattlesnakes, by the sound.

But it wasn't snakes. Or castanets. It wasn't the stir of bones in a crypt or rolling dice.

It was the ball bearings.

The tiny metal spheres were rising from the road. All of them. Slowly, almost tentatively. Within a moment, they began circling Cameron like a lazy tornado. Assessing without threat. The little BB-like objects seemed to be wondering about him, just as their larger brothers had been wondering about those cables, and about that building to the road's left side.

The building, Cameron knew from Benjamin's attempts to reach an uncensored network, housed operations for MultiPlexity: the leading wired Internet provider for the western United States.

Something about that building made the Astral ships — or possibly those inside it — extremely curious.

Cameron watched the tiny spheres circle him.

A line of the things seemed to reach out like an arm — like a column of insects swirling above a body of water. Cameron felt a nudge at his backpack. He shrugged it from his shoulder. The balls pushed their way inside the pack then used their bulk to force the zipper open from the inside.

The cylinder of what Benjamin had called Canned Heat rose from the backpack on a floating cushion of ball bearings.

"Hey," Cameron said, reaching for the cylinder, dimly aware that he should be frightened, worried about discovery ... basically any emotion other than the numb and stupid curiosity he felt, inherited from the air and its psychic alien activity.

The cushion of tiny balls flinched playfully back. They held the cylinder away from Cameron then covered it in a writhing, moving mass. Its surface became a roiling storm of beads, then drained away and opened like a blooming flower. The bearings held the Canned Heat above his hand and let it go. Cameron caught it.

The swarm moved away, heading toward the five shuttles under the braid of data lines leaving the MultiPlexity building.

Cameron, feeling as if he were in a trance, followed.

His feet found the road's hard surface. There were now no ball bearings on it at all — no hazard for the weary motorcyclist on his way to sabotage. And yet here he was, facing emissaries of those he planned to disrupt, still holding his instrument of destruction. The Astral occupation had bugged and filtered the network, keeping lines of communication between people like Benjamin closed while allowing only population opiates to escape in a parody of freedom. The tiny balls had held the device he'd use to undo all they'd done then let it go.

Just as they were letting *Cameron* go.

*What is it?* said a voice inside his head.

But the voice wasn't his own. Or in English. It wasn't words. Only a feeling, the same one he'd been feeling since he started standing in the grass.

*What is it?* he wondered.

*They* wondered.

Cameron could feel tendrils wanting to infiltrate his mind. Searching for his plans, perhaps — his intentions with that strange metal cylinder he was transporting to the capital from nowhere. But Cameron had felt the intrusion before and thought he could deflect it. He thought of Piper. He thought of Dan, who'd last made this trip at his side. He thought of Vincent, who'd been there too, before he'd been murdered while protecting a family of strangers.

*What is it?*

*It's nothing,* Cameron tried to reply.

The shuttles moved upward, approaching the wire streaming its billions of data bytes drifting side to side to side in rhythm, as if trying to find resonance. Now rising, circling the cables. The ball bearings approached Cameron, and for a blink he thought the cloud of tiny spheres formed a Titan's face, but then it was gone.

*What is it?* he wondered.

*They* wondered.

*It* wondered.

The world, itself, seemed to wonder.

But Cameron wouldn't answer. They could kill him if they wanted. The shuttles could release their death rays and turn him to ash. They could open up and release their terrible black-skinned, blue-glowing creatures with needle teeth. The tall, hairless Astrals could come from the shuttles, walk forward, and snap his neck like a twig. The ball bearings could surround him again, then squeeze the life from his body, clog his throat, or fill his lungs.

They could do anything they wanted, but Cameron wouldn't answer. He could fail at his mission, but he'd never willingly give it up.

*What IS it?*

Now the curiosity was frustrated, borderline angry.

Cameron felt emotion surround him like a cloak. He was so close to something, yet he couldn't solve it. He was a man with four sides and sixteen squares of a Rubik's Cube solved who couldn't move the last two squares into place. He was a man playing solitaire, almost finished but unable to find the final ace. Something felt very, *very* close.

But it was their feeling, not his.

Just as Cameron was considering running after all — as if *that* would make a hair of difference — the bead-like spheres began to float upward like a cloud of hornets. They roiled in a tiny tornado again, now spilling upward instead of down. They coated the lines above, hugging them, making them sag and bounce. They flicked up and down with the eerie speed of their larger counterparts. The five large shuttles rose up and swapped positions, one for the others, like a dealer shuffling cards for three-card monte.

Then all at once, five shuttles and countless ball bearings formed a giant circle in the air, pausing, seeming to send Cameron a silent message. What it was, Cameron had no idea.

Then the formation exploded, flew into separate directions, and was gone.

Cameron stood in the middle of the now-deserted highway for a few more minutes, his foggy mind slowly returning to normal. Then, feeling hypnotized, he slipped the cylinder containing Terrence's communication virus back into his pack. He zipped the bag, shrugged it back onto his shoulders, and took a moment to wonder what the hell had just happened.

Five minutes later, Cameron was again motoring eastward in shredded jeans, with a bloody leg and shattered helmet, unable to radio anyone about his suddenly more interesting mission.

But it was okay. For a while, Cameron was content to have only his own voice in his head.

It took Cameron another hour and a half before the capital gates entered his view — but when they did, a single ball bearing was still rolling along behind him, unseen, like a tiny escort.

# CHAPTER 18

Piper felt acutely aware of the slip drive's presence in her pocket but forgot it once the abbess started discussing things she couldn't possibly know.

"This church represents a diverse group," Gloria said. "There are those like me, who seek the spiritual. There are those like the people in this room and Thelonius here (whose real name is Franklin, by the way) seeking rationality. There are people like Terrence, adept with their minds and hands, easily able to fix things. There are malcontents — people who never quite fit, rarely satisfied with the status quo. But of all the people who know and visit this church, most will never see what you're seeing now."

"Why?" Piper asked.

"Because most people are looking for someone to follow. Others? They're searching for something to believe in. Many want someone to tell them that everything will be fine. Those last are usually lost. I can spot them on sight."

"How?"

"Because *everyone* is lost." The abbess smiled. "I was reverend of a small Methodist church, back before it all. There are many schools of religion and spirituality, but

SEAN PLATT & JOHNNY B. TRUANT

we all have something in common, organized or not —
congregation, bedside, or the depths of a mind."

"What one thing?" Of course, Piper already knew.

"Faith."

Piper repeated the abbess's out-of-place word, deadpan:
"Faith."

"Belief in the absence of a sure answer," Gloria
elaborated. "But you see the trick there, don't you?"

"What trick?"

"Being lost becomes necessary if one is to ever be
found." The abbess shifted in her chair, still smiling in spite
of their strange surroundings. "See, in order for any of us to
get on in life, we must have faith in *something*. And in order
to have any faith, there must be something we cannot *know*
that requires our trust. That leap of faith might be small,
and for most it is. But regardless, *it is still a necessary leap.*
A leap past uncertainty. A leap you took in coming here,
Mrs. Dempsey. A leap you're taking right now in listening to
me, believing I am who I say, and that my words are worth
hearing."

"But you said most of your ... your *congregation?* ... would
never come here. To this room. To know what you really do
at this church."

"There are many things this church does. This room
represents just one. The only one your friend Terrence cares
about, perhaps, and probably the only one you care about
— but merely one of many nonetheless." The abbess looked
toward the closed doors to the chapel's body. "If this bit of
rebellion isn't what they're seeking, they may stay out front
for our services."

"But it's all a sham. A cover."

"Our services are as true as what happens in this room,
helping Terrence reach his friends in Utah."

Piper took a breath, held it, then exhaled with a feeling
of deep fatigue. She must have been running on adrenaline

when fleeing the mansion, then evading the Reptars. Now she was crashing. Piper realized how beaten she was, how frightened she'd been, how alone she was starting to feel.

"What does any of this have to do with Meyer? You said something about my husband."

"I've spoken to enough of those who were taken into the ships and later returned to guess at what compelled him," Gloria said. "But you tell me, Piper: Did he seem strangely driven to come to this place? *Unduly* driven, like a compulsion? Like he was being *told* to come?"

"Are you saying he was in communication with the Astrals from the beginning?" The idea was a little offensive. Piper was split on how she felt about Meyer today, but her root — especially relating to the Meyer of the past — was still in unwavering love. He'd never been a traitor. But he'd surely been compelled.

"Not consciously," Gloria said, seeing Piper's discomfort. "But below the surface, maybe? The accounts I've heard and read — both from the 'lesser abductees,' as they're called, and from people who know the viceroys — all point to a feeling like an itch. Each of the Nine traveled to a place that is now a capital and waited for contact. But if you ask me, it wasn't that these people saw the Astrals coming. I believe the Astrals *saw them.*"

Piper sat up straighter.

Gloria nodded toward the computers, to the scientist working at his bench under the rolltop. Thelonius — Franklin, apparently — had wandered over to stand beside Gloria's plush chair. The abbess nodded, and he brought over a stool then sat atop it to form a rough circle.

"This is a *rational* church," he said. "I taught high school science before coming here. I've never been a religious person, or even believed in God." The monk pointed at the ceiling. "But I do believe in *them.*"

"The Astrals?"

He nodded. "Gloria will tell you that a higher spiritual being watches over us all. I'd say it was a bunch of alien ships. There's room for both our beliefs, but there's no question we've been observed from the start, as if by Gloria's god. Because they've been here before, you know."

Piper nodded, knowing that particular theory from her time in Moab.

"Many people — especially now, given what's happened — believe that some of what ancient people thought of as gods were actually alien visitors. Beings who 'descended from the sky in chariots' and did remarkable things that seemed like magic. They built colossal, impossible structures. They wielded fire and light. They could fly and communicate by thought. To ancient people, they must have seemed *plenty* godlike. It raises questions about so many of the old stories. Maybe the biblical flood was caused by ancient aliens. Maybe there was a real-life Noah's Ark that's nothing like we've imagined before. We can only guess. All we know for sure is that this isn't their first time here. And if they were once interested in us, it makes sense that they'd want to keep an eye on us."

"Which is why there are UFO sightings, right?" Piper was still unsure where this might be going.

"Some, I imagine," said the monk. "Some of those are probably wackos, like everyone's always assumed. But that's not what I'm referring to."

"What then?"

Gloria looked at Thelonius and said, "Go ahead. This is your stuff, not mine."

The monk turned back to Piper, wobbling a bit on his stool. "Look, I could go into a lot of stuff that would bore the hell out of you, but for now let's just say that quantum physics tells us a few things about the universe that are as confusing as they are amazing. Just one of those crazy things is that our world is made up of more than the three spatial dimensions we know: length, width, and height."

"What else is there?" said Piper.

"The math says there are probably seven more. Maybe twenty-three. It's either ten or twenty-six dimensions total, but the point is there are more than we think. We can't access those extra dimensions because they're rolled up too tightly ... but maybe the Astrals can. It would explain how they arrived at Jupiter without us ever having seen them out there before. Maybe they appeared from somewhere else after traveling through one of those higher dimensions. What might commonly be called a wormhole."

He waved his hand like a conversational eraser.

"That's not even my point. To what Gloria was saying, we think the Astrals can't only *travel* through those compressed dimensions. We think they might be able to *see* through them as well."

"See through them?" The words made Piper's skin crawl. She felt watched by an invisible voyeur.

"We argue about this," said Gloria, patting Thelonius companionably on the leg. "But at this point, our rational contingent hits a wall because the next step has to be a leap of faith."

"I don't know about that," Thelonius said.

"It's okay, Franklin," Gloria replied, clearly enjoying the scientist's predicament. "I do, and some day you will, too."

Piper looked from one to the other. "What are you talking about?"

"Even their science holds many things that seem almost spiritual," the abbess explained.

"I wouldn't say it's—"

Gloria cut him off. "His quantum physics basically says that energy responds to intention and thought. That sounds *spiritual* to me. The universe behaving like a giant hologram? Also *spiritual* to my ears."

"The math is more than—"

"You go on, Franklin. Keep trying to calculate my soul." She turned and took Piper's hand in hers. "Honey, they've told me stories about supercolliders being used to smash things together to try and find the universe's secrets — to open up that tight little ball of something they can't understand. But there aren't any of those machines around anymore — and still we know those holes in space are opening today."

"How?"

The abbess tapped her head. "Thought." She eyed Thelonius. "*Prayer.*"

"Meditation," the monk added, his word like a correction. "Altered states of consciousness."

"I hate to admit it," Gloria said, "but it does seem like there's a shortcut to spirit."

"What?"

"Drugs," said Thelonius.

"Not drugs."

"*Drugs,*" the monk repeated. "Not just anything. Most drugs just fu—" He cut himself off, seeming to remember he was a monk in a church. "—just screw you up," he finished. "But of the abductees who've returned, a surprising number report having felt their abductors before, in drug trips. The strongest connections seem to have come from a plant-based hallucinogen called—"

"Ayahuasca," Piper finished. Something she knew all about. Knew her husband's fascination with. Knew how driven and purposeful he felt after those hallucinogenic sessions, and how the aftermath made him do strange things — like purchase unremarkable land in the Colorado mountains and build an end-of-the-world bunker beneath it.

Thelonius nodded. "Precisely."

"They've been watching us," said Gloria. "They've been peeking through the eyes of people like your husband. Maybe through people who are deeply connected without substances, too, like monks." She looked over at the man beside her. "*Real* monks, I mean."

"They know everything then," Piper said, thinking again of the information she'd taken from Meyer's computer and what it might mean. What would the people in this room make of what was on the slip drive? What would Benjamin make of it, if they could, in fact, get it to him? The idea that the Astrals had been peeking over humanity's shoulder filled her with a sinking sense of futility. Organizations like this church were playing rebellion. There was no way to evade an enemy who knew you as well as you knew yourself.

"They don't know *everything*." Impossibly, there was a tiny smirk in the corner of the monk's mouth. He looked at Gloria, who gave him an indecipherable look.

Piper watched them both. "What?"

"The Astrals have come to Earth many times before," Gloria said. "From what we can figure — and from what people like Benjamin Bannister tell us — they've done so when instruments they left behind to guide us have nudged our social evolution forward to a point of critical mass. The Egyptians, the Mayans, the Incas — all cultures who were highly spiritual, highly connected at the level of mind or soul. Cultures who Benjamin thinks were able to call to the Astrals through the combined force of their minds, albeit without realizing they were doing so. But this time, we're different. For the first time, they seem to have arrived and been surprised by what they found."

"Surprised how?" Piper asked.

"This time," said Thelonius, "we've formed a rational society instead of a spiritual one. We've built our own magic devices and a highly advanced technological culture — contrary to past cycles, in which we'd developed more mental connection rather than gadgets, and had *those* tricks to show them when they appeared to check on us."

"So what?"

"Diverting toward technology — and away from mental or spiritual development — has thrown our visitors for a loop," said the monk. "We don't have the group mind they expected — and might need in order to fully understand us. That's why they spent so much time building a network of stones: to fill in the blanks. But it's only partially working. So far, they can't quite comprehend the way modern humans have chosen to store and utilize their collective consciousness. Our current group consciousness is too new — too totally foreign to them."

"What are you talking about?" Piper asked.

The monk smiled. "The Internet," he said.

# CHAPTER 19

Trevor stood at the door to his father's study, wondering if he should dare to follow his instincts.

The computer was right there. *Right friggin' there*, not ten feet away. Trevor had been in this room plenty of times, to grab books from the shelves or look something up in the home's digital library, which was clunky to access anywhere other than at the main console.

He had no business on the computer now. But that could, if he was discovered, be explained. There were no Titans in this part of the house; they were all closer to the dining room, helping to prepare for the evening banquet. Reptars didn't enter the house. The human kiss-asses who did his father's bidding had mostly gone home for the day. Only members of his family might find him tinkering. Trevor could make up excuses for them — maybe say the catalog interface was acting funny. He'd just hopped over for a second. And so on.

Trevor stared at the thin screen, still leaning rather conspicuously in the doorway. Whatever made Piper run had come from inside. It might *still* be there. He'd passed his father earlier and seen him agitated, mumbling about folks sticking their noses into things that didn't concern them. Surely, he'd have known what she'd taken. And it's not like computers were filing cabinets. You copied files, then only deleted them if you had a good reason and knew how to do it without alerting anyone. Piper would have had neither.

Trevor could go to the computer now, poke around, and maybe discover what Piper had found. *Maybe.* It felt worth a stupid, foolish, futile shot, given his current inner turmoil over his missing stepmother. If Trevor got caught? Well, he could play dumb. Nobody would assume he'd intentionally done anything wrong.

Except maybe for Raj.

Trevor's palms were sweating. Not good for secret agents trying to get in and out undetected. He was about to leave, thinking himself a coward, when his father brushed by him to enter the study.

"Hey, Dad," he said, his voice almost breaking with nerves.

"Hey, kid." Meyer opened one of his desk drawers and began rifling, glancing up just once.

Those two simple words felt like a sigh. Only after he'd felt himself relax did Trevor realize how strange his father had seemed lately. He'd tried getting used to the new Meyer Dempsey and convincing himself that nothing had changed. Yes, he seemed to be mentally connected to Earth's invaders, but what father didn't have his eccentricities? Meyer had been powerful and arrogant before, same as today. No biggie.

But hearing him greet Trevor so casually now made Trevor realize how odd that simple greeting sounded. Meyer sounded like Trevor's dad ... which made Trevor think of how he *hadn't* seemed like his father for much of the past two years.

*It doesn't matter. Either way, he's becoming his old self again.*

A second voice inside Trevor contradicted the first: *Or*

*maybe you're finally getting used to his new self.*

"I was going to grab a book," Trevor said, realizing he should probably explain his presence.

Meyer looked around at the study's dusty old volumes. "One of *these*? Why don't you download one on your Vellum?"

"I don't feel like running down to the public library."

"The download sites are back up. You didn't know?"

Oh. Right. Trevor did know. The net had been coming up little by little — progress always being made in the land of the viceroy.

"Oh. Yeah, I forgot."

His father opened another drawer and searched anew.

"So," Trevor said, "that dinner thing tonight."

"Yes?" Meyer closed one drawer and opened another. His tone was short, sliding downhill from where it had been when he'd entered.

"Do I have to go?"

"I told you. Yes. Everyone needs to go. There will be press for at least an hour at the start. You can go when they go."

"Do I have to dress up?"

Meyer slammed the last drawer, his face frustrated.

"What?" Trevor asked.

"I can't find my signet cufflinks."

"Do you need them?"

"For an official dinner, yes, I should wear the seal. God*dammit.*" He said the last syllable to his desk, as if it had wronged him.

"Maybe they're in your bedroom."

"They're not in the bedroom."

"Did you check in Piper's—"

Trevor stopped when his father vented a frustrated grunt and kicked a cardboard box beside the desk hard enough to impale it with his wingtip shoe. A tiny rain of leaflets fluttered out — probably more useless pro-Astral propaganda.

"I'm sorry," he said, fighting for control.

Trevor blinked. "No problem." But it was strange, all right. His father prided himself on unfettered calm, and Trevor could count on one hand the times he'd seen him lose emotional control.

"It's this banquet. This fucking banquet. Why do we have to have it *tonight*? You know about this thing with your stepmother?"

Trevor nodded slowly.

"It's all a big misunderstanding. She's always using my connection to grab shows for her juke because the net is ... well, you know how it's been. Problems with the wires or something. Which is why I've been on Raj to find a way around the issues with the city net, at least for connections in the house."

Trevor said nothing. That seemed wrong, too. After two years, you'd think that intergalactic travelers who'd built the pyramids could do some basic electrical repair. Or for that matter, properly secure data on a computer.

"She tripped an alarm or something — some bullshit security they have on this thing. But then she chooses *right now* to go off somewhere, and it looks bad because they think she did it on purpose and is running away."

"Did what?"

"Something was accessed that shouldn't have been. Nothing terribly important. I keep telling them it's a mistake; that's not like Piper to do something underhanded. But they ..." He trailed off then touched his temple. "Well, it's hard to explain, but since I'm tuned in to their groupthink or whatever you want to call it, I don't just get answers like talking to a normal person. I can *feel* their disbelief, as if I didn't believe her myself."

"Oh."

"But I do believe her, Trevor. Or I mean, I would if she were here to tell me what I already know."

"Sure." Again, Trevor felt a new sense of familiarity in his father, reminding him that it had been missing before.

Meyer's perfectly combed hair had come slightly askew after kicking the box. His tie had flapped out of his coat. But it was more than those simple bits of disorder that caused Trevor to wonder. His father looked momentarily lost.

"Never mind," he said. "I'm sure it'll be fine. But the *last* damned thing I want to do tonight is have dinner with a bunch of ambassadors."

"The other viceroys?"

Meyer shook his head. "Just ambassadors."

"Couldn't it be handled over Skype or something?"

"Banquets like this are never to talk business, Trevor. It's a PR thing."

"Why?"

"We're still a human society. New power structures don't change that. People have to believe in all of this. Believe in the system."

Trevor resisted the urge to ask if he meant "believe it" instead of "believe *in* it." So much of his father's job as viceroy seemed like acting rather than politics. The new government and social infrastructure was all human, with the Astrals supposedly acting only as supervisors. But the visitors weren't merely observers, and everyone knew it. Too many humans had been killed, and the old governments had been forcefully rebuked when they'd attempted nuclear mutiny. But the public image machine kept churning, spitting out *colonization-is-good-for-all-of-us* propaganda, broadcasting fancy dinners like tonight's as the new and elegant norm. Trevor would have rolled his eyes if he hadn't seen his father's mastery of the public eye in the past, and his fervent belief that reality was simply whatever someone declared and repeated. Enough dinners with smiling human dignitaries broadcast to the population, and people would eventually believe all the lies.

"Sure," Trevor said.

Meyer looked at the kicked box. He seemed baffled by his actions, as if unable to fathom why missing cufflinks had roiled his stress into a momentary loss of control.

"Dad?"

"Yeah, Trevor." He smoothed his hair, retucking his tie.

"You said the Astrals were digging below the Apex. And that's why the rebels tried to blow up the city with that plane."

"Not exactly in that way, but yes, that's what we think."

"*Why* are they digging?"

Meyer looked into Trevor's eyes from across the room. He seemed to be warring with a decision. "I guess there's no reason I can't say," he finally said. "There's a structure underground here. Something that got buried by time."

"And they have to *dig* to reach it?"

"That's how you get below dirt, Trevor. You dig."

"But they're aliens."

"There's still dirt between them and the structure. And the Apex is on top of it anyway."

"Why did they plant a giant glass pyramid on top of something if they meant to dig it up?"

"I don't know. They're building at *all* the capitals."

"But *right on top* of a dig site?"

"I don't know. Why does it matter?"

"What's the structure underground?"

Meyer's eyes had narrowed slightly, but he answered without hesitation. "A temple, I think."

"But they're being so slow."

"They're trying to find its door then search it carefully."

Trevor felt less than satisfied. Each answer birthed ten more questions. What exactly was down there? What were the new monoliths for? Were the Astrals just digging to get at an old structure or digging around it for artifacts? The compulsion to keep asking was a horrible itch, but Trevor knew he had to pull back. His father could sense prying, and so far he was still in the realm of curiosity. If he connected the rest of the dots for his father, asking how a discovery at the dig site could possibly have attracted Piper's attention and launched a citywide manhunt, Meyer's demeanor might change from paternal to guarded — maybe suspicious. He'd been betrayed by one member of his family already, and his denial would only stretch so far if a second joined the first.

"Oh," Trevor said. "Okay."

His father's eyes had hardened, his momentary weakness now gone. "Have you heard anything from Piper?"

Trevor fought the urge to swallow, knowing it might be misinterpreted. "No."

"You're sure? Not just *from* her, but *about* her? No idea where she might be?"

Trevor saw a Reptar's vision of Terrence in his mind. He saw the police captain, talking about bad camera feeds near one of the churches. He saw Terrence in the flesh, revealing things he shouldn't have known.

"No."

Meyer met Trevor's eyes. His fingers trailed along the desk as if in search. "Was there anything else then?"

Trevor swallowed. "No. I guess I'm good."

"You came in for a book. Aren't you going to look around for one?"

"I can download one. I just forgot."

After a pregnant moment, Meyer nodded slowly. "Good."

At the door, he called Trevor back.

"Yeah, Dad?"

"If Piper can't make dinner, I'll need you to be my second. The person I turn to as my right hand when the press asks questions."

"Oh, sure," Trevor said, feeling a bit blindsided.

"Because you *are* my right hand. My best man. And I know you'll stand beside me no matter what."

"Sure, Dad."

Meyer nodded. "Then I'll see you in a bit."

Trevor walked back down the length of the rear hallway, the clacking of his hard-soled shoes echoing off the stone floor. He needed to prepare for dinner, and an evening as the viceroy's right hand.

His father's greatest ally, whether he liked it or not.

# CHAPTER 20

Benjamin shuffled the windows on his largest monitor, dragging them to adjacent screens, trying to make sense of it all. Nothing quite fit — but in a maddening almost-there sort of way, something was definitely about to break the surface.

He looked from window to window. From screen to screen. Limitations in the public network had become an even bigger problem than restrictions in the underground web he used to communicate with the other rebel labs worldwide and the church in Heaven's Veil. *That* network might (might!) be free and secure, though Benjamin still had his doubts. But regardless, Wikipedia was on the public net, not the private one. As were conspiracy blogs, with millions upon millions of pages packed with the puzzle pieces Benjamin needed. And who controlled the public net, at least until Cameron could get into Heaven's Veil and plant the virus? Astrals, of course.

And the Astrals, unsurprisingly, were stingy about the alien-related information they allowed through their filter.

It shouldn't have mattered. Benjamin knew most of this by heart and had untold terabytes of data culled from a lifetime of paranormal and extraterrestrial research. He knew history better than most historians — the *real* history, he often thought, rather than the official bullshit. He had his photos and videos, materials traded with others through the years. A smart and properly paranoid person didn't rely on the Internet to answer his questions; Benjamin made copies and backed them up. But even his local records didn't tell the whole story. Since the occupation, every amateur UFO researcher had become a serious investigator. Every conspiracy theorist, duly vindicated, had sprung into action. But with the worldwide network neutered, there was no way to share and parse new research. He had all the old information in the world, but little of the new. It was frustrating.

That's part of what Cameron had set out to fix. The Canned Heat virus, properly unleashed, should give Benjamin and his prepared colleagues a cache from which to grab handfuls of unrestricted data as fast as they could. They wouldn't get anywhere near all of it unless new Internet activity had been surprisingly light or the Astrals proved to be surprisingly inept at plugging the hole Cameron was about to drill, but they'd get enough. They'd get the most important sectors. The story behind the story. Then, maybe, this puzzle would begin to make sense.

Something with the Templars begged attention, for instance.

Benjamin knew the basics. He knew about the Rose Stone in Hertfordshire. He'd even been into the artificial cave below its original position. He had archive photos of the carvings inside that cave, and his own photos, samples, and rubbings. But what else might have been discovered? Were people still heading into Royston Cave, or was it too far into lawless outlands? Were there wild barrens overseas like there were here? Did shuttles guard the cave? A deep hunch swore it was important.

But Benjamin didn't think Astral shuttles would guard

Royston Cave. It was, he thought, entirely possible that the aliens didn't even know the cave was there. It had been dug a millennium ago, well after the last evidence of a widespread alien occupation. And although the Astrals had proved they could scrape the surface of human thoughts, they didn't seem to understand the electronic networks at all. They weren't stupid; they knew what those networks were and had cut them on arrival. But they'd reactivated them just as suddenly, their only known attempts to access having proved no more skilled than any user who sat down in front of a terminal. In their shoes, confronting an unknown as baffling to Astrals as their technologies had always been to humans, Benjamin supposed he'd have put native experts on the case. But seeing as the Astrals wouldn't know what they were looking for in this foreign soup of electronic information, it seemed entirely possible that nobody — alien *or* human — had stumbled across information about an obscure English cave. Or had any idea what it might mean.

Even Benjamin didn't know what it meant — to either the old story or the one currently unfolding. But the Templar carvings at Royston had always been considered a kind of codex — and if Benjamin's hunches were right, that codex might be needed to decode something after all.

Now ... as to what that something might be? It was impossible to tell.

He didn't even know what to ask. Nobody did. But the Knights Templar had been the Benjamin Bannisters of their day, and there was plenty in biblical times — even during the Crusades — that smelled extraterrestrial to Benjamin. If the Templars had known something about that last occupation, there were only so many ways they'd have chosen to pass that information along to those who'd need it in the future. In code, surely.

A loud rumbling rolled in from outside. Benjamin looked down and saw the water ripple in his glass. There had been a few rumbles minutes ago, but he'd been too focused to pay them much mind. Earthquakes, perhaps, if those happened in Utah.

There was a louder noise. Sharper, rawer. Not deep like the others, but tinged with treble notes.

Ivan burst into the office, his eyes wider than usual. It took Benjamin a moment to realize what was different, but then it hit him: even during the capital attacks, he'd never seen the hard man frightened.

"Benjamin! Get out here!"

"Where? What's going on?"

Another sound outside — this one deadly similar to a distant explosion.

"Just come!"

Benjamin tumbled out the lab door behind Ivan, finding the courtyard between the lab and the ranch house in chaos.

The entire staff was outside, techs milling in their casual clothes and occasional lab coats as if unsure where to go or what to do. Ivan's small band of military roughnecks and the minor delegation from the nearby rebel camp were climbing into an electric Jeep, one hard-jawed man with a crew cut yanking the charge cord from its rear before piling in. The lab wasn't military, so there were few guns, but people piling into the jeep and the low transport beside it were packing and racking, cleaning their weapons and loading shells by the box.

On the horizon, there was nothing but fire, like napalm. East. Toward the resistance camp.

"*What happened?*" Benjamin shouted.

Ivan's head only cocked, unhearing. Benjamin's voice had been drowned by a helicopter thundering by to the south, moving at what had to be maximum speed. Ivan turned to watch it pass then flinched hard when an Astral shuttle appeared in front of it from nowhere. The shuttle didn't bother to fire its weapon. Instead, as had happened above Heaven's Veil, it allowed the copter to plow into it, detonating in a plume of rolling flames and spinning debris.

The crowd half ducked; the explosion was nearby, and the rotors had been spinning fast enough that the lab's grounds were peppered with the outer halo of shrapnel on detonation. Ivan ducked with a hand on Benjamin's back then straightened as the copter's remains pounded the desert and the shuttle zipped away.

"*What the hell happened?*" Benjamin shouted.

"We don't know! Carter saw it going down. Tried to run toward camp with the Jeep still tethered and about fucked our only vehicle charge port in the process. He has family over there." Ivan's lips formed a line. "*Did* have family anyway."

Benjamin looked. Black smoke eclipsed the fire. Whatever had happened was already over. The ships had left them alone until now because they were barely a threat. The just-concluded ninety-second solution ran that point home.

"What did it?" he asked, knowing the question was unnecessary.

"Shuttles."

"Just the one?"

"Carter said there were three. But they ..." He looked around. "They seem to have bugged out already."

Benjamin scanned the sky, seeing nothing. They'd left the lab untouched. Why? They knew it was there, just twenty minutes west in an electric Jeep. The Vail mothership had spent six months suckling from the money pit on the property, and shuttles had buzzed the place repeatedly. The lab wasn't an Astral mystery.

Yet they were all still alive, free to sabotage the capital another day. It didn't make sense, just like the Astrals' refusal to destroy the nearby rebel camp until now. There'd been no warning. Five minutes ago, Moab had been at peace. For a flash, it had been in the grip of a one-sided war. Now that skirmish was over, and the survivors could only bury their dead and wonder.

Two vehicles screamed across the parched soil, headed toward the pillars of black smoke. Ivan sat heavily on one of the outside chairs — in the shade during the afternoon and evening, where techs tended to take their breaks while pretending the world wasn't ending. Benjamin doubted there would be many sitting outside this evening. Being inside didn't make anyone safer from the shuttles' return, but sitting outside would feel like spitting in Fate's eye. They'd been on this spot for years, several spent in the aftermath of an alien occupation they'd been working to subvert. Being left alone so long had lulled them into feeling charmed, as if there were a bubble above that made them invincible. That illusion was gone. For days and weeks and months, residents would live in a throbbing state of quiet panic.

Benjamin watched the lanky man sit. He looked out across the pan, watching the flame and smoke of what used to be the resistance camp. Despite his fear and sense of loss (he hadn't known many in the camp, but people were people), Benjamin couldn't help but feel sorry for Ivan. What woke him in the morning and kept him going through the days was the dream that, eventually, brute force might be able to settle humanity's grievances. But now it was more obvious than ever that the Astrals had merely been letting them play their ineffectual games — and that at any point they could tire of the irritation and end things with a snap.

What would drive Ivan now? What did he have to live for?

"Jesus, Ben," he said, not turning his head. "They're all gone. Every one of them."

Benjamin didn't bother to say that there might be survivors. It might make things worse rather than better.

"What now? That's all the equipment. All the people who might know how to get more jets, tanks, anything at all. There must be other camps, but ... what now?"

Benjamin sat beside Ivan, unable to summon a fitting platitude to make it all better when he knew things were only getting worse.

"I think we should go inside," he said instead.

Benjamin rose, but Ivan didn't seem to hear.

So he went back inside alone with the horizon still on fire, a pair of engines purring their way toward the charred atrocity. Benjamin could only leave the man to his loss, knowing that all anyone could do was to reach the next day ... then the one after that.

"Cameron," he said to his empty office once the door had closed behind him, "you'd better give us something to believe in, Kiddo."

Cameron didn't respond.

# CHAPTER 21

"Sir?"

"I told you not to call me that."

"Nathan?" Coffey repeated.

Nathan's hands fell from his face. He looked at his second in command, trying to make his features stoic and hard. It wasn't difficult. His default face had always been sort of impassive, and years of running a rogue paramilitary state had helped him to hone it. She didn't ask what was on his mind, but Coffey was, of course, smart enough to intuit — and to allow no emotional inflection into her voice about that intuition when news went sour. There was a no-bullshit policy between them. Nathan always respected directness over tact.

"I'm afraid they've identified your wife's body."

"I know," Nathan said.

He didn't know, but he'd assumed. It was usually best to assume the worst. The upside was that the only two possibilities, if you planned like a pessimist, were neutrality or pleasant surprise. Optimism, on the other hand, had a way of clearing the path for defeat.

"No news on Grace," Coffey said.

"Keep searching."

"To be blunt," she said, "there's not much searching to be done. The camp is in cinders. It looks like they might have got a few minutes' warning because most of the intact bodies were in their meeting hall structure. You know, the circular roof near the stream."

Nathan nodded. He'd looked at a few satellite images since Cameron Bannister's visit in the way most husbands and fathers looked at beach photos from family vacations. He knew his late wife and possibly late daughter's home from above: all rectangles and circles, the peaks of trees appearing as shrubs.

Coffey looked like she might be waiting for dismissal. She'd been better at not being subservient — being the hard-nosed number two he could respect. She'd informed him of deaths and losses, but never like this, never his own family. He couldn't blame her hesitance, but didn't like it. Showing him sympathy meant she felt he needed or wanted it. Either that, or Coffey just couldn't help it.

Served him right to let her see him with his face in his hands after hearing the news.

"You can go."

"Anything you need?"

"Just keep searching."

Coffey looked like she might be thinking about repeating that searching was pointless, but thankfully she kept the message in her mouth. If Nathan had to repeat himself to earn compliance, he might very well snap. He was already barely forestalling a desire to throttle her. She was right, of course; he'd seen the after images of the camp. It wasn't much more than a smoking hole in the ground — a few hundred square feet around the collapsed meeting hall being all that remained unburned. If they hadn't found Nathan's daughter yet, it meant she'd been in the torched areas when the shuttles had come. Maybe sleeping as death came from above.

Coffey paused for a final moment then turned to leave. The door closed. Nathan waited until his lieutenant's footfalls were no longer audible on the steps before pulling the tall bookcase against the wall over on its face.

For a few delirious seconds, a red rage of fury subsumed him. He shouted in the mostly soundproofed room; he ripped a television screen from its mounting and smashed it on the ground. He kicked the desk, doing little more than chipping the wood and stubbing his toe.

Nathan paused, chest heaving. After a moment, he launched into another tantrum, knowing how his impotent rage would appear from the outside, not caring.

Glass vases detonated. Office items were hurled. Picture frames were shattered.

Nathan stood in his ransacked office once it was finally over, shoulders bobbing up and down with his heaving breath, unable to dominate an enemy he couldn't see, hear, or touch.

Broken glass littered his chair. He brushed it away, suddenly delicate, and sat. Again, he planted his face in his palms then pulled himself upright.

*No.* He wouldn't mourn. Not yet.

Someone had fucked him. They'd fucked him *hard.* It didn't matter who you were; you didn't fuck Nathan Andreus. Unless you were looking to get fucked right back. Step on Nathan's land and lose a foot. Kill an Andreus warrior and get friends or family slaughtered before your eyes.

He knew who'd done this, and why. Obviously, it had been the fucking Astrals. On their own. They didn't need permission or a tip-off. So far, their needing Nathan to control the outlands had kept their fucking ET hands off the camp, meaning the Astrals had somehow known where Nathan's people had fled before he himself had. Choosing now to decimate a camp that couldn't dent Astral armor was spittle in his eye. An intergalactic fuck you, as repayment for ... for ...

Well, Nathan wasn't sure *what* it was for. For letting the camp survive until now rather than raiding it? That didn't seem like a good reason, considering the Astrals had proved they could raid that camp fine without his help. Same for Benjamin Bannister's lab.

So: Was this comeuppance for helping Cameron Bannister? That didn't seem right either. One man headed to the capital was hardly an insurgent threat. Besides, if they knew Cameron was on his way (something Nathan didn't imagine was likely), they could easily stop him without sending a message to Nathan.

Unless they wanted to remind Nathan that they could do whatever they wanted at any time, and that they were allowing *him* to keep living, too.

Unless this was a reminder ... and deeply personal.

He stood and paced. He had to do something. It didn't matter that the aliens were responsible. He was in bed with the Astrals, but Nathan Andreus of all people knew to keep one foot on the floor no matter who shared his bed. He followed their orders but kept his own. He controlled the area's outlands in his own way, not just as their puppet.

If they'd done this to spite Nathan and teach him a lesson, then it was game on. The shuttles destroying the camp rather than Andreus HQ or his co-opted residence told Nathan that even though he'd done something the aliens didn't like, they still needed *him*. His army, his Republic, maybe even his mind. They'd given him access to the unrestricted net before he'd even worked out the back doors that allowed him to peek in on Moab's chats with ...

Nathan stopped. An interesting idea flitting inside his mind.

Thanks to snooping on Bannister's communications,

SEAN PLATT & JOHNNY B. TRUANT

he knew Cameron was on his way to the capital *not* just to snoop around the Apex dig site but to sabotage the network.

A good plan: it might seriously punch the Astral below their cosmic belts, right in their interstellar testicles.

But only if Cameron could get into the city.

Which, of course, he couldn't.

Or maybe he could.

Nathan had told Cameron that the conversations Benjamin thought were private weren't secret to someone like Nathan, who'd once made his living in communications software.

Including conversations involving the whereabouts of certain city fugitives who might, properly leaked, act as a fine distraction for extraterrestrial minds. Distractions that might draw forces away from an intruder at the gates.

Intruders who, according to satellite, were outside the city now, trying to figure a way in.

The Astrals wanted to fuck Nathan Andreus? Well, fuck *them*.

Nathan's portable computer was smashed, but this could be handled by someone else, easy as pie.

Nathan tapped a wall unit. Coffey answered.

"Jeanine," he said. "I want you to have Greg send a message to Heaven's Veil Viceroy. Not to the house, but to him personally — right into his goddamned pocket, so he can't possibly miss it."

"Of course. What would you like the message to say?"

Nathan smirked. "Tell him where his wife ran off to."

# CHAPTER 22

Raj dabbed the linen napkin at the corners of his mouth, realizing that doing so was excessively decadent and not caring. Everything about this official banquet was excessively decadent. They were eating wagyu steak and Yubari melon while the world roiled in chaos. None of the ambassadors from the other cities would look at Raj and think him pompous for dabbing with a napkin — and if they did, who cared? *They* were pompous.

The slope graphing inequity in modern America (modern *Earth*, really) was sharp, and they all stood at its top. The outlands were lawless; outposts were poor and exploited for resources; larger cities were filled with opiated labor. Only the capitals were prosperous — and within the cities, you only had to go a few miles from the viceroy's mansion to find the poor. This well-set table was the *crème* of even the elite *crème*. Nobody would fault the commander of the guard for being dainty when they were all (let's be honest) fluffing their beds with human lives.

The woman across from Raj was giving him suggestive glances. She was an assistant to the Giza ambassador and had an exotic look that Raj couldn't help but see as his personal vision of Cleopatra. Maybe she wanted him. Maybe he could have her. And why not? His marriage was a sham. He was only at the table because he was Lila's husband, and only married because he'd accidentally fathered a girl who'd essentially become a princess. People only knew Raj as the brown guy standing beside the girl with the baby in press photos and public interviews of Meyer Dempsey, but so what? Family was family, and power was power. It no longer mattered *how* Raj had arrived; he'd done it and now had what others wanted. He couldn't be kicked out of the family, even if Lila tried to leave him. Because how would that look? People turned to the viceroys for cues. Dissent in his family would look horrendous to the citizenry.

Raj spotted Lila from the corner of his eye. She'd attended this event with the greatest reluctance, bemoaning the need to dress up, to wear her fine jewelry, to be paraded in front of tabloid cameras and presented as if their lives were a fair representation of life on Earth. But where was her moral superiority now? She was dressed to the nines, looking damn fine in Raj's opinion. Jewels dangled everywhere. And now that she'd been dragged to the table with gemstones dripping from her wrists and neck, Lila was having a grand time. Laughing while the outlands burned.

Of course, it wasn't just Lila's clear lack of fortitude that would give Raj permission to play footsie under the table with the fine woman across from him — and whatever else later on. He also had an ace in the hole.

Raj had Piper.

Everyone knew by now that Piper had gone missing. She wasn't at the table, of course, but she'd also been acting strange beforehand. She followed Meyer like a puppy, but everything recently had left her mouth sideways, as if she were parroting what everyone else (especially her husband) wanted to hear. Raj had been thinking of saying something about Piper for a while, but raising suspicions about the lady of the house was a fine line. Done right, it would earn him more respect than a yes man like Christopher because it would show he was willing to make tough choices for the greater good. But Meyer was also attached to Piper, and might not appreciate Raj suggesting the treason they all now knew was true.

Plus, Lila might be involved. Trevor, too.

Farther down the table, the ambassador of somewhere-or-other (Raj hadn't paid attention and didn't care) asked Meyer about construction on the Apex — as if human hands had anything to do with *that*.

Meyer gave a suitably PR-appropriate answer.

People behind the cameras smiled and nodded. They knew where their bread was buttered. They knew who funded the press. They knew who controlled all information into and out of the city.

Raj ate his scallop sashimi with lemon confit steak, glad to have good food but failing to appreciate why *this*, of all things, was what the mansion served when it had important guests. But whatever. He was where he needed to be, with a hot woman sitting across the table, clearly into him. He merely had to wait out the dinner.

How much longer would this all drag on?

When the cameras finally packed up and left, Raj relaxed, knowing he could stop posturing. The cessation of the media circus meant they were at the meal's halfway point, maybe more. Now tongues would loosen. They could all drink more freely. And Raj could get up and leave the table if he wanted to — which he would, if he could get the Egyptian ambassador's assistant to follow.

But the Giza ambassador distracted the girl's attention before Raj could send signals, demanding this or that bit of information that the ambassador could have extracted her damned self.

The discussion droned on, making Raj's head hurt with

its dullness.

Progress of the South American monoliths.

Unrest in Asia, quelled in seconds by shuttles.

There was talk of human power structures — slightly guarded because there were Titans at the table, silent but seated among the humans for appearances. Everyone was greedy. Everyone wanted a grab at the brass ring. The Astrals clearly planned to stay, to let human society regrow under its thumb now that it had governments back in place. The Astrals needed to be here for reasons that were none of Raj's business (To teach? To advance humanity? It sure didn't seem to be harvesting organs, and the Astrals could be peaceful if people would just do as they were fucking told), but supposedly the Astrals didn't want to rule and would leave such things to the humans.

There were viceroys today. Maybe in time — perhaps when things had stabilized enough to spread into the outlands — there would be presidents. Or kings. Everyone at the table was well positioned to accept those roles, the viceroy's family and friends (and sons-in-law) prominent among them.

There was a lull. Raj made sure nobody was looking and winked at the girl across from him. She winked subtly back. A half wink, but definitely there. He whispered an unnecessary excuse to Lila, who barely heard him and didn't bother to act like she cared, then gave a final look to the girl, set his napkin on his seat, and left the room.

He was in the hallway before realizing the girl hadn't followed.

Raj peeked his head back into the room. The Giza assistant was still where she'd been, giving no indication of moving anytime soon.

*Bitch.*

Unable to return immediately lest he look stupid, Raj made his way to the bathroom. He was about to go in and wash his face when a dinging farther down the hall, like an old-timer's spit striking the bottom of a brass spittoon, grabbed his attention.

He waited. The noise repeated.

Curious, Raj walked forward. The sound chimed a final time then stopped.

After a moment, it started again.

It was a ring. A strange ring, but a ring nonetheless. A single ping, like an incoming message.

He found himself at the door of Meyer's office. It was open because this was a house first and a government building second, and everything on the computers was supposed to be protected. You could only access them if you had clearance to be in the house, and could only access anything sensitive with a palm print. The Titans didn't seem to understand Raj's recent changes, and he'd been embarrassed to realize that at least part of the problem was that the Titans didn't *have* palm prints. But for human-to-human communications — and certainly for storage — everything was secure. No need for closed doors around here.

But the ring wasn't coming from the computer. It was coming from Meyer's phone.

His *phone?*

Raj didn't like using the phone anymore because he had the distinct impression that everything he said was being captured and analyzed. But ever since the network had returned, phones had regained their status as a necessity, even for the viceroy.

The phone chirped again. This time, Raj was close enough to see the screen light up. It read:

*INCOMING TEXT MESSAGE FROM*
*ANONYMOUS*

Well, which was it? A call or a text message? Raj didn't text anymore. Text was worse than voice calls. The feeling that the Astrals were reading texts was even stronger than with calls — especially given Raj's better-than-average understanding of such things from his vantage as ad-hoc network engineer.

Raj picked up the phone. It chirped again.

Meyer was busy. He wouldn't want to be interrupted. And besides — if this were an Astral thing, they'd talk directly into his head. Nobody liked to admit that Meyer could hear the aliens in his thoughts, but he obviously did. He'd even admitted it to the media. Hell, the media *played it up*. Part of Meyer's image as slightly supernatural. A god, really, that people shouldn't just love and adore and be fascinated by, but worship. Like a pharaoh.

The phone chirped again. This time, Raj felt like the thing was talking to him. *Ordering* him to take the message. That was his job, if he wanted to be the viceroy's right hand. Or maybe, if he proved himself, the viceroy's second in command. Possibly his eventual successor.

He could answer it. The phone would unlock on his thumbprint, seeing as he was the home's sysop and had administrative access to the system. And what was even better: if the call turned out to be something that didn't concern Raj in any conceivable way, he could relock the phone. The sysop could do that kind of thing, too. Meyer would never need to know.

Raj pressed his thumb to the screen.

He read the message and smiled.

He wouldn't need to bother Meyer with this trifling matter at all.

He could send the peacekeepers after Piper Dempsey all by himself, and accept the viceroy's gratitude once it was over.

# CHAPTER 23

Piper thought she heard it again: a distant sound filled with a dry but somehow gurgling rattle. The sucking sound of a vacuum — not the kind you used to clean a carpet but the vacuum of space, where there was no air, life, or anything but endless miles of gas and rock and fire and nothing.

"Do you have cameras on this side of the church?" she asked Thelonius, indicating the place she may or may not have heard the strange noise.

The monk looked up. He'd plugged in the slip drive of pilfered data from Meyer's computer and was dragging files over to the church system. Piper had been lucky, finding what she'd found. Human records were encrypted and locked down at all times, but the Astrals were sloppy because they didn't understand the system. They worked on thought and biological energy. Codes and electronics weren't beyond them in concept but did represent another language. A custom the aliens hadn't yet learned.

*You were lucky to have seen this before anyone else*, Thelonius had told her.

*Lucky* indeed. Now she was up to her armpits in shit. Piper could do with less good fortune.

"Of course," he said, "I'll just need to pull up the surveillance program on this monitor. I want to abort the copy first because sometimes we have fidelity issues here when too much is running at once. Hang on."

He moved to stop the file copy process, but Piper waved him away, feeling stupid. She'd felt stupid for exactly as long as she'd felt lucky. An odd combination that left her all alone because it meant she was probably a fool.

She was standing beside a monk, jumping at noises that, the harder Piper listened, the more she realized probably weren't there. She kept imagining pursuers at every turn, even though she was safe. Piper was among holy people who were also rationalists, wearing her dainty little dress, her almost-black haircut and styled with fashionable bangs, her giant blue eyes probably making her look like a doe in headlights. She couldn't find a comfortable position for her body and kept crossing and uncrossing her legs as she sat, and her arms at her waist to match, fluffing her hair, propping her chin on one hand, the elbow below with nowhere to rest.

She couldn't get comfortable. Her mind wandered.

Piper was certainly unwelcome back at home by now, based on the way the peacekeeper had come to Terrence's before she'd fled through the back door. Where would she sleep? Could she *ever* go home? Was she now a member of this dissident church? Should she trade her dress for a robe, so she'd be appropriately modest rather than flaunting her deposed status as city royalty?

What had she got herself into?

"No, no, don't bother," she said.

"It's no problem."

"It's fine. I just thought I heard something."

"What did you hear?"

"Nothing."

"What did you *think* you heard?"

"Oh, nothing." Piper giggled nervously, hating how weak it must make her sound. "One of them. A Reptar. But I hear them everywhere now, after a near-miss."

She laughed again. Thelonius watched her. "I know what you mean. I think I hear them sometimes, too."

Piper didn't want to dwell on her petty fears. She changed the subject.

"Why did they use stone?"

The monk looked up, confused.

"Before, when you were talking about old alien construction," Piper said, trying to orient him. "When they first showed up, they plunked down all those big stones. Then they cut all those big bricks — or *someone* did anyway — and started making the Apex out of stone at first. So, I mean … why *stone*? They're an advanced culture."

Thelonius watched her for a moment then said, "Our best guess — and by our I mean us here and your friends in Utah — is that they used stone because they thought that's what we expected."

"But they changed. They took away the stones before the first row was finished and began using that blue glass instead. Or at least, it *looks* like glass."

"It's definitely not glass. I'd love to get my hands on a nice big chunk of it to be sure, but so far we think it's something they grow."

"*Grow?*"

"A crystal. It can be seeded and grown. Interestingly, it would have been far easier five thousand years ago to just *grow* the pyramids instead of building them, but it would have been too jarring to us."

"Wouldn't the arrival of aliens be jarring enough to those ancient people? What's the harm in building blue pyramids after that?"

Thelonius shook his head. "No. I meant to *us*. Jarring to people *today*, not the people who were around back when the pyramids were built. Today, we can almost explain pyramids. Archaeologists content on kidding themselves have been trying to do that forever. But if the ancient structures had been like the Apex back then, what would we have thought?"

Piper felt like she was missing something. "I'm not sure I follow. Are you saying that they didn't build blue glass pyramids in ancient Egypt because it would have been jarring to us today, in modern times?"

"That's my theory, yes."

"But how — ?"

"Believe me, you don't want me to go into it." Thelonius smiled. "Let's just say our perception of time is dependent on the human experience. Mathematically speaking, it's more accurate to say that every time is now."

"So they know the future?"

"I wouldn't go that far, but don't get me started."

Piper decided he was right. She *didn't* want him to elaborate. Heather had all of the *Back to the Future* movies from the 1980s and '90s on the juke, and they'd watched them a few times through as a family, both pre- and post-Astrals. Thinking about time always hurt her head.

"Then why are they building with glass now?"

"Crystal."

"Whatever."

The monk shrugged. "They must think it's more in line with what we expect today, and that it won't shock those who find them in the future, given all our society has done on its own without Astral help. We're not ancient stonecutters ourselves anymore. But what's particularly fun, and gives me hope for what you've got here—" He tapped the screen, where the files had finished copying. "—is that if you ask me, I'd say they're making it up as they go this time."

"Don't *you* make life up as you go? Or are you implying that they know the future again?"

"No..." The strange monk turned his body toward Piper's. She'd already surmised that he only wore his robe as disguise, to make him fit into the church's cover. Inside, he looked as straight-laced and rational as they came: an egghead in any clothing. "I mean, they seem to be adjusting their plan on the fly to account for new information they hadn't anticipated."

"Is this what you said before about the Internet?" Piper hadn't really understood that the first time.

"Our worldwide network is just an effect, but yes, it's one thing. Didn't Benjamin tell you about the past alien visitations when you were in Moab?"

"Yes, but ..." Piper didn't want to finish. She was embarrassed to admit that as nice as Benjamin seemed, his theories had always struck her as convenient, paranoid, and decidedly wacko. But even more than that, Piper was embarrassed to admit that she still didn't really believe those wacko theories, even though Earth's occupation proved her version of history to be the wackier between them.

"Ask Gloria about it when you get a chance," he said. "I was never a churchy guy, but in this case some of the hard facts make me want to believe. I can tell you all about quantum entanglement, but that's not much different than what she'd call 'the energy of connection.' I used to think that 'Law of Attraction' bullshit was ... well ... *bullshit*, but really it sort of reflects what theoretical physicists have been seeing in the way intention and observation affect reality. It's a bit outside her sweet spot, but Gloria will tell you that ayahuasca might have opened real doors for Meyer rather than just showing him hallucinations. It might have allowed him to see other worlds ... and, more importantly, allowed those other worlds to peek in on *him*. My first instinct is to roll my eyes about that (the idea that we're all somehow connected through an invisible god energy), but it's the same phenomenon we see with quantum flux and the holographic universe theory as calculated by Susskind and 't Hooft."

"Okay," said Piper, not at all understanding.

The monk laughed. "It's just funny. History has always moved back and forth between periods of spirituality and rationalism, each a reaction to a previous period of the other. But both sides are arguing for the same stuff in different languages. The point is that in the past — when the Astrals were here before — human society had more or less reconciled the two. Those old societies all seemed to have developed high degrees of spiritual connectivity while remaining rational — something someone with my nerd background would probably try to explain as 'nonlocal energetic phenomena' and other big words. But it boils down something between church and science — or more accurately, both. The records imply that ancient human societies had learned mental tricks that the Astrals use without being taught — which makes sense, considering that the Astrals clearly seeded life here in the first place. But the thing is, what happened in the past — the development of a deeply connected human society, like the Egyptians or Mayans — didn't happen this time around."

"Why not?"

"Who knows? But it didn't. Instead, in the false dichotomy of spirit and intellect, intellect won. The Astrals have been able to peek in on us through people who learned how to reach some of those far-away worlds with their minds — doing the things the Mayans did every single day — but could only get glimpses until they crossed space-time see our society in person. We're far less spiritually connected than they seem to have anticipated, but we're *far more* technologically advanced. I don't think the Astrals quite know what to do. In a way, we went wrong this time around. We failed to grow into what they seeded us to become. But still, something deep down in modern humanity seems to know we should be connected and still yearns to build the mental bond we *should* have in another way — a way that suits what our minds became, more rational than spiritual. Hence computers: our attempts to recreate brains. And networks, which allow us to connect in a way our souls seem to crave."

"It's strange to hear a scientist talk about souls," Piper said.

Thelonius flapped the loose arms of his robe. "Hey, I'm a monk, too."

Piper smiled, feeling herself relaxing, descending from her paranoia about Reptars coming to get her.

"So," he went on. "Let's see what you've got here, shall we?"

He clicked on an icon indicating the archive's primary image. It was *the* image, Piper saw as it opened, that had led her to commit theft and seek a second opinion.

The picture showed what looked like a stone tablet, indeterminate in size because there was no point of reference. It had been taken (probably with an iPhone; the Astrals had given up using their own technology for anything that had to pass through human hands) somewhere dark. Piper could make out a dark corner, as if of an underground passageway. The light seemed to have been provided mostly by the flash. The stone was covered in strange glyphs that Piper had never seen in any museum.

Propped below the tablet, visible as an apparent way of marking the object within the photograph, was a tablet computer, its screen filled with large white text on a black screen. The text — again, probably for the benefit of human toadies who'd file and analyze the image — was in English, likely typed by human hands.

## EXHIBIT 401
### EAST CHAMBER LOWER LEVEL
### FOUND IN ARCHIVE CRADLE
### ** DEVICE MISSING **

"What does it say?" Piper asked.

"Exhibit four oh—"

"No. I mean the markings on the tablet. Is that a language?"

Thelonius squinted. Then he enlarged the image, pinched it in and out, scrolled around at the scratches, drawings, and indecipherable markings.

"I have no idea. But like you said, if anyone knows, it wouldn't be the science teacher. It would be Benjamin."

Looking at the image, Piper felt her creeping dread return. The image was only one of many files bundled into the drive's package. Her heart had been pounding with hurry, but she'd popped open a few of the other documents before creeping intuition had sent her from curiosity to espionage. Some of the language (again in maddeningly readable English) in those files that had made her sweat, but seeing this one image sent it all rushing back. It renewed her sense of dawning hopelessness — a certainty that her husband, whom she loved and wanted to trust, was playing for the wrong team.

"What do you think this means," the monk asked, "*device missing?*"

A booming erupted from the front of the church, as if the doors had been blown open.

Then screams.

Around the enclosed back room, the scientist monks traded stares with wide and frightened eyes. Then they scurried like ants, grabbing drives and shutting down screens, every move purposeful and rehearsed.

Thelonius yanked the drive from the computer and shot

a glance at the others. Across the room, Gloria stood.

"They found us," he said, his voice barely calm. "Grab what you can in ten seconds, then get to the passage."

# CHAPTER 24

"Mom."

Heather waved Trevor away. She was watching Meyer at the table's end. He'd behaved strangely for long enough now that she'd finally grown used to it, but this was unusual for even the new and improved Meyer Dempsey.

A man with a gray beard was speaking to him in a rather self-important manner, but Meyer was pressing a finger to his head, barely listening. As Heather watched, his hand rose until the finger was straight out and parallel to the ground. Meyer looked like he might be pantomiming a gun to his temple and was soon to pull the trigger, completing the visage of blowing his brains out with boredom. Heather didn't think he was making an attempt to show the table how dull the conversation in front of the man, but it would be hilarious if he was. It was the kind of thing Heather would have done, if this banquet had been in her honor rather than his.

"Mom. I need to talk to you about Piper. I think she might be—"

"*Shh*, Trevor. I'm watching something funny."

From the corner of her eye, Heather saw Trevor's head

tick toward Meyer. He looked back at her and set his hand on her arm, begging for his mother's attention.

"Now. I need to talk to you now."

"Hang on."

At the end of the table, Meyer's eyes settled. The last of his attention turned from the man. This wasn't lost on the orator, who all at once seemed to realize he was being ignored but appeared similarly reluctant to call the viceroy on his lack of manners. Instead, he kept speaking, hoping the moment might pass.

Meyer's finger pressed harder to his head. Wrinkles formed against his perfect dark-brown hair, graying at the temples. His finger paled from pressure. It trembled, the digit giving at the knuckle.

"Mr. Viceroy?" Heather heard the man say.

Meyer stood. He didn't look at his inquirer or any of the dignitaries who broke from their conversations at the sound of his squeaking chair. Instead, he looked down at his own chest, pressing harder, seeming to focus intently on something that no one could hear.

"*Mom!*"

"Shut up, Trevor. Look at him. What do you think he's doing?"

"Who knows. Listening to alien radio?"

"I'm serious."

"I know you're serious, Mom. But I need to tell you something about—"

Meyer left the table, exiting to the hallway. Baffled heads turned to watch him go.

Heather stood. A few people turned to look at her, but no one cared about Heather Hawthorne. She was something of a matriarch at this table, like a retired queen kept around to feign respect. She probably wouldn't be here at all if Lila hadn't given birth to Goddess Baby Clara, who so fascinated Meyer's adoring public.

"Mrs. Hawthorne?" said the man to her right. He'd already offered his official title, but Heather had given so little of a shit that she'd actively forced herself to forget it.

"*Mom?*" Now Trevor sounded more curious than urgent.

Heather pressed a finger to her temple then followed Meyer from the room, trying to mimic his zombielike walk. Those who'd been watching the viceroy's strange, out-of-the-blue departure turned to Heather instead. She was wearing a long green dress that might have been at home on a Hollywood red carpet. Her days on real red carpets were probably over, but at least the stiffs at the table could watch her still-fine ass on its way out.

Trevor came behind her, snapping at her heels like a terrier. She found herself safely out of the dining room with her seventeen-year-old son now demanding her full attention. Some of that attention was still on Meyer, who'd gone farther along the hallway and rounded a corner. So far as she could tell, he'd yet to notice her behind him.

"Mom!"

"Not now, Trevor! Can't you see that your father is having an episode?"

Heather pushed past him. She reached the bend in the hallway where, thankfully, Trevor took a hint and fell silent. A good thing. The minute Heather arrived at the corner, she heard voices trickle around it: Meyer and someone else.

She peeked around the corner. The other voice was Mo Weir, Meyer's aide. Meyer had beelined directly to him as if he'd known precisely where the man was, despite Heather assuming Mo had left for the day.

"Mo. Where's Christopher?"

"The guard captain?" Still spying, Heather watched Weir shake his head. "I don't know. I can radio out. Or if you'd like to go into your office—"

"No, no. Look. There's been some sort of a breach."

"We know that, Meyer. Your wife—"

"Not her," Meyer said in an irritated, impatient voice. "Jesus Christ, nobody's told you?"

"Told me what?"

"Fucking hell, Mo. You need one of those earbud things."

"Maybe you could just *tell* me, Meyer."

Heather liked Mo. He didn't take shit, just like her. Half the world was awed by Meyer Dempsey, and the other half was afraid. Weir was neither. When Meyer said stupid things, Mo threw them back. If the fabled emperor had employed a right hand like Mo Weir, he'd never have embarrassed himself by parading naked in his new clothes.

"It's hard to say. Nobody's really talking to me."

"*I'm* talking to you, Meyer."

"In my head. It's all just confusion. I'm not hearing anything direct from Divinity. It's like trying to listen in on a cocktail party."

"This is fascinating. But until you give me something I can use, I'm at a loss as to—"

"Someone's outside. Someone at the gate."

"Okay. Do you want them let in?"

"No. He's not supposed to be there. He's ... he has something."

"Jesus, Meyer. This is like playing charades."

"They're pissed off. Just hang on. I'm ... I'm trying to sort it out."

"Maybe they sent you instructions. Have you checked your computer or your phone?"

"They're in my office."

"Well, let's go there then."

Meyer turned forward. Heather fell back and rammed Trevor.

"Wait," she heard Meyer say.

"What?"

"There's a few things happening. That's why it's

confusing. Something in the desert. Did we launch an attack?"

"We? Nothing I know about, but they don't ask my permission."

"It has to do with the person at the gate. From Utah? He's here to ... shit, I can't tell."

"Go check your messages."

"Fuck that. Hang on. I can get it if I focus."

Heather had caught this particular tone a time or two from Meyer and recognized it plain as day. If there was one thing Meyer Dempsey hated, it was being excluded as if he were an idiot incapable of making his own decisions. Meyer was no one's toady. Heather could hear his irritation at being kept from the loop, and his natural defiance to subvert the authority keeping him out.

"Meyer ..." said Weir.

"*Shh!*"

Silence. Heather looked carefully around the corner and saw Meyer with his hands on his head, eyes closed. Mo Weir was beside him, arms crossed in obedient annoyance.

"Okay. There are a few things."

"The thing with Piper ..."

"No. They don't care about that. At least not right now. It's ... the man outside, he has something. He's ... being watched."

"If he's a problem, they'll kill him."

Meyer shook his head. "They can't. Something to do with ... dammit, I can't tell. They ... sent a message? Something. But they don't want to kill him. Just stop him. Where did you say Christopher was?"

"I didn't."

"Get him."

"Okay, let's go to your office."

"They've sent peacekeepers to the gates," Meyer said. "They know right where he is."

"And you want to send the guards? Christopher?"

"No, there's something else. *Shit.* This is impossible."

"Sometimes, I wonder if you're just making these things up to fuck with me," said Weir.

"Dammit." Heather watched Meyer open his eyes and shake his head. "Wait. My office."

"Your office," Weir repeated.

"Did I get a package today?"

"Like FedEx? They're out of business, I think."

"A data dump, I mean. About the Apex. There's something about the Apex." A look of recognition crossed his eyes. He seemed almost frightened.

*"What,* Meyer?" Weir sounded tired.

"Shit. I wonder if that's what Piper saw."

*"What?* Hell."

"I missed something. The archive. Under the Apex."

*"What archive,* Meyer?"

"Did anyone tell you that they're digging under *all* of the capitals?"

"No, but why do I care?"

"It's not just here, Mo. Hell. That's what I'm feeling. That's what I'm hearing; they're not just searching here in Heaven's Veil. They've lost it. They can't find it, and now they're looking all over."

*"What* can't they find?"

Meyer pinched the bridge of his nose. "I don't know, but it's a problem. Is it related to the guy outside? I don't know."

"Meyer ..."

"Come on, Mo. We have to leave."

"Where? Aren't you still in the banquet?"

"Not anymore." Meyer bit his lip. "Come on."

"I could help you more if I knew what you were planning," said Weir's voice.

Heather flinched back, preparing to slide into an alcove.

"Whoever's outside is a problem, but they're not telling me why," Meyer said.

"So?"

They turned to head away, toward Meyer's office. "So we're going to find out for ourselves," he said.

# CHAPTER 25

Piper ran.

She'd been in low heels when leaving the house, but she'd discarded them a while back, content to walk the streets in bare feet like a kid. Now running, bare feet were painful. Enough that Thelonius (*Franklin*, she felt compelled to call him in her mind now that they were sharing the same peril) had doffed his sneakers and handed them over during their flight.

Piper didn't know what was funnier: that a monk would wear sneakers under his robe or that this particular monk's shoes didn't fit her all that badly. They were far from perfect, but stayed on as the group traversed the underground tunnel, accessible by the hidden doorway and staircase in the church.

Piper ran, her questions mounting.

How had this tunnel been built? Heaven's Veil was an alien city. It had grown from a collection of hippies in tents, before the trees had been razed and the ground leveled. Work had been shared equally. The Astrals had used their energy beams to ease the burden, but human dignity seemed to require that they not all sit around and be waited on. Even so, it was hard to believe anyone had missed the tunnel's creation.

But there were other questions, too. Like: *How had the Reptars found her?* And really: *Had* the Reptars found her, or had she merely had the horrible misfortune of being in the building when the Reptars just so happened to find the dissident church instead?

What about the monks in the chapel's large main room? Piper, Gloria, Thelonius, and the others in the back had run without hesitation, moving with the smooth precision of a practiced drill. She'd heard the rattling, purring Reptars. She'd heard the screams. So were the others dead? And if so, why didn't any of those running in the tunnel seem to care? They'd turned tail and sprinted, yanking removable drives from computers, grabbing samples. There would be no mistaking the church's true purpose once peacekeepers breached the back room; there hadn't been time to right the room or silence the artificial choir. They couldn't return, and they'd left the others to die. Like cowards.

Piper ran, listening for pursuit behind her.

The tunnel wasn't long. After a few minutes, they reached a set of stone steps, and Piper got the answer to at least the first of her questions: the tunnel existed because it wasn't a tunnel at all. It was a series of interconnected basements with doors knocked through adjoining walls, supports added to hold back the soil between them.

They emerged in the home of a small old woman with a shock of white hair. She was wearing thick glasses — one of the stubborn few people who'd refused vision correction and kept the eyeglasses industry afloat. They stormed up through the basement door with a crash and found themselves staring right at her. She was in a wheelchair, a shotgun leveled directly at one of the lead monks' chests.

With a clucking tongue, the woman raised her weapon's barrel, pointing it at the ceiling, then slid it into a makeshift holster on her wheelchair's side. *That*, Piper had many new questions about. Did the woman just sit here all day, waiting? Who kept a shotgun in a holster, especially on a wheelchair? And how had she kept the weapon from the police and peacekeepers?

Gloria pushed to the front and nodded briskly to the old woman.

"Mary."

"I'd say it's good to see ya, Gloria," the woman said, her voice carrying a slight Appalachian accent, "but I guess tha'ad be a lie."

"Peacekeepers," Gloria said, out of breath. The abbess wasn't a small woman. Piper was winded, and she'd maintained a decent yoga routine even in her new station as Queen of Sheba. Gloria, who didn't seem to be in peak condition, was probably knocked flat.

"Yeh, I saw. Ran by an' raised a helluva holler. I guess you're retired now, ain't cha?"

"I don't know if they followed," Gloria huffed.

"I guess if they did, they'll get a chest fulla buckshot," the old woman said mildly.

Gloria nodded. Without a parting word, they ran again, leaving the woman to her apparent duty.

Out in the streets, Piper saw a pattern in their duck-rush-duck movement. She fell into step without effort, but again: it had the feel of something the monks had rehearsed — on paper if not in life.

"The others," Piper said, catching a glimpse of the distant church. Still just a steeple, nothing unusual. But what did she expect? For it to be on fire? The church was only a building and, in itself, had committed no crimes. The peacekeepers would appear and keep peace. It's what they did. It's why Heaven's Veil had so little crime despite its heavy air of malcontent.

"They knew what they were signing up for," Thelonius

said, his tone short.

"You can't go back."

"No."

"What will you do?"

"We'll have to head into the outlands. That's the plan."

"The plan?"

"It's always a good idea to know your exits," Gloria said. "On a plane or in life. I didn't want any of this, but it's hard to feel bad. Everything happens for a reason, and is right in the end."

Piper thought that sounded like an icy answer. She glared at the abbess, her sneakered feet pounding concrete. Like the others, Gloria had discarded her robe in the old woman's home. They were all in the normal clothes they'd been wearing beneath: jeans, tees, and sneakers. As if they spent their days ready to run at a moment's notice.

"How can you say that?" Piper hissed.

"No matter what I say ... nothing changes," Gloria said, still searching for her breath.

"The outlands," Franklin repeated. They paused along the side of a building, his gaze asking for peace. "We'll need to get out of the city."

"How?" Piper asked.

"It's not hard to get out. I doubt they'd chase us."

"You *doubt they'd chase us?*" Piper said.

"Not us," said Gloria, pointing at the entire group. Then she pointed instead only at the former monks, excluding Piper, and corrected her: *"Us."*

"So just you, then. Not me." Now feeling colder, angrier. Apparently, this was a group that just cut and run — *all for one and* ... well, and apparently that was it.

"Not you. You're the viceroy's wife." Realizing how she'd taken her exclusion, Franklin rushed to clarify. "You have to go back home."

Piper assumed she'd heard wrong. "You think they'll

just let me go back to him?"

"No," Franklin said. "You're not understanding me. You're the viceroy's wife, so you have access to the mansion."

"Access? What the hell do you mean?" Piper wanted to scream. She'd heard gunshots a few seconds ago, and was hearing Reptars purring nearby. They were barely concealed, nowhere near ... well, nowhere near wherever they were going, as a group or in pieces. The issue felt undecided, hanging by a thread.

"The drive," said Franklin, pointing at Piper's pocket, where she'd restowed it. "The information we were about to send to Moab before they broke in. You can get it to the network hub. We're fairly sure it's in the mansion."

Piper's patience broke. She'd nearly died a few times today and would live with the screams of others who hadn't been as lucky. The world had been turned then turned again. She couldn't keep up and longed for it all to stop long enough to get her head straight. These weren't her enemies. But they were the only people she could shout at, and the number of things they were taking for granted was stupid.

She didn't know what the network hub was.

She didn't know *where* it was.

Even *they* didn't seem certain exactly where it was.

And besides, Piper didn't know what she was supposed to do with this hub if she found it, the drive, or anything else. Send the information to Benjamin? Okay. But how? Astrals controlled the networks, and the Astrals wouldn't be happy that Piper was trying to share her contraband. Even if there was a way to send a signal — and she had a clue how to do it — the Astrals would surely block it.

How did mansion access matter? If the peacekeepers had been sent to pursue her, there was no chance she'd be allowed back on the grounds. Even if she was, there was no way she'd be left to roam free. There was no way she wouldn't be searched. There was no way — no way in the deepest pit of Hell — she'd be able to take what she'd shown to the monks and magically deliver it to anyone outside the city. Worst of all: Franklin had left a copy on the church computer. There would be no question of what Piper had taken from her husband. She was caught red-handed, and the evidence — whatever it was evidence *of* — would die with her.

"It's the best chance we have," Franklin said. "The tablet in that photo—"

"Might not mean anything!" Piper almost shouted. She felt near tears. They were tying knots with her arguments. So what if some device was missing? It didn't mean a damned thing, and wasn't worth the loss of more lives.

But even as she screamed at Franklin, Piper knew she was fooling herself. She hadn't just seen the tablet. She'd seen the other files, too: a plan nearing completion. A clock that would soon start ticking. Repetitions of some of the stories Benjamin had told her in Moab, only this time from many years past. Whoever had written what she'd seen, he or she had been human. Alien work done by human hands, before the hammer fell. And it was indeed a hammer meant to fall.

She remembered what Charlie, Benjamin's colleague, had said a long time ago.

*Contact has only ever been phase one.*

*What's phase two?*

*Extermination.*

Yes. That's why she'd stolen. That's why she'd run. The Astrals meant to use whatever they'd left behind.

"Then we can just *take* it to Benjamin. We can ride to Utah. Or walk, if we have to."

"Something tells me they won't just let us go if we have the drive." Franklin looked at Piper. "Or if you're with us."

"But I can't just — !"

Piper stopped protesting when she heard a low, rattling

growl from around the corner in front of them. She stepped back to feel the press of bodies behind her. For a moment, she wondered why the monks wouldn't back up too, but then she turned and saw the problem. They'd taken shelter to catch their breath and plan in the most closed-off place they could find: a dead-end alley that would soon be their grave.

"Go. We have to get out of here right now," Franklin said.

"It's out there."

"We can't go back. We have to run. We'll split up."

But they couldn't. By the time Franklin was finishing his sentence, the alleyway's open mouth end was eclipsed by an enormous, slinking black shape. It moved into view, almost too wide to enter. It entered anyway, its powerful haunches taut, its black-scale skin shifting with that strange luminescent blue glow bleeding from beneath.

Despite its sheer bulk, Piper's attention was drawn to its eyes — its double-lidded, color-shifting eyes.

First, they were yellow.

Then black, vanishing into the churning skin of what passed for its gruesome face.

Then red.

Then a blue as bright as the deepest ocean.

The Reptar came on tapping claws, its body like a beast, its movements like an insect. Its mouth opened. Piper saw rows upon rows of needle-tipped teeth, arranged in concentric rings. The jaw seemed to unhinge too far then almost flatten. Its core made a noise like specters stirring. An inhaling, grating rattle, something wet and boiling into a gurgle.

Piper raised her hands in surrender, knowing it was futile.

"I'm the viceroy's wife." She tried to keep her voice even, fighting panic's downward drag.

The Reptar roared, its breath rancid like soured meat.

It coiled its twisted haunches to spring.

There was a noise like thunder, and the thing's head disintegrated. Piper found herself spattered in gore — a curious blend of red blood threaded with glowing blue, like something squeezed from a firefly.

Christopher stood at the alley's mouth, just behind the Reptar's body, holding something that looked like a sawed-off shotgun that had been somehow modified, covered with tubes and gears. Terrence was behind Christopher, with Trevor beside him. To Trevor's other side — unbelievably — stood Heather.

"It works." Christopher handed the weapon to Terrence with a satisfied nod. "What d'ya know?"

# CHAPTER 26

Meyer stopped, his head cocked, Mo Weir dashing to his side. Mo never ran. It was odd to see his blazer flapping, the man nudged into urgency against his will.

"What was that?" Mo asked.

Meyer wasn't sure. It had sounded like a gunshot, but it felt like forever since he'd heard one, back when he'd almost felt like another Meyer Dempsey. He remembered the sound concussing his eardrums and the way it made everything sound muffled as if by ill-fitting earplugs for a while afterward.

"Was that a gun?" Mo asked.

They were still inside the house, nearing the front door. The sound had been like the striking of a mallet and had definitely come from ahead, but that only told Meyer it had happened outside. The house had no sense of auditory direction. All sounds that didn't originate inside came from the door, from all over the city, above and below.

"So you heard it," Meyer said.

"Of course I heard it. Why wouldn't I hear it?"

"I thought it … never mind." Mo wouldn't understand. Plenty of what Meyer heard these days came from inside his head. He could hear the Astral discussions even now: Reptars on patrol, curiously disturbed, quiet Titan minds, Divinity's overarching judgment — and, when Divinity saw fit, its orders to the viceroy.

Mo was moving forward. Meyer hung back, curious. Christopher carried a pistol. It wouldn't thump like that, and since Meyer had ordered him to the gates where there'd be Astrals, gunfire didn't make sense. You didn't hear guns inside Heaven's Veil. Peacekeepers used their teeth to enforce order, and shuttles blasted silent energy rays. Humans hadn't been stupid enough to fire their primitive weapons inside the city in months. It was possible Christopher had run off to the gate as Meyer had asked then fired a shot, but why? And besides, Christopher's pistol would have made a distant crack, not that low, heavy thumping sound.

Mo shook his head, approaching Meyer. He'd been willing enough a few seconds ago, but that simple report had taken the wind from his sails.

"I'm going back. We can monitor this from your office."

Meyer rubbed his temples. They'd both seen the new message on his phone. Meyer didn't know if he could trust whoever had sent him Piper's whereabouts, but he *could* easily believe that her disappearance at this specific moment wasn't a coincidence. Piper had trekked through what was now outlands with Cameron Bannister then spent months with the man and his crew at the Utah lab the Astrals perpetually ignored. If the man waiting outside had come from some sort of rebel camp, perhaps Piper was on her way to meet him. *Especially* given the information she seemed to have stolen.

Meyer didn't know how he felt about any of it. A sense of betrayal? Anger? Crushed dignity, owing to the Astrals cutting their human viceroy from the loop and handling everything themselves? Or was it jealousy? Everyone talked readily enough about Cameron Bannister, but Piper was tight-lipped despite knowing him best — at least around Meyer. What did that say about their relationship in Meyer's absence?

"No, Mo. Come with me."

"We're not soldiers."

"And it's not a war. I just want to see."

Mo shook his head, still heading away from the front door. "If you want to see what's happening around gunfire, you're on your own."

Meyer wasn't sure he wanted to see what was happening after all.

But he ran through the door anyway, feeling the skies open and exposed — nervous and conflicted for the first time in what felt like forever.

# CHAPTER 27

Cameron heard the loud, low thumping report echo to his position from inside the city. Immediately afterward, he saw the shuttles stir and shuffle without leaving the gates.

Cameron swore from his concealed position behind a burned-out car. This had always been the plan's trickiest part. Crossing the outlands — especially with Nathan Andreus's permission and offer of a vehicle — had been easy. But getting past the gates and its guards, even after ditching the bike and approaching slowly on foot? Now that felt downright impossible.

He heard a low, deep stirring in the distance. The sound of Reptars, seeming to scream out in unison. He looked toward the shot's apparent location, somehow expecting a flock of birds in startled flight. But nothing happened beyond that growl. No movement of shuttles.

He'd been here for over an hour, staring at the gates, waiting for a solution to surface from nowhere. He had no way to communicate with Moab; his helmet had shattered when he'd rolled through that field of (apparently alien) ball bearings. He had no way of speaking to anyone inside the city. He had no line to Terrence, no line to anyone friendly in the Heaven's Veil resistance. He could go around to where Terrence's church stood against the wall (and now that he thought about it, probably should), but that would mean approaching through a razed, baked pan of land, passing the massive statues denoting artists' attempts to capture the face of Divinity. Heading around to the church would mean moving in plain sight, and if any shuttles or Astral guards were in the area, he'd be dead. Besides, he'd be giving away more than just himself if he went to the church. The Astrals weren't stupid. They'd let him make contact before striking — and that would spell the end for Benjamin's contacts. And for Terrence.

He sat back against the destroyed vehicle, trying to think. Cameron had a singular mission: to get the Canned Heat to Terrence. He could hook the thing to the hub on his own, with or without Cameron's help. He liked the idea of taking a rest and perhaps staying hidden in the city for a while before heading back (ideally leaving a newly freed Internet behind) but didn't need to do anything beyond making contact and delivering his parcel.

Stripped to its basics — getting the Canned Heat over the wall and into Terrence's hands, without taking a Heaven's Veil vacation — the idea sounded more manageable. But regrettably, even *more manageable* didn't take him to possible.

Maybe he could sneak up to the fence and throw the thing over when no one was looking.

Maybe he could lure a hawk to the ground, tie the Canned Heat to its legs, then somehow train it to find Terrence.

*Shit.*

He had no idea how to do what needed doing. He'd anticipated improvisation, but now that he was here, Cameron found himself clueless.

He was about to walk a wide circle around the city, searching for weak spots (or possibly carrier hawks), when several loud sounds boomed from behind him.

Cameron turned then stood enough to peek through the car's shattered windows. His breath caught in his throat.

The double set of gates were opening wide, and the shuttles were moving out of the way, circling around toward the city's center and rear, out of sight.

Ten minutes passed. The gates stayed open, seemingly unguarded for no reason at all.

Cameron stared at the wide-open gate for what felt like an hour before deciding that the shuttles seemed to be gone, and the gates would stay open.

And worst/best of all, he knew the gates hadn't merely *opened*. They'd opened *for him.*

It didn't matter if it was a trap. If the Astrals knew he was here, flight was futile anyway. If they knew he was here, he'd have to take his chances at a trap or die running.

There were still things they didn't know. There was still a chance, no matter how slim.

Between a thin chance and none at all, Cameron's choice seemed clear.

He stood.

Walked forward slowly.

And waited to see what would happen.

# CHAPTER 28

Raj watched the guard shack's security monitor, seeing a red dot appear a handful of blocks away. Whether the red dot indicated a shot fired to match what he'd heard or something more, he didn't know. Christopher knew exactly what all of the grid map's symbols meant, but Christopher wasn't here. He was off picking his ass, like always. Captain of the guard indeed. What was higher? Captain or commander?

*Damn right.*

The oddity of the commander not knowing how to read the map occurred to Raj, but he brushed the notion away. He didn't know how to read it because that sort of triviality was beneath him. Raj was head of security, in name if not in practice. Meyer trusted his judgment. That made Raj a strategist, whereas Christopher was one step above a grunt. Human guards were pointless anyway, like Christopher.

Still, the red dot held his attention. The map was fascinating to watch. It tracked the position of Reptar peacekeepers and other forces. Raj had entered the shack to watch the detail he'd dispatched using the viceroy's command string roil toward the church at the city's edge.

186

There'd been a shot and that mysterious red dot just down from the gate. That seemed to have stopped his patrol. They'd regrouped, now headed more or less back in this direction. Toward the Apex, toward the house. Maybe toward the red dot.

Raj watched the screen, fascinated and annoyed in unison. He hoped the fucking Reptars had at least grabbed Piper before turning back. They'd certainly had the time. He'd seen them surround and enter the church. He'd seen them stream throughout the sector afterward, focusing in a narrow line pointing away from the besieged church, as if tracking or retreating. There were twenty or thirty peacekeepers out there now — plenty to catch one disobedient woman.

He hoped they'd at least stop by the guard shack on the way back and drop her off before running toward this whole red dot incident. Raj wanted credit for the bust, and he might not get it if too much happened between then and now.

Raj waited.

His eyes rolled. The stupid animals were heading toward the front gate, apparently not planning to stop at the mansion.

He exited the guard shack. He touched the pistol at his hip.

Raj nudged the shack door closed behind him, making sure it locked, and headed off the mansion grounds into the buildings ahead, following the running peacekeepers' purrs.

# CHAPTER 29

"Jeanine," Nathan said into his intercom.

"Yes, Nathan."

"Is Bannister inside yet?"

Coffey hesitated a moment for replying. Then: "Almost. But ..."

"But what?"

"He's literally just walking into the city, Nathan."

"So? You sound like that's a bad thing."

Another pause. "I'm sending you the satellite feed. Take a look, and see what you think."

Nathan looked at his shattered laptop, victim of his earlier tantrum. Seeing its dead screen reminded Nathan why he'd destroyed half of his office. Remembering made him think of Julie and Grace, dead merely because they'd chosen to hide in the wrong place. To hide *from Nathan* in the wrong place. He'd been vacillating in his anger for the past hour while milling through his destroyed office, trying to decide whom he was angriest at. Did he most hate the rebels who'd sheltered his wife and daughter? It was hard to hate them, seeing as they were dead themselves. That left two parties left to loathe: the Astrals who'd murdered them

188

— and Nathan himself, for driving his family away.

But self-pity could come later. Vengeance was his target for now.

"I can't see the feed."

"You'll find it under—" Coffey began.

"I'll be right down."

"Yes, of course."

Nathan found his lieutenant in front of the communication room's large screen, pinching and swiping to view various parts of the satellite feed. Normally, the feed wouldn't warrant the biggest monitor, but Coffey might have heard his earlier destructive spree.

"Look," Coffey said, hearing Nathan's approach. She pointed at a lone figure approaching a pair of wide-open gates like a gunslinger tromping into a showdown. Or an ambush.

"Are you kidding me?" Nathan asked. "Are the Astrals still over by the church?"

Coffey pinched out, then back in on another section of the city. "They're here." She tapped the screen in a few places, her fingers leaving small, irregular blue dots to mark her touch. "Reptars. Maybe twenty or more." She tapped again. "There are Titans here and here."

"*Titans?*"

"Looks like it."

"Where is this?"

She scanned and pinched back out. "Around 400 meters from the front gate."

"Of the viceroy's mansion?"

Coffey shook her head. "Of the city."

"The fucking aliens are going *toward* the front gate? Why aren't they at the church?"

"Only a small peacekeeper detail was sent. The shuttles stayed where they were but have now rolled back to here and here—" She touched the screen. "Probably out of his line of sight. Hiding, like they're waiting to pounce. You didn't see any of this up in your office? I assumed you were watching, since you—"

"I wasn't watching," Nathan snapped, his lips pressing bloodlessly together. His fists clenched. He wanted to pick one of the people in the communication room and beat the living shit out of him just to vent his frustration. There wasn't anyone in the room over thirty years old, and all were fit and well trained, but none would lift a finger against him. It wasn't safe to beat Nathan Andreus in anything he cared to win if you cared to see another sunrise.

"You're saying the Astrals didn't divert at all?" Nathan stared at the overhead view. "They didn't even *care* to chase down Piper Dempsey?"

"Just the small detail, Nathan. The rest of what you see moved toward the gate."

"Titans." He exhaled. "Why are they sending Titans?"

"I don't know."

"When Bannister was on the move, did someone spot him?"

"We weren't able to watch him the whole way. I don't know."

Nathan chewed his lip. "They knew he was coming."

Coffey nodded. "Yes."

"And now they're waiting. Opening the gates and slinking out of sight ... and this stupid asshole is dumb enough to just walk right in, as if they left the door open by mistake."

Coffey's head tipped: a half shrug. "Looks that way."

Nathan's head slowly moved side to side. "He's carrying that device. The one Bannister mentioned over their channel a while back when he was talking to his man in the city. Terrence."

Coffey looked shocked. "You mean the virus? The one Terrence created? How do you know he has it with him? Did he tell you about it or see the device when he was here?"

"He's headed into the city, Jeanine. They wouldn't try something so dangerous just for reconnaissance."

"But what makes you so sure he's—"

"It's what I would do," said Nathan, cutting her off.

Coffey's head returned to the screen. Cameron Bannister was still making his way slowly toward the wide-open city gates, right out in the middle of everything like an asshole wearing a bull's eye.

"They know," Nathan said, deciding. "I have no idea *how* they know, but they know he's carrying the virus. They're letting him in so they can take it away without destroying it, so they can study it and see how the network ticks. Once they have what he's holding, they'll kill him."

"Well then," said Coffey, "I guess we're about to see the end of Bannister's resistance."

Nathan reached toward the screen, pinched it wide, then wider still. Maybe five to eight miles away, the computer had laid an Andreus graphic over a small clump of dark boxes.

"Not if they get reinforcements," he said.

# CHAPTER 30

"Not that way," said Terrence.

Piper looked at Terrence, now with the enormous modified weapon Christopher had used to dispatch the Reptar in some sort of holster behind his back. She had to stop running because Terrence was behind her, and she didn't know what "not that way" meant.

"I don't know for sure," he said, breathing heavily as he caught up with her, "but given the way they all seem to communicate mentally, I'll bet they know a Reptar was killed. First time that's happened inside the city since the occupation, I think," he added.

"And?" Piper could feel seconds ticking away. The peacekeepers' rattling purrs seemed to come from all directions and had since they'd resumed running. The group was uncomfortably large, but there wasn't much point in discretion. They'd either make it or not. Their loud weapon rang the dinner bell, and it seemed miraculous that they hadn't been overtaken yet. They'd rounded a few corners, stumbled through someone's piled up trash bags, and nearly broken their necks on a spill of what looked like tiny silver BBs on the far side. None of it had been quiet, and yet they'd been fortunate so far, surviving only on speed and luck rather than skill and evasion.

"I'm pretty sure they were already onto me," Terrence said. "From earlier."

"And if they weren't," Heather added, "they probably are now that Chris here so subtly discharged an illegal weapon."

"Maybe I should have let it eat them," Christopher said, turning to face Heather.

"Maybe you shouldn't've come, Mom," Trevor added.

"You told me to!"

Trevor ignored Heather then turned to Piper. Of course he hadn't *told her to come*; Piper knew from past experience that she'd simply tagged along unwanted. For the half second before he spoke, she was struck anew by his change. Trevor wouldn't be legal to vote in the old world, but the past years had already turned him into a man. She saw shades of Meyer in Trevor's eyes — a kind of merciless practicality that told Piper he'd leave anyone behind if they slowed the group. Better for some to survive than none at all.

"You need to go back, Mom. I keep telling you, it's not safe." He pointed back toward the house, where they'd been about to go. "They'll let you back in, no problem. Christopher will go with you." He turned to Christopher as he would an underling. "Make sure she gets home safely."

Trevor looked at Piper and extended a hand. For a crazy moment, Piper though he wanted her to give him five.

"What?" she asked, staring at the hand.

"You took something from Dad's computer."

"I–"

"Give it to me, Piper. I heard Dad say there's someone outside the gates and the Astrals know it. They're all worked up."

"And?"

"And that tells me it might be someone from Benjamin's lab. Or the rebels at least. If you give me what you took, I can get to them. I'll tell the cops I want to join the contingent at the gate then sneak out or at least toss it somewhere safely beyond the fence for someone to find later."

"Why would I take anything from your fa—" Piper began.

"I don't like what Dad's doing any more than you do." He jabbed the outstretched hand toward Piper again, insisting.

Piper looked at Trevor then at Heather, who of course hadn't moved. Her jaw worked. "I'm going with you," she said.

"They won't let you out. I'm technically Apex Guard, so I have options. But they're looking for *you*, Piper."

She gestured toward the monks, who'd trailed behind in an untidy bundle. "What about them? They have to get out of the city, too."

"Not now. They'll need to try and hide in here, then sneak out later."

"I'll hide and then sneak out with them."

"No, you won't," said Christopher, shaking his head. "They're looking for an Astral killer, and you're already a fugitive. The shuttles will be circling for a while. Running is the worst thing you can do."

"So you want me to—"

"Go back home," said Trevor.

Piper felt her eyes widen. Exactly what the monks had been saying, and this from her stepson. How could they be so stupid? He'd just said she was a fugitive. Did they really think she'd be welcomed back?

"It's you they're looking for, Piper, but mainly because of Dad," said Trevor. "He's upset, sure it's a misunderstanding. They wouldn't do anything to unsettle their viceroy. Some eyebrows will raise, but they won't hurt you."

Piper felt abandoned. She glared at Terrence — her last chance at sanity.

"Sorry, Piper. I agree with Trev. Give him what you have

to deliver, then come back with me and Heather."

"*You?*"

"Yes, me too," he said, nodding his huge head of hair. "Gotta take the chance that they'll keep buying what I'm shoveling. So far, so good because I'm still here after my little visit this morning."

"They aren't stupid, Terrence."

"We need someone inside. It's the only way."

"Not you." She turned to Trevor. "I'm talking about *me*. I won't go back."

"You have to."

"I don't have to do *shit*."

Trevor flinched; Piper rarely swore.

"If you think *you* can get outside, you take all of us," she said.

"Piper, I'll be walking right through lines of guards and police and Astrals! I'm not getting out; I'm just taking your delivery!"

"Take us too."

"There's no way! It's—"

There was a loud humming sound behind them. Piper spun to see the edge of a shuttle hovering low, now visible between the buildings. They never flew this low. It seemed as if it hadn't seen them yet, but she could already hear another on its way.

"*Give it to me, Piper!*" Trevor hissed. His hand shook. His eyes seemed panicked.

Instead of answering, Piper looked toward the gate then back at Heather, who was now dragging Christopher toward the house. She began to move. Terrence had joined Trevor behind Piper rather than going with Christopher and Heather. Monks in street clothes brought up the rear in a second group.

As Piper looked back, a second shuttle loomed behind Franklin and the others.

There was a bright flash, a chorus of screams, and a waft of hot flame.

In that flash, the party of fugitives had dwindled to three: Piper, Trevor, and Terrence.

They ran, the deadly alien sphere moving into position behind them.

# CHAPTER 31

Cameron could hear a commotion ahead, but the path between gates remained deserted and still.

He'd seen Heaven's Veil many times on the various hacked camera views Terrence had given them access to over the years, but he hadn't seen it with his own eyes since leaving the house with Piper all that time ago.

The surrounding area was still thick with trees and hills, but Astral terraforming had denuded the city's land itself and a wide ring around it, grinding rock and soil to make it flat. He'd heard and seen that the city was mostly concrete, slab stone, and the odd patch of grass for opulence (especially around the viceroy's mansion), but the apron was almost baked clay.

The gate was wide. It scrolled backward into recesses at the opening's sides. Between the two edge posts lay a wide area cut lower into the rock, like the vast drainage systems Cameron had seen in urban California. The valley continued forward to a second set of gates, also left open.

Halfway between the two gates, walking steadily through the center of the recessed valley, Cameron wondered if the Astrals would simply close the gates and trap him between them.

A new question rose to match it:

*Why?*

They could have killed him a dozen times already. He'd stood in front of five shuttles a few hours ago, before being surrounded by millions of floating BBs.

They knew he was here. For whatever reason, they'd decided it wasn't in Cameron Bannister's fate to be killed out of hand. Why, he didn't know.

But really, did it matter?

He couldn't run.

He couldn't ask Benjamin, Danika, or Charlie for advice.

He couldn't get in touch with Terrence.

If the Astrals knew he was in Heaven's Veil, Cameron was doing all he could hope to do. If he played along, he might find a way to hand off his true purpose. He wasn't carrying a nuke, which they might suspect. He wasn't here to assassinate Meyer Dempsey, which they also might suspect. He was carrying a small cylinder. He merely needed to plug it into the right holes, or hand it off to any one of several right people.

That might still be possible, even in the throat of a trap. There still might be a way.

Cameron walked forward, heart in his throat.

# CHAPTER 32

Meyer was stopped by the massive muscular arms of two Titans as he tried entering the main thoroughfare near the gate. He'd passed several circling Reptars already, all eyeing him with what he thought (and definitely sensed) was anger. But they'd let the viceroy by. He'd seen two shuttles, both practically parked as they hovered in their out-of-the-way positions in two of the better city back yards. They hadn't even twitched.

But the Titans stopped him.

"I'm the viceroy," Meyer said unnecessarily. "Let me through."

The Titan on the right gave Meyer a soft, pleasant smile without moving his arm. The smile was maddening in his agitated state. It was impossible to anger the Titans. You could drop your drawers and shit on their feet; they'd smile blandly down while you did it. Reptars would correct your *faux pas* with teeth and claws.

"Let me through," he repeated.

The second Titan shook his head, also smiling. Meyer's mind filled with an image of a green circle, its edges outlined in black. The symbol meant nothing to him, but he understood its meaning from a warm sense of emotion wafting from the Titan: the area was controlled, somehow restricted. And he wouldn't be going through no matter who he was.

"My wife is in there. Piper. You know Piper Dempsey?"

Meyer saw a flash inside his mind: Piper, as she appeared on the occasional broadcast. He was annoyed to be reminded of his wife's identity, but he understood. He'd asked the question. They'd answered.

"One of the rebels, too. One of them is outside. I know something about him, if he's who I think, you might not know that—"

Again, Meyer saw the green circle with the black outline. This time, the image came from higher. From Divinity, aboard the mothership.

"You're just going to let him in?" Meyer tried to summon pointless indignation. "What if he has a nuke? What if he plans to blow up Heaven's Veil? I don't know if you know much about nukes, but if they get close like this, it doesn't matter how much you try to—"

The Titan on the right cut him off again, still pleasantly smiling. He held up a tiny sliver object. It looked like a stainless steel pearl.

To accompany it, again, Meyer saw the green circle in his mind. He sensed his earlier panic starting to subside, as if the Astrals' collective will was pushing it down. He could still sense something in the group mind that felt like Reptar rage but could no longer feel the discordant sense of unraveling plans, and panic about the man outside the gate. Whatever had alerted them earlier, it wasn't bothering them now. And he couldn't sense any worry over Piper, as if all that alarm over her disappearance had ceased to matter.

*Move along,* the Titans seemed to say. *Nothing to see here.*

At the far side of Meyer's vision, just beyond the Titan's shoulder, he could see a single, young-looking man with untidy brown hair appear in the valley between the inner gates. The aliens were staying back, mostly invisible from the approaching man. Meyer could see him, but the Titans were doing their best to stay hidden from the walking man.

Still the Titans' pleasant expressions seemed to say: *Move along. Nothing to see here.*

Behind him, in the blocks to Meyer's rear, a contingent of Reptars circled and prowled, thinking alien thoughts of murder.

# CHAPTER 33

A shuttle flashed, discharging its weapon two blocks up. A woman screamed, and Raj swore he could smell charred flesh. Then he heard running and saw the shuttle's pursuit.

He thought to flee in the other direction, but that was old Raj thinking. He was no longer a scared little Indian, running from alien ships while dodging emasculating abuse from Lila alongside her mother's racist barbs. He wouldn't pretend he commanded those ships (though he sometimes dreamed of a day when he might), but he didn't have to run from their danger.

They shared a side, the Astrals and Raj.

What they pursued, he could pursue.

What they incinerated, he more or less wanted incinerated ... or at least understood.

Instead of running from the shuttle, Raj ran toward it.

His mind showed him the map he'd seen back in the guard shack. He knew where the red dot had been and where the flash must have occurred relative to it. If he added the city's double front gates and the long sunken valley sloping between them, the three points drew a straight line.

The conclusion was obvious: something was happening

near the gate, and the Astrals were headed to intercept it, apparently blowing things up along the way.

Was it Piper? What if she'd fallen in with malcontents, and whoever had fired the weapon earlier — whoever was running from the shuttle — was one of them?

The shuttle rose above the buildings ahead, seeming to give up its chase. Raj stood still, making no effort to hide, watching it fly directly overhead.

He stood indecisive for a minute after the ship passed, torn between investigating whatever the thing had just blown up and the survivors it had lost (or lost interest in) and discovering what commotion lay at the gate.

Before he could make a decision, Raj heard the shuffling of feet: the runners he'd heard earlier. The ones who'd been fleeing the shuttle, running right toward him.

This time he *did* slink back, pressing himself into a doorway.

Peeking around a corner, Raj saw Piper.

Terrence was with her, apparently helping the deserter. That made sense; Raj had been watching Terrence for a while now, sure he was up to something.

The party's third member was harder to account for, and would definitely be more difficult to explain to the viceroy. It was Trevor Dempsey.

Raj let them pass then turned to follow, keeping low and staying hidden.

Raj mostly liked Trevor, but this was business.

These three may have somehow evaded the shuttle and peacekeepers; they wouldn't escape the commander of the guard.

And wouldn't the viceroy be thrilled when Raj caught loose ends missed by the Astrals' best efforts?

# CHAPTER 34

Trevor took the lead.

His breath was short and fast. He remembered playing paintball in his youth, before the world had ended, and the way he'd ducked around a faux warscape in a protective helmet to play it. The helmet had only been a hat with a face shield, more or less open, and he'd been playing a harmless war game — and yet he'd still felt suffocated by his breath.

This was like that. Trevor felt as if a cotton wad had been stuffed down his throat.

But this wasn't a game. He was on the losing side, no doubt. It might not even matter that he was the viceroy's son. The Astrals kept Meyer because he was well liked by what remained of North America and was now known to the rest of the world. Meyer was a face that humanity seemed willing to trust, but Trevor had no illusions; the Astrals were in charge and would only keep partners for as long as those comrades stayed out of their way.

Piper was in their way now. Terrence had already told Trevor that whatever she'd stolen had been worth going to the dissidents for. Piper's behavior rammed that point home. She'd stolen something from Meyer's computer, and that something had been troubling enough to trigger a rather violent reaction. He'd seen their trailing knot of people turned to ash by the shuttle. Trevor, Terrence, and Piper were only alive now because they'd been twenty feet farther down the street when the weapon had discharged.

Trevor looked back, expecting to see the shuttle. But it wasn't there; they'd somehow eluded their pursuer. Shuttle attacks didn't fire like bullets or rockets. They used quick-cook heat rays. It didn't take long to bake what they aimed at, but it did take a second or two. And in that second — against all odds and hope — they'd managed to sneak away.

It seemed too good to be true, but it was their reality nonetheless. They were alive, but they couldn't expect that kind of luck to hold out.

They had to keep running. Stay hidden. Conceal themselves from prying eyes.

Despite what he'd told Piper, Trevor wasn't positive he could talk his way out of the gate at all — let alone with a fugitive and another hanger-on. Still, he had to try. It was all they had. Either the shuttle had seen the three of them with the party they'd killed, or it hadn't. Either the Astrals knew flight was afoot, or they didn't. They'd either shifted their attention to whoever might be waiting at the gate ... or they'd split their search in two, now looking for this knot of bandits as well.

There would be no going back to the house for Piper. Not after that shuttle blast.

Trevor could only try.

He *had* to try.

And if they could reach the gates clean — if Trevor could keep Piper away from Astral eyes for long enough to figure his angle — then maybe they'd survive. Maybe *she'd* survive.

If they could reach the gates undetected.

But Trevor couldn't shake a sinking feeling that their luck was already gone.

# CHAPTER 35

The area around the gate was entirely deserted.

Cameron almost wanted to raise his hands, feeling like a lone cowboy sauntering into an enemy camp in an old western. He wanted to take his fingers away from his guns and hold them high, telling the sentries who had him in their sights that he meant no harm.

But there were no sentries.

There were no guards.

There were no shuttles, no animal-like peacekeepers, none of the big white beings the press called Titans. No human guards, from the viceroy's detachment or otherwise. No police. No vehicles; no automated weapon systems; no locks; no slots or scanners to verify Cameron's ID or rights to be here.

There was nothing at all.

Cameron walked through the gate and up the slowly rising valley between it, waiting for the other shoe to drop. He felt fatalistic, like he had no choice. His actions were stupid. But really, how stupid was it compared to the mission's idiocy in general?

Benjamin had given him a communication virus that

SEAN PLATT & JOHNNY B. TRUANT

he knew full well might fry the network rather than freeing it. Cameron wasn't deaf. He'd heard the discussion, both from Terrence's end during their original journey to Vail and back at Moab. Canned Heat had a fifty-fifty chance of working, at best. The wrong 50 percent left them worse than cut off, of no use to anyone, deader than they'd already been.

Cameron's first stop had been with Nathan Andreus — the despot whose minions had nearly killed him and Piper on their way to Moab. Since that meeting, he'd crossed hostile land, along open roads, without so much tree cover for most of the trip, daring their airborne foes to challenge him.

Yes, walking directly into the enemy city's beating heart at the end of that trek was stupid beyond belief.

But now he was in the city without a hint of harassment.

He still had the canister in his pack, despite the intense interest of those strange flying balls.

He was in the lion's den and could be killed at any second. But hadn't that been true from the start? Wasn't that true, even now, every day, for the Moab lab?

They could jump out with drawn guns to take him.

Peacekeepers could appear and rip him apart with their teeth.

They could simply surround him and tell him to stop walking. That would be it for his mission. An end with no pomp, circumstance, or ceremony.

But around Cameron, there was nothing. Nothing at all.

He entered the city.

Nothing rose to stop him.

# CHAPTER 36

The alien signals inside Meyer's mind were confusing. He couldn't ever quite make sense of his soupy thoughts; now was no exception.

The Astrals all seemed to hive-think around him. Sometimes, he could catch their moods, but even the moods, now, seemed conflicted. Normally, it took the filter of Divinity — unseen archivists who never left the mothership — to turn all that messy Astral thought into something Meyer could understand. But even without collating and parsing, he could usually get a sense for how the Astrals were feeling.

And they did have emotion, contrary to what most humans thought. Meyer should know; he was there with their mind, absorbing it all.

They felt sympathy, though it was tempered by superior knowledge — like a parent might feel sympathy for a child even in the midst of administering discipline, for his own good.

They felt anger, though it was always blunted by logic.

They felt joy ... *maybe*. Meyer could sense an emotion like pleasure, but it was like something seen far beneath a pond's rippling surface.

There were even times when Meyer suspected the Astrals felt love.

And Meyer — slightly more evolved than his fellow humans even before this all began, certainly more evolved than nearly every human now — usually found he could sort it out in the end. He caught the scents of their thoughts, enough to feel the patterns. Even without Divinity's help, he could spot their loudest edges, though the dots between were often muddled and harder to connect.

But not now. Now, discerning the thoughts and quiet emotions surrounding this standoff was so much harder.

Emotions were noisy as Meyer stood behind the Titan guards, watching a man he believed to be Cameron Bannister disappear behind the first row of buildings.

He could sense anger in them.

He could sense their worry that everything, despite careful planning, might not go correctly.

He could detect a slight fear of chaos — of the uncertain and unknown.

There was concern for those involved in this standoff, too. That was unusual. Meyer had never sensed remorse from the aliens because remorse carried the baggage of doubtful action. As far as he'd seen, the Astrals were never doubtful. Why would they care — even in their tiny, slight alien way — about doing the wrong thing (or having done the wrong thing) now?

Most perplexing of all, though, was the emotion Meyer could sense below all the shallower surface sentiments. It felt like the left-behind stink of burned toast in a recently used kitchen. He couldn't even begin to name it. Something to do with Cameron Bannister — a man that Meyer, for one, had never met. For some reason, the Astral collective didn't quite trust Cameron — not as a possible rebel, but in another, harder-to-define way. They also wanted to hurt him a little — not for logic, but for spite.

But Meyer's thoughts dissolved as Cameron vanished into the city. He'd been certain the Titans would stop him. He'd been sure the Reptars would leap out and chase the man down before he exited the valley. But no, the standoff had ended without confrontation, and now Cameron Bannister was gone.

Meyer, feeling alien emotion as if it were his own, not pausing to understand his words, turned to the closest Titan and snapped, "You're just going to let that motherfucker go? After what he's done?"

The Titan smiled blandly, again holding up a single silver pearl.

"Go after him! Catch him! Don't you know who that is? Don't you know what he did?"

The Titan continued to smile.

With Cameron gone, a gap formed between the Titans, apparently content to let Cameron get away with everything.

Meyer forced his way through the gap.

The Titans raised silent arms, shouting inside Meyer's head from behind. But the viceroy was already off and running, and nobody was going to stop him.

# CHAPTER 37

The house guard communicator crackled in Raj's ear. Seconds later, the viceroy's shouts blasted into his head. Meyer sounded out of breath and nervous. Two things Meyer Dempsey never, ever was.

"*Christopher!* Christopher, do you hear me?"

There was a beep.

"Yes, sir. I hear you."

"Where are you?"

"At the house."

Raj, listening, made note of Christopher's tone. An *of-course* way of speaking, as if he wanted Meyer to know he'd have no reason to leave the grounds. But Raj knew that Christopher had left; he'd seen it himself. He'd even seen Meyer talking to Christopher, and then — oh yes, now this was staring to make sense — talking to Trevor.

Trevor seemed nice enough, but thinking about it, Raj supposed Trevor had always been against him. He'd allied with Christopher, even back in the bunker days. It had been Christopher and the crew against Raj, Heather against Raj, even Lila against Raj. Trevor hung with Christopher or with Lila, and that stayed true today. Raj had thought for a while that something fishy was going on — with Trevor, with Lila, with Christopher. Some secret they were keeping. Here it was again, except now they were keeping it from the viceroy: a step too far. Raj would have to call them out — and would delight in doing so.

"Do you have your weapon?" Meyer asked Christopher.

"Of course. What's — ?"

"Get to Junction Road and—" A heavy pant, an intake of breath. "—and Vine. Near the gate. You know it?"

Raj looked around. *He* knew it just fine. That intersection was a few blocks away.

"Near the gate?" Christopher asked.

*"YES, NEAR THE MOTHERFUCKING GATE!"*

"Okay, okay, I hear you. Is something wr — ?"

"Bannister." *Puff. Inhale.* The swishing of fabric. "Your old buddy Cameron."

"What about him?"

"He's here."

"Here in the city?"

"Yes, goddammit!"

"Where are you?"

Meyer resumed, now huffing harder, as if he was running. "Behind him. But they ... fucking Titans ... just let him go. Right up the ... the central valley and ... inside. They held me back and ... now I'm going to lose him in—"

"What about the shuttle patrols? The peacekeepers?"

"Are you listening to me?" Two heavy breaths then, *"They let him go!"*

"Why?"

"Okay, okay," Christopher said in Raj's ear. "I'll head out there now. But I'm on foot, and that's a hike. You still might reach him before I do."

Raj's hand touched his weapon.

Junction and Vine. Not far at all.

He could be there in no time.

# CHAPTER 38

"Oh my God," Piper said.

Trevor turned toward her, as did Terrence from her other side. Their faces were curious, waiting for her to continue.

"That was ..." Piper paused to regroup, still not believing her eyes. She finished the thought: "That was *Cameron!*"

Terrence looked around. "Where?"

"Up ahead."

Terrence looked like he wanted to tell Piper she was seeing things but couldn't quite bring himself to say it.

"Why would Cameron be *here?*"

Trevor swallowed. "Dad said someone was here. When he was talking to Mo Weir. Someone at the gate."

"But *Cameron?*"

Piper felt her feet beginning to move faster. They'd been creeping, heavy with a sense that hurry would end them. She hadn't allowed herself to consider the monks' deaths, but that had happened while rushing. They had to be careful, tend every step lest they be discovered.

Still, Piper's feet shuffled beneath her, trying to glimpse what she'd seen a block ahead before her quarry got too far away.

"Slow down, Piper," Trevor hissed.

"Why would he be here?"

"They don't know why he's here," Trevor told her.

"Who doesn't know?"

"The Astrals."

Terrence, from behind Piper: "What are you talking about, Trevor?"

"I just heard that word came down. They knew someone was outside, but not who or why."

"Well, he's not outside now."

"That doesn't make any sense." Trevor sounded baffled. "Dad said they seemed panicked. Like everyone had to rush to the gate and keep whoever was outside from coming in no matter what."

Piper kept hustling, something pushing her toward Cameron. She desperately needed to reach him, and soon. She hadn't seen him since Moab, and even though her memories of Cameron were tinged with guilt, he'd been in her life when she'd been more innocent, less quietly complicit in something so terrible. Back then, Piper had been hiding from the Astrals and hoping to fight them. Today, they circulated in her house like guests while her family dined on fine china. Today, her husband was in charge of sending Reptars into the streets to hunt people who refused to do as they were told.

"They let him in?" said Terrence, now almost running behind Piper.

Trevor said, "Maybe someone else was outside."

"And Cameron just happens to be here, in the city? *Right in front of us?*"

It felt like fate. Piper reached the corner and, with barely a glance for alien pursuit, turned to follow the departing man's back. She had to reach him. She was *meant* to reach him. She'd been all over the city today; she'd hidden with insurgents; she'd seen those same short-time friends vaporized in front of her eyes. They'd barely dodged peacekeeper patrols from the church, then more peacekeepers after they'd turned toward the gate. Those near-misses had steered her group toward this inevitable reunion.

That's what fate felt like: *inevitability*.

"Piper!" said Trevor. "Stay low!"

She barely heard him. Instead, Piper pattered behind her old lover in a dead monk's sneakers in the deserted street, finally raising her voice to yell after him.

# CHAPTER 39

When Meyer heard Piper shout Cameron's name, he accelerated despite his empty lungs. The Titans had held him back for too long; he was lucky to have not lost his quarry. He almost had. Piper's shout was a fortunate beacon. A good thing, considering that Christopher wouldn't be here for minutes, and Meyer was on his own.

He rounded one corner, then another, just in time to see Bannister turn, and for Piper to crash into his unabashed embrace.

Meyer ran harder toward them, but was almost clotheslined by a new pair of Titans who stepped out from the shadows to stop him.

He was still two blocks back. His target was ahead, mockingly visible as he clung to Meyer's wife. They broke after too long, then Cameron embraced two others in turn: Terrence, whom Meyer knew had a history with Cameron ... and, wrenchingly, Trevor. They were in the middle of the street, hugging, slapping backs and seemingly smiling (though that was hard to tell from a distance) as if they were merely reacquainting in a mall.

Didn't Cameron know he wasn't supposed to be here?

Didn't he know the Astrals hated him? Couldn't he feel the atmosphere's creeping pall of negativity? Didn't he know that the Titans, if they could stop holding back well-intentioned viceroys, were dying to wrap their giant powder-white hands around Cameron's neck and squeeze until something snapped?

But nobody was stopping this inappropriately joyful reunion. The four celebrants were in the middle of the goddamned street, hugging and shaking goddamned hands, smiling and practically goddamn laughing because this was all a big goddamned joke on Meyer Dempsey and the city under his command.

And the Astral guards holding him back were letting it happen.

"Let me through," Meyer said.

The Titans smiled like courtly bouncers.

"Let me through! Don't you see what's happening down there? Right in the middle of the fucking street? Don't you know who that is? *Don't you know who I am?*"

The Titans fixed Meyer with their infuriatingly accommodating expressions, as if waiting for him to tire himself out and stop his tantrum.

"That's Cameron Bannister! Benjamin Bannister's kid! The people in the desert who keep working with the rebels to attack the city! You knew he was out there! You sent guards to stop him! He might be carrying a bomb! Are you really going to let him pow-wow with his man up there? Aren't you going to send the peacekeepers? Aren't you going to go after him? He's an insurgent! *He fucked my wife!*"

The Titan on Meyer's left gestured at the street. They were still mostly hidden in the alleyway's shadowy mouth, but he could plainly see the stone between their position and the others. At first, Meyer didn't know what the alien was pointing at, then he saw a small stir of leaves — one of those whorls that get caught in the eddies wafting between city buildings.

Except the swirling wasn't leaves. Even from several buildings away, Meyer could see the objects in the vortex. They were tiny balls of metal, like the object the other Titans had shown him earlier.

"I'm warning you," Meyer blurted, wondering at his own mounting, spiraling anger. "If you don't let me through, you'll be *very* fucking sorry!"

The Titan nodded pleasantly as if Meyer had wished him a good day.

He couldn't break through their muscular arms.

So Meyer started screaming.

# CHAPTER 40

Cameron looked up at the sounds of shouting.

He still had Terrence's hand clasped in his, and the stubborn smile wouldn't leave his lips even though his animal brain had already keyed his system to alarm. Piper's expression was subtly different. Her joy shared other emotions. It was hard to believe it had been two years since he'd seen her. If his comrade and Meyer's boy weren't here, he'd probably still be holding her, refusing to let go.

Their heads turned. Shouting was coming from a few blocks back, rolling down the middle of the wide-open street like floodwater.

Cameron felt stupid, exposed, terrified. For himself, sure — but mostly for the others. Terrence was tough; he'd traveled with Vincent and knew peril like an old friend. But the boy was seventeen, if he remembered right, and had always struck Cameron as sweet and a little naive. Piper was almost as strong as Terrence, but she looked beaten by the intervening years, and Cameron couldn't help wanting to leap between Piper and danger, to take its brunt and spare her.

All at once, Cameron realized he'd been lulled into a

spell. He'd emerged from behind that burned car on high alert, passing through the open, unguarded gates with the greatest of trepidation, his every nerve on fire. But time had passed, and it was hard to maintain vigilance for more than a handful of minutes. As one innocent block surrendered to another, he'd begun to subconsciously feel that maybe it was all a mistake. Heaven's Veil had become a peaceful colony, open to all. Benjamin's preparations and Ivan's estimations had proved themselves paranoid. There were no guards. The gates stood wide for all who cared to enter, or leave in peace.

But now they were surrounded by stirs of activity. Cameron could hear rustling down a dozen dead ends. Shouts stabbed the silence. Back the way he'd come, there was a tremendous banging and a crash, muffled by the distance he'd paced off like a man nearing execution.

Heaven's Veil's sleeping defenses were waking.

Starting with whoever was shouting.

"I know who you are!" the shouter bellowed. "Motherfucker, I know who you are!"

A deep voice. One Cameron almost recognized. Piper was staring, her huge eyes wide, her dark bangs far too sweet for mortal peril.

She knew.

Or rather, she *saw*.

Cameron couldn't tell who the man in the suit was, screaming profanities from two blocks away. But he *could* clearly see the white shapes of two enormous Titans holding him back.

The second assault approached from the rear. Cameron turned in time to see that, too.

# CHAPTER 41

Raj wondered for two seconds — the precise interval between the onset of Meyer's shouting and the loud noise from the city's entrance — how he could summon assistance.

Then he realized something that was both terrible and liberating: he was here alone, and the only one able to do a thing.

The viceroy needed help, and the target of his displeasure was no more than twenty feet from Raj. But Meyer didn't carry a gun.

The Titans Raj saw holding Meyer; for whatever reason, weren't willing to intervene.

Raj had been able to issue a command to the Reptar patrols, but he wouldn't be able to do so again. For one, technically speaking, that wasn't his domain. And secondly, Raj had no idea if any were in the area.

Christopher — who, Raj was beginning to feel certain, was some sort of a traitor — hadn't arrived, if he ever would.

Even if Raj had a line to the police like Christopher, the area had no obvious human patrols.

It would have to be Raj. A blessing, considering how easy it would be.

He'd been watching them for twenty minutes. Trevor had a pistol on his belt, but Raj had never seen the kid try to fire it. Terrence had some sort of a giant rifle, but it was on his back, and there was no way he could draw it in time. Piper didn't have a gun unless it was in her panties. And Cameron? He had that big backpack. He could draw his weapon, but Raj didn't think he'd do so smoothly.

Raj unholstered his own weapon — a plain old lead slinger, same as all human peacekeepers wore. He felt its heft in his fist, fingering the trigger. He flicked off the safety and racked the slide, knowing there was little point in quiet with Meyer shouting his lungs out down the street.

Given the awkward position of Terrence's rifle, Raj only needed to worry about Cameron and Trevor. And if he shot one right away, it would be easier to disarm the other with confusion.

He raised his weapon and stepped forward, heart thumping, ready to prove his worth to the Viceroy.

Raj wasn't a great shot, but he was good enough for this.

# CHAPTER 42

Too much happened too fast.

Commotion at the gate hadn't stopped. There had been that large booming noise, followed by more — a kind of crashing, shambling, chaotic hustle.

Meyer was still shouting, his efforts in struggling against the two albino hulks finally bearing fruit. He was past one, now held only by the other. Piper could see his red face, thinking it strange. She'd seen him angry before, but Meyer swelled with silent fury. She'd seldom seen him lose his cool, be it to scream or panic or cry. But she saw it now. Everything he'd held inside bubbled to the surface, turning him into another man, foreign and frightening.

Then a crack from the rear. At first, Piper thought it was a snapping stick — one of their party knocking something over in the confusion. Then she saw the uniformed figure marching forward, her mind having trouble slotting it into any parody of meaning: Raj, here, pistol in hand, his once-soft, now-often-petulant brown eyes focused, his bearing upright. Her mind caught the tiniest detail — a drift of white smoke escaping the pistol's barrel. It was almost not there. But Raj had fired, all right.

Cameron slumped into her. Something in Piper sprang to alarm. She grabbed him under the armpits, his front pressing into hers, his superior weight making her wobble, her inappropriate dress tugging its straps into her shoulders. There was a bloom of red on him — not in his center, thankfully, but in his shoulder, near his collarbone.

Even in the next partial second as Raj came closer, Piper knew what had happened. She'd fired more guns since Astral Day than she'd liked and knew you had to grip with both hands and stand prepared. Raj, inexperienced and recently insecure, had fired one-handed like a cinema cowboy, surely flinching with the blast. If he'd been farther than ten feet away, he'd have missed entirely.

Another half beat. Another sixtieth of a minute. Another one thousand milliseconds of eternity.

Piper's life didn't flash before her eyes, but she had time in that second to see every nuance.

Raj had shot Cameron without hesitation, almost literally in the back. He was already moving his sights from Cameron's now-neutralized form to his right, toward Terrence. It was all happening in slow motion. She would need to take Cameron's weapon. She would need to do what had to be done all over again because —

Another flash of minuscule time. Meyer broke free, his feet pounding pavement at tenth gear, his tie flapping, his face red, his mouth open. Titans behind him began to move. One had a finger to his temple. Calling help.

Raj coming. His gun hand swinging like a machine's armature.

His swing was too wide; there was movement as Piper started the impossibly slow job of finding Cameron's weapon on his sagging form as it dragged her knees to the stone street.

A blur of fabric. A new arm.

Trevor dove between Piper and Raj, tackling him

**224**

around the waist. A shout came from somewhere — possibly from Trevor's lungs. A cry of fury. Almost desperation. Something from nowhere. And in the face of it, Raj didn't stand a chance.

But as Raj's body smacked the ground, a new sound filled the air around them.

Piper thought of the Titan with his finger to his temple. Calling the Reptars that must have been in the shadows all along. They sounded a block away, no more. Rattling purrs pricked her skin, Cameron's nearly dead weight heavy in her sagging lap.

Terrence had pulled the strange rifle from his back. Unsure where to aim it, he pointed at Meyer. Who skidded to a stop with raised hands.

Trevor punched Raj in the face, twice. Piper whispered his name, and he looked up, his face momentarily crazed. His knuckles were red — with his own blood or the gusher now streaming from Raj's nose and lip, she wasn't sure.

Time sped back to normal. Piper felt seconds ticking, seeing herself in the center of a frightening diorama.

Meyer, still forty or so feet away, his hands raised in the face of Terrence's drawn weapon.

Trevor, kneeling half-on, half-off Raj's chest, his right fist red and raised, Raj's gun lying harmlessly on the stone three feet away.

Cameron in her own lap as her hand paused on his gun, momentarily afraid to draw it.

Titans leisurely approaching.

And, around them in a ring, the shifting blue-and-black forms of at least twenty Reptars.

Piper finally drew Cameron's weapon. Remembering, she flicked off the safety. Cameron was still against her, but his weight was shifting away, allowing Piper to sight from her knees — though specifically on what, she couldn't have said. She looked down at him. He seemed to be regaining awareness. The bullet had taken him in the shoulder, but blood was everywhere, as if spit through an artery.

Wincing at his wounded shoulder, Cameron slipped off his backpack. It had come partially open, its zipper sagging in a plastic-toothed mouth. He came to his knees.

"Terrence," he whispered. "Help me up."

Trevor reached for Raj's gun, slipped it into the back of his pants near his own weapon, and extended a hand to Cameron.

"*Terrence*," Cameron repeated.

Trevor looked momentarily wounded by Cameron's rebuke but straightened anyway. In his place, Terrence shifted the big rifle to one shoulder and used his free hand to grasp Cameron's, palm on palm. He yanked Cameron upright ... but as he did, Piper saw Cameron slide something into Terrence's pocket.

"Now hit me," Cameron whispered.

Terrence blinked, understanding seeming to settle in his eyes. Piper thought he'd hesitate, but he released Cameron's hand, pivoted the big rifle to hold it longwise with two hands, and drove the heavy stock hard into the side of Cameron's head.

"What the *hell*, Terrence?" Trevor blurted as Cameron went down.

Piper swallowed, wondering what came next, then saw the new man arrive beside Meyer — the man Cameron and Terrence had apparently already seen: Christopher.

He whispered into Meyer's ear. The viceroy visibly calmed then tucked his tie back into his coat. Piper watched as Meyer whispered something indecipherable to one of the Titans.

Beside Meyer, Christopher gave Terrence a tiny, barely there nod.

Terrence walked toward Meyer then stood beside Christopher.

Meyer pointed to Terrence and announced to one of the Titans, "This one is with us."

The Titans looked at Meyer, a less pleasant, more confused than normal look washing across their smooth faces.

"On the viceroy's order, you'll take my son into captivity," he added, wearing a look of disappointed, angry regret as his eyes met Trevor's.

Meyer looked around at the circle of Reptars, prowling like sharks. In turn, he locked eyes with Cameron, Piper, and Raj. He looked once more at the Reptars and finally back to the Titan.

"The other three," he said, glaring at Piper — a hurt, tortured strain of knowing in his eyes, "you may handle however you'd like."

The Titans moved to respond, but the alley's mouth exploded in a hail of stone before they could, unleashing a new breed of hell.

# CHAPTER 43

Trevor stared at Terrence's back, concentrating on whether he'd been inexplicably betrayed, when something massive crashed through a wall two blocks down. Or crashed through the *alleyway* ... but because the alley wasn't wide enough, there was no reason to let two little things like brick walls stop it.

The crash was like a bomb exploding — which, Trevor thought once the intruder passed the dust cloud, might've actually happened. The thing was all thick steel plating, down to the wheels. There *were* wheels, but the vehicle was otherwise a twisted class of tank. It had four turrets around its revolving cap, and despite the ample dust and confusion, Trevor's first random thought was to wonder what the things fired — or *had* fired, if explosives cleared the alley's mouth. But his thoughts were lost as the street descended into chaos.

What looked like hundreds of Reptars were behind the vehicle, climbing, prying at every plate as if trying to worm their way in.

A strange thought occurred to Trevor: this thing — whatever it was — seemed to have crashed the gate and barreled through the city, demolishing anything in its path. It had been, apparently, chased by most of the city's peacekeeper force.

But it had attracted no shuttles. The notion filled him with foreboding.

Looking up between buildings, Trevor could only see the usual Colorado blue, marred by a corner of the massive mothership off to one side, centered on the under-construction Apex. The motherships had a bounty of weapons, but again: the ship wasn't flinching, letting the armored car do as it wished.

No time to ponder. Whatever the tank-like vehicle was, it had drawn the attention of every member of the street's standoff — every Titan, Reptar, and human on both sides of the traitorous coin. It was a loud, insistent distraction. And without shuttles to end it, the thing barreled forward.

Trevor moved to flinch back, but the motion brought him close to Terrence. There was a chance he was playacting, but Trevor wasn't sure. Terrence hadn't hesitated a whit when Cameron had said to strike him, as if he'd meant to do it all along. Trevor wondered if he'd judged the man wrong. They'd all been under the Astral thumb for the same length of time — but *being under the Astral thumb* was almost the same as being under Astral protection. Ironic; he'd begun this adventure with his father by fleeing the ships, and now people flocked to them. The world's safest places were under alien occupation.

Maybe Terrence was more comfortable in his new life than Trevor.

Maybe he'd misjudged Terrence, and the man had always been on the Astrals' side.

Maybe, when Trevor had run to him for help finding Piper, Terrence had flipped, running to Christopher ... who, it turned out, might also be a traitorous sack of shit.

Or maybe not. It could be a ruse. Perhaps these were

small plans nested in larger ones, and they were all sharing a side.

It took six seconds for the tank car to reach them, and Trevor found himself adjacent to Terrence for three. Adrenaline still flooding his system from beating Raj, he punched Terrence hard in the throat then ripped the modified rifle from his holster.

Its barrel centered on Terrence's chest for a beat, but there were bigger — and more obviously hostile — fish to fry.

The vehicle arrived with a carpet of Reptars. Trevor made the mistake of thinking they might be more than animals long enough for one to see him hesitate, then it leaped. The thing was on him as Cameron, somewhat comically, thrashed with his good arm. Trevor recovered smoothly, righted the rifle, and blew a hole through the alien's chest. An obscene shower of gore sprayed the tank.

The Reptars startled backward at the sight — their preference for living kicking in. Trevor stood and aimed at the nearest monstrosities, meeting each in its ugly shifting eye, his implied threat perfectly clear.

It didn't last long; one of the Reptars came from behind, taking him broadside, its mouth already open and purring in Trevor's peripheral vision as he again hit the concrete.

Piper managed a shot — not enough, seemingly, to kill it, but enough to twist its interest from Trevor to her. Again, he aimed and prayed, having no clue what his weapon fired and when it might require reloading. It discharged faithfully, tearing the upper half of the monster's mouth to memory.

Trevor got to his feet.

He looked at the vehicle in time to see the air around it pulse, a low buzz thrumming into his bones. He felt his hair want to stand on end. Every Astral clinging to the vehicle tensed, and Trevor heard several loud cracks. Then the pulses stopped, and the Reptars slunk away from its metal skin, wounded.

A hatch popped on the armored vehicle — which looked, now that it was close, as if it might be a short bus prepared for combat. The turret was still a mystery.

A head wearing an enormous orange mohawk emerged, beckoning furiously, casting glances at the cast-off Reptars, large earlobes impaled with swinging rollers the size of a toilet paper core. Trevor had a moment to think that this guy had taken the term road warrior to the limit, but then Cameron was behind him, pushing. Piper was already halfway in.

There was no way to know who these people were, but going with them was better than being dinner.

"*Get the fuck in here, or we're leaving you!*" the man shouted.

"*Go!*" Cameron urged behind Trevor, still shoving.

Cameron swung his pistol around between shoves, aiming at Meyer and his two henchmen, at Raj still on the pavement, at the onlookers now appearing at what passed for slit-like windows in the vehicle's sides, at the unmoving Titans, at the swarming, furious Reptars.

Then Trevor was in. Cameron was in. The mohawked man dragged the hatch closed with a clang and took a seat behind some sort of steering mechanism that may once have been a wheel.

Piper was across the dark interior, looking cold and out of place. In addition to the mohawk, two others shared the space, both with similar hairdos. One was a woman with what looked like a massive ivory fang through her septum, her face half covered in tattoos.

The second man stood inside the turret. The vehicle leaped — somehow *sideways* to the direction Trevor had thought its wheels were oriented. There was a shudder and a loud series of crunching noises outside. They'd run over a few Reptars, but the thing barely shook, as if it weighed several tons — and had spherical lead wheels to match.

"*Haul ass!*" the woman yelled.

The first man mashed his foot to the ground. The tank-like thing accelerated much faster than anything this size had any business doing, and Trevor watched through slits in the metal as they passed back through the detonated alleyway. The man in the turret did something, and several fireballs erupted around the thing — to the sides, to the rear, to the front. Trevor spilled from his seat onto the floor, and as she came down from her standing position, the woman with the tattooed face stepped on him without apology. She merely cast him a look of extraordinary inconvenience and shifted to where she needed to be, firing what sounded like a normal firearm through the slits. The noise, inside the enclosed and echoing space, was painful.

Trevor tried to stay still, casting glances at Cameron (who seemed pale with blood loss) and Piper (who looked terrified and sick) as the thing screamed back through the now-decimated gates and into the outlands. Soon, the rumbling stopped, and they were screaming across the hardpan, no words traded among the tank's occupants, no idea — in Trevor's mind, at least — where they might be headed.

The woman picked up something like an old-fashioned CB and spoke into it.

"Base? This is Tarantula."

A radio replied. "This is base."

"Tell Lieutenant Coffey we've successfully picked up our passenger. The big man's most wanted and—" She looked over as if needing to count. Her expression soured. "And two others."

Trevor's eyes found one of the slits in the thing's side, peering upward, now able to see the blue skies from his slouched position near the metal floor.

"The ships," he said as the engine roared. "Why aren't the ships coming after us?"

The woman looked at him with something like hatred

then turned back to the vehicle's front. Her voice returned, somehow angry, resenting Trevor for a reason he'd never requested and couldn't understand.

"Because until we got called into this bullshit, we've kept a truce." She sighed heavily and shook her head. "But if I were them, after what we just did? I'd say it's game on, any minute now."

# CHAPTER 44

Lila was crossing the upstairs hallway, returning from Trevor's room, when she heard Clara stir. Going downstairs could wait. After what she'd seen through the window, Lila could use the distraction of playing mother. Half of the city looked like it had gone up in smoke. Her entire family might be dead. Only her mother was for-sure still alive, but only now had Lila summoned the courage to learn what Heather might know.

Her daughter's small, innocent noises were more compelling. Soon, she may have to hear what Heather had to say. But for now, she could keep pretending.

Lila went to the crib then watched as the girl stirred from her nap. The crib was an embarrassment, and her two-year-old daughter had even said so, using that exact word: *Mommy, this crib is an embarrassment.* But what was Lila supposed to do? She'd had the crib before Clara was born. Normal mothers had a few years to use a crib. Taking her out now felt like admitting failure — or, strangely, a twisted breed of motherly success. Who else got a walking, talking, somewhat spooky kid before two? What other young mothers heard "Mommy, this is an embarrassment" so early? Usually, you had to wait until you had teenagers to hear that sort of thing — and then hear it about everything you did. That's how Lila remembered her own teen years, now barely twelve months distant.

Clara rolled over and opened her eyes. They were big and blue — as big, in fact, as Piper's. But Piper wasn't blood to Clara. Lila's eyes were brown, and Raj's were browner. Of Clara's four grandparents, only one had eyes that weren't brown: Meyer, whose pupils glowed with a greenish breed of hazel. Lila remembered from high school science that brown eyes were supposed to be a dominant trait, blue was recessive. And yet here were her daughter's bright eyes, as deep as any ocean.

"Hi, Mommy," she said, not rising.

"Hey, baby."

"Are we still going to play with Grandma?"

Lila thought of the chaos outside. She'd heard explosions, seen fire and smoke, and might be attending several funerals this week, if she could summon the guts to find out. They should go to Grandma, all right — but definitely not to play on the lawn. Jets and bombers had failed to harm Heaven's Veil, but someone had finally managed. And so far no one in the family, other than her mother, had returned.

"Maybe. Not outside, though, okay?"

"Oh. I wanted to play outside."

"We can do that tomorrow, maybe. How about we play a game?"

"A game with Grandma?"

"Sure."

"Okay! I dreamed about Grandma."

Her heart skipped. Lila thought of the smoke. The fire. The strange itching sensation she'd been feeling for hours.

"What about her?"

"She had a thing."

"What kind of a thing?"

"It was like Daddy's salt shaker."

Lila thought of the implement sitting on the grand dining room table. Only Raj would have a favorite salt shaker. There was a pepper grinder too — both stainless steel, far too expensive in the old world for something designed to hold salt.

"Oh. Well, that's interesting."

"Did you talk to Uncle Trevor?"

"Sure. Earlier. You were here."

"I meant before he left," Clara said.

Lila felt a chill. For some reason, she flashed back to the strange sensations she'd had while Clara was still growing inside her — that sense that felt like a mainline to some sort of under-the-current intelligence. She'd found ways to ask Clara about those things since she'd begun talking and understanding, feeling foolish every time. The girl had no recollection of any of it. And why would she? Fetuses didn't speak any more than most kids Clara's age did. Not beyond babbling and kicking uterine walls.

*Before he left?* If she'd heard that back in the bunker, she'd have thought it was a metaphor. For death, maybe.

"He's just with Chris, Baby."

"I mean after he went with Uncle Terrence."

"Trevor didn't—"

"And Grandma," Clara finished.

"What about Grandma?"

Lila thought she might hear about Raj's salt shaker again, but Clara stood and beckoned to be picked up. Lila obliged, appreciating the comfort of Clara in her arms now of all times, but the minute she was up, Clara flapped her arms to be put down. Maybe Lila needed comfort, but her daughter didn't. Her mother was transportation. Beyond that, nothing was terribly disturbing to Clara because (and this, Lila realized sometimes with a feeling of creeping dread) nothing was terribly surprising to her. Just another day at the office for the girl in the upstairs crib.

Clara sat and started pulling two dolls apart. One had dark skin, the other's was white, their dual colored hair intertwined in a tangled nest. Racial harmony by force in this dollhouse, if not by design.

"What about Grandma, Clara?" Lila repeated.

"I'd like to play a game with Grandma."

"Do you think Grandma would like to play a game?"

Clara shrugged. "Maybe. It'll make her feel better."

Lila sat slowly. This was always strange, and Lila felt like she was balancing whenever speaking to Clara about events she couldn't possibly know. Until someone drew her attention to the differences between herself and other young children, Clara would probably think that what she could do and know was normal. Lila didn't want to point it out, or for her tone (or the tenor of her hesitant questions) to frighten her daughter. But Clara's gift — if that's what it was — startled Lila plenty.

The gift, yes. And in her quietest moments, Lila sometimes admitted to herself that she was a bit unnerved by the girl who held it.

"Why does Grandma want to feel better, Clara?"

"Everyone likes to feel better."

"But why today?" Lila tried to make herself smile. "I didn't talk to Grandma yet." She swallowed then forced herself to finish the sentence: "To ask her about what she did today."

"Oh. Well, Uncle Trevor is gone. Them and Grandma Piper."

"*Piper?*" Lila's hand went to her mouth. Where were they? She didn't know how to ask if they were dead. She also wondered what it said about her that she'd reacted more to news about Piper than about her brother. Her stepmother seemed so innocent. She'd become her dad's quiet companion again the moment he'd returned — always a bit unhappy perhaps. Trapped. Dragged along for the ride.

But then she remembered Clara's plural. "*Them* and Piper?"

"Mr. Cameron too."

But Clara, of course, would have no idea who Cameron was, if it was the Cameron Lila suspected.

"They'll be happy there," Clara said, finally separating the dolls' hair.

"Where?" But she didn't want to know, if the answer was Heaven — not the city but the place she'd grown up believing was somewhere out there in the clouds, beyond the reach of spherical spaceships. She didn't want to know that any more than she wanted to head downstairs for her mother's report.

"With Mr. Cameron's daddy. Where Grandma Piper was happy."

*Moab?* Was Clara talking about the lab in Utah? Why not; she'd covered so much unknown ground already.

"So you know Mr. Benjamin," said Lila, playing along.

Clara made a little *mmm-hmm* noise and began dressing the dolls, sticking purses into their claw-like hands. Apparently, the discussion was over.

Lila stood, casting her daughter a final glance. She really should talk to her mother and face whatever music needed facing — good, bad, or indifferent.

"I hope Mr. Benjamin doesn't help them find it," Clara said.

"Find what, Clara?"

"If he helps them," she said, "I guess we'll *all* be leaving."

Lila didn't think Clara was being literal. This time, she felt sure that leaving was something she wouldn't want to face.

# CHAPTER 45

Benjamin watched the vehicle approach. It was a refurbished Jeep Cherokee from years before Astral Day — probably not even auto-drivable; hardly a suitable vehicle for outlands royalty. But as much as Benjamin feared Nathan Andreus, he couldn't help but respect the man even before properly meeting him. He ruled the outlands like a despot but didn't court luxury. He'd done what he needed to do, from beginning to end, mass murderer or not.

The Jeep stopped. Again, Benjamin expected the driver to let Andreus out through the rear doors, but instead he walked a few feet away and took in the open desert surroundings, allowing the passenger to get out on his own.

The rear door opened, and instead of Andreus, a woman emerged in a black Andreus Republic uniform, same as Benjamin had seen on broadcasts about the outlands. He tried to contain himself, but the uniform's sight gave him a chill.

The vehicle's driver walked forward, the woman fell into place beside and slightly behind him. The pair reached Benjamin, and the man extended a hand.

He wasn't merely a driver. The man from the driver's

seat was Nathan Andreus himself.

"Are you Benjamin?" he asked.

Benjamin fought a hard response. He made himself grasp the man's hand then meet his icy eyes. They were buried in wrinkles as he squinted in the bright Utah sun, hard and unyielding. His grip, for a man who'd left his thirties behind quite a while ago, was strong. He had a trimmed goatee and a shaved head that practically glowed in the sun.

"Yes."

"Nathan Andreus. This is Jeanine Coffey."

Benjamin shook the woman's hand.

"Thanks for coming," he said, unsure what else to say. This was an awkward meeting, but Andreus had given him a choice: They could meet at Andreus Republic HQ or in Moab — but (and Andreus didn't need to say this; it had been implied in bold type) *they would be meeting.* Andreus had given his estranged wife and daughter their space for long enough. Now that the elder in that pair was dead, Andreus was through being an absentee father, even if it meant grabbing responsibility by its quivering throat.

If they had to meet, Moab was better than Andreus's turf every day ending in Y.

"Is Grace inside?"

Benjamin nodded, trying to fight the feeling that Andreus claiming his sixteen-year-old daughter was being handled like a hostage exchange.

"Yes. Come on in." He didn't want to ask the next question because it sounded untrusting, but there was something missing — something that intensified the feeling of a hostage exchange. "Where are our people?" he added.

"They're coming," Andreus said.

Benjamin looked at the Cherokee. There would have been room in the vehicle for five.

Andreus followed Benjamin's gaze. Then, blessedly, a

seemingly genuine smile cracked his weathered features. "It's too tight in the back if it's three wide. Besides, I don't ride with anyone I don't know. No offense."

"Of course," Benjamin said.

The way people talked about the Republic, Andreus had his people trained and fiercely loyal. But outsiders might take it upon themselves to rid the outlands of a warlord, jumping forward with a garrote to strangle him while crossing the desert.

"There," he said.

Benjamin followed his finger. At first, there was just the sound of an engine and a brown plume of dust, but after a few minutes the distant noise changed pitch. The cloud got bigger. Sunlight winked off a windshield. Tires ground on packed clay. Then a second Jeep SUV pulled up beside the first. Cameron was the first one out, his shoulder wrapped in a white bandage, his arm in a sling. Piper followed, holding his arm as if to lend support where it wasn't needed. A Hispanic driver emerged next but didn't come forward. Last to exit, via the passenger side door, was a young man Benjamin assumed must be Trevor Dempsey.

They came forward. Taking care with Cameron's shoulder, Benjamin wrapped his son in an embrace. He hugged Piper too, finding her smile all too grateful, as if she'd wanted to be here all along, having suffered a two-year prison term. He shook Trevor's hand, introducing himself unnecessarily, while the young man did the same.

He took a moment to survey the new arrivals: the outlands leader and his lieutenant, the three prodigal sons and daughters, and the second driver who, it turned out, apparently meant to stay outside, on a picnic table in the shade. Benjamin led the others inside, wondering what he'd managed to get himself into.

Piper Dempsey, wife of the viceroy.

Trevor Dempsey, son of the viceroy.

And their new mutual, reluctant allies.

For better or worse, the Andreus Republic and the scientists now shared an enemy. The Astrals might need Andreus's control of the outlands, and might hold their retaliation until all arguments were considered. But Benjamin felt deeply that the laboratory's luck, which had held for far too long, was now finally numbered in days.

He looked up before holding the door open for the others to enter.

The sky was blue, wide, and empty.

But soon that would change.

# CHAPTER 46

"I'll need some time to analyze this." Benjamin pointed at the stone tablet's projected image and its strange legend Piper had seen on Meyer's computer. "For now, let's not assume anything. Assuming, on this scale, is a terrible idea."

"What do you mean, on this scale?" Cameron sat beside on another of the lab's plastic-and-tubular metal chairs. It felt better than Piper had expected — better, perhaps, than she wanted to admit — to be back in Moab. She'd never have wanted to vacation in Utah back in her New York City days, but the time between her last Moab visit and now had been spent somewhere more comfortable and yet far less bearable. Returning to Benjamin and even Charlie — with Cameron by her side, guilty as it felt — was like a warm fire after a long, cold winter.

"You've played the telephone game, right?" Benjamin said. "Where one person whispers a phrase to the next person, and that person passes the message along. And by the time the message makes it around the circle, it's always wildly distorted?"

"Sure."

"This," Benjamin said, tapping the projection, "is at

least a thousand-year-old game of telephone. Maybe much older than that. The oldest ruins we know of — and that ancient astronaut theorists would point to as evidence of extraterrestrial visitation — go back twelve thousand years and effectively double what most archaeologists admit is the history of civilized humanity. Everything we're dealing with here — everything we might use to make sense of the Astrals' actions today based on their actions in the past — is thousands of years of hearsay at best. And before we can analyze something like this, it's guesswork threaded through speculation."

Piper felt disappointed. Part of her had hoped Benjamin would take one look at the tablet and know exactly what to do with it. Worse: Deep down, she realized she'd been seeing getting the slip drive's information to Benjamin as the end of this adventure rather than one of its many midpoints. But that was ridiculous. What had she thought — that the language upon it would reveal a recipe for a universal Astral poison that, once brewed, would cause the aliens to flee the planet and allow it to regain its feet without harm? She dimly remembered watching an alien movie with Meyer, what felt like a thousand years ago. The aliens in that movie had been allergic to water. In the famous *War of the Worlds*, the more sensible culprit defeating the aliens had been Earthbound bacteria. That's what she'd been foolishly hoping for: a quick fix. But of course life was never that easy.

"But it does tell us something we need to know, right away," he continued.

Piper's chin lifted. From the corner of her eye, she caught Nathan Andreus and Jeanine Coffey. He looked stoic, and that was frightening to Piper. Nathan's daughter, on their reunion, still wouldn't talk to him. She supposed that would make anyone unfriendly.

"It tells us," Benjamin lectured like a natural professor, "that what they're looking for — the weapon we call Thor's

Hammer — probably isn't as readily accessible to them as we'd thought." He touched the screen where the placard read, *DEVICE MISSING*. "What Trevor overheard seems to corroborate this. They're searching at every capital, under all the new structures. Which, I'm proud to say, at least ties up one loose end."

"Which loose end?" Cameron asked.

"The question, 'What's special about Vail?' There's something under that mountain after all."

"What?"

"Don't get ahead of me, Cameron." Benjamin flashed his usual smirk. "I said something under the mountain. Give me credit for that before more questions are asked." His affable expression flicked toward Andreus, but the man didn't return his smile.

"I don't know what's under there," Benjamin continued. "Nobody does. It's not in any of the records. If I had to guess — and this is only a guess, you understand — I'd say it's a temple of some sort. Some place of symbolic intent where they left their doomsday device."

Nathan said, "Why?"

"That's what we can't quite figure out." Benjamin's voice went a bit jittery as he answered Andreus. "One theory is that it's something necessarily Earthbound because of effects it has on the planet. A means of tipping our rotational axis, for instance."

"You think there's some magic box under that pyramid that will knock the Earth off kilter?" Nathan wasn't really asking; Piper could hear the difference. He was expressing disbelief in a ridiculous crackpot idea — which, for most of Benjamin's life, was how his ideology had always been seen.

"Maybe literally, maybe symbolically," Benjamin said. "Think of some of the legendary disasters of the past. The *Bible* is full of examples."

"The *Bible?*"

"Stories," said Benjamin. "Again, I'll refer you to a game of telephone. Maybe some of what's in there is totally true. But maybe some of it has simply been told enough times that it's become distorted. Certainly, extraterrestrial visitations of ancient peoples would appear godlike. Think of some of the stories we know: a great flood, for instance. A man tasked with preserving history beyond what was essentially a biblical reset."

Piper had been raised with plenty of religion. She couldn't help it; Benjamin's theories rankled her. "You think Noah's Ark was meant to survive ..." She could barely say it, and paused for effect. "An *alien apocalypse?*"

"We can't know, Piper. That's my point. Maybe a literal god came down and made it flood. Or maybe those ancient people recounted their interpretation of those events: powerful beings from the sky who decimated humanity then tasked some with preserving heritage to try again. I won't give you all the details, but there are plenty of theorists who believe there really was an ark — but that instead of taking two of each animal, that Noah of legend took genes instead."

Nathan looked like he might walk out in boredom. What stopped him, perhaps, were two things. First, nobody else, disbelief notwithstanding, seemed willing to budge. And second, Nathan had taken a rather decisive stand when he'd burst into Heaven's Veil to rescue Cameron — along with Piper and Trevor. He'd been playing the middle and was now clearly on humanity's side. Piper could practically see the Astrals above, weighing his benefits and transgressions, trying to decide if they could stand to lose Nathan Andreus and leave the Colorado/Utah outlands to chaos.

"There are a lot of mysteries here," Benjamin went on. "Is the missing device truly Thor's Hammer? From what I can tell of the drive's other data, I'd say it's likely. There's talk in there of completeness — of a ritual the Astrals may be going through now, and may have gone through every time in the past. Before making first contact with us, landing that first day and disembarking the nine worldwide viceroys, they established networks to harvest our thoughts. Even the viceroy selection process feels to me like a filtering down — like a tournament almost. They abducted a lot of Earth citizens then eliminated a few from consideration over time each day or week before sending them home. They were left with chief selections: all high profile, all highly respected or at least known prior to their abductions. All authorities — the kind of people humanity has a track record of listening to, but also possibly representatives of the best our species has to offer. So this, too, looks to me like a ritual."

He tapped the screen, still showing what seemed to be a keystone tablet that had frustrated the Astrals as much as it was frustrating Benjamin. That tablet was causing the Astrals to scramble in a worldwide dig.

"They'll do what they're going to do. An ice age, a flood — maybe they'll incinerate us all. Maybe they'll eat us. But they're planning something malevolent, and all that's stopping them is finishing this ritual — finding this one thing they need. Again, literally or figuratively. They either need this device before they can push the button, or they're looking for the button itself."

Trevor looked cold. He looked, Piper thought, as desperate and afraid as she felt. She wanted to tell Benjamin to keep things less dire — there were children present. But Trevor, the youngest among them, was seventeen. Plenty old enough for war, and well past adulthood in countless cultures across endless ages.

"Let's focus on what we know, not what we don't," Charlie said from the corner.

"Right," said Benjamin, seeming to remember himself. "What we know is that the Astrals' intentions are not good—"

"Thanks, Sherlock," Coffey said.

Andreus shot his lieutenant a look. Apparently, disbelief was okay, but jocular sarcasm was over the line.

Benjamin stuttered for a moment then continued. "We know they're digging under all nine of the new monoliths. So whatever they're searching for, they seem to be riffling through their pockets as if searching for keys."

"Any idea what those big monoliths are for?" Trevor asked.

"It's hard to say. None are complete. And they're not hurrying either. It makes me think of a ticking clock. Something they know needs to be done and will take time, so there's no need to rush. Maybe that's good for us and maybe not. But as to what they're for? Who knows? I'd ask the same questions about the Apex. But as our departed friends at the church in Heaven's Veil pointed out, they've had to scramble. They started with stone, presumably because that still seemed to make sense. They've only glimpsed us while they've been gone, through the eyes of select people. They may have made assumptions about us and the way we'd be based on past visits and peeks, but those assumptions turned out to be false."

"Like the Internet thing," said Piper.

Benjamin nodded. "Old visitation evidence suggests we used to be much better at using our collective minds. Today, not so much. We must seem especially foreign to them. Let's say the monoliths are hubs of a worldwide network, possibly using orbiting motherships as repeaters to connect them. It even makes sense. But if that's the case, they can't just tap into us as a collective. They need to make sense of individual minds, which may be slowing them down."

"Are you saying," Nathan began, "that our apathy and alienation is protecting us?"

"Maybe." Benjamin shrugged. "This seems tentative and methodical to me, though again, it's impossible to say for sure what things were like thousands of years ago. But they seem to be feeling us out. Adapting as they go. The Apex and the other monoliths may be part of that. An attempt, in conjunction with those first stone networks, to connect us. But they could just as easily be intergalactic antennas. Or big arrows that say, 'Dig here.'"

Andreus shook his head. "Why am I here? I can't do shit with guesses."

"Then focus on what we know for sure," said Benjamin.

"You said that before," Andreus countered. "And here we are, still with the guesses."

"What we *really* know for sure," said Charlie. "Brass tacks."

"And what's that, Mr. Cook?" Andreus asked.

Charlie pointed at the screen. "We know they've lost something they need before they can do what they have to do."

Andreus waited. Finally, he said, "So what?"

"So," Charlie continued, "we have to find it first."

# CHAPTER 47

Lila entered the small house on the mansion grounds as if she owned it then looked around its living room for Raj. Finding only the home's owner present, she fell into Christopher's lap, kissing him.

"Whoa. Wait," he said. "What's this?"

Lila kept kissing Christopher. She held him. She hugged him tight enough that he dropped his bottle of hydrogen peroxide and inadvertently rubbed the already-wet cotton ball he'd been using to dab his wound against her bare arm.

"Good to see you too, Lila."

She grabbed both sides of his face, squishing his cheeks. Lila was on his lap, awkward in the way she'd fallen against him, putting herself at an odd angle. She kissed him again.

"I thought you were dead."

"Why would you think I was dead?"

"I heard explosions. Gunshots. I saw fire and smoke."

Christopher exhaled. He looked at the front door, which was as closed as it should be. Lila followed his gaze, remembering the way she'd glanced around the room. Paranoia had trained them both.

"Did you talk to your mom?"

"Yes. Just now."

"Then she told you I wasn't dead."

"I was still worried. What the hell happened out there?"

"Heather didn't tell you?"

"She told me, but ..." Lila realized that she'd been hoping Christopher's story would be different. She'd thought on some level that his version could undo her mom's. Heather had been grim — so unlike her old self, increasingly like her new one. Lila didn't like the way they lived but abided it. Piper clearly hated it enough to flee. But Lila's mother would never run. She'd live as they did, hating herself and making jokes that somehow always boomeranged back at the joker. She'd spent two years inadvertently insulting herself (or maybe *intentionally* insulting herself; she'd come from self-loathing parents), and it had stripped much of the mirth from her biting wit.

"She told you about Trevor and Piper?"

"That they climbed into a tank and ran off? Yes. Should I be glad or not? I honestly couldn't tell."

"Glad in that they didn't get eaten by peacekeepers, yes. But as to the rest?" Christopher sighed. "They went with Cameron Bannister. I assume Heather told you he showed up, rather surprisingly, after I brought her back here the first time? Based on what Terrence told her afterward, I mean."

Lila nodded. She chose to see Christopher's return to the chaos after dropping off her mother as heroic rather than infuriating. She'd heard them arrive downstairs, but Christopher hadn't stayed. If he'd been called back by her father, she should forgive him. If that was true, there'd have been no other way.

"She told me."

Christopher looked around yet again. The fear, even inside his small, private house, clanged on Lila's sense of right and wrong. Why were they here? Why did they live like this?

"I don't know where he came from. Terrence doesn't know either. We found Piper with some others, and I thought that was it. Your dad put us on alert about an intruder at the gate, but the Astral command, which usually rubber-stamps the viceroy's orders or vice-versa, called us back — and back was where we were when Trevor and your mom came to me. I assume Cameron must've been the intruder, but he was alone when we found him. No one was chasing him. We saw two Titans holding your dad *back*, not coming at us."

"Titans don't fight, do they?"

"No. I don't even think they can. But they're always in communication with the mothership and the peacekeepers, and there's no obvious reason to keep your dad back. It doesn't make sense. There's this big alarm about an intruder, but it's like they opened up, invited him in, then let him run right into us and Piper and Trevor."

"Maybe he snuck in," Lila said.

"How?"

"They let people out all the time on the borders."

"*Let*," said Christopher. "There are always shuttles. People can go, and authorized people can enter. But never unaware."

"Maybe whoever was at the gate was a distraction," Lila proposed. It didn't matter, and she didn't care, but Christopher always volleyed the ball to straighten his thoughts. She was happy to feel settled on his warm lap. After her afternoon of terror and worry, just being here was enough.

"I don't know."

Lila sensed Christopher's discomfort then moved away to sit on a soft chair near rather than directly on him. She saw conflict in his eyes: familiar, after having seen so much in the mirror.

"What's bothering you?" Lila asked. "Not just Trevor and Piper. They're following Cameron back where he came from, right? And I know how it sounds, but I didn't see or hear anything blowing up since, so they must be safe, at least for now. So what's getting you?"

Christopher bit his lip. "Did your mom tell you ... ? No, of course not. She was gone."

"What?"

"Unless Terrence told her that too. Which I seriously doubt."

"Christopher, *what?*"

He looked at Lila as if assessing her discretion. If there was one person on the grounds he had to trust, it was her. And of everyone besides her brother, Lila most trusted him. After the way things had ended at the old bunker, she had more confidence in Christopher than even her own mother.

"Okay," he said, still seeming to wrestle with divulging a secret. "When the Astrals showed, they did it all at once. From everywhere. As if they'd been hiding and waiting. Your dad too; he just kind of started yelling from down the street, then he and the Titans holding him finally came down. This was right before the ... the *whatever it was* that took Trevor and Piper. Before that thing showed up. I saw some of it start to happen as I was running in. But the thing is, we kind of caught them red-handed. Terrence was right there with him, but Terrence ... well, he couldn't go with them in the tank thing."

"Why not?"

"Because Cameron gave him something before he left. Something that Terrence — specifically Terrence — needs to have. And he has to have it *here.* In Heaven's Veil, not out wherever they were going. Terrence had to stay. He says Cameron said to hit him, so it would look like he was a plant. Like we sent Terrence with Trevor (I don't think any of them knew I was there earlier, too, thankfully) as some sort of a spy. Hitting Cameron was supposed to be Terrence coming back to our side after the cavalry arrived to catch the fugitives. But the thing is ... well, I don't know if I'd believe it, myself."

Lila felt her heart beating harder. If she'd heard Christopher right, that wasn't the kind of thing he should have said so plainly. Or maybe he should have. When doctors gave patients news of a terminal illness, Lila imagined they did so in the same way: *Here are the facts. You'll die soon, but at least now you know.*

"What do you mean you don't know if you'd believe it?"

"Terrence is great with gadgets, but he's not an actor. He looked *caught*, Li. Cameron whispered something when Terrence picked him up off the ground then slipped this thing into Terrence's pocket. But then Cam says, 'Hit me.' To Terrence's credit, he got it in an instant. No hesitation. I did what I could to back him up, but your dad isn't stupid, and neither are the Titans. Or probably the Reptars."

"So?" Lila didn't want to say more.

"I can't shake the feeling that Terrence is being watched. That your dad doesn't trust him at all but is going along with the bullshit for some reason." He shrugged then added what Lila had already surmised: "And if he thinks something's fishy with Terrence, he'd have to suspect something was up with me, too."

"Raj ..." Lila began.

"He's fine. He's with the medics. Just a broken nose and a lot of bruises and cuts."

Lila almost rolled her eyes. That was very much not what she'd been asking. She could give a shit about Raj. He seemed to have sicced the peacekeepers on Piper, and started the melee across town. *Fuck* Raj.

"I meant, what will he do when — ?"

"Him, your dad." Christopher stood and pressed the cotton ball and its peroxide against a gash on his forehead. "Who knows? It's not like I can ask. I'm not gonna run. Terrence *can't* run. He has to be here. So we wait and see if

I'm being paranoid."

"And if you're not?"

Lila wanted him to tell her he had a plan — a grand scheme that got her out of the house and to safety, away from Raj, while somehow turning her father from his apparent position on the Dark Side. That was, in a way, the worst thing of all. Until Meyer Dempsey stopped being Heaven's Veil's viceroy, Lila would always face a choice between her father and dignity as a human.

But instead of revealing a grand plan to magically solve everyone's problems, Christopher repeated what he'd said a moment before: "We'll just have to wait and see."

"Why does Terrence have to be here?"

Christopher looked off into the distance — into the empty space past Lila. As if he was trying to wrap his head around something. Something necessary. Something perilous, vital, and impossible, given the eggshells underfoot.

"The thing Cameron gave him," he finally said. "It has something in it that he built in Moab, before he and Vincent and Dan met up with the rest of us in Vail. Something that will open what the Astrals have been hiding on the network. Terrence says it's something that could either work or fail spectacularly — but that if it doesn't work or isn't tried, the resistance won't get another shot.

"Okay."

"But how he's going to do it — how he's going to get it into the data center, where it needs to go? There's just no way. I don't even want him to try because it feels like that's what they may be waiting for — to catch him red-handed for sure this time."

Without thinking, Lila blurted, "Give it to me. I'll do it."

"Terrence has to do it. It's not something he can explain."

"But if they want it, why don't they just take it now?"

Christopher gave Lila a look that said, *Why keep wondering about questions no one can answer?*

"I'll keep it then. Let's go to Terrence's now and get it."

"Terrence already gave it to your mom."

Lila wasn't sure she liked that. Her mother had once been Lila's best friend, and she hoped one day that trust could return, but it was hard to forget their fights in the final days of living underground. The energy pit access Heather had protected then handed to Meyer and the Astrals as if rolling out a red carpet. The way she'd fought with Lila, who'd wanted to destroy it so the Astrals couldn't dock to Vail.

Lila, who even then had felt Clara broadcasting the future, and what she needed to do.

Clara, who'd told Lila of her dream, about Grandma hiding a *thing* like her father's favorite salt shaker.

Clara, who'd said they might be helping the Astrals whether they wanted to or not — in, Lila thought, the same basic way Heather had once helped them without meaning to, back at the bunker.

Whatever Cameron had given Terrence, it might be the resistance's last hope.

But Lila couldn't shake the feeling that Heather's possessing it now — controlling who saw it, who touched it, and where it would end up — might be exactly what the Astrals wanted.

# CHAPTER 48

Trevor waited until both women were in the bathroom before walking over and carefully locking the door.

The space was small but clean. Trevor realized with an odd strain of surprise that he'd never been in a dedicated women's restroom in his seventeen years of life. Even in this lab staffed by a few dozen scientists and techs, it was maintained like a sacred space. There were flowers on the back of the toilet and beside the sink. By contrast, the men's room wasn't much better than a gas station's. He had a moment to be fascinated and another to be inappropriately aroused by the intimate territory's foreign nature. But it broke when Danika fixed him with a stare that seemed to suppose she could read his thoughts.

"So," she said, "is everyone ready to start having sex?"

Coffey, Andreus's lieutenant, looked at Danika with something like disdain. Trevor felt himself blush. Danika was super cute: straight brown hair in a no-bullshit ponytail, an elfin nose, little lips and a wiseass smile that always showed a few teeth. She was shorter than him, tiny, easy to pick up. He wanted to joke back about lifting her up onto the sink, but it wasn't just wrong; it was also impossible

257

to force through his lips with the harder, much-*less*-bullshit Jeanine Coffey staring daggers at them both.

"I needed to talk to you in private," Trevor explained.

"Talk to us in private, or talk to our privates?" Danika countered. "My *office* is private."

"Not private enough."

"Mysterious."

Coffey looked supremely annoyed. Trevor had only managed to nudge her into this meeting after he'd told her that Andreus had commanded it with implied urgency. That wasn't technically true. Andreus had, after taking certain precautions and sweeping the room with a handheld comm device of his making, asked Trevor to have this discussion with Coffey and "anyone other than Benjamin," but he hadn't ordered a thing and certainly hadn't specified the meeting occur in a bathroom.

But this was the only room that met Trevor's criteria. First, it wasn't the kind of place anyone — or any*thing* — would think to barge into. Second, it had a door with a thick rubber edge that formed an almost airtight seal against the top, bottom, and sides of the doorjamb, leaving no gaps. Owing to the lab's in-cave construction, the bathroom's location inside it, and the thick metal door someone had repurposed from a much heartier application elsewhere, the room would be relatively soundproof. And, perhaps most importantly, it was away from Benjamin's lab.

Andreus had refused to give him the device he'd made to sweep less awkward meeting rooms, so Trevor had done his best.

But now that they were in the room, its confinement felt more like a detriment than an asset. They were close enough for Trevor to smell both women's shampoo, for him to see more of Danika than he'd noticed before, and to feel Coffey's harsh, militant disapproval.

"I want to show you something."

"Okay, but I'm not showing you mine back," Danika said.

Trevor pulled the phone from his pocket. It had stopped working as a connection device in the outlands, but was still an excellent multipurpose device. It somehow kept time in the absence of a strong signal and still worked as a music player, a game repository, and a camera.

"This is what Nathan asked me to show you." Trevor zoomed in on the photo he'd surreptitiously snapped in Benjamin's lab then handed it to Coffey. Danika leaned in, jockeying for a better view.

"What is it?"

"It's a circle," said Danika.

"Oh," said Coffey. "Do you mean this?"

Trevor looked at the screen. One of them had touched it and scrolled to the side. The object was still visible, but now Coffey was pointing at a grainy blur that might be a banana sticker Benjamin had stuck on his desk forever ago.

"No, this."

"The circle," Danika said.

"No." Coffey pointed at the wrong thing again. "This."

"This." Trevor reached over and stuck his finger on the thing Danika had called the circle. He had to push against Danika's side. She turned, and Trevor felt the soft swell of her small breasts.

"Like I said," Danika told Coffey. "The circle."

"But what is it?"

"We don't know."

"*We?*" Coffey said.

"Nathan and I."

"So now you're working with Nathan."

"He just asked me to show you."

"Well," said Coffey, her voice sounding increasingly impatient, "*what the hell is it?*"

"I just told you I don't know."

**259**

"You actually said *we* don't know. You and your pal Nathan. You know, the warlord?"

Coffey gave the smaller woman a stare. "He's not a warlord."

"Like I'd trust a statement like that from a warlord's lieutenant."

"We're on the same side whether we like it or not," Coffey said. "Thanks to Cameron."

"Who was delivering a device your boy agrees is genius."

Trevor seemed to remember Danika thinking that the Canned Heat plan was risky and stupid but said nothing. She seemed to like losing less than holding firm to her convictions.

"But he didn't tell Nathan he was carrying it at first, did he? And when we ran in to save his ass, he hadn't even kept it so Nathan could use it. No. He'd handed it off to your guy in Heaven's Veil. Which was really fucking smart."

"Which was the plan to begin with," Danika retorted. "Because Terrence designed it."

"And now hopes to deploy in a police state, on a controlled and protected hub, rather than via Nathan's pirate setup far outside harm's reach."

"We didn't know he had that set up."

"Which proves my point," Coffey snapped.

Trevor held up his hands. "Okay, just ... just hang on."

"Yeah, hang on," said Danika. "I'm in a bathroom with a bitch here."

Coffey glared at her.

"The reason we don't know what it is," Trevor continued, wincing at his repeated use of the plural, "is because we can't get a proper look."

"Why?" Coffey asked.

"Because we don't want it to know we can see it."

Danika gave Trevor a long look. "Well now. That's a normal thing to say."

Trevor looked back. Despite the small space, Danika was standing hands to narrow hips and wearing a sarcastic smile.

He could have chosen anyone other than Benjamin. He couldn't stand being this close with even Piper for lingering and obvious reasons, but why hadn't he picked Cameron?

Instead of answering directly, Trevor flipped back to his image gallery and surfaced the first of the waveforms Andreus had sent him. He'd told Trevor exactly what he was looking at — pulled from something that was kind of like an oscilloscope but not quite, using components from an RF something-or-other. He'd stopped trying to memorize it when the bald man said that Coffey would recognize what she was seeing and wouldn't require an explanation.

"Here," he said, handing her the phone. "He wanted me to show you this. It's a screenshot from his—"

Coffey was scrolling side to side, up and down. Her face changed, moving from annoyance to something stuck between fascination and curiosity.

"This is coming from that ... that circle thing you can't look directly at?"

"It's 'in the room,' is what he said."

Danika craned up and looked, apparently unable to make sense of the lines onscreen.

"But he *thinks* it's coming from the foreign object."

Trevor nodded.

"Is it stationary? Or does it ..." She made a little squiggle in the air.

"It's hard to tell without being obvious, and it's way too small for the security footage, but yes, it moves. Like *they* move."

Danika stared at Trevor as if offended by her exclusion. She glared at Coffey's downturned face then back at Trevor. "What are you talking about?"

"While trying to restore communication with Terrence,"

Trevor explained, "Mr. Andreus noticed that there was a second signal in the next room — Benjamin's office — in addition to the one he was trying to create. Like there was a little television station or something. So he went looking with a handheld detector, and before long he noticed this ..." He reached for the phone and flipped back to the shot of Benjamin's desk, then zoomed back in on the tiny, blurry circle. "Floating nearby."

"*Floating?*" Danika repeated.

Coffey turned the screen so Danika could see. "Remind you of anything?"

"Not really."

"Imagine it being a lot bigger."

"Okay."

"And shooting death rays."

Danika looked up, shocked. "You mean like a shuttle?"

Coffey nodded. Trevor felt himself nodding along.

"We've suspected this," Coffey said. "We've never seen them, but we imagined they'd have a means of surveillance. I know it would be on my punch list as a campaign coordinator, if I had their tech. And after hearing Cameron's story about all those 'BBs' he found on the road, it makes perfect sense that one might follow him." She exhaled, her face thoughtful. "This is why they let us go. They knew where we were going, and that they could watch us. But why?"

She asked a second question before Trevor could answer, effortlessly slotting into her strategist role. Knowing what was at stake, Danika had dropped her sarcasm.

"Is this the only one?"

"He thinks so," Trevor said. "He's swept the place and only found the one source. He says that means there's either just the one, or there are a few close together. But why would they bother, if they didn't separate?"

Coffey looked like she wanted to pace, but the room was too small. "He doesn't want to tell everyone, does he? That's why he just told you, and told you to tell us."

Trevor nodded. "He said he doesn't even trust himself. It moves like the shuttles, so it could pop in on him at any minute and hear him having this discussion with you. He can't wall himself off without giving away that he knows it's there but figures it's probably not interested in me. He says that as long as we know it's watching but it doesn't know we know, we have an advantage."

"A *big* advantage," said Coffey. "It means we can show one hand and hide our real intentions on the other. But the question is, what can we show it? It's watching us for a reason, and somehow that's a better alternative than just destroying this place."

Something was falling into place in Trevor's head — something Coffey wasn't seeing because she didn't know the lab's history like he did, through Cameron. Danika wasn't seeing it because she didn't know Heaven's Veil — and importantly, those who'd begun this journey. Trevor knew both. He knew what this lab was capable of and what the bunker had birthed. He could only think of one good reason for all the fortunate turns of events that had fallen in line. The reason they'd been allowed to live and operate. Watched in secret.

"They've played us."

Both women turned to Trevor.

"This isn't just about the lab," he said. "It's about Piper, too."

# CHAPTER 49

Meyer looked down at his computer screen, wondering if his old or new method of communication was worse. The Astrals were capable of paring their collective thoughts into bulletins meant for mostly disconnected (and unfortunately human) beings like him, but they were unpracticed and terrible. Other human authorities had men and women in their command chain. The police captain, for instance, got his orders from Mo Weir, who translated commands handed down from Meyer as he walked and talked. Meyer was capable of articulating human thought, and Mo was more than used to turning his hyperactive mishmash into actionable directives. But Meyer had nobody in the chain above him. No one human anyway. And so he had to deal with bullshit like this.

His screen read, *SUBJECT PROGRESS NULL CONTINUE TO WATCH.*

Meyer knew what that meant. He probably wasn't originally supposed to know this part of the Astrals' plan, but Divinity had informed him (mentally this time — perhaps the slightly less terrible of the ways they communicated) after Piper left the city. Meyer understood why. They seemed to have anticipated her actions, assuming she'd be curious enough to look at the images when they flashed magically onto Meyer's screen while she'd been in his office, then traitorous enough to copy them and flee. They'd seemed to understand that Piper wasn't the sort of woman to stand around and watch Rome burn once she'd accidentally discovered evidence of the Astrals' nefarious plans. But in spite of it all, they'd seemed to understand — possibly by siphoning off Meyer's own emotions and thoughts — that Piper loved Meyer Dempsey. She might return to him even though she should run to someone who could help her translate the stolen info. And if that happened, it was important that Meyer knew how to react. If Piper came back to confess to her crime, Meyer had to understand that her taking that information had been the Astrals' intention all along.

Of course, she hadn't returned. Meyer had seen her flee. In fact, he'd watched her *hug Cameron Bannister* then run. She'd delivered that information to Benjamin Bannister just as they'd wanted — despite Raj's jackassed attempts to help by sending Reptars to the church. Meyer hated Raj for that. If she'd been allowed to simply send the information, she'd at least have stayed in the city. Raj forced her hand. His idiotic actions sent her past the gates. Now Meyer might never see her again.

He resented being a pawn but told himself that it was the best he could expect under the circumstances. He was still human, and as far as humans went, he was at the top of the chain. There were only eight humans in the world with his power, and none with more. But he was still shuffled to the side to make way for Astral strategies, invited back into the loop only when they needed his help or compliance. Or when they needed him to dance for the camera like a stooge, wearing that giant Meyer Dempsey smile that told the world that everything was under control and would, in the end, be just fine.

He looked at the screen.

*SUBJECT PROGRESS NULL CONTINUE TO WATCH.*

Jesus Christ. They couldn't even use punctuation. They knew the vocabulary but had a foreigner's lack of understanding, clueless about how to string things together. Language had always been important to Meyer. Whenever people sent him misspelled or poorly punctuated messages in the old days, he'd handed them mental demerits. He'd always thought less of people who wrote *they're* when the proper word was *their*. It was even possible that the "Meyerness" the aliens had sucked out of him during his abduction was the only reason they could form sentences at all. Maybe he should give them credit for being able to do any of it, when mental communication was their norm. But then again: *fuck them.* A seed of imperfection, in the form of human mind, had in this case made those perfect beings better.

But the message was still the message: a notice to their puppet in the viceroy's mansion, giving him all the information he needed to know. Meyer once ran empires and answered to no one, but now he was someone barely worth a download.

Bannister still hadn't cracked the human code on the tablet, as far as the droid had seen.

And, Meyer thought cynically, they'd just CONTINUE TO WATCH because they sure as hell couldn't do anything more. After finally excavating their buried temple only to realize some lowly human had stolen their lucky charm and hidden it elsewhere, what had they done? Had they used the vast, superior intergalactic brain to find what was lost? No. They'd turned to a human for help, playing Bannister (and Piper, for that matter) like strings on a banjo.

Letting humans do their dirty work.

Just like Meyer had been.

*Yes, sirs. No, sirs.*

Meyer was on the receiving end, never planning. Powerful only because the Astrals allowed it.

He remembered how angry he'd been when the Titans wouldn't let him run to Piper.

He remembered how stupid he'd felt when he'd come home and they'd invaded his mind to explain why.

And right now, he found himself wondering how far their mental juju extended. He was already fairly sure the Astrals had been using him as a window for years, manipulating what he'd taken for existential experiences into devices for spying on humanity — or Meyer's slice anyway. He knew they'd placed those rocks everywhere to take humanity's temperature and know their intentions as an aggregate. He knew that sometimes, when they passed too near the rocks, they gained a temporary ability to exchange discreet individual thoughts with others. But could they do that without someone knowing? Specifically, could they read his mind right now and know exactly how disobedient he felt? How little he wanted to keep taking their orders in front of the world?

Meyer forced himself to sit. This state of mind was impractical. He'd never been especially emotional, and the floods he'd felt recently were more mounting evidence of the situation's intolerability. He was feeling emotions from outside; he was feeling his own emotions; he felt himself, in fits of anger and malcontent, wanting to do stupid things.

But he was better than that.

Meyer Dempsey had always been a logical man.

He breathed deeply. Closed his eyes.

Anger was pointless. Meyer's ability to see that made him more evolved. It, along with his other outside-the-box mental abilities, was probably what had made the Astrals choose him as one of the viceroys. He'd gone through a gauntlet. He'd been tested and found worthier than the tens of thousands before him. He should have more dignity than this. He should be less stupidly impulsive.

He was the viceroy. He couldn't change their power structure and raise humans above even his own position, so there was no point in trying. No point in struggling. Was his place ideal? No. Could it improve? Also no. But on the other hand — if Meyer stayed emotional, fretting about things he couldn't change — could his situation decay?

Oh, yes. Most certainly yes.

His family was safe. Even Trevor and Piper, in Moab, were safe. The Astrals wouldn't raid the lab like they'd raided the rebel village until Benjamin cracked the code and showed the watchers to their missing prize. Even then, Meyer seriously doubted they'd respond with violence. The Astrals didn't want that. Sometimes, it was necessary because humans were violent by nature. But the point of colonizing and judging had been to avoid unnecessary strife — at least as humans understood it. But they wouldn't act senselessly. They'd protect Trevor and Piper because that's what Meyer desired. He had that much power at least.

But doing something stupid would change that. If Meyer rocked the boat, he might not stay safe.

Lila and Clara might not stay safe.

Piper and Trevor might not stay safe.

Even Heather, whom he still had feelings for despite her recent icy exterior, was safe for now ... but might not remain so if he disobeyed willy-nilly.

And really, just about the stupidest thing Meyer could do right now would be to ignore what Mo had shown him — to keep that information from the Astrals, who had enough to juggle without sending their little ball bearing spies into every single room. They wouldn't know what Meyer did — what he'd seen and heard on the surveillance camera hidden in Christopher's lamp.

He'd been right to doubt Terrence and Christopher's

loyalty, after the other day's display.

He'd been right to have his own devices planted to watch them.

And now that he knew Terrence and Christopher's secret, he shouldn't keep it all to himself.

But he wouldn't share yet. The Astrals hadn't known what to make of that little silver cylinder, and neither did Meyer.

As with Benjamin and the tablet, Meyer would watch.

And wait.

And when they did whatever they were going to do, he'd stand ready to do all he could to keep his family safe ... even if it meant throwing humanity to the wolves.

# CHAPTER 50

Benjamin stood at the front of the room.

Piper watched from her seat. Cameron was beside her, their hands casually linked.

On her other side was Nathan Andreus, who still frightened her but whom she'd nonetheless found herself getting used to. Meeting Andreus's daughter, Grace, had humanized the man in Piper's eyes, and when he'd brought her back to the Andreus camp, that feeling of humanization had lingered. Piper knew he'd done horrible things. She still sometimes had nightmares of two years ago, hiding from his minions in a drift of fetid leaves and mud. But she couldn't help seeing him as a man who'd done what was necessary to keep his family alive. Just as Meyer had done for her.

A wave of guilt rippled through her. Cameron clenched her hand and smiled, as if he knew and wanted to grant her forgiveness on the universe's behalf.

"Templars," said Benjamin.

No one responded to his dramatic declaration, and he continued with an air of disappointment. "The writing on the tablet is very much like the drawings and code left in Royston Cave, found under the Rose Stone, by the Knights

Templar." He tapped the projection the entire room had already seen, and which was no more enlightening now than the first time.

"That tells me that the Templars wrote this tablet," he said.

"In Colorado?" said Cameron.

"There's a lot we don't know about the Templars," Benjamin said. "It does seem unlikely that they crossed the oceans in wooden boats during the Crusades to leave this tablet buried under Vail—"

"Unless extraterrestrial ships took them over the ocean," Danika said. It was the kind of sentence Piper would normally expect to precede laughter, but the world had changed. Now the absurd was sensible.

"Not in this case," Benjamin said.

"Why not?"

"Because of what this says." Benjamin paused to see if anyone would ask him then continued, seemingly disappointed. "I'm paraphrasing, but it basically says, 'Ha ha, suckers, we took your prize, and you'll never find it, nyah nyah nyah.'"

"You're sure you're paraphrasing?" Danika said.

"Astrals didn't place this tablet. If I had to guess, they probably have no idea what it says."

Danika shot Trevor a look.

"And?" said Cameron.

"And so, that gives us an advantage. They don't know where their device is, but we do."

"So the tablet tells you where it's hidden."

"Sort of," said Benjamin. "The Templars loved codes and deception and riddles, so this doesn't actually tell us where the device itself is. It just leads us to the next link in the chain."

"Chain?"

"Kind of like a scavenger hunt, where one thing leads to

another," Benjamin explained. "I suspect it's a sequence of riddles, and what we're after explains them, like a decoder ring. But I know more about history and alternative archaeology than most people. Once Terrence plants that virus in the network hub, we should get some clear time to reach colleagues we haven't been able to talk openly with for fear of being overheard. After we get this — this *codex*, I guess you might call it — we should know where the hammer's been hidden. And if we can reach it before they do, we might be able to destroy it ... or hide it again."

"I still don't see how there were Templars in Colorado," Cameron said. Piper looked at his profile. If Benjamin knew the most about alternative archaeology, Cameron came in second. It was a distant second, because Cameron had spent most of his youth disbelieving then disavowing his father's work, but even Piper didn't think there had been Crusaders on this side of the ocean.

"It may have been moved several times," he said. "We can't trace the history. The last move might have been recent. Moves of the codex, not the tablet, I mean."

"Moved by whom?"

"Descendants of the Templars."

"Who is that?"

"In this case," said Benjamin, flipping to the next slide showing an enormous church, "the Mormons."

Two of the rebel camp's leftovers (Taylor and Olivia, Piper thought their names were) laughed, but Benjamin gave them a remanding look.

"I'm serious. Those of us who are on the outside of the Templar organization as it existed — and I'm sure that's all of us here — can only guess at the organization's trajectory through the ages. We know they were highly, *highly* secretive and ritualistic. Any number of modern-day secret societies are believed to be linked to those roots. Like the Freemasons. Or the largest power structures in any society: the churches."

"I could believe the Vatican," said Cameron. "But the *Mormons?*"

"The Catholic church of course has its ties," Benjamin said. "But think about it. There's always been a secret elite. The elite makes the rules and pulls the strings. For a long time, those were the religions. *All* the religions. Call me cynical, but it's hard to believe even the most stalwart holy people back in the day failed to notice their relative wealth, their relative power, and the way they could get others to do what they wanted."

"Now hang on a second." Piper hadn't practiced any religion in years, but old roots went deep. That had sounded like an insult, and she felt the need to defend what she'd once believed with all her heart.

"It's not a wholesale judgment, Piper," Benjamin said, holding up a hand. "But it's objectively true that modern politicians and institutional figures of *all* stripes, across *all* faiths, are in the business of controlling hearts and minds. Many do so honestly. Plenty do not. But all hold control in their palms, to a greater or lesser degree. The Mormons, in America, would be no exception. And the Templars' descendants, be they Freemasons or the friggin' Rotary Club for all we know, would be foolish not to make contact. To bring them into the secret at least. And honestly, is it really surprising that there's a connection? We now know there's been a prominent Astral contact site in North America all along, and that Vail was one of their cornerstones. Utah's next door, and just so happens to be home to the Latter-day Saints. Joseph Smith talked about alien life all the time. Their planet of Kolob and all that. Hell, in the twenty-teens, there was even a public art project erected in Salt Lake City showing two Mormon missionaries arriving in a flying saucer, one with blue skin. They got details wrong, but the artists building statues outside Heaven's Veil probably have it wrong too, and they're right there among them. After all we've seen, is it really so crazy to believe that there's a connection, church to stars?"

"You said it was church to Templars."

"Sure. Enough of a connection to the idea of alien visitation that, when the Templars or whoever came knocking, the church would listen. And would, perhaps, help hide something they believed in enough to fear its return."

The room was momentarily quiet. It dawned on Piper that most everyone who worked at the lab and the few who'd survived the camp massacre were all present and listening. It was probably overkill to explain all this theory to the rank-and-file grunts — but the fact that there *were* grunts where there had previously only been workers gave her goose bumps. It meant that they might be through studying and analyzing. Piper had brought them information, and now Benjamin knew what it meant. The time to act was nigh. Now, while they were still ahead of the game, before the Astrals solved the puzzle and fell into pursuit.

"So where does your analysis suggest this codex is hidden?" Trevor sounded stilted, as if reading from a script.

Benjamin smiled and clicked to the next slide: a sheer cliff with a wide parking lot at what the shot showed of its base. Several vehicle-sized tunnels were cut into the rock, yawning into darkness, their mouths muffled with gates.

"Little Cottonwood Canyon, outside Salt Lake City. Kept safe in the hidden tunnels of the Mormon Genealogical Archives."

Beside Piper, Cameron's mouth fell open. So did Piper's. They knew about Little Cottonwood Canyon. Benjamin wasn't wrong about that particular Mormon connection to extraterrestrial life, and nobody here needed convincing.

"That's an Astral outpost," Cameron said.

"Unfortunately, it is." Benjamin nodded. "According to the tablet they found under the Apex pyramid, the Astrals are practically sitting on what they've lost." He shifted uncomfortably then continued. "This mission's success, then, depends on us snatching it from under them before they realize it's there."

# CHAPTER 51

"I don't like this," Benjamin said.

Nathan Andreus smirked across the table. The room's door was closed but not impervious to the intrusion of small, pearl-sized silver spheres. Nathan's signal detector was in the table's center, still declaring the room clear. But the detector was a rubber stamp, not a deterrent or a protection. If the BB entered this room, they'd be sunk. They'd be alerted to its arrival with no time to hide. They were clearly plotting something, and Benjamin had never been good at keeping a straight face and a secret. Andreus had only told him about the spy among them because Benjamin was the linchpin that would make their deception possible. Without that, he'd be as much in the dark as everyone until the big reveal beside the Great Salt Lake.

"Of course you don't," said Andreus.

"We should at least tell Ivan. He's the muscle. Ivan has the survivors from the rebel camp who are hot for revenge. They can at least stay ahead of us and—"

"Nobody's hotter for revenge than I am." Andreus recrossed his legs and leaned back. "But this will only work if the Astrals don't think we're expecting problems with this plan of ours. They know we don't think they're stupid. If we go out heavy, they'll know we're assuming the shuttles are watching from above. Then it's a big game of who knows what. Trust me." Nathan's disturbing smile bunched his goatee. "I've done this sort of thing before."

"So we go in unarmed?"

"Not unarmed, but not heavy. We can't take any of my biggest, best vehicles. Remember, this is cat and mouse. After your little performance, explaining the mission to everyone, they'll assume we're going into the front lateral tunnel of the Cottonwood archive. They'll get out of our way when we arrive — trying to make it look like we just managed to sneak by without being seen — because they *want* you to take the supposed codex." Nathan laughed. "Where did you get that photo you showed of the codex we're supposedly looking for anyway?"

"It's a back stock photo from the Smithsonian. I think it's an ancient adding machine, like an abacus 2.0, but I'm not totally sure."

Andreus laughed again then settled. "So that's where we have to go: into the front lateral tunnel. And that adding machine — our decoy — is what everyone in the group other than the few of us who know the truth needs to believe we're after. Everything has to go exactly by the supposed book. The BB will follow you, and I can hang behind to verify that it does. Then we branch off: Cameron, Trevor, and I going for the plate the tablet actually talks about.

"How can you know the BB will follow me?" Benjamin asked.

"Because I've been watching it for days, and it *always* follows you. It's only with Cameron now because he's out in the front room delivering 'important mission information' while it thinks you're asleep. It even hung out in your room well after you *were* supposedly snoring. Believe me, I'd been hoping it would just leave and we wouldn't need Cameron's distraction. I didn't want to have to tell him about this, too."

"Cameron can keep a secret."

Andreus assessed Benjamin, who felt X-rayed.

"I sure as hell hope so. Because if someone looks directly at that BB, we won't be able to trust any of this from that point on. Even now, part of me thinks they're playing a long con: trying to trick us into lying in front of the spy BB so we'll show our true hand elsewhere, the way it played Piper to deliver that information then *almost* played you to decipher it for them."

Benjamin nodded slowly. That near-miss had occurred to him with some ferocity. If Andreus hadn't noticed the signal and its source, Benjamin would have given the same basic briefing, but telling everyone the truth instead of the lie.

"If we're trying to mislead them," said Benjamin, "why don't I just stay in the lab, pretending to work while you sneak out to Salt Lake and grab the plate unseen?"

"Because we won't *be* unseen." Andreus pointed at the ceiling. "The trick here is to almost show them what we're after — *almost*, but not quite. Haven't you ever lied to someone, Benjamin?"

"Sure." But staring into Andreus's eyes, he felt like a rookie masquerading as a veteran.

"Little lies sell deception. Big lies get you caught. If you're not greedy, you can get away with a little lie here and there. It's like warming an ice-cold bath one degree at a time."

Andreus sat forward and continued. "The shuttles will see us leave this place, so we have to explain *why* we're leaving, and do that part of it openly. The Astrals knew you'd crack the Templar code when they couldn't, so you had to do that, too. We'll have eyes on us the entire time. This mission has to succeed, and all on the sly. So no one can know. We have to go in numbers. Not because we need them to get the book from the archive, but because going in numbers is what we'd do if we thought they weren't watching, and if we were truly pulling a trick we thought they'd never see coming — while simultaneously pulling a *different* trick they *actually don't*."

Benjamin planted his head in his palms. "This hurts my brain."

"Oh, come on now. That big brain of yours? You're humanity's salvation, Mr. Bannister."

"Or its downfall."

"We get the plate." Andreus tapped the table for emphasis. "I've communicated with your man, Terrence. He'll inject his virus in time with our finding the artifact. When the network opens and we're again topside, we can broadcast our find. We'll grab the artifact and smuggle it out then rejoin the group on the decoy mission to try and find your typewriter thing (and 'unfortunately' fail) then leave. We'll act disappointed that the tablet steered us wrong and go home. They'll never know it steered us right and gave us what we needed. If we're lucky, no one fights."

"Can't the Astrals intercept the messages you're sending to Terrence?"

"The Astrals know about our new channel of discussion," Andreus said, "but that's okay because reestablishing a channel to Terrence is what crafty people like us would do if we didn't know the Astrals were watching. So yes, they'll hear whatever we say to each other. But fortunately, Terrence and I have worked out a simple code so I can tell him what I really want him to do, out in the open, without raising alien eyebrows. If they had them."

"How did you manage that?"

"Did you ever tell a kid, 'Don't you *dare* mop that floor, Timmy' because you want him to do the opposite?"

Benjamin stared. "You're kidding."

"The Astrals are terrible at understanding the nuances

of human communication. This is safe, especially given how little needs to be said. Remember, the Astrals let my people use our comm channels openly as part of our deal. Yet we've been talking behind our hands, to some degree, the entire time."

Benjamin chewed his lip. It would work. If the channel was already established, Terrence only needed a signal. A command of "Now" would suffice. But he still didn't like it, with so many ways to go wrong.

"You're afraid," Andreus said, watching him.

Benjamin didn't respond.

"It's okay, Benjamin. Everyone's afraid. It's not bravery to act when you're sure everything will be fine. Brave is being scared shitless and acting anyway."

"I don't want to be brave."

Benjamin didn't think it was cowardice holding him back. He flat-out *didn't want to do this* — not because of his or anyone's fear but because it simply wouldn't work. The people they had for this mission weren't fighters. With the exception of the rebel leftovers, they were all scientists. The Astrals had disposed of their fighting force, leaving Ivan and a few others in possession of a killer instinct. Ivan would agree to this plan in a bloody instant and arm everyone to the teeth if he knew its full truth, but that was *why* nobody had told him.

Andreus's plan, unfortunately, relied on stealth and deception, with no room for error. They'd be armed, but not sufficient to handle any potential problems. Benjamin had heard Cameron, Piper, and Trevor's tale of escape from Heaven's Veil, but he also knew they'd made that escape in what was essentially a tank — and now that Benjamin knew about the BB, it also sounded like the Astrals had *allowed* them to go. This Salt Lake mission would be different. If their subterfuge was discovered and they had to scrap at Cottonwood — if they had to scrap *at all* — they'd be massacred.

The game would be over. If the Astrals discovered what the tablet had really led them to find, they'd have drawn an engraved map to Thor's Hammer and delivered it to them. Nothing could stand in their way after that. No one could stop them.

"I changed my mind," Benjamin said, even though Andreus was practically staring him down.

"You don't get to change your mind, Ben."

"We'll find another way. We know where the plate is, and the Astrals don't know we know. We can take our time, figure out a way to do it right."

"You're letting fear get the best of you."

"It's not that. It's stupid to act when we know we'll fail."

Andreus shook his head.

"What?" Benjamin asked.

"The die is cast. You made your speech, and the Astrals were listening. If we don't go, they'll know we know something."

"I'll make another speech. I'll tell everyone I changed my mind. Cottonwood's an Astral base, for Christ's sake. They'll understand if it looks like we want to think twice about running into the lion's den."

Andreus shook his head. "No."

Benjamin met his eyes. "I'm sorry?"

"It's not just you in this anymore. I stuck my neck out there to save your people in Vail."

"They weren't actually in danger." Benjamin said, knowing his response sounded lame.

"We didn't know that. And the Astrals *know* I didn't know but went in anyway. I've had amnesty, but those days are numbered. They could show up at any time to destroy my camps, like they did for the rebel base. I lost my wife to this. Do you know how hard it was to decide whether to send Grace to the Republic or keep her here? Two terrible choices. Shuttles could burn either one without any notice."

He stabbed a finger into the table. "This? This is our *only* chance. You don't get to make the decision alone. We're partners now, like it or not."

Benjamin watched him, feeling chastised. He'd never been so frightened — and so sure they were merely lining up for execution. He felt helpless. He didn't just fear death. Its *inevitability* prickled his skin.

"Then we have to arm up," Benjamin said. "We have to take one of your tanks."

"They'll know we're up to something if we do that."

"Our *official version* is that we're up to something!" Benjamin blurted. Andreus was infuriating to talk to. He pretended to be having a discussion while delivering orders.

A small smile had grown on Andreus's lips, despite his shaking head. Benjamin wanted to leap across the table and punch him. Benjamin was out of his mind, and this bastard was *enjoying* himself, keeping secrets because he thought it was *funny*?

"Benjamin," Andreus said. "Do me a favor."

Benjamin stared.

"Take a deep breath."

"What's so goddamn funny, Nathan?" It felt reckless to say his first name. Assuming familiarity. It was the kind of thing that local rumor said could get you disemboweled to teach you a lesson. Drawn and quartered, or beheaded.

"We have to get in and out, pretending to look for one thing while searching for another, without breaking our illusion. But the lack of fallback seems to be bothering you. No chance of surviving if things go wrong, and we can't maintain that illusion. Sound about right?"

"If we're killed," Benjamin said, "we won't get a second chance to get Thor's Hammer before they do."

"Would it make you feel any better if I assured you there's no chance we'll be killed?"

The flat, statement-like quality of the lie left Benjamin

momentarily speechless. Andreus hadn't inquired as preamble to a pep talk. He'd stated it like a fact — the way he'd declare that there were two men in the room. He'd implied it as a mission objective. Datum a commander might use to plan an assault.

The only question was how Andreus could possibly think Benjamin would believe something so absurd — or, possibly, just how stupid Andreus thought he was.

"How could you *possibly* think that heading *directly* into an Astral-controlled area won't entail risk?"

Andreus told him.

# CHAPTER 52

Heather clenched the silver canister between her breasts. Terrence extended his hand. "Heather."

It had taken Terrence time to get used to Heather's caustic nature the same way getting used to her took everyone time. But Heather's house on the grounds was on Terrence's other side, opposite Christopher's. Years of having her as an obnoxious neighbor had taught him that there was no winning. Brevity was the only way to argue — not because it worked, but because it meant you'd put yourself out there less when she eventually made fun of you before walking away, having done exactly whatever the fuck she'd wanted.

"You gave me this thing," she told him. "So now, if you want it back, you have to tell me what you plan to do with it."

Terrence looked around Heather's small living room. He wasn't wearing his trademark glasses, so his worry and urgency were clear.

"I told you," he said.

"You just told me it's something you made for Benjamin.

Having to do with the Internet. But I know you were talking to Benjamin through that church that got blown up, maybe with the help of that big pile of black ashes that Piper had been hanging out with."

"So what?"

Heather held the canister tighter. Terrence kept beckoning with his fingers. "Come on, Heather. Give it to me." He was much bigger and stronger but wouldn't pry it from her. He was oddly polite, and Heather strangely intimidating. Like a tiny spider with giant fangs.

"So a lot has changed since the original plan. You don't know for sure what Cameron was going to do with this before he handed it off. Piper and my son are out there somewhere! How do you know Benjamin's plans don't require saving them from the desert instead of hacking the Internet and—"

"Do you know the Andreus Republic?"

The warmth left her skin. Of course Heather knew about the Andreus Republic. They were animals. People claimed they skinned their enemies — or at least, that's what the news said. Andreus bands were the main reason nobody left Heaven's Veil or local outposts. She didn't want to hear what followed. She'd mentioned Trevor, and Terrence had replied by broaching the Republic. A chilling implication. *Advantage: Terrence.*

"Turns out, Nathan Andreus and I have a lot in common," Terrence said, clearly enjoying his conversational coup on the Queen of Wry. "He's a lot smarter than people give him credit for. I was sitting in the guard station the other day when my radio started giving static bursts of Morse. Long story short, I changed a few settings in my web browser code, and now Andreus and I are pen pals."

Heather still didn't trust herself to speak. Terrence

wasn't getting to the point, unless the point was that he'd turned traitor and wanted her to know he was about to join a group the news painted as practically cannibals.

"He's a tech guy," Terrence said, taking mercy, his smarmy look relaxing. "He's had an in all this time. Understands all my network stuff, including the general idea behind Canned Heat."

"Is that a saucy women's prison movie?"

"Trevor is fine, Heather. He and Piper and Cameron made it to Moab okay. The tank thing we told you about? Turns out that was an Andreus Republic vehicle. Now Nathan Andreus and his people are working with them. And they're ... planning something."

"What are they planning?"

Terrence reached for the silver cylinder. Heather clenched it tighter and pivoted away.

"The Astrals are watching Internet traffic, such as they're able. And that's not a problem for someone like Andreus or me, who know where to hide messages in the deluge, then couch them so they aren't terribly incriminating if discovered. The bigger problem is the wholesale severing of channels. What you have there—" he pointed, "—is a virus that I think will disrupt their blockages, opening some of those channels for at least a little while. Long enough for people like Benjamin to share some information in order to ... to do other stuff."

"What other stuff?"

"That's need-to-know information."

"Well, guess who needs to know?"

Terrence got a few fingers on the canister, but Heather slapped him away. Soon, he'd tire of the game and simply pin her despite his nature, but she could weasel some more secrets before he did.

"Fuck off, Terrence. If I'm good enough to hide this for you, I'm good enough to know what you're doing."

"The more you know, the more you could get in trouble."

"More trouble than running off and killing one of the peacekeepers? More trouble than helping Piper get away after stealing some CIA secret shit from His Lordship the holy motherfucking Viceroy of Heaven's Veil?"

"Time is a factor, here, Heather. You're not helping."

"No way. You thought they were suspicious of you, so you gave me this thing to hide. Then you come here, to my house, rubbing your suspicious ass all over my face. Now I've got suspicion on my chin."

"Wow. Vivid imagery."

"Look. Just let me help. I'm in it this far anyway."

"There's no way for you to help."

"Why not?"

"Because I just need to plug that into a port and execute."

"So it's a program."

"It's complicated. It can't just be emailed. I need that actual canister you're holding."

"Is it complicated or simple? Make up your mind, Terrence."

Terrence sighed. He kept himself from rolling his eyes, probably because Heather would take it as a sign of victory. His hand fell to his side.

"It's simple in execution. It really is just plugging in and executing it. But if it works, it'll uncensor the Internet for just long enough, at least, to help Benjamin send information to colleagues worldwide who can help him find something."

"And he needs to do it ASAP. Which is why you're so eager."

"Not ASAP. They need to find something first."

"I thought whatever you were doing would *help* them

find it."

"They need to find one thing *then* the other."

"Like a scavenger hunt," Heather said. "Fun."

"But as soon as they find the first thing, that's when this needs to go. *Right* then. No sooner and no later. Satisfied?" He reached again.

"Not at all. You haven't told me how I can help."

"Why do you need to help?"

Heather took the canister from her chest and waved it in the air. "Because I want to get into trouble! Because I'm sick of all this! Look at me! Lila and Trevor get to live in the big mansion. Piper gets to live in the mansion with Meyer. Shit, even *Raj* gets to live in the mansion. But where does Heather end up? Out in the shitty guest shacks with the help!" She considered adding "no offense" for Terrence but decided not to bother. "I went out with Trevor to help there, and *still* that little bastard ran off without me. Now he's in Utah, probably living it up and going to all the best parties, while I'm stuck here, bored!"

Terrence looked like he might suggest that there probably weren't any parties in Moab worth going to. Instead, he sighed.

"The node that plugs the mothership into the network seems to be in the house. I'm sure it's up on the fourth floor, with all the other computers. If you really want to help, you can figure a way to get in there. I have some tricky ideas on how to do it, but they all introduce complications and unknowns that I'd rather avoid if possible. Best-case scenario is walking right up there, plugging in, and accessing a terminal. But it's restricted. I don't suppose you have access, as family?"

Heather laughed. She was Lila and Trevor's mother and Clara's grandmother, but nobody seemed to understand that those things made her family.

"No, I don't have access."

Nobody would give Heather access. She lived in the guest houses, for God's sake.

Even Piper, who'd managed to steal from Meyer and the Astrals, wouldn't have access to something like that.

Heather felt her usual flash of bitterness.

Piper didn't share blood but lived in the house.

Even Raj didn't share blood but lived the house.

Heather's resentment turned to inspiration. "When do you need to be in there?"

Terrence frowned. It looked like he'd asked a titanic favor but now had to admit that his unreasonable timeframe was icing on an imposition cake.

"Tomorrow. Three o'clock."

Just over twenty-four hours. That was enough time to sharpen her knives then determine the best ways to twist them.

"I can get you in," she said.

"How?"

"It's a surprise."

Terrence looked like he might pry further but knew he was talking to a performer. He extended his hand, and this time, Heather slapped the cylinder into it.

"Thanks," he said.

Terrence was halfway to the door when Heather called his name. He turned back, waiting, tired of her shenanigans.

"You keep saying, 'If it works,'" she said.

"Yeah."

"You think it might not work?"

Terrence nodded. "I'd say it's fifty-fifty. If I'd had more time, I could get to seventy-five-twenty-five, but I don't. Tomorrow. Three p.m." He sighed. "Unfortunately."

"If it doesn't work," Heather said, "maybe you can try to uncensor the Internet later."

Terrence gave her a humorless smirk.

"If it doesn't work, there'll be no Internet left, and the resistance will be cut off from any possible help. Totally blind."

# CHAPTER 53

Cameron was reclining in the rear of a rather lavish converted recreational vehicle when his father stumbled back, rapping his thigh on a protruding table, to join him.

"Nervous yet?" Benjamin asked.

Cameron lifted his head. He had his fingers interlaced just above his collar, flat on his back, staring at the ceiling. It wasn't so much that he needed rest as the fact that the RV's bed was more comfortable than the one he'd been sleeping on in the lab. Ever since the camp's survivors had joined them, it had only seemed right to surrender the house. Nathan's daughter, Grace, had lived out there before she'd left, despite her not getting along at all with Taylor, Olivia, or the other rebel remainders. Nathan had been sleeping in the lab, like Cameron. Even after more than a week in the same place, Cameron didn't think the father-daughter pairing had exchanged more than twenty words.

The RV's bed, however, was comparatively plush. The minute it had arrived and he'd fallen into its mattress, Cameron had wondered why Andreus hadn't brought RVs from the start. They'd all been converted to run on solar and could go a few hundred miles on a charge, but even dead they'd have made for nice little houses. They weren't fast, owing to the solar conversion's lack of torque, but it hardly mattered. Considering that the Astrals thought they knew what the caravan was up to, they had all the time in the world.

"No, I'm not nervous," Cameron answered.

Benjamin sat atop one of the padded benches near the bed. "*I'm* nervous."

Cameron sat up. The bed was in a rear recess, designed to be closed off as a miniature bedroom. If he stayed put, he'd be talking to his father through a slit. Sitting, they were two feet apart. There was also a pair of feet from Danika, who'd been uncharacteristically painting her fingernails outside Cameron's co-opted bedroom with a worried air, but that was fine. Danika, like Trevor and Andreus, already knew anything they'd discuss.

There were somewhere between twenty and twenty-five people on this errand across various vehicles, but the rest of them thought they were pursuing something that didn't exist. Something, Benjamin had told him, that might be an ancient adding machine from a Smithsonian photo. Something that most certainly wouldn't be in the Little Cottonwood Canyon genealogical archives.

It was cruel to send so many people into the beast's mouth then send them away feeling like failures when they came up empty, but deception was necessary. The detector in Benjamin's hand suggested the BB was elsewhere (possibly with Charlie, conducting another decoy lecture in a separate RV), but any gaffe could give them away and blow the whole thing.

Danika looked at Cameron. "*I'm* nervous. How can you not be nervous?"

"When all of this started, I was on the road with Dan. I headed to your lab, to find Dad. Dad's message sent me to Vail. So I was on the road through the beginning and stayed on the road — or at least out in the open, once we reached Vail — for months. I was used to traveling in the fringe places Dad took me as a kid." He set his hand on his father's shoulder. "I guess I got used to the idea that everything is at least a little dangerous, and that the tide could change at any time."

Cameron, hearing himself articulate the thought, found it profound. Danika looked unimpressed. She frowned and resumed painting her nails. To Cameron's knowledge, she'd never had painted nails. She'd probably found the polish in the RV, and was whistling in the dark.

"Hmm. Very macho. Maybe they could put you in an Old Spice ad."

"Old Spice? Who still wears Old Spice?"

"I wore Old Spice until I ran out."

Danika cocked a thumb at Benjamin. "See? Macho."

Cameron watched her for a moment. It took him a while to see what was off about her, given her usual sarcasm, but then he had it. Her movements were overly slow and precise — because the moment she stopped focusing on painting straight lines, her hands started shaking.

"We'll be okay," Benjamin said.

Danika frowned, not looking up. "I'm a scientist. I'm supposed to be in a lab, maybe in front of a computer. Maybe Rambo here grew up walking the desert and killing game to eat over an open fire, but I grew up reading my mom's old Judy Blume paperbacks. Later, I graduated to sitting safely inside and reading cozy mysteries. My dad didn't even let me date until I was practically out of the house, and by then I was afraid of boys, too. Probably Dad's intention." She looked up, and Cameron realized, for the first time, that Danika had no idea how pretty she was. She'd spent her life staring at data. Everything else had been an untrustworthy distraction.

"It's okay, Danika," Benjamin repeated. "Really. I

wouldn't have okayed taking so many people if it wasn't."

"We *had* to take this many people so ..." She stopped, looked at the BB detector to make sure it wasn't alarming silently, then went on. "So it's not overly obvious if three of us split off."

"I still wouldn't have allowed it. I promise."

Cameron found himself looking at his father, waiting. He knew the man well enough to sense more in the story. Benjamin hoped, yes. He fantasized, yes. He had his head in the clouds in terms of his work and leaped to many unfounded conclusions in pursuit of excitement, definitely. But he didn't promise lightly.

Benjamin saw Cameron's stare but spoke to Danika.

"The Astrals at the archive will be conveniently absent when we arrive because they're letting us in. They'll be around so it doesn't look too fishy, but they'll allow us to sneak by and pretend they don't know we're there. They needed me to read the Templar tablet because they couldn't, and because they know the adding machine thing I projected during our fake meeting isn't what they're looking for; they'll know they have to *stay* out of the way and *keep* leaving me alone so I can keep doing what they want — what they think I'm doing all on my own, without knowing they're watching everything I do."

"Why?" Danika asked.

"Because we haven't finished our job," Cameron said before Benjamin could answer.

Benjamin nodded then resumed talking to Danika. "We've shown them what we're after. They plainly saw it's not the object they want to find — the device that was missing from the excavation site under the Heaven's Veil Apex. But because they believe I'm reading the tablet faithfully, they have to assume our supposed codex is just a link in a longer chain. They need to stay out of the way so we can locate this first object ... and then lead them to the *next* link in the chain, which they're hoping will be Thor's Hammer."

"But it won't be."

"It *will* be," Benjamin said. "But they won't know we've found this first stepping stone. Which means that later, we can go after the hammer without them being wise."

Danika put her fingers to her temples. Benjamin laughed.

"I know, right? That's how I felt when Nathan explained it. We have a big game of chicken. There's the thing we're *pretending* to be after, which is different from the thing we actually are. We're too smart to come in plain sight like this, and they know *we* know they can see us in their shuttles, not via that little spy BB and—"

"Stop," Danika said. "Just stop."

"My point is that they won't interfere. They *can't* interfere."

"But that's what's been bugging me, Dad." Cameron watched Benjamin perk up at his rare use of the familial term. "*We* know they won't interfere because we've learned we're doing what they want us to do: find something that will lead them to their lost hammer. But in *their* version of what we must be thinking, what we're doing is stupid. Because officially, they think we'd have to assume they were hostile. And yet here we are, heading into one of their protected outposts."

Benjamin shook his head. "Not protected. *Preserved.* There's a difference. That's what Nathan explained when I was feeling like you are, Danika. We don't know exactly what the Cottonwood archive meant to the Astrals once upon a time, but it's carved into Utah cliffs, so there could be anything down there that the Mormons aren't telling anyone about. The facility's always been secretive — in human hands, I mean. Like the Templars. Like the Freemasons." He smirked. "Like the Mormons apparently."

"So?"

"There's a reason this archive exists." He made a face. "*Genealogy?* Seriously? Does anyone here believe that a secretive organization bored a series of massive tunnels in a canyon wall to store *microfilm genealogical records?* The idea's absurd. There have been tours, just like there are tours of anywhere secretive and mysterious, but they smell like distraction. Racks and racks filled with tiny, impossibly long drawers of microfilm. Supposedly, there's never been a digital storage system that's as long-lasting, but I have a hard time buying that. So in the end, I have to ask: What's really stored at the Little Cottonwood Canyon archive? And more importantly, why do the Astrals care?"

"You think Thor's Hammer is right there? At the archive?"

Benjamin laughed hard enough to turn Ivan's head from the RV's passenger seat up front. He lowered his voice, wary of the military man's attention.

"Oh, I know *exactly* where Thor's Hammer is, Cam. You do too. That's what kills me. As far as historical jokes go, it's a doozy."

"Where?"

Benjamin laughed softer. "If you haven't figured it out by the time we leave to chase it, I'll have to tell you. But think about it, Cam. A weapon from the ancient alien theorist texts. Where would it go?"

"Jesus, Dad. I got tired of your guessing games a long time ago. Did you read it on the tablet?"

"The tablet confirmed it, but it's the sort of thing I kind of always knew."

"If you read it on the tablet," Danika pointed out, "that's cheating."

Benjamin waved it away. "It's not at Cottonwood. The Templars would have to assume the Astrals would occupy Cottonwood."

"Why?"

"Because of the records."

"Records of what?"

"This is Charlie's guess," said Benjamin, "though don't go asking just yet because remember, he doesn't know what we're really after. But you know all the research he's done into panspermia? The idea that life here and other places was seeded from a common source — from Astral DNA, or their equivalent genetic material anyway?"

"Sure," said Cameron. "You think the archive contains *those* records?"

"It's genealogy, isn't it? Lets the human keepers of the place say what they do there with a straight face. But the place would have been built — and by built, I mean the original catacombs we assume were initially in those cliffs, behind the archive, then surely expanded by Masons in ways the original creators didn't know about because Masons like to hold an ace — with alien help. An ancient partnership. The newer tunnels were added, giving the thing a face and access. But the Astrals would know exactly what it was and why it mattered. But do you understand the difference now? A simple archive of records is the kind of thing you *preserve*, not necessarily *protect*. It's informational, not strategic. They didn't know the Mormons had hidden something new right under their noses."

Cameron felt like he was missing something. "So what?"

"Nathan's people have analyzed every speck of back satellite data they've ever had on Cottonwood. There's also an Andreus Republic outpost near Salt Lake, and Salt Lake City itself is largely Andreus controlled, seeing as it's not a capital and doesn't have a mothership. And they're positive that there are no Reptars at the Cottonwood Canyon facility. Why would there be? It has no strategic significance, and even now that they know there's something there that matters, they want us to take it." He tapped the table. "There are only Titans at Cottonwood. Only the intellectual, record keeping class of Astrals, whose panspermatozoic genetics we obviously share and are hence most equipped to curate such a place."

Cameron looked at Danika, who seemed as unimpressed as he was.

"Again," he said. "So what?"

"Something I've suspected, something that Nathan's people have proved," said Benjamin. He winked at Danika. "Titans couldn't hurt a fly."

# CHAPTER 54

Meyer opened his eyes to find Mo Weir standing in front of him.

He jumped; Mo clearly hadn't expected the viceroy to snap out of his communication at the exact instant he'd been studying his face. Mo had told Meyer that he looked like a yogi when he was talking to Divinity (or rather, Meyer thought resentfully, when Divinity talked to him), and now it looked like Mo had decided to investigate his trance a bit closer. He'd looked about ready to snap his fingers in front of Meyer's closed eyes.

"Oh ... hey, Meyer."

"Where's Raj?"

Mo blinked, as if he were the one who'd been doing some sort of a weird, micromanaging mind-meld.

"Raj?"

"Yes, Raj."

"You mean Christopher."

"I mean Raj. Do you think I have some sort of weird aphasia where I confuse normal people with conniving little shits who knock up my daughter?"

Mo hesitated a second, probably trying to decide if that

had been a joke. It almost had been, but right now even Meyer wasn't sure. Back when he'd taken the drug that opened an alien window inside his mind, he'd felt like he was joining a kind of collective intelligence. Communing with Divinity on the mothership was something like that. Readjusting to the sense of renewed singularity took a while — sorting out the others' thoughts and emotions from those that remained uniquely his own.

Mo half smiled — something that could be seen as joining in if Meyer was joking or played as cynical if he turned out to be serious. He hadn't had proper time to be angry at Raj when he'd first found out about the pregnancy because he'd discovered the truth while still aboard the mothership. Earthly matters — even those involving whose dick went into which off-limits place — had seemed trivial compared to everything else.

"I don't know. Want me to call around and find him?"

"Yes, Mo. Why else would I ask if I didn't want to know?"

Mo nodded, accepting the order without insult. Meyer reminded himself to stand down. He was impatient with Mo because he wasn't reading Meyer's thoughts. Literally. It wasn't the sort of thing to anger a reasonable man.

Mo spoke into his communicator then turned to Meyer. He wouldn't speak first. He could sense the man's mood. Mo was no more psychic than anyone other than the freaks who accidentally stumbled through the few remaining stone nerve lines, but he was intuitive as hell — especially when it came to working with Viceroy Dempsey.

"They're on their way to Cottonwood," Meyer said.

"Hmm. Good."

"Trevor is with them. Piper too."

Mo gave Meyer another one of those looks, seemingly unsure how to respond. Maybe he wasn't as intuitive as Meyer had been thinking, if he couldn't read him now. Or maybe Meyer, in the past, had been easier to read.

SEAN PLATT & JOHNNY B. TRUANT

"I see," Mo said. "I don't suppose they told you what they're looking for."

Meyer wanted to reply by saying, *No, of course not, I'm just the fucking leader of North American humanity, no need to tell me more than the basics.* Instead, he said, "No."

Mo nodded. He didn't know all that Meyer knew, but he'd been informed of a lot. Meyer wasn't sure if he was allowed to tell his right hand what he learned from the Astrals, but he could only be efficient when Mo knew enough to do his job. And also, fuck them if they had a problem with it.

There was a knock on the doorframe. Both men turned to see Raj awaiting acknowledgement.

"Come in," Meyer said, indicating a chair.

Raj sat, followed by Mo, preparing to take notes on a tablet. Meyer stayed standing.

"Raj," he said, "I'd like you to post a guard at the network center upstairs on four. Another where the stairs and the elevator come out."

"Two separate guards for the elevator and stairs?"

"They come up ten feet apart. What do you think?"

Raj didn't respond, clearly having no idea what the correct answer was. Meyer let it go.

"What are the doors up there. Glass?"

"Hybrid synthesized sapphire glass," Raj clarified, seemingly happy to have an answer. "Like on a phone's touchscreen. Unbreakable."

Meyer suppressed his lack of enthusiasm. The Apex was made of transparent bluish glass that some thought was sapphire too, but Meyer bet that alien stuff could withstand a direct ICBM hit. And yet the Astrals weren't sharing, even though the network center they were discussing was more important to the aliens than the Viceroy's office.

"Obviously, keep it locked. I don't have to tell you that, do I?"

"No. No, of course not."

"Keycard access or what?"

"To get in? No; it's a palm print. State of the art."

Meyer wished Raj would keep the brochure listing of features to himself. "Who has access?"

"Just me and those above me."

"Does that include Christopher?"

Raj's eyebrows furrowed for a fraction of a second. On paper, he outranked Christopher, but everyone (including Raj) knew his position was honorary. Raj got to wear a uniform when he wanted and act like a big shot. No biggie. As long as Raj could keep from ordering Reptar patrols without consulting a subordinate who actually knew what the fuck they were doing, his implied power was harmless.

"No. Christopher is just a captain."

"So he can't access the network."

"No."

"What about Terrence?"

"Terrence doesn't even have a rank."

"Just answer my fucking question, Raj."

"Sorry. No. When we've needed him in the past, he's been given terminal access. The on-duty center supervisor lets him in."

"Do they watch him?"

"You mean stand over his shoulder?"

"Yes."

"No, not normally. But—"

"When was his last access?"

"I don't have the logs. I'd have to check."

"You're the supervisor's supervisor, Raj. It's the one job you have that you're actually qualified for. Try not to have your head up your ass."

Meyer almost felt sorry for Raj. Almost. He seemed to be reeling from the punches. This way of talking was cruel, but he didn't feel like wasting time with bedside manner. He needed answers. Maybe it was wrong to experience power by belittling another, but doing so now — especially when the subject was Raj — felt impossible to resist.

"I ... Okay."

"Nobody gets access for now. Not even the supervisor. I want that door always locked, guards out front, nobody inside. Restrict access to two people: you and me. Anything goes wrong, I'll know I didn't do it. That knowledge will add a lot of clarity to whatever comes next."

"Yes, sir," Raj stammered. "Of course, sir. Can I ask a question, sir?"

Across from Raj, Mo laughed. Raj sounded ready to ask if he could lick Meyer's leather loafers. Meyer was almost tempted to request it, just to see if the kid had a molecule of dignity.

Raj glanced over at Mo's laugh then turned back toward Meyer, looking just as servile.

"Okay," Meyer said.

"Is this related to what happened the other day? Are Terrence and Christopher ..."

Meyer raised his eyebrows expectantly.

"Are they ... you know ..."

"I don't."

"When you showed up ... and then afterward ... when I was saying how Terrence seemed like he was with them in some capacity other than as a ... you know, like not under direction but as a ..."

Meyer wanted to put his face in his palms. He couldn't decide if Raj's floundering was more amusing or embarrassing. He couldn't say what he thought, even though the answer was plain as day. After the dust settled and the tank vehicle had gone, Raj hadn't been able to shut up about Terrence (and, by extension, Christopher) playing both sides. Now, when it mattered, he couldn't say those same words.

Meyer wanted to let him dangle until he hanged himself, but time was wasting. Still, he wished Raj would finish a question because Meyer was dying to tell him it was none of his fucking business.

"I'm short on guards," Raj finally spat in apparent surrender.

"How is that possible?"

"Christopher has almost all of them. Out by that destroyed church."

"The *house* guards?"

"I guess they were all he had."

Meyer rolled his eyes. Raj had just missed a perfect opportunity to point out how poorly Christopher was doing his job. Meyer, watching Raj, wished he had a third option for his security. The choice between a traitor and an idiot was no choice at all.

"I'll put you in touch with Capt. Jons of the police. He'll get you some officers to act as guards. They don't get access, though. To *any* locks, including incidental house locks. They need to go to the bathroom, you or whoever you have left lets them in."

"Sir?"

Meyer sighed.

"Are you anticipating ... trouble?"

"Maybe." He didn't want to tell Raj more. Right now, Meyer knew for sure that Terrence, Christopher, Lila, and Heather were either involved or knew what Terrence was planning with his communication virus. Letting Raj know any more than he already did — even the names of those he suspected — was begging for a clusterfuck.

"Then is it possible to get some ... *other* guards?"

"I told you I'll set you up with police."

"I was thinking of ... of peacekeepers."

Meyer looked directly at Mo Weir, who just shook his head.

"You're kidding."

SEAN PLATT & JOHNNY B. TRUANT

"If there might be trouble, they're the best equipped to—"

"I'm not having Reptars in the house." He stopped himself from adding the codicil: ... *you catastrophically stupid fucking moron.*

"But they're supposedly highly intelligent, right? Not like animals, and—"

"Absolutely not. Don't ask again, or I'll take you outside and feed you to one. Feel free to explain all sorts of things to it before the thing starts ripping you apart."

"Then maybe some of the Titans. There are a pair outside now who could—"

Meyer shook his head.

"All due respect, sir, if you're expecting anything like I think you might be, I have my doubts that *any* human guards will be able to help. At the risk of stepping out of line, I think there may be something in the works that involves Astral technology, and if that's the case, there's no way that human guards with human weapons could possibly—"

"I'll get you cops."

"But the Titans ... there are a bunch of them around, doing nothing, and ..." He trailed off.

Meyer finally sat.

"I don't suppose you ever saw an old movie called *The Dark Crystal?*"

Raj shook his head.

"You'll see its influence in a handful of Fable's films. It was a puppet movie, but good. There was this ancient race, and they split into two derivative races: the Skeksis and the Mystics. The Skeksis were these twisted, evil things that fought and were generally walking piles of shit. The Mystics were like old men with nothing to do other than walk around slowly and draw magic maps in the sand with canes, crap like that. They were all Zen. Peaceful."

"Okay," said Raj.

"The Reptars are their Skeksis."

"Okay."

"And the Titans are their Mystics."

Raj gave a small nod of assent.

"You ever see a Titan fight? Ever?"

Raj seemed to think then shook his head.

"You could punch a Titan in the face, and he'd just smile at you. You try to get past a bunch of them and they'll stop you with those giant arms, but they'll never hurt you. You come at them with guns that might actually be able to hurt them and they'd hide or do what they could to prevent your passing, but they won't shoot back. They'll try to reason with you then call for Reptars to fight. Their guns are props. They're vital to everything that happens here, but the Titans are useless as fighters because they seem to be the half of Astral consciousness that deals with peaceful discourse."

Raj looked at Meyer for a long moment. Meyer could have counted to five slowly before Raj spoke next.

"Okay."

"So you understand?"

"What does that have to do with puppets?" Raj asked.

Before Meyer could reply — and it was possible his response would have come in the form of a backhand slap across the face — Mo put a restraining hand on Meyer's arm.

"I'll get him some cops," he said.

# CHAPTER 55

Piper was lying flat on a dusty expanse of sand and grit, somewhat behind a large rock. Nearby, the others were also horizontal, somewhat behind other boulders.

She looked at Cameron, surprised by his proximity. He must have scooted closer while she'd been focused on the expanse of concrete not far ahead. A slight decline lay before them, followed by a corresponding rise. A parking lot sprawled beyond that then a cliff of fractured gray stone. There were three semicircular tunnels in the rock, just as they'd been on the image Benjamin had shown them in Moab. There were no cars in the lot. Piper thought she knew why. If this were an Astral place staffed exclusively by the hairless white Titans, they wouldn't arrive for work in cars.

The thought made her roll to look upward. The sky, bordered on both sides by wide canyon walls, was blue and empty. It could have been another average afternoon before Astral Day, hanging out in the rock scree by the entrance of the Mormon Genealogical Archives.

Cameron looked back then smiled at Piper.

"This is a terrible idea," she said.

307

Cameron tried to bolster his smile, making it crawl higher on his cheeks. He partially succeeded.

"Did Charlie explain on the way over?"

Piper nodded. But she'd wondered why Cameron had beelined for the RV with Danika, Ivan, and his father, allowing Nathan to lead her into the other. She'd wanted to ride with him. Her insecurity had even entertained the idea that her desire led to refusal. Cameron had been keeping his head low for most of the day. Piper didn't like it. If there were secrets, she wanted to hold them.

"Like I'm sure he said — Charlie and Nathan; this was mainly Nathan's plan, but don't tell Ivan that — Nathan's been watching this place on his satellites for a while. Best he can tell, there's only a handful of Titans watching, and they mostly stay outside. They don't know it contains the codex that used to be in Vail." Cameron's eyes flicked away momentarily as if distracted then returned to hers with sharper focus. "Point is, that's just a few Titans for what might turn out to be miles of tunnels. Like anything secretive, there's the official version and the truth. This place is officially quite large. Benjamin says it's surely much larger."

Cameron looked over his shoulder. A small Asian woman was crouched behind a fallen boulder, eyes wide and trying not to tremble. Piper barely knew her as more than one of the lab techs named Tina. She wasn't a stranger simply because Piper was new to the ranch this time around. Tina had been at the Moab facility Piper's first time staying there, and they'd lived in close proximity for three months. But Tina was shy, like many of the techs. They kept to themselves and did their work, seemingly frightened of shadows.

And *these* were the people Nathan Andreus wanted to use as troops, to storm an alien base.

"I know what you're thinking," Cameron said, again

drawing Piper's eyes. "But remember, we're not expecting to fight. Like I said, the Titans probably only patrol the outside and the main tunnels. There'd be no reason to go deeper. The site interests them, but in the end there are only records in there. It's low security, and in their shoes, I'd never expect an attack."

He ticked his head toward Tina.

"Everyone here is scared, I know. But we need runners, not fighters."

"Runners?" Piper asked.

"For all the tunnels and rooms we know about and all the ones we don't. We need to get in and out. That's what matters: speed and stealth. We don't need to be strong, tough, or brave. We need to be fast and quiet. Everyone here can run, and keep a low profile. God knows they're quiet enough in the lab."

For the third time, Piper looked at Tina. This time, she waved back and tried to smile. Tina was maybe five-three with practical short hair and glasses that were too small for her face.

"They're going to change shifts in ..." Cameron looked at his watch, which he'd had rebanded and kept faithfully wound. "Six minutes. And—"

"They punch a clock?"

"Actually, it took some time to figure that out," said Cameron, peeking around before spotting Andreus and Coffey maybe twenty feet away. "They seem to be watching a blade of light made as the sun passes behind a series of holes in the rock farther up. Today, it lines up in six minutes."

"They flew through space," Piper said, "and they tell time with rocks."

Cameron smiled. "They built a worldwide brain with rocks then started building pyramids. Just because we don't do it doesn't mean it's not advanced."

Piper eyed the Titans near the tunnels' mouths. They

were milling casually, like night watchmen going through the motions. It sure didn't look like the Astrals were expecting an attack — or whatever it was they were about to attempt.

"Nathan's footage shows a sort of slow regrouping every day when some Titans leave and others come to replace them. We should be able to get around *there*—" He pointed. "—and slide inside *there*."

"All of us."

Cameron nodded. "All of us."

"This big group of human meat."

"We only have to run and look. We brought this many people so we could break into groups and cover as much ground as possible in very little time. We need eyes. If Benjamin's right, there will be plenty of other relics here that nobody's told the public about, and it could be with any of them. Maybe in an old tunnel because he suspects there was something here before — something alien, from long ago, just like the temple under Heaven's Veil — that this was built to mate with. It may look like a dig. But if the Templars and their modern cousins moved this thing from where it was supposed to be and hid it from Astral eyes, it would have been maintained — kept somewhere accessible but hidden. We know what it looks like. *They* may even know what it looks like."

"If they've seen it," said Piper, "why wouldn't they know what it was, and that it should have been at Vail?"

Again, Cameron's eyes flicked away before returning. This time, Piper identified the mannerism. She knew him well: he was either lying, or about to.

"The Templars must've put it inside something else."

"So we're not looking for the thing in Benjamin's photo. We're looking for something else, with that inside?"

"No, we're looking for that."

"So the thing he showed us — that's the case, and the real device they want is inside it?"

"Right. Maybe. It's unclear."

"How did Benjamin find a picture of the case, if it's just a case?"

"You'd have to ask him."

Piper fixed Cameron with an assessing glance, but he was looking at his watch, at the Titans, at Nathan Andreus and Coffey.

"What are we really doing here, Cameron?"

Cameron didn't seem to hear her.

"Two minutes," he said.

# CHAPTER 56

Raj was sitting in one of the extra rooms off the fourth floor corridor, feet up, using an old business card to clean the undersides of his fingernails. He stopped between the ring and middle finger to look at the card. It was for a lawyer whose card declared *FAST SETTLEMENTS GUARANTEED.* Raj wondered at it. He'd found the card under the desk, but the building, like almost everything around Heaven's Veil, was new and had never been occupied by lawyers. There probably hadn't been any lawyers anywhere since before Astral Day, though Raj could imagine many jokes about lawyers attempting to sell their services to the planet's new overlords.

How the hell had that card ended up here?

Pondering the card's journey was more appealing than wondering what Meyer might do to him if his perimeter failed.

Maybe this was a blessing in disguise. The viceroy had beaten him up verbally, but on the bright side, he'd been giving those insulting commands to Raj, not Christopher. Christopher was *persona non grata,* apparently. Whom had the viceroy gone to when he needed security handled, even if he'd been kind of a dick about his faith in Raj's ability to handle it? Well, he hadn't gone to Christopher.

Not when Christopher and Terrence were the problem.

Raj had spent a fair amount of his time up here thinking about that. Outside the door, just twenty feet farther down the hallway, were the deceptively strong and impregnable double sapphire-glass doors leading into the network hub. There were three cops outside, all carrying sidearms and shotguns. Raj, who was forward thinking, had even found a gas mask for one of their belt clips, just in case the clever pair of Terrence and Christopher (whom Raj had seen in full jailbreaking mode back in the bunker) decided to smoke their way in. If they somehow got past the cops, there was the lock, which literally only Meyer and Raj could open with their palms. Their *live* palms. Raj had thought of that one, too. He didn't think Terrence was the type to hack a guy's hand off (or kill him) to open a door the cheater's way, but Christopher might. He'd suspected Christopher since the day he'd met him, and now Raj had been proved right.

He wondered what Lila would think of *that*. She'd always defended both men, and now they were about to pull something stupid and get themselves arrested (or, ideally, killed) in the process.

Terrence was just a spy? Terrence had been acting on Christopher's orders to infiltrate Piper Dempsey's group when Raj found him ... with Cameron Bannister, whom he'd also never really trusted? Yeah, right. The viceroy had seen through that bullshit as easily as Raj.

Raj stopped picking under his nails and listened. Someone was coming.

The someone revealed herself a few seconds later. Annoyingly, Heather had walked right into the off-hallway room where Raj had stationed himself as a backup, as if she'd known he was here all along.

"Hey, Beef Jerky."

Raj let his feet fall to the floor and sat up properly in the chair.

"I need to use one of the computers."

"I know you own two. Check your house."

"I can't get a signal. Terrence told me to find one with a hard line."

"There are several downstairs. You shouldn't even be up here."

Heather shrugged. "I live here, don't I?"

"No."

Heather walked closer. "I just want to check on something for Lila, okay?"

"Lila didn't tell me about anything. What is it?"

Raj could smell the bullshit. Especially since Meyer had basically warned him about this, almost exactly.

"It's a surprise, Kumar."

"So why are you up here? Seem like overkill, to use one of the nerve center machines to check a website."

Heather sat on the edge of his desk. "I don't need one of the computers. I need you."

Was she coming on to him? *While* insulting him? That wasn't possible. She must be bad at this.

"You're good at computers and stuff."

"I am, huh?"

"Computers and math."

"Uh-huh."

"Possibly outsourced tech support or customer service."

"Okay. Thanks. I'm busy here."

Heather looked down. "I can see that."

Raj stood. Heather moved, as if to block his way. That set Raj's nerves on high alert. His eyes narrowed, and he looked past Heather into the hallway. Where, he now thought, he'd just heard a small noise of indeterminate origin.

"What are you doing here?" He took a step to the right. Heather did the same, parrying to match him.

"Clara got one of her psychic flashes about some old kids' show featuring trains with fucked-up creepy faces. I need to see if I can figure out what it is."

Raj moved a step to the left. Again, Heather moved to block.

"I think it might be *Rapey the Train Engine*. Does that sound right to you?"

"Okay," Raj said. "Step aside."

"I found another kids' show where the characters look like sex toys. I say conspiracy. Thoughts?"

"Out of my way."

"You know what I could go for?" she said, now sounding nervous. "A game of backgammon."

Raj shoved Heather away and marched double-time to the hallway door.

At the network center doors, with the cops unconscious at his feet and a set of tools in his hands, was Terrence.

# CHAPTER 57

Meyer took the small device from Mo then wiped the thing's end before plugging it into to his ear. The guards all wore them on duty, and Meyer could access their protocols to give orders, but didn't normally listen. Raj trying to reach him through security guard channels made Meyer want to punch him.

"What?"

"You asked me to let you know if anyone tried to get into the network center," Raj said in his ear. Meyer could tell by his voice that the kid was smiling. What the hell did Raj have to smile about? He didn't get to be smug or self-satisfied. Not until he'd erased the fuckery of sending Reptars out without consulting anyone. Piper could have been killed. Meyer didn't care if she *had* stolen from him, *was* being used, and *might* think he was the enemy. Anyone who messed with Meyer Dempsey's people — whether he was a viceroy or not — was asking for a fist down their throat.

"So someone did."

"Terrence and Heather. Just like you thought they might. They had *tranquilizer darts*, if you can believe that, but I was here as a backup."

316

Meyer considered telling Raj to wipe the smile off his face because that's right, it *had* been Meyer's thinking, not Raj's. But telling him to stop smiling when Meyer couldn't see him would freak Raj out.

"My ex-wife, Heather?" He knew perfectly well which Heather, and didn't currently know any others.

"Y ... yes. You said you thought she might be—"

"Fine. I'll be right up." Reluctantly, he added, "Thanks."

Meyer handed the comm back to Mo. "You want help?" Mo asked.

"He said they knocked out the cops with darts. If he's calling, he cuffed the other two. Unless he's an idiot, which he is."

"That doesn't answer my question."

"I don't need help," Meyer said.

"Then how about props for embarrassing photo opportunities?"

Mo smiled, but Meyer left the room. He often volleyed with Mo, especially on the topic of idiotic underlings, but he wasn't feeling it. Everything felt backward.

He was allying with Raj against Christopher, who'd served him well for years.

He was doing what the Astrals would want him to do even though he was annoyed at the way they kept withholding information, as if *he* were the idiot.

He was about to send Heather away — his friend and (if he admitted it) soul mate — while clapping Raj on the back.

But Meyer had to do it. He could get Heather off easy. She had a history of doing dumb, impulsive things, and everyone knew it. But preserving their station mattered because not many people these days were truly safe, but the Dempseys were. He had Lila to consider, and his granddaughter. Plus, Trevor and Piper, who'd return once they came to their senses. It was fun to play with the rebels, but what happened once those ill-conceived acts of rebellion petered out? You came home to Meyer, who'd done what was necessary to keep the house of cards from collapsing.

He rounded the staircase on the third floor and heard the scampering of startled feet behind him. Then, unwelcome at this of all times, he heard Lila's voice.

"*Dad? Dad! Where are you going?*"

Meyer ignored her. He began taking the steps two at a time, determined to face whatever needed facing so he could avoid looking into his daughter's eyes.

Meyer reached the upstairs hallway and found Raj sitting on Heather's back, her face to the cool tile floor. Terrence was beside them, upright, in restraints. Three policemen were on the ground, facedown and drooling. Lila arrived at Meyer's side, panting from exertion. From the corner of his eye, Meyer saw her lance Raj with a look of hate.

"They tried to break in, just as you said they would," Raj said with an infuriating smile.

Lila ran to her mother, shoving at Raj, having to rock him a few times before he finally moved aside. Heather rolled, and Lila cradled her head like a child's, now down on her knees, sending that same disdain-filled look back at Meyer. He almost heard her say inside his mind: *Look what you've become. Look what we've become.*

Raj, annoyed at having been thrown from his perch on Heather's back, stood. He crossed to the viceroy, but Meyer's eyes were still locked on his daughter's.

Lila wasn't speaking. He couldn't hear her true thoughts, as he could hear the Astrals. But still he could sense the message in her look, clear as anything.

She seemed to say: *Traitor.*

Raj held out an unmarked silver cylinder. Terrence watched it change hands with jealous eyes.

"He had this," Raj said.

Meyer took the cylinder, feeling the weight of Lila's stare. Feeling the burden of Divinity's expectations. Knowing that

**318**

no matter what Lila thought and how much she might hate him, he'd done everything for them. For the family. For everyone's benefit, whether they appreciated it or not.

"He also had this," Raj added, handing over the tranquilizer pistol Terrence had used to incapacitate the guards. It was something new that Meyer had never seen — classically Terrence-modified to hold a clip so he'd be able to fire multiple darts without needing to reload.

Lila still sat with her mother, her shoulders rising and falling, brown eyes bolted to Meyer's.

*Traitor.*

Meyer took the weapon in his other hand. Then, still looking at Lila, he fired two darts into Raj's stomach.

Lila's eyes grew wide. Heather tried to sit up, speechless for the first time ever.

"Do it quickly," Meyer told Terrence, tossing the silver cylinder into his still-bound hands.

# CHAPTER 58

"Here," Andreus said.

He was talking to Trevor because Trevor had inexplicably taken the lead, but Cameron turned to look as well. The bald man held his hand out, indicating a passage in the rock that looked exactly like all the others.

"You're sure?" Cameron asked.

Andreus took a step toward Cameron. He probably wasn't trying to be intimidating, but he didn't seem able to help it. The step said, *How dare you question my judgment?* and had probably served him well over his years taming unruly followers, but Cameron found himself immune. They were three people with a mission, same as the other small groups running through the much larger, more carefully mapped tunnels. Andreus's quest was real, and the others were decoys. But that meant nothing. Everyone inside this hollowed-out mountain, from the moment they'd sneaked past the surprisingly (but not really surprisingly) easy-to-infiltrate perimeter, had proved his or her bravery. In here, Nathan Andreus was nothing special, and Cameron wouldn't take his word for anything without an excellent reason.

After a moment's challenging stare, Andreus held up his palm. For a moment, Cameron thought the man might strike him, but then he saw the smudged markings on his skin.

"Bird, bird, turtle, guy with a hat," Andreus said, apparently translating the legend B-B-T-GH he'd written on his hand. He pointed back toward where they'd come from. "The concealed door was right where Ben said the tablet put it. The first branch was bird, then bird again." He pointed above the mouth of the passage he'd indicated to Trevor, at a turtle carved in the rock. "Turtle." Then he tromped down the passage alone, and Cameron heard his voice add from farther down, "Guy with a hat."

Cameron shrugged at Trevor, who managed a smile in spite of his obvious nerves. They followed the warlord's voice to the short rock-walled passageway's end and found him pointing above a new — and apparently final — tunnel.

Cameron looked at the glyph above the door.

"I think the sun is setting behind him."

"*Guy with a hat,*" Andreus repeated, again pointing at the glyph. "Time?"

Cameron looked at his watch. "Three minutes. It's 4:17."

"Three minutes since we broke away."

"Since we broke into groups."

"Not when we broke away from Piper's group."

"Yes. Sorry. Three minutes from then." The large group had split immediately upon entering the front tunnel, having found the facility's interior surprisingly (but again, not surprisingly at all) deserted. There hadn't been enough tunnels at the first branch to justify Nathan, Cameron, and Trevor taking their own path, so they'd waited a bit then slipped away. Piper would assume they'd split later, when they'd reached another fork — though Cameron, for one, thought it was possible she might not notice at all.

Everyone had been nervous, including Piper. The facility was comprised of row upon row of tiny-drawered filing cabinets stuffed with microfilm, but they were all acting like a mothership could descend at any moment. Right now, everyone felt selfish. If Piper had noticed and was worried, she'd see them soon enough. If Benjamin's reading of the tablet was accurate (and so far, it had been), they'd find what they were looking for and rejoin the tour in ten minutes, maybe five.

"Okay," said Andreus. "I sure hope this is all there is, because my hand's out of symbols."

Cameron pushed past him into the tunnel, inexplicably irritated by Andreus's air of authority. This was his father's research. Only a handful of people could have translated the tablet, and Benjamin Bannister was one of them. Not Nathan Andreus. Not even the Astrals themselves.

"Your detector still on?" The passageway had narrowed, so Cameron had to turn both head and shoulders to ask.

"No," Andreus answered. "I figured we'd go on faith that the BB was with Benjamin instead of us."

"I didn't hear it making noise."

"It makes noise when detecting a signal."

"Any noise at all." The detector normally chirped and crackled with static. It could be silenced, of course, but they'd all nonverbally seemed to agree that in here, any sounds of life were good.

"There must not be any signals in here. Makes sense. We're in a goddamned mountain. I'll bet the BB signals can't even get out. It's probably recording to broadcast later."

"And your signal to Terrence about releasing Canned Heat?"

"Also prerecorded. I left a modified phone in the RV."

"So we need to do it on time, seeing as you can't change when it sends Terrence the signal."

"I may have overstated the timing. As long as we have

a signal to the open Internet within maybe five minutes of surfacing, we'll be able to broadcast whatever we manage to record of this thing we're looking for to your dad's buddies. And call for help if we need it."

Trevor's voice came from the rear. "Do you think we'll need help?"

Cameron was about to revolve on the spot and answer, but the passageway widened into a chamber and they could all see one another. For the first time, looking around the chamber, Cameron wondered how deep into the mountain they were. This part of the tunnel system was impossibly old, and there would be no ventilation. The thought made Cameron claustrophobic.

"Just making sure all bases are covered, Trevor," Cameron said.

"But if we had to escape ... just in theory ... how would we? You know, because you were talking about getting help. I mean, just curious."

Cameron resisted a strange impulse to kneel before Trevor as a way of conveying comfort. But that was absurd. Trevor would take it as pandering, and the boy was taller than him.

"Our friends the Templars took care of all of that," he said. "There are even exit instructions on the tablet. Lieutenant Coffey, Danika, and Benjamin know those instructions same as we do, and each of them is either with one of the other groups or in shouting distance. But remember, Trevor: They want us here. They know the object they lost isn't here. It's something they need to *get* what they lost."

Andreus seemed to have lost interest and had gone around a bend, farther into the chamber. Cameron heard him call back to them.

"What?" Trevor said.

Cameron wanted to see what Andreus had found, so he

walked backward a few paces then held up a finger, asking Trevor to wait.

Around the bend was a small, humble altar. On the altar was what looked like a small clay plate decorated with a swirl pattern. Andreus was holding up the printed image Benjamin had given each of them, comparing. They'd found it. It was here.

With the reverence he'd seen in Benjamin many times throughout his youth, Cameron picked up the plate. He held it in front of Trevor's eyes, using his index finger to indicate a complex set of grooves circling the rim, like the knurling on a coin's edge.

"A key," Cameron said.

Andreus gave him a questioning look, but Cameron was talking to Trevor.

"You asked what it was," Cameron continued. "The Templars didn't store the device they took from Vail here, but they did store this: a key needed to unlock — or possibly *activate* — the actual device, wherever it is."

"Possibly?" Trevor repeated.

"My father's the expert. I think he even knows where it is. But for now, I can just tell you one thing for sure."

Trevor raised his eyebrows.

"Whatever the Astrals lost and the Templars hid from them," Cameron said, slipping the plate into a satchel he'd prepared and carefully padded before leaving Moab, "it can't be used without this."

"I'll tell you another," said Andreus. "If the BB decides to inspect that bag of yours on the way out and finds what's in it, we're seriously fucked."

Cameron wanted to smirk at Andreus's paranoia, but he'd picked a bag with a tight-sealing zipper for exactly that reason. The BB could force its way in, but not without Cameron's knowledge.

"Okay," he said instead. "Then let's go."

Cameron led the way down the tunnel, suddenly eager to find the others, rescue them from their wild goose chases in the name of showmanship, and gather their group of ill-prepared intellectuals back home. There were still mysteries (how to inspect the key plate without the BB seeing, how to rid themselves of the BB, and how to find and disarm Thor's Hammer were only a few), but for now, the first big hurdle had been crossed.

Cameron stopped when there was a small, almost inaudible beeping sound to his rear.

He was thinking he'd imagined the noise when it chirped again.

Cameron turned to see Nathan Andreus — torturer, gang lord, conspirer with the enemy — staring at something in his hand with an expression of unabashed terror.

"What?" Cameron asked, feeling his heart beating harder as if it already knew. "What is it?"

Andreus held up the detector, which beeped again.

"The Astrals' little spy BB," he said, his voice disarmingly neutral. "It's coming right at us."

# CHAPTER 59

There was a noise from somewhere near Terrence's belt. Meyer looked at him with questioning eyes, and there was a moment where Terrence looked like he might pretend the noise hadn't come. But then he seemed to remember who'd opened the hub door, who'd tied Raj's hands with one of the policemen's zip ties, and who'd unbound his own. The viceroy had been on the wrong side for a long time and still might be now, in Terrence's mind. But all three of the room's occupants knew that if Meyer was playing a con at this point, it was so long that its duplicity failed to matter.

Meyer had broken them into the network center with his own palm, and Terrence had what he'd called Canned Heat in his hands.

Meyer wasn't sure if he'd done the right thing or not, but he was in with them for sure: lock, stock, and smoking barrel.

Without waiting for Meyer to ask about the noise, Terrence held up something that must have been another of his odd inventions. A communicator of some kind — maybe even the thing he'd sort of been told about by Divinity. The thing that allowed him to communicate with the other

326

group while the Astrals feigned ignorance.

"That was my signal. If we're going to install the virus, we need to do it now."

Thinking of the signal from outside Salt Lake City—from Piper and Trevor's group — made Meyer recall something that bothered him, though Divinity hadn't explained more than the basics. The Astrals knew what the other group was up to. Meyer had no idea what they planned to do about it, but instinct told him their knowledge was good for no one.

"You're in contact with them?" Meyer extended a hand, standing from his perch at the edge of what might be a rack of servers. Heather watched, uncharacteristically quiet. "Let me talk to someone."

"It's automated," Terrence said. "On a timer. They're underground now and can't send or receive signals."

Meyer had thought of that. Not even the Astrals could talk through a mountain. Given that Meyer seriously doubted ships couldn't get into the archive he'd seen through Divinity, it seemed the others were much safer now than in Moab. The irony.

"Why do you need to sync whatever you're doing with them?"

Again, Terrence regarded Meyer with doubt. Unlike Terrence and Christopher's disloyalty and the Moab crew's incursion into the Mormon archive, this wasn't something Divinity understood. The droids had inspected the cylinder once, and they'd been aware of its general function. But the specifics — as, strangely, with the details concerning a lot of mundane human technology — were still a mystery. Telling Meyer now would mean popping the last advantage Terrence's group had. Until he plugged his strange canister in to do its job, there was still a chance that Meyer was only pretending to have flip-flopped. He might be trying to get information the Astrals didn't have before flip-flopping back, and Terrence knew it.

Still, taking a very human leap of faith, Terrence's dark eyes — unshielded by sunglasses, for once — met Meyer's.

"What this does," he said, shaking the canister, "is something we're fairly sure the Astrals will be able to counteract once they see the way it works. The network will be open for a window, but not forever."

"And?"

Another assessing stare. He could refuse to answer or make something up, but Meyer would know if he lied. The Canned Heat was near its intended port, as if he might be preparing to shove it and run if Meyer's honor fell suspect.

"We need the window open when they come out. So they can transmit data other people need to help solve a problem." His jaw worked. "And because if they need help, an open network will help them get it."

Meyer looked at the canister. Heather and Terrence looked at Meyer.

"Do what you need to do," Meyer said.

Terrence stuck the end of the thing into a terminal port. A dialogue box appeared. He clicked around then entered something on the keyboard. A progress bar replaced the box as the software unpacked and began to do its work.

Heather stood while they waited. Meyer watched, her eyes on something else. Searching.

"Where's Raj?"

"By the d—"

Terrence had been about to say "by the doors." That's where Meyer had left him before binding his wrists. But Meyer looked over and saw the spot vacant.

"He was there," Terrence said.

Heather looked at Meyer. "Did you let him go?"

"I shot him. I've been here the whole time."

"But you touched him last."

"You *saw* me, Heather. When would I have let him go?"

"He's not there now."

**328**

"I can see that."

"Jesus Christ, Meyer. Why weren't you watching him?"

Meyer's mouth opened in disbelief. It was easy to forget that he was the viceroy, that he was feared, that they were all doing something they shouldn't be. Here was Heather, behaving like her usual bitch self, reprimanding him the way she always had back when they'd been married.

"He was right th—"

"Oh," Terrence interrupted. Meyer looked down at him, seeing him tapping the keyboard. "Oh, *shit.*"

"What?" Heather asked.

"No. No no no no ..."

"What the hell, Terrence?"

"No, you bitch." Terrence slapped the terminal with his palm. "No!"

"Will you just fucking say what's the matter?"

Terrence looked back, his face crushed with worry and loss. He pointed at the screen, filled with rapidly scrolling information in a white-on-black screen window that Meyer couldn't come close to deciphering.

"It's failing," Terrence said.

"What's failing?"

"The network. All of it."

"You killed the Internet?" Heather looked more annoyed than panicked. "How did you *kill the Internet?*"

"The Canned Heat. I thought I'd worked it out, but it's aggressive. The virus is only supposed to attack targeted sectors, and there's no way and *I thought of everything and* MOTHERFUCKER!"

His face clenched and he kicked the server bank, as if brute force would erase the mistake.

He looked at Meyer, his features grim. "We have to disconnect it. Cut it off. Unplug it from the network."

"Will that stop it?"

"It's all I know to try."

Meyer would have to take his word. He nodded curtly. "Then do it. Whatever you need."

"Where are the main fiber lines?"

"I have no idea."

"Or some sort of a data gate."

"Can't you just turn off the power?" Heather asked.

"Where?" Terrence ignored her.

"I ... I don't know."

"Who does?"

"Raj?"

"We have to find him. Heather, find him."

"*You* find him!"

Meyer and Terrence turned back toward Heather's irritated shout to find Raj by the door, his wrists unbound, flanked by two Titans and a pair of Reptars.

Beside them, visible from the corner of Meyer's eye, the terminal's screen flashed as the network began eating itself alive.

# CHAPTER 60

"Wait a minute," Piper said, turning. Benjamin was behind her, along with a few of the rebel camp survivors and a tech she didn't recognize. "Where's Trevor?"

Benjamin looked back, but he only shrugged.

"And Cameron. He was here too. And that bald guy. Andreus."

"I think they broke off," Benjamin told her. "There was another tunnel."

Piper didn't think so. First of all, she was sure there hadn't been another tunnel. The Mormon Genealogical Archives had turned out to be grand but boring. An accountant's wet dream of a secret hideout. Buried in a mountain and mysterious, but still just a series of identical rooms packed with endless rows of floor-to-ceiling filing cabinets, stretching from one end of a room to the other, filled with small, square, carefully labeled drawers. She'd pulled out a drawer or two. They were long and narrow, filled with thousands of sheets of microfilm.

The place simply wasn't the labyrinth they'd all been led to believe it was.

There didn't seem to be anywhere old enough to house

Benjamin's codex relic.

And there certainly hadn't been a branching tunnel since she'd last noticed Trevor and Cameron. The archive's floor plan wasn't that complicated, despite its underground location. She could even see another group down the wide tunnel, milling about more of the endless filing rooms ahead as if on a slightly earlier tour.

"They were right behind us. In this group," Piper told Benjamin.

"I told them to split off."

"When?"

"Originally. The plan was to break into a bunch of smaller groups."

"But when were they supposed to split off?"

"When they ... I'm not sure. But I know I can't see them, so clearly they did."

"Could they be lost?" asked the nameless tech.

Piper looked at the tech, then at the group farther down the hall. Impossibly, someone from the other group waved. Because this was nothing at all. The entire errand was one big, useless dead end.

"I couldn't get lost in here," Piper said, peering into the obvious, wide-open tunnel.

"Maybe they went into one of the rooms," Benjamin said.

That sounded unlikely. The rooms held no interest. Unless one of the filing cabinets turned out to be fake and there was an ancient trove behind it, Piper couldn't imagine what would have drawn Cameron's attention enough to linger. Benjamin had made this sound like a hike through the past. He'd suggested they might find old passages behind new ones, littered with relics that would make a museum director drool. But this was something between a vault and an office, nothing more.

Piper pushed past Benjamin, headed back the way

they'd come. Benjamin shuffled behind, protesting. Finally, after realizing they were rejoining other groups with similar discoveries of nothing, Piper met the scientist's eye.

"You know where they went," she said.

"Maybe into one of the rooms," he repeated. But Benjamin was a terrible liar.

Piper gave the other members of her group a look then pulled him aside.

"What's going on here, Benjamin?"

"What do you mean?"

"We uprooted the entire lab to run around in here. There's nothing."

"I guess I made a mistake."

"We didn't have to create a distraction to get in. We didn't have to pick a lock. We ducked behind some rocks and came inside — and now that we're in here, there's nothing. Nobody at all."

"It's just an archive," Benjamin said, his lie becoming more apparent with each passing second.

"You said this was one of the places the Astrals made sure to occupy when they showed up. That Andreus guy has all sorts of footage. But they just walk around outside? I swear I thought one of them glanced over and saw me outside then looked away."

"We've been lucky."

"You didn't expect to find the codex here, did you?"

"What? Of course I did."

Benjamin was squirming, his eyes darting around, uncomfortable.

"Why aren't you telling me the truth, Benjamin? You and Cameron both."

"Of course I'm—"

"You knew there was nothing here. Nothing for us to—"

"Shh!"

Piper's head cocked. Her eyebrows bunched. They

were away from the group, and she'd been softly talking. If Benjamin feared losing face — most everyone seemed to have made their way back into one big harmless, useless knot — her inquiries wouldn't do it. What was the point of shushing?

Piper fixed her gaze on Benjamin, biting her lip. Rather than trying to worm more lies out of him, she simply marched farther down the hall toward the facility's front, without bothering to stay quiet. The place was theirs. They could throw a party, and the Astrals would supply the punch.

Piper stopped when she reached their first branch, hands on her hips. There were some final stragglers down the last passageway she hadn't been able to see from her old position, but now they were coming forward to join the others. Trevor and Cameron had been with them, so where had they gone? Her first instinct was worry, but a look at Benjamin nixed it. They weren't lost. Their fearless leader knew exactly where they were, but he wasn't telling.

"What's really going on here, Benjamin?" Piper was loud enough for almost everyone to hear.

He flinched, looked around, then rushed forward, holding up his hands.

There was a cracking sound. Piper looked over to see an invisible seam crack the wall open. A hidden tunnel made from the kind of hewn stone they'd all been told to expect but hadn't found lay behind it. Inside the tunnel were Andreus, Trevor, and Cameron.

Something shot past Piper's line of sight. At first, she thought it was something someone had thrown, then realized the object stopped, hovering between her and Cameron as the trio emerged from the tunnel, their eyes wide, apparently still feeling the fear Piper had long ago lost from her shoulders.

The object was a tiny silver sphere, about half the size of a pearl.

After its moment of hesitation, it buzzed around Cameron like a light-speed hornet. It had no face and made no noise, but Piper knew shock and anger when she saw it.

There was a small noise of ripping fabric. Piper and Cameron looked down to see small movements inside of the bag slung around Cameron's shoulder. There was another small ripping sound, and the BB re-emerged, again stationing itself between their faces.

Cameron's wide eyes met Piper's, his face flushed.

"We have to go," he managed to say.

Alarms screamed from every direction.

# CHAPTER 61

Titans and Reptars watched Raj bind Heather's and Terrence's wrists. Meyer shook him away when he tried to tie him. Heather thought Raj would force the issue, but he didn't. That gave her a sliver of hope — the idea that if Meyer remained free under the guards' eyes, they might yet survive to fight another day — but it was only a spark. Meyer wasn't a runner, and Reptar peacekeepers were fast. Free hands meant little. They were giving Meyer the Viceroy's dignity of walking out unrestrained, but that didn't mean he wasn't in custody.

As they walked down the main stairway, Heather thought about how glad she was that Meyer had sent Lila off after shooting Raj. How glad she was that Lila was probably in her room with Clara instead of being led away with her parents. And, as the cherry atop a bitter sundae, that Clara hadn't seen a thing.

Except that Clara, Heather knew, probably saw everything anyway.

Meyer paused when they reached the front lobby. He didn't stop moving and wait for the others to notice him. Meyer moved to the group's front — ahead of Raj and even

336

the Astrals — before ceasing his feet and challenging the others to run into him.

Raj recovered too close, barely avoiding crashing into Meyer's chest. He stepped to the side and brushed fussily at his shirt and the canvas undershirt beneath — thick enough, as it turned out, to keep all but the darts' tips from breaking his skin.

"We're not walking them out like this," he announced.

Raj looked at Meyer in disbelief. Heather wanted to laugh, despite her bound wrists. Being caught in the middle of intergalactic treason didn't stop Meyer from showing Raj who was boss.

"Them?" Raj repeated.

"Heather is mother to my granddaughter. Even walking Terrence out in restraints shows unrest in the viceroy's mansion at a time when we can't afford to appear unsettled, given the recent turmoil. Many Heaven's Veil citizens saw that, and right now we can't afford to—"

Raj straightened.

"Who are you talking to?" He looked at the Titans, enormous but still so blandly polite. The Reptars had their mouths closed and were quiet, seeming to behave in deference to the sanctity of the viceroy's residence. Heather supposed both classes of aliens must understand human speech, but neither spoke. Meyer talked to the Astrals through his mind somehow. This posturing meant nothing.

"Not to you, Raj," Meyer said.

Raj shook his head, disbelieving. He turned to the first Titan, who seemed to cordially nod.

"The viceroy is under arrest," Raj said. "As are these two. As Guard Commander, I hereby order you to take them away or whatever you do with criminals, when you send down shuttles and ... well, do whatever. And as systems administrator, I can report that the viceroy and his accomplices have not only breached a secure area—"

"Using my authorized palm print," Meyer added.

"In order to install malicious software into the system that has already caused irreparable damage to—"

"Damage that you were too busy with us to worry about," Meyer said. "Which is a shame, since protecting our systems is your job."

Raj jabbed a finger toward the door, glaring at the Titan. "Take them away."

There were footsteps from Heather's side. She turned to see Mo Weir, Meyer's aide, approaching without any hurry.

"What's going on here?" he asked.

Meyer looked at Mo then at the Titans. Finally, his eyes settled on Terrence, and Heather saw him make a decision. A normal person would feel bad about what Heather realized he was about to do, but Meyer believed in big rights and big wrongs, and the small ones to match. It was always fine to commit a small wrong in the service of a larger right … even if that right benefitted mainly Meyer and those he cared about while sacrificing others. He'd done such things for their entire marriage. Heather hated how much it had always turned her on. He was willing to make hard decisions, and make unfortunate sacrifices when there was no other way.

"Heather and I caught Terrence doing something to infiltrate the house system, which has since spread into the city network," he said.

The overhead lights flickered as if in agreement. Heather had no idea if the network's failure would kill the city's power, but it might be possible. Their computers would stop being able to connect to other computers, and those still wired in (or connected over the air) might be irreparably damaged. Phones would stop working. They'd be cut off — an island in the middle of hostile outlands.

Terrence glared at Meyer but said nothing. He must realize, Heather thought. Someone had to take the fall, and he was half there already. Lying about Heather and Meyer's involvement wouldn't change his fate, but still she could see Terrence's resentment as it bored into Meyer — as it bored into her.

"That's not true," Raj said.

"Take him to confinement. Let me know when it's done."

*"That's not what happened!"* Raj put his face close to the nearest Titan's. "You saw! You were there! They were all around the terminal, all three of them! They're all in this together. *He's a traitor!"*

Meyer gave Mo an eye-rolling smile. "He's misinterpreting my talk with Terrence upstairs."

Mo's returning look said, *Oh, that silly Raj.*

Raj was staring, stewing, boiling hot. His already dark complexion reddened. He didn't seem to know where to aim his plea — at the Astrals, who should have seen what was right in front of their faces, or Mo Weir, who'd never liked Raj any more than Meyer or Heather had.

"Take him," Mo told the Astrals, pointing at Terrence, "but leave them." He flicked his finger between Meyer and Heather.

One of the Titans widened his eyes slightly — a look Heather had come to interpret as, "Are you sure?"

Mo nodded. "Ms. Hawthorne is a ... well, she's a character. They have a complicated history."

The Titan continued listening, making no sign that he understood the subtleties of either "character" or "complicated history."

"We'll detain her," he said. "I'll let you know if further action is needed."

Raj looked ready to leap from his skin. "Are you kidding me? You're *letting them go?* You can't let them go! Don't you know who I am? *Didn't you see what they were doing?"*

The Titans made short, simultaneous nods. The Reptars'

currently yellow eyes flicked toward Heather, but they didn't move or make any of their terrible noises. Then all four, with Terrence in tow and Raj following, remonstrating like an angry Rumpelstiltskin, walked through the front door to what Heather now saw was a waiting shuttle inches above the lawn.

When they were gone, Mo looked at Heather then turned to Meyer. "Everything okay then, boss?"

Meyer nodded. "I'll handle her. Thanks, Mo."

Mo curtly nodded then walked back the way he'd come.

Meyer reached into the drawer of a hallway side table and removed a small pair of scissors. He snipped Heather's plastic tie and met her eyes.

Outside, the shuttle rose from the lawn, taking Terrence away.

"We count to fifty," Meyer told Heather, taking her hands. "Then we run."

# CHAPTER 62

The room came alive with Titans, surrounding them in an enormous semicircle, having poured from dozens of unseen rooms and offices. Cameron was reminded of gophers rising curiously from their holes — except that instead of gophers, the just-now-diminishing alarm inside the archive had attracted the attention of scores of bland-faced, albino, hairless bodybuilder accountants. An odd combination, and plenty intimidating. But this had always been their worst-case scenario, and Benjamin had thought of everything.

The Titans could call for reinforcements, but the tunnels were still at the group's back. They could pile in and run. Benjamin's analysis of the tablet had given them an escape route that the leaders — including Cameron — had memorized. It was a route that the Templars who'd built this vault's predecessor had expanded between Astral visits, without bothering to let their intergalactic partners know.

The ring of Titans moved closer. Slowly.

"It's okay," Cameron whispered to Piper. "Titans don't attack. They can't."

"Shuttles," was her reply.

Cameron nodded toward the exit, where he could see daylight teasing through an encroaching line of white giants. "Shuttles can't get in here. The doors are too small."

"They'll shoot their way in. They'll—"

Cameron took her arm, silencing Piper before tugging her gently backward. Benjamin was shooing people toward the concealed tunnel, but the door had closed and nobody, yet, had summoned the nerve to break the stalemate by reaching to open it.

"We have to go."

"Where?" She eyed the domed entrance beyond the Titans.

"The tunnels we came out of. There's another exit."

"They'll come after us."

Behind them, Andreus was reaching for the door, never moving his eyes from the Titans. The room and passageway were large. The hidden rooms the Titans had spilled from — inside which they'd apparently been hiding so the groups could do their work, until their deception was uncovered — were kissing the edges. Andreus could open the door right now. Cameron imagined that Titans could sprint, but it was hard to believe they would ... or if, once they caught up, the intruders would get more than a stern shake of a disapproving finger.

They could block their way, though, and push them around.

They could grab them then call for Reptars.

Cameron and Andreus had played that scenario out, too: how long, once a signal was sent, would it take for reinforcements to arrive?

Minutes, surely.

But it would be enough time to reach the tunnels and lose them down further hidden doorways and labyrinthine passages.

Cameron looked back. Andreus's hand was on the

concealed door's latch.

"Let's go," he said. "Hurry. Before they call for help."

Cameron gently nudged Piper and turned toward the door. His skin prickled, sensing something behind them that couldn't be heard or seen or felt.

Around the room, white-skinned Titans were bending at the waist, touching their hands to the ground, beginning to change.

Cameron watched their limbs elongate. Their movements become more insectile. They grew the long torsos of animals, their skin now black scales laced with a haunting blue glow.

Every Titan in the room turned into a Reptar and started to purr.

Then the screaming began.

# CHAPTER 63

Out the back door.

Across the lawn.

Past Heather's small house, which she'd so resented.

There was a rear guard house, but Meyer raised his hand to the man inside with his usual charming smile. The guard didn't look at them twice. Why would he? Meyer was the viceroy. He could leave his house with whomever he wanted, and take them wherever he pleased.

They didn't run. Meyer didn't want to take any of the home's many vehicles because he preferred to stay nimble, and vehicles could box you in — something Piper had vividly described to Heather from their time on a Chicago expressway when the Astrals were still on their way. Nor did he want to run because flight was an admission of guilt. So they walked. Fast. Staying out of sight.

Heather let him lead but felt their actions amounted to trying to have their cake and eat it too. Meyer had come over to Terrence's side in the end — humanity's side, really — but he was still proceeding on viceroy's eggshells, hoping his authority might protect him. They couldn't stay in the mansion (that house of cards was top heavy; Mo Weir

344

had either been protecting his man or genuinely ignorant, though Raj would find plenty of evidence to damn them eventually), but they weren't yet fugitives.

They were in that curious in between: something not quite rebel and not quite sympathizer, not quite complicit and not quite insurgent. They had to keep moving, knowing they could never return, trying to find their way out and into the wilderness beyond the fences — where being world famous as Heaven's Veil's viceroy was a detriment rather than an asset.

But they could worry about that later. For now, there was only flight, guilt, and cold sweat.

Maybe a quarter-mile from the fence, they were almost sideswiped as a motorcycle screeched into the street ahead. The rider dismounted then removed his helmet. He drew a pistol from a holster and centered it on Meyer's chest.

*Raj.*

Meyer raised his hands. Heather could see the lack of compromise in Raj's eyes. Meyer wouldn't be talking his way out of this one. They had to flee, or they'd be arrested then put on trial for treason for sure. The other option was being shot dead.

"I never had a chance, did I?" Raj said.

Meyer's head cocked between his raised hands. Whatever he'd expected Raj to say or do, that wasn't it.

"If none of this had happened, you'd never have accepted me as Clara's father. You'd have pretended I didn't exist."

Meyer stammered the beginning of a response, but Raj went on.

"I tried to protect her while you were gone. After you abandoned her. I did my best, but it wasn't good enough. Just like I wasn't good enough for you even before you knew about the baby. Just like you wanted to leave me behind, before Lila forced you to take me. But I always did what was right. Even after people broke in, and everyone made friends with the intruders. The same people who betrayed you, before you turned on the rest of us. The same people who, I'm pretty sure, included the man who slept with your wife."

Heather looked at Meyer's face. Meyer Dempsey was never at a loss for words. Meyer Dempsey was never bested in conversation. *Never.* But he was speechless now.

"I always wanted to help. Always tried to protect this family. I kept the guard even while you ignored it. I played second fiddle to Christopher even though I was supposed to outrank him. And when the chips were down, it was me — not Christopher — who kept stepping up. When Piper went missing. When they were plotting against you. When they did exactly what you said they'd do with the network center, and I dutifully reported it just as you'd asked."

Raj's eyes bored into Meyer's. The gun was rock steady, aimed at his chest. Heather remembered a few Raj gunshots gone awry, hilarious in the past like a best-of bloopers reel. But there wasn't a chance of him missing this time.

Her eyes searched the street. There were a few bricks in a pile near an adjacent building, but they were just bricks. If she went for them, he'd turn and shoot her.

"I'm going to watch you burn, viceroy," Raj snarled.

Meyer, seeming to sense futility, tensed for a pointless fight. Heather saw it happen, but Raj somehow missed it, his glare intent upon Meyer's face. It was a stupid, stupid thing to consider, the gun leveled as it was.

Heather was about to shout for Meyer to knock it off — blowing his cover to Raj but saving his life — when Meyer struck. He did it when Raj's eyes flicked toward a sound down the street, gaining a partial second's advantage. But it wasn't enough, and Raj wasn't close enough to grab or strike.

Meyer lunged forward.

Raj took his shot.

**346**

In the moment of shock that followed, Heather leaped for her brick — with all the fury of impending, righteous loss — and smashed it into the back of Raj's head.

Raj collapsed, unconscious.

Heather rolled Meyer over, down on her knees in the street, finding her hands wet with spreading blood, in time to see him form two final words before dying.

Meyer didn't make sounds, but she could read his lips just fine.

The last words she'd have expected from the great Meyer Dempsey's final breath.

"Love you."

# CHAPTER 64

The Reptars came for them.

Cameron was breathless beside Piper, staring toward the advancing horde of black, panther-like shapes, his breath leaving shallow and fast. His hand, on her arm, had gone slack.

The nearest of them leaped. It moved shockingly fast, scuttling across the space like a spider. Its mouth opened, revealing concentric semicircles of needle teeth. The inside glow that bled between the creature's scales shone brighter within its throat. Piper stood frozen, seeing how its mouth seemed to disengage past 180 degrees, the top of its head becoming invisible as it presented only tongue and teeth.

The thing gave its rattling purr as it came forward, its Titan reticence entirely gone. It struck at one of the rebel survivors, Taylor, and tore her arm off at the shoulder. She screamed, her motions jostling Andreus from the only partially ajar doorway.

They came. *En masse*, they came.

No hesitation. The Reptar that had started with Taylor finished her off, its bite ripping the head from her shoulders. Her friend, Olivia, battered stupidly at its body, but her ministrations were cut short when a second Reptar ripped her in half at the waist.

Cameron yanked Piper away, dragging her through throngs of humans and black alien limbs whirring like the churning blades of a food processor. Blood sprayed Piper's face, her bare arms, her chest. She saw Ivan ripped apart in front of her then nearly lost her footing as his blood drenched the concrete underfoot.

They were headed the wrong way, sprinting to duck behind a truck left in the entry cavern following its final delivery. Cameron pulled her down, wrapping his arm around her from the back, clamping his blood-streaked hand over her mouth without delicacy. The air left her lungs.

The group had dispersed. The door to the tunnels was still ajar, but Piper had no idea if anyone had managed to get through. The first Reptar — the one that had ripped Taylor and Olivia apart as if holding a grudge — had panicked the group. Maybe its desertion was good. Right now, Reptars seemed occupied with slashing their party to pieces and were ignoring the unused doorway — a positive development if anyone hoped to use it without being followed like snakes chasing mice through their furrows.

"They're shapeshifters," Cameron said, breathing heavy, his eyes bulging with fright. "Titans. Reptars. It's just an illusion. All this time, they've been able to change from one to the other."

*Maybe*, Piper thought. But the ability to shift forms was something no human had ever seen and lived to report. It was a secret the Astrals had kept carefully guarded — pretending to be harmless Titans at all costs instead of revealing their nature. Surprising the Astrals into changing now meant that before today, nobody had seen them angry.

No one would be leaving alive.

"We have to reach the tunnels," Cameron said, his panic apparently forgetting that he'd dragged them *away* to hide behind the truck.

With a tremendous crash, their hiding place was torn into the air. Piper saw three Reptars behind the truck, all with their front limbs up as it flipped through the air in a tight spiral and struck the concrete ceiling, making rain from shattered pebbles. It crashed back down as Cameron leaped atop Piper and drove her to the ground.

One of the three beasts turned then shot after a male lab tech — Piper couldn't tell who. He fell apart like sliced meat. With horror, Piper saw Danika with her hands shielding her face behind the fallen tech. Her eyes met Piper's before the thing impaled her with one of its claw limbs.

The two remaining Reptars over Piper and Cameron reared like horses then came down just feet away. Both opened their mouths to purr then flicked their heads upward as something heavy struck the one in front. Piper's eyes followed the object's trajectory (it turned out to be a small tractor tire, pulled from somewhere on a gantry) above and saw Benjamin with his arms out, post throw. Charlie was beside him in his usual buttoned shirt and bland tie, a solid right-hand man to the end.

The struck Reptar turned then jumped upward in two giant bounds. It made quick work of the climb, on the gantry in seconds. Benjamin and Charlie were already sliding down a ladder like firemen. The thing followed, but at the bottom its eyes lighted on Tina, the tech Piper had seen earlier. It went through her like mown grass as Charlie and Benjamin dove behind a pile of boxes.

The final Reptar struck, charging them with a wide open mouth, unhinged like the one from before. The alien looked like the head of a hairbrush: a large, flat oval studded with spines sharp as knives. It shoved toward them, but Cameron had scrambled for a push broom in the corner. The thing had a heavy metal handle, and Cameron jammed it into the Reptar's mouth. The creature bit on the pole, momentarily stymied, but the skin on Cameron's right hand was flayed as it brushed one of the razor-sharp teeth, skin hanging in a flap, a torrent of blood spilling down his arm.

Piper spun toward a loud banging and saw Cameron wrestling with the Reptar. It was a shotgun report, from one of the few large weapons they'd brought. Nathan Andreus turned after his shot and shoved the shotgun's barrel practically down a new Reptar's throat. There was a new report, and a blue-black spray covered the wall behind it as he pulled the trigger.

Piper waited for Andreus, having cleared himself a circle, to aid Cameron's rescue. Instead, he slipped through the tunnel doorway, followed by Coffey.

She pulled the door closed behind them, leaving everyone else to die.

Cameron was weakening. The Reptar's strong jaws were bending the bar, and it was backing up to strike anew, from a different angle. But with Coffey and Andreus gone, nobody had more than a small-caliber sidearm except for Trevor, who in a fit of panic Piper realized, she hadn't seen since this all started.

There was a jolt. She looked over to see Cameron rolling the Reptar aside, somehow besting it in a wrestling match. All of sudden, Cameron was winning, having beaten the monster because it was inexplicably dead, or dying. Something massive and sharp had been driven through its eye. She looked up to see Benjamin standing over the Reptar, his chest out like a proper savior.

Charlie was running up behind Benjamin, shouting, panicking, not giving Benjamin credit for his kill and his son's rescue. But Benjamin saw none of it; he smiled down at Cameron and said, "Bet you didn't think your old man could—"

Too late, Piper, still on the ground, realized why Charlie had been running. The truck had fallen back into place, once more shielding them from the rest of the room. A second unseen beast had sneaked up behind Benjamin.

Benjamin's face changed from triumphant to confused. The Reptar ripped through him and started to chew.

Cameron and Piper were mostly to their feet when it happened. Cameron, his face shocked, tried to jump on the beast, but Charlie struck him like a linebacker, his moderate frame easily trumping Cameron's slight one. The pair struck the ground, all three of them now mostly around to the other side of the flipped truck. They couldn't see the Reptar or Benjamin's body, which was a blessing. But they could see the rest of the space, and that was a curse.

Piper had lost track of any gunshots, but she could see two or three dead Reptars. By contrast, she saw scads of dead humans — or, at least, *pieces*. There were arms and legs and torsos and heads, indistinct chunks that could've been anything. Some of the Reptars were finishing off the few remaining humans remains; the rest were leaping across the room like apes in cages. Charlie had knocked them behind a kind of standing desk — possibly a check-in station for incoming vehicles — but between them and the door Coffey and Andreus had sneaked through were twenty feet or so of gore-streaked open floor.

Cameron was still trying to rise and take his revenge. Charlie slapped him.

"Don't be an idiot!" he snapped with more emotion than Piper had ever heard from him. "Don't thank him by jumping into the same thing's mouth!"

Cameron's eyes cleared. Charlie pointed at the garage-bay-like doors to the outside, clotted with patrolling Titans-turned-Reptars. Beyond them were the heavy metal bodies of waiting shuttles, ready to clean up anything hoping to flee.

When he was sure Cameron and Piper saw what had happened outside, Charlie pointed at the concealed door in the room's wall.

"We all know the way, through tunnels they probably don't know anything about. Your father's final helping hand. Don't insult him by not taking advantage."

Piper wanted to say, *Like Coffey and Andreus took advantage by leaving us all behind?* But she stopped herself and nodded. Cameron, making his face grim but settled, nodded too.

"They're heading to the doors. They know we're mostly finished." Charlie pointed again. It was true; the Reptars were falling into a slow patrol, apparently looking for loose ends. No one was left. Piper wanted to believe Trevor had made it out somehow, but she didn't see how.

"Stay low. Now," Charlie commanded.

Cameron went first. When the way seemed clear, he waved to the others to follow. He made the door in seconds, flinching whenever one of the Reptars purred while crossing nearby, barely seen. He looked around again before opening it then waved Charlie in, followed by Piper.

She moved to comply, but something had her leg. Piper turned to see it in the clawed appendage of a Reptar that had been hiding, waiting, maybe knowing the door was there all along.

It moved to strike, its mouth open and gut churning. Cameron had been frozen; he moved his arm for some futile reason but wasn't close enough. Piper tried to curl up and protect her middle.

Cameron stretched. The door yawned open as his hand dragged it. Inside, Piper could see Charlie, the moment frozen, his mouth open in a shout, his bug eyes wide.

A shot ripped through the now mostly quiet space as the thing's head exploded.

"Trevor," she breathed, noticing him more than her own salvation. "Thank God you're—"

Every Reptar turned at the shot. A grim expression crossed Trevor's face, and he raised a foot to kick her hard in the chest, into Cameron's arms as they tumbled backward against Charlie, through the open doorway.

She had time to see Trevor's eyes meeting hers as at least five of the beasts descended on him at once, all teeth and claws and fury.

Cameron closed the door, latching it somehow from the inside.

Charlie, too close to Piper's ear in the small, rock-lined space, shouted for her to run.

So she did, leaving acres of death behind her.

# CHAPTER 65

It took hours to find the way out.

Cameron's mind kept wanting to dwell on his father's death, but he wouldn't allow it. The emotion was too raw, and if there was one thing Cameron Bannister had learned throughout his life, it was how to bury uncomfortable feelings about his father.

But Benjamin hadn't just been Cameron's dad, he'd also been the group's best historical mind. The last of their hope might have died with him. Charlie was an extremely competent research scientist, but his focus was on the science, not the history. He'd followed Benjamin on many of his later adventures, but his focus had been on lichens, carbon dating of artifacts, how acids might have been used in the Queen's Chamber of the Great Pyramid to send out some sort of energy beacon. Charlie didn't know half of what Benjamin had — information essential to finding Thor's Hammer before the Astrals.

But most of all, Cameron tried to be strong for Piper.

Piper was usually an open book, but the final seconds she'd glimpsed of the Cottonwood archive had killed her emotions like a cut connection. Cameron didn't like it. Her big, blue eyes rimmed with stubborn tears that refused to fall. He tried to hug her or offer a strong arm to lean on when they stopped to rest, but she shook him away and sat alone. He tried talking to her (about idle things, like the types of rock the tunnels had been bored through), but she stayed mostly silent. When he asked her what was wrong — a stupid question if there'd ever been one — Piper said "Nothing." An answer to match his inappropriate query.

Still, Cameron told himself that staying tough was his job. It was always easier to maintain strength for others than to face the demons inside. That's probably why Cameron, on his band's tours through so many borderline places later in life, had always made room for charity. Helping others fostered a sense of control. It made a person feel that some day, he might find the strength to help himself.

He shut down, and so did she. Charlie was as unreadable as ever — perhaps, for once, a necessary rock amid the storm. Over the past few years (even before Astral Day), the recently slaughtered had composed the entirety of Charlie's existence. He'd interacted with no one else. Even Cameron and Piper had been relative latecomers. Now they were gone, save the few who'd stayed to attend the Moab lab while they were away. Cameron doubted that the facility had survived the Astrals' anger.

It sounded as though the Reptars had quickly broken the latch on the hidden door and made their way into the tunnels behind them, but spent minutes to do so. By then, they'd made it through two more intricately concealed doors in the rock. Cameron had quietly thanked the Templars, the Freemasons, the Mormons — whoever had earned his gratitude.

After that, they could only move forward.

They found Andreus and Coffey about thirty minutes after entering the tunnels. To their credit — and contradicting the cowardly way Cameron felt they'd left — the pair had found the first of the linked chambers throughout the tunnels and waited for anyone who might follow. When Cameron told them that no others would be coming, they all left together.

The air was stale. The way was hard and dirty. Whoever had made the system had courteously pocked it with air shafts, like holes punched in a jar's lid made to trap a butterfly. But since that day, several of the tunnels had caved slightly, and twice they had to move rocks one by one before they could proceed.

Finally, they reached an underground lake. After some searching, Cameron found a hole in the wall under the water's surface. All five of them waded in and moved through it, thinking it another of the tunnel system's many sumps. But this time, instead of coming out in another tunnel past a low-hanging obstruction, they emerged into muted sun in the small pocket of a little lake near the mountain.

Piper, who surfaced just after Cameron, flinched back and looked upward. He sympathized; they'd been assuming for much of the journey that the only reason the shuttles weren't leveling the mountain to find and kill them was because the Astrals cared slightly more about the archive than the escapees. Instead, their thinking went, the shuttles would simply patrol the mountain and wait. Eventually, the remainders would burrow out ... and be dealt with.

But there was nothing above them.

After a while, they climbed onto the shore and into the sun to dry in what remained of the day's heat. When dark came, they ventured away from the rock to look around, and waited just far enough into the desert that retreat into the tunnels – if necessary – would be possible.

But nothing happened. There were no Reptars. No Titan patrols. No shuttles. No motherships.

Their final egress had been rushed. It felt possible that the Reptars either hadn't seen them dash through the door or (and this seemed more likely) simply had lost that information in the day's shuffle. The Astrals, after all, had proved that they weren't infallible. Sometimes, your average Titan-turned-Reptar soldier simply forgot, or didn't bother to report.

They were — so the expression went — only human.

The idea gave Cameron an ounce of hope as they slept through the night, huddled for warmth. If they could be tricked, defeat was possible. And if Cameron, Piper, Charlie, Nathan, and Jeanine Coffey had been lucky once, they could get lucky again.

If the key Cameron still held unbroken in his satchel could activate the Thor's Hammer device, perhaps it could deactivate it, too.

In the morning, Andreus held up his cell phone and waved it around, every motion betraying futility. He repeated the motions with the BB detector. He'd kept both dry inside a sealed bag in his backpack. They worked. But there was nothing to detect.

"No network means no help," said Andreus.

"And Terrence?" Cameron asked.

Andreus shrugged. "He must not have made it."

"Can you contact him on ... on whatever you were using before?"

Andreus pointed at his dead cell phone. "No network," he repeated, "means no help."

What Andreus didn't bother to say because they all knew it was that no help didn't just mean help for the five of them, in terms of finding safety. It also meant help in solving the Thor's Hammer puzzle. It meant help in terms of reaching Lila, Clara, and Meyer, who were the only remaining survivors in the world Piper likely still cared about. It meant help in terms of knowing anything that might be happening in Heaven's Veil, Moab, or anywhere at all.

Nathan sat on a rock, looking defeated. Coffey put her hand on his shoulders. Seeing the tenderness of two ruthless people sank Cameron deeper into his helpless despair.

There was nothing left in the world. Nothing but the quest.

Cameron stood. Piper looked up, her enormous blue eyes unfathomably sad, yet somehow more normal than they'd been throughout the exodus.

He extended his hand. Piper took it.

They walked, passing Charlie, Nathan, and Jeanine on their rocks. Headed vaguely south, toward Moab and whatever of his father's records might have survived.

"Where are you going?" Andreus asked.

Cameron didn't turn.

"The only place we can go," he said. "To try and save the world."

# CHAPTER 66

"You *do* understand, correct?" the woman asked.

Alpha straightened, attempting to heed the strange way the being in front of him was communicating. Beta and Omega were flanking his sagging body, still holding his arms.

Alpha looked down. The hands of the two others, on his white flesh, were like his own. Their arms were like his arms. The fact that he noticed this told Alpha that something had already changed, and he wasn't sure he liked it or could even abide it. He'd always been one among many, but with a unique sense of identity necessary for finding his place among the others. If none of them truly understood separateness, they'd be unable to do the simplest things. They wouldn't be able to work their positions in the city below, because none would know where to go if all were truly the same. They wouldn't be able to form a line without knowing who had to go first. But still, through it all, there had been the collective. He had a concept of *his arms* and *his hands* now, same as always. But that sense of "his" was twisting into something impure as seconds ticked. He didn't just notice *his arms*. He was also beginning to feel that he didn't want the others to put *their hands* on *his arms* because they were *his* and nobody else's to touch or possess.

The human woman looked at Omega, on Alpha's right. Alpha turned to look as well. Omega had the same hairless head as Alpha. The same strong features. The humans claimed they couldn't tell his kind apart, but the humans also felt that the Titan form appeared large and strong. From their perspective above, things had tilted in the other direction. Rather than seeing himself as large, Alpha thought the humans seemed small and fragile — mere shadows of their proud genetic stock. But humans were their children nonetheless, and worth the attempt at understanding.

Alpha, even as tired as he felt, found he could still catch the flavor of groupspeak running between the woman's mind and Omega's. Beta would hear the groupspeak as well — but Beta, like Alpha, was not whom the woman was groupspeaking to. Noticing such difference in *who* was speaking to *whom* wasn't something Alpha ever remembered noticing. Of course groupspeakers needed to have primary recipients in mind or nothing could be communicated, but it had always just sort of happened. Only now was Alpha noticing the duality. They were all one, but also separate.

Alpha didn't like the realization. The humans — this time anyway — were an almost entirely separate species. Their way of existence seemed isolated to Alpha, like a dark room with no potential for light. How did they live without the emotions, thoughts, and assistance of others on their frequency? And worse: If the humans had the capacity to be like their progenitors (something they'd proved in past epochs), why had they turned out so foreign in this one? Time, such as humanity understood it, had marched forward. But did the society on the planet below represent progress? Alpha didn't think so, and the idea made him uneasy.

The woman's groupspeak to Omega — duly translated

by Alpha's sluggish cortex — sounded like, *He does not understand.*

*It is early,* groupspoke Beta.

The woman looked at Alpha. Out loud, using her human voice, she said, "You *do* understand. We can hear your interpretations."

"Interpretations," Alpha repeated. Speaking aloud felt strange. He'd tried it before — all of them had at some point since arriving at the planet — but he found it clumsy and almost destructive, like a bludgeon.

"We have animated this surrogate—" The woman, wearing a blue dress and bright-orange hair, gestured down at herself. "—to facilitate groupspeak in a way that will be easiest for you to comprehend and internalize as the process takes hold. *Do you understand?*"

"I understand."

"And you understand the medium we are using to communicate," she added, almost a question.

"The language," Alpha said.

Now that he'd spoken a few words aloud, he found spoken words coming more easily. Beside him, Beta and Omega were looking over with curious eyes. They were very like the woman's human eyes. Alpha hadn't noticed *that* before either.

"The *language*, yes," the woman said, duly corrected. "We are less familiar with its nuances, perhaps, than you are at this point."

"It is their language," Alpha said.

"*One* of their languages."

"But your surrogate speaks the language."

The woman took a moment before responding, possibly assessing the truth of Alpha's statement. Divinity could animate surrogates to do just about anything, but speaking always came easier when the human puppet held a tongue's raw materials in her brain ahead of time.

"Yes. We are not used to it. It is strange to us."

It was strange to Alpha, too. He tried to shake off his odd fog, which he could feel deepening.

"I request direct audience." He didn't like communicating through the surrogate. It was clumsy. It felt wrong.

"You would no longer understand us if we groupspoke natively. Do you understand?"

Alpha looked behind the woman. In the nest, he could just see the subtle glow from the true speaker's body — translucent, sparkling, teeming with light. He found himself understanding why the few humans who'd seen the beings called them Divinity. The word finally held meaning, whereas in the past he'd translated it into something that meant space — confusing because space was empty, and the mind was the opposite. Now, standing before the human woman, Divinity made sense to Alpha. It suited the humans' perception of gods. Which also made sense, because many *had been* humanity's gods, as Earth's ancients had seen them. The perception was its own loop, curling back on itself.

"I understand," Alpha replied.

"The process will continue. Soon, use of a surrogate will be the only way you'll understand. The capacity for groupspeak will remain dormant inside you. We will train you to use it again once you are ready. But you will not recall how or why, or what it means when the time comes, and you will not realize that groupspeak was once normal to you. Do you understand?"

"I understand."

"You will become less able to see your true nature — the true nature of others like you, as those beside you now. You will experience that which you shut away, yet will have no control. It will consume you. You will at times sense only darkness. Do you understand?"

"I understand."

"You will be filled with falsities, things you must know.

But in that dark state, as many go when the time comes, you will not remember these events. You will not recall that when you were among the light, this fate was chosen by you. Do you understand?"

"I understand."

The woman looked at Beta. She said nothing, but a small nod passed between them. Alpha felt a new breed of fear, realizing they had groupspoken but he'd heard none of it. The new fear was hollow and sharp, frightening atop his existing terror because there were none to share his emotion. He was alone, and darkness was descending. Soon they — those he now clearly thought of as *others*, having no part of Alpha himself — would add more darkness to him, filling him to the brim like an overflowing vessel. He wanted to take it all back, but the darkness was heavy, like a drape. He was alone. And that was how he would die.

"You will adjust," the woman said. "In time, it will become as you are, and you won't remember that there was ever a difference. Do you understand?"

"I und—"

Alpha couldn't finish. He bent at the waist, feeling his face contort.

He flopped onto all fours from the pain. At his sides, Beta and Omega let him fall. They were separate. They were not him. The woman was not him. The true speaker behind the woman was not him. Nobody was Alpha but Alpha.

Every muscle seemed to tighten at once. His bones might erupt from his skin.

"It is within your control," the woman said. "The change. It is always chosen, by any who shift. It is necessary that you focus. That you do not *allow* it to happen, but in fact *cause* it to occur. To welcome the darkness. Do you understand?"

The darkness seemed to momentarily part. Finally, Alpha truly *did* understand.

He focused.

He allowed the change.

He stopped fighting the darkness and instead allowed it to change him.

He finished shifting then straightened. Everything was different. He seemed to know where he was, but his surroundings were strange. Somewhere he'd never been. He could seem to sense a force — the woman? — pushing thoughts toward him. It was odd and unusual. But he could learn to accept it, if this was how they communicated across distances, different as they were.

The woman looked to the muscular being on his left. "Take his robe. They will not accept it."

The hairless beings removed the robe from his body. Once bare, he felt cold. But then the beings returned and laid a fine set of clothing on the table at the room's center. He found he knew how to put the garments on and did so.

"The clothing is called a — " the woman began.

He cut her off. "I know a suit when I see one."

"When you are sent to your post, you will—"

"Let's just take it one step at a time," he said impatiently.

The woman looked at one of the other beings. Some sort of tentacled thing, barely visible, danced with light behind her. But he'd had enough of this, and of them telling him what to do.

"The memories," said the woman. "Have your donor's memories settled?"

"I don't know what you're talking about."

"There was an imperfection. A chain of events. In the forebear, there was an unspooling. It was regrettable but is now rectified. We have taken care in this iteration to remove discursive stimuli from the stream before passing the donor's essence into you."

"Great," he said, not understanding.

"Do you remember your forebear?" the woman asked.

"My father."

"Your predecessor, to use their word."

"Who the hell is my predecessor?" he asked, annoyed.

"The one whose life force was terminated by a human weapon. Below. An hour ago."

He didn't bother answering. He wanted to go home — enough with the stupid questions.

"Is there a mirror around here?" He'd pulled on most of the human garments already but now threaded the long cloth around his neck and began to tie an intricate knot that required no effort. He straightened the strip of fabric hanging down his front and ran a hand through his immaculately combed hair.

One of the Titans waved at a panel along the wall. It slid aside. He walked to the mirror behind the panel and wiggled the tie into place. He inspected his green eyes. His white teeth. His close shave.

"Do you know your name?" the woman asked from behind him.

Of course he knew it. But he wouldn't play parlor tricks. Alien stooge or not, he wasn't about to jump through hoops. That hadn't changed. Not through the Astral ships' arrival, not though the flight from New York to Vail, not through his first marriage or his second.

"A shuttle will transport you to the mansion below," the woman said. "You will understand it as your home. But it may take another hour or two before the donor's memories fully settle, but they will resolve with less potential for chaos than the corrupted set did within your forebear. It is important, during that time, that you do not interact with other humans who may have known the forebear. The forebear's updates haven't fully assimilated with the donor's root memories following the untimely but necessary life force cessation. You must not interact with those who may have known your donor before the sampling until gelling is complete. It is possible they will recognize undue differences between you and the donor, and we will be required to remote-terminate you, draw a new sample from the donor in his cell, and spawn a new copy to replace you. Do you understand?"

He nodded, wishing they'd get on with it and take him back down to the viceroy's mansion. He'd had a long day, and a granddaughter he wanted to play with.

It was stupid of the woman to keep asking him the same insulting question.

*Of course* he understood.

He was Meyer Fucking Dempsey, and nobody had better forget it.

# GET THE NEXT BOOK IN THE INVASION SERIES!

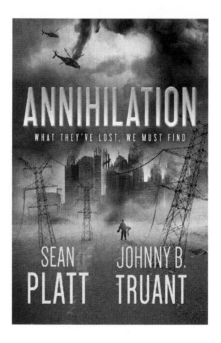

# ABOUT THE AUTHORS

**Sean Platt** is the bestselling co-author of over 60 books, including breakout post-apocalyptic horror serial *Yesterday's Gone*, literary mind-bender *Axis of Aaron*, and the blockbuster sci-fi series, *Invasion*. Never one for staying inside a single box for long, he also writes smart stories for children under the pen name Guy Incognito, and laugh out loud comedies which are absolutely *not* for children.

He is also the founder of the Sterling & Stone Story Studio and along with partners Johnny B. Truant and David W. Wright hosts the weekly Self-Publishing Podcast, openly sharing his journey as an author-entrepreneur and publisher.

Sean is often spotted taking long walks, eating brisket with his fingers, or watching movies with his family in Austin, Texas. You can find him at www.SterlingAndStone.net.

**Johnny B. Truant** is the bestselling author of the *Invasion* series, the political sci-fi thriller *The Beam, Fat Vampire, Axis of Aaron, Unicorn Western,* and many more fiction titles in addition to the nonfiction bestseller *Write. Publish. Repeat.*

He is also co-owner of the Sterling & Stone Story Studio, and along with partners Sean Platt and David W. Wright hosts the weekly Self-Publishing Podcast, openly sharing his journey as an author-entrepreneur and publisher.

Johnny and his family are thrilled to finally call Austin, Texas their home after far too many years of planning to move and complaining about life in northern Ohio. You can usually find him hanging out at www.SterlingAndStone.net.

For any questions about Sterling & Stone books or products, or help with anything at all, please send an email to help@sterlingandstone.net, or contact us at sterlingandstone.net/contact. Thank you for reading.